Betrayal

Betrayal

RITA POTTER

SAPPHIRE BOOKS PUBLISHING
SALINAS, CA.

Editor - Tara Young
Book Design - LJ Reynolds
Cover Design - Fineline Cover Design

Sapphire Books Publishing, LLC
P.O. Box 8142
Salinas, CA 93912
www.sapphirebooks.com

Printed in the United States of America
First Edition – July 2022

This and other Sapphire Books titles can be found at
www.sapphirebooks.com

Dedication

For Terra: Who shares this journey with me.

Acknowledgements

Thanks to Chris and Sapphire Books for letting me tell my stories the way I want to tell them, even when they aren't conventional.

Thanks to my editor, Tara. I appreciate your sense of humor and love that you seem to *get* mine. I was especially gleeful that I was able to put misspelled words in that you couldn't correct.

To all my family and friends who have been beside me for so many years, I appreciate your support and your willingness to let me ramble on and on about my books.

To my new friends, my writer buddies, you guys are the best and have made this journey so much better. There are too many of you to list, but you know who you are.

To my mentor Jae, you set the standard that I strive to meet. Not just in my writing skills, but in how I conduct myself in the writing community.

To Terra, I still think you should have let the pterodactyl carry CJ away to zombies, although the readers will probably thank you for it. Thanks for loving me and all my idiosyncrasies.

To Chumley the cat, who believes he is the reason for any of my writing success.

To my readers, I appreciate every one of you who reaches out to me, shares your thoughts with me, writes a review, or reads my stories.

I hope you have enjoyed the series as much as I have enjoyed writing it. As I wrote the final chapter, I was shocked at the emotion that bubbled inside me. These characters have become a part of my life, so even though this is the end of the series and I am saying goodbye to them, who knows maybe someday we will meet again.

WHITAKER ESTATE RESIDENTS
Commission Members

Name	Role	Relationship
Dillon Mitchell	Leader	Skylar Lange
Cynthia Cramer	Doctor	
Karen Foster	Supplies	CJ McCormick
Renee Lipinski	Food	Katie Grogan
Jake Stein	Defense	Lily Stein
		Nancy Thornton

Other Key Members

Name	Role	Relationship
Skylar Lange	Nurse	Dillion Mitchell
CJ McCormick	Communication	Karen Foster
Maria alvarez	Attorney	Tasha Nicks
Leslie Freeman (Deceased)	Tower Security	Denise Freeman
Anne Templeton	Asst Communication	Tiffany Daniels
Willa Andrews	Filmmaker/Photographer	
Alaina Renato	Kidnapped from Amarillo	

Deceased

Denise Freeman	Died at beginning of crisis	Leslie Freeman
Dee Devonte	Died in battle	
KC Campbell	Died in battle	
Tiffany Daniels	Died rescuing hostages	Anne Templeton

Chapter One

The room was quiet except for the rhythmic *thunk* of the unbalanced ceiling fan. Everyone around the table gaped in stunned silence at the mysterious, dark-haired woman.

Dillon Mitchell's gaze swept past the faces of the other four Commission members before her stare locked on the piercing blue eyes of Alaina Renato. Who was this woman, and what was she trying to tell them? Her words reverberated in Dillon's mind, but she struggled to make sense of them. Alaina's expression gave nothing away.

"Did you just say that someone here, other than CJ and Jake, has been talking to Babcock's people?" Dillon asked.

"No." Alaina held her gaze.

Dillon's shoulders relaxed. *Thank god.* She started to voice the sentiment, but Alaina cut her off.

"They haven't been talking to his people. They've been talking directly to Braxton Babcock."

"Who's been talking to him?" Dillon tried to keep her voice calm, despite her racing heart.

Alaina shrugged. "I wasn't privy to that information."

The initial shock subsided as the others found their voices. Questions were hurled from all directions, and due to the modest size of the meeting space, the volume filled the room. Alaina sat back in her chair, eyes narrowed, as she studied her questioners.

"Hey!" Cynthia Kramer called out and waved her hand. "Everyone," she said louder. "We can't get answers if we all talk at once."

Dillon turned to Cynthia. Since Tiffany Daniels's death two weeks ago, Dillon found it hard to meet Cynthia's gaze. While much of the time Tiffany had been a thorn in Dillon's side and did little to help the community, in the end, she'd died a hero. She'd sacrificed her own life to save the people she loved, including Cynthia, who'd once been Tiffany's best friend.

Dillon's heart clenched every time she saw the pain in her friend's eyes, but today was different. While a hint of sadness remained, there was also a spark of life.

"She's right." Dillon gave Cynthia a smile. "Let Alaina tell her story."

Alaina bit her lower lip. "I'd prefer questions since I'm uncertain what it is you want to know." Her low voice held a note of reserve. "That is if you can ask one at a time."

Cool. More like ice. Despite the circumstances, being surrounded by people she'd only known a short time, Alaina appeared to be in complete control. She showed no signs of being intimidated by the Commission's inquisition.

She'd been enigmatic since her arrival, although Dillon suspected Cynthia might have cut through a tiny piece of her armor. Alaina's arrival at Whitaker Estate hadn't been by choice. Since the upheaval that left most of the people in the country, if not the world, dead, society had broken down.

Nearly six months had passed, and still they were no closer to understanding why everyone who wasn't underground or above a certain altitude had perished; however, they had learned that the world was a much more dangerous place. Without a police force, it allowed the lawless to take what they wanted.

A gang of young men had attacked Whitaker Estate, after they had snatched several women from the group living in Amarillo. Alaina was one of those taken. A battle ensued, leaving all the attackers dead, and three of their own: Dee Devonte, KC Campbell, and Tiffany.

Dillon shuddered at the memory. After the attack, she could no longer view their new world in the same way. Because of Whitaker's planning, they'd been living in a protective bubble, which didn't match the experience of the hostages from Amarillo. Their existence at Whitaker Estate had been near utopia, compared to the dystopia that existed outside the walls of their sanctuary. Dillon knew that soon life as they'd come to know it would change again, but now, she needed to focus on what Alaina was trying to tell them.

"I think we should let Dillon ask the questions," Jake Stein said, pulling Dillon out of her reverie.

The other Commission members around the table—Jake, Renee Lipinski, Karen Foster, and Cynthia—nodded.

Cynthia swept her hand out. "The floor is yours."

Gee, thanks. Dillon didn't voice her sentiment. "Would that be okay with you, Alaina?"

Alaina nodded. Her piercing blue eyes steady, almost challenging.

"Let's start with you. We'd like to get to know

you a little better." Dillon gave what she hoped was a disarming smile.

Other than a tiny vein that throbbed in Alaina's neck, she showed no reaction. "Very well. What would you like to know?"

"How long had you been at Braxton Babcock's, um, his compound?" Dillon avoided saying *cult*.

"As I said previously, a little over four years."

"Please, humor me." Dillon smiled, but Alaina's expression remained closed. "I want to make sure everyone heard."

Alaina nodded.

Dillon took it as permission to continue. "And why were you there?"

"That is of a personal nature and not relevant to the issue at hand." Alaina held Dillon's gaze.

Dillon took a deep breath. She needed to keep her composure. Knowing that someone at the estate could possibly be betraying the group had left emotions high. Surely, Alaina wasn't intentionally being evasive. Besides, she was right—her personal story was not their business. Anyone who valued her privacy wouldn't want to tell her life story to a group she'd just met, and Alaina appeared more private than most.

"Fair enough," Dillon said. "When did you leave the compound to join the group in Amarillo?"

Alaina looked up and to the right as if doing calculations in her mind. Dillon suspected she knew exactly when she'd left but didn't want to answer too quickly. Alaina returned her gaze. "It was nearly two months after the *crisis*. The chaos turned out to be a good time to slip away undetected."

Telling. Dillon decided against pursuing why

Alaina wanted to *slip away*. Besides, she didn't believe Alaina would answer the question, anyway. "Was it your intention to flee to Amarillo?"

"Yes."

"May I ask why?"

"They were the closest group I was aware of. Remaining alone didn't seem to be a safe option." A hint of pain danced in her eyes but disappeared as quickly as it came. "Little did I know Amarillo wouldn't be safe, either."

Dillon thought of offering reassurance but doubted it would be well received. From the stories the women told, they'd been treated brutally, which made Dillon glad that the attackers had all been killed during their raid on Whitaker Estate.

"Did you tell the group from Amarillo that you'd come from Babcock's community?"

"No."

No. That was it. Alaina wasn't going to make her job any easier. As Dillon contemplated her next question, a loud bang interrupted her.

Renee's palm hit the table. Her ruddy face gave away her frustration. "Why not? Why wouldn't you tell them where you came from?"

Alaina shifted her gaze toward Renee and studied her without speaking. Slowly, she turned back to Dillon and gave her a slight nod.

Seriously. Fine, she could play this game if that is what it took. Dillon cleared her throat. "Why didn't you tell them where you came from?"

Renee let out a snort. Cynthia, who sat next to Alaina, shot Renee a look as if to warn her from saying more.

"It didn't seem important," Alaina answered.

"So why did you decide to tell us?" Dillon said quickly, hoping to cut off anything Renee might say.

"Because it did seem important. There was no indication that Babcock intended any harm to their group, but I fear he may have designs on yours."

"So why wait?" Renee called out. "If we're in so much danger, why did you say nothing for two weeks?"

Dillon turned to Renee and scowled. "I believe I was given the task of asking questions. If the Commission would like to assign someone else, please make a motion to do so." Scolding Renee in front of the group wasn't ideal, but she didn't want Alaina to stop cooperating, either.

"Sorry," Renee muttered. Her full cheeks flamed against her blond hair.

"I apologize, Alaina," Dillon said. "Please, can you tell us why you waited to tell us?"

"I didn't know you. The world isn't exactly a safe place anymore." Alaina paused. "If it ever was," she said in a quiet voice. Her jaw hardened. "I wanted to assess the situation. Babcock has known your location for several months, so I doubted a few more days would make a dramatic difference."

"So it was a calculated risk?"

"Exactly." Alaina offered a slight smile. "Decisions have become a game of calculated risks, haven't they?"

"No doubt," Dillon said. "I suppose your first impression of us wasn't the most reassuring." A bigger understatement couldn't have been spoken. Dillon flinched at the thought. Her introduction to Alaina came after Dillon had shot a man point blank in the temple. Granted, he had been responsible for Alaina's kidnapping and was trying to disarm Dillon, but her sleep had been haunted since.

"Although I was thankful to be saved, in the moment, your reactions seemed...ah, shall we say, excessive."

Another understatement. Gunning down the entire group just for driving into their haven would seem to be a gross overreaction. "But you do understand that we'd been in touch with your friends in Amarillo and knew who they were?"

"And what they'd been doing to us," Alaina said without emotion. Cynthia patted Alaina's hand but quickly drew back. Alaina turned to Cynthia and smiled. "After having several conversations with Cynthia, I understood the actions you took. It likely saved many lives. There would have been no negotiating with the bastards." The word bastards came out in the same tone as if she were saying kittens or puppies.

Alaina's reactions were fascinating, and Dillon would have loved to explore them further, but now was not the time. They needed to get a handle on Babcock's intentions. "Now that we've established that you trust us."

Alaina held up her hand. "I never used the word trust. I said I've assessed the situation and felt I needed to tell you of the dangers. I believe focusing your questions on the traitor would be more productive than wasting your energy analyzing me."

Controlled. Dillon nodded. "Fair enough. Do you know when the traitor, as you label her ..." Dillon stopped. There were only two males, Jake and his son Tad, but she would be remiss in not suspecting everyone. "I'm assuming it is a her."

"Yes. Your assumption is correct."

"Okay. Do you know when the traitor first made contact with Babcock?"

"I can't tell you the exact date, but I believe it was within a few weeks of the crisis."

"How did you first discover this?"

Alaina narrowed her eyes. "Once again, may I ask the relevance? Focusing on me won't help you find your traitor."

Warmth spread up Dillon's neck. Alaina wasn't wrong. Agatha Christie had always been one of Dillon's favorite authors, and Alaina reeked of mystery. "Do you have any insight into what was said to Babcock?"

"From my understanding, it started out as a casual conversation about the crisis. Babcock is a master of luring people into his web." Alaina bit her lower lip. "The conversation went on for several weeks before Babcock subtly switched the narrative. He began to seek information and led the proverbial lamb to the slaughter."

No doubt, her disdain for Babcock ran deep. Knowing the context of Alaina's involvement with the ministry would lead to a better assessment, but Dillon accepted, for now, she wouldn't be allowed access to that information. "And what did our traitor reveal to Babcock?"

"Your general location and the nature of the... the...shall we say the type of women at the estate. He was repulsed but didn't let his little Birdie know. The man is a master poker player."

"Birdie? Is that the name she gave?"

"Actually, it was Bertie, but he took to calling her his little Birdie." Alaina sighed. "Cynthia informs me that there is nobody by that name here."

"What makes you so sure the woman was from here?"

"My bad." Alaina raised her eyebrows. "I suppose he could have been talking to another group of lesbians at an estate near Lake Piru."

"Point taken. What were his plans?"

"To wait in the weeds until the time was right. He wanted to build his army first."

"Army? Seriously, he was assembling an army?"

"An army for God. You," Alaina swept her arm around the table, "were to be his prize. The righteous warrior for Jesus would rid the world of sin." Her nose crinkled as if she'd smelled something foul. "At least his definition of sin."

"So he plans to march into our home and exterminate us?"

Alaina shrugged. "Extermination. I doubt it. Reform would be more his style. Or should I say conversion?"

Dillon's mouth went dry. *Conversion.* A word that caused shivers to run up her spine. "You can't mean...." Dillon struggled for words.

"What bigger triumph than to cure the sinner?"

"What the fuck?" Renee said. "What kind of bullshit is this?"

Alaina turned to Renee, and they locked gazes. "Dillon asked the question. I didn't say I agreed." She turned away.

"Do you have any indication when his army would be ready for an attack?" Dillon said, reestablishing herself as the questioner.

Renee muttered an apology and slumped against her chair.

"You must understand, Babcock is a very patient

man. He doesn't behave rashly. He will not act until he believes his victory is all but ensured."

Finally, a bit of hope. "That's good. So we have plenty of time?"

"I wouldn't go that far. I've been gone from the compound for nearly three months. A lot can change in that span. They were broadcasting their message around the clock. Each day, more people *answered his call.*"

"But we've stayed in contact with them. They've only reported a few additions to their numbers."

Alaina's poker face dissolved. If she wore glasses, Dillon was sure, she would have looked over them with a look of disparagement. "Apparently, you're not the only ones that know how to lie."

Dillon chastised herself, embarrassed that she'd come off so naive. Of course, she knew Babcock wasn't above lying, so why was she determined to make a fool of herself in front of Alaina? "You obviously know Babcock better than we do. Won't you tell us your assessment of the danger we're in?" Why hadn't she just started with this question?

Alaina appraised Dillon before speaking. "The threat is real. The timeline is uncertain. Being a *mere* woman, I wasn't in the room when these discussions occurred. However, I was able to pick up bits and pieces."

Interesting. Was Alaina's husband or lover one of Babcock's inner circle? Another question that Dillon knew would remain unanswered.

"What you're saying is that an attack is a foregone conclusion, the only uncertainty is when?"

Alaina nodded. "I would tread very carefully if I were you."

Dillon cocked her head. "Meaning?"

"If Babcock suspects that you know of the traitor, the danger to this community rises exponentially. You must be discreet in your search and not let the traitor know you're looking for her."

"Oh, is that all?" Dillon said and rolled her eyes. "Piece of cake."

"I know that's not what you wanted to hear, but you needed to. He is a dangerous man. An evil man. He was bad enough when there were still laws. Without laws, I fear what he and his followers may do."

"I appreciate your candor." Dillon propped her elbows on the table and rested her chin on her hands. "There's much the Commission needs to discuss. Is there anything else you would like to share?"

Alaina shifted her gaze to Cynthia, then back to Dillon. She bit her bottom lip before speaking. "Babcock's army is well prepared. They'd been stockpiling weapons in their compound well before the world crumbled. And they know how to use them. You will not be able to defeat them alone. I believe you can trust the group from Amarillo. While they are God-fearing folks, they are true Christians. Not the crazy brand of Christianity that Babcock spews."

"Thank you." Dillon nodded with a half-smile. She gazed around the table. "Does anyone else have any questions for our guest?"

Everyone shook their heads but didn't speak, not even Renee.

"Very well," Dillon said. "Ms. Renato, we may have further questions, but for now, I believe the Commission has plenty to discuss."

"Is that your way of dismissing me?"

Damn it. Why did this woman make her feel so inept? Dillon smiled, hoping to appear casual and regain some sense of control. "Perceptive. Yes, we would like some time alone to discuss our next moves. You understand that the Commission was elected to represent everyone at the estate, so we take our duty very seriously." What the hell? Why did she feel the need to explain herself?

"I understand completely. I will take my leave." Alaina stood. "Thank you for hearing my concerns."

Cynthia leapt to her feet. "I'll walk you out."

Alaina's eyes flashed before the cool shroud descended. "Very well."

Nobody spoke as they watched the pair depart.

Chapter Two

Cynthia put her hand on Alaina's back as they exited the room, sure that all attention was on her. She didn't turn; her sole focus was on Alaina. Something made her want to comfort a woman who didn't seem to want it. Although the last couple of days, Cynthia had sensed a subtle shift in Alaina, or maybe it was just wishful thinking.

Once the door closed behind them, Alaina snaked her arm through Cynthia's as they walked down the hallway. Alaina was a couple of inches shorter, which still placed her well above average in height.

Neither spoke until they arrived at the end of the corridor that spilled into the massive library. One of Whitaker's indulgences and Cynthia's favorite place inside the sprawling mansion.

"You should get back to the meeting," Alaina said. "I have a feeling there's going to be a lively discussion."

Goosebumps rose on Cynthia's arms. Something about the low tone of Alaina's voice frequently caused the reaction. No doubt, Alaina fascinated her. Made her want to spend countless hours getting to know the elusive woman. *Duty calls.* But she wasn't ready to return quite yet. "Are you okay?"

Alaina's lip curled slightly. "Yes, I'm okay."

"You think I'm silly." Heat rose in Cynthia's cheeks.

"I think you're sweet." Alaina squeezed Cynthia's arm and gazed into her eyes. "I'm just not used to it."

Warmth spread across Cynthia's chest. Why did a simple touch from Alaina make her feel this way? They'd only kissed. Nothing more. Although, she suspected Dillon thought it had gone much further. Probably because she had trouble focusing on anything else when Alaina was nearby. Alaina's kiss was the most sensual thing she'd ever experienced. It went far beyond any of her previous sexual encounters. How could she explain it to her friends? They'd think she was a hopeless romantic.

"Cynthia?" Alaina said. "You're a million miles away."

Cynthia shook her head as if to clear her thoughts. "Sorry." She had no intention of telling her what she was thinking. "I know I should get back to the meeting, but I wanted to make sure you're okay."

"I'm good."

"Can I see you later?" Cynthia spoke the words quickly, before she second guessed herself.

"I'd like that."

Three simple words set her heart racing. "Where will you be?"

"I thought of going into the reading room. What do you call it?"

"The Athens Room."

"Yeah, that's it." Alaina smirked. "Do you think I can find a book?"

Cynthia gazed around the library that spanned three stories. She shrugged and smiled. "There might be something around here."

Halfway down the corridor, Cynthia heard raised voices. She sighed. A threat of this magnitude, on the inside, would surely have everyone on edge. The Commission agreed on many things but feared the issue would challenge their cohesion.

She took a deep breath and counted to ten before she pushed open the door. She slid into her customary chair and let her gaze circle the room.

Renee slammed her notebook onto the table. "Who are we going to believe? Some woman that just dropped in our laps or the people we've spent every day with over these past several months?"

"What reason would she have to make up a story like this?" Jake asked.

"Plenty." Renee's voice raised as the redness crept farther up her neck. "What better way to stir up trouble than plant this crazy seed and make us fight amongst ourselves? Ingenious."

"We just ignore it?" Jake shrugged and turned up his lip. "Yep, real responsible. Let's just let Babcock march in here and take over the estate."

"Damn it, Jake. That's not what she said," Karen said, her soft Texas twang softening the irritation in her voice.

Cynthia plopped against the back of her chair. Her thoughts drowned out the voices. The Commission couldn't afford to argue like this, especially with a threat closing in. If anyone could unite the group, it would be Dillon. Even though Cynthia no longer felt like an outsider, Dillon still had a longer history with the others.

She gazed at Dillon, who had also sat back and stopped talking. Their gazes met. Dillon nodded in acknowledgment. Cynthia smiled and motioned for Dillon to take the floor.

≈≈≈≈

Dillon waved her hand. "Hold on. Let's look at this rationally, not emotionally."

Renee glared but stopped talking and leaned back in her seat.

"What's the worst-case scenario if we take it seriously and Alaina is lying to us?" Dillon ignored Cynthia's glare and Renee's pout. She needed to bring the temperature in the room down. Karen with her sweet disposition and Texas charm was her best bet. "Karen, you've been quiet. What bad could come of us taking this stance?"

"Well..." Karen looked thoughtfully around the room and then settled her gaze on Dillon. "It could drive a wedge. Everyone looking over their shoulder and accusing each other of something...something we don't even know is true."

"Our cohesiveness had been getting better." Jake ran a hand through his short dark hair. *Jake's tell.* Dillon had grown to know the gesture well over the past several months. It signified his frustration. "Even before, um...with..." He glanced at Tiffany's empty chair.

"Just say it," Cynthia said, the pain evident in her eyes. "After Tiffany died, it gave everyone a wakeup call. We need to stick together and not fight amongst ourselves."

"Kinda like 9/11," Dillon said. "Remember how

the country came together?"

Renee crossed her arms over her chest. "And remember how it all went to hell, and we went back to the same infighting? Even worse."

Damn it. What had Renee so worked up? Normally, she was cooperative and jovial. Quick with a joke and a smile, but today, she was loaded for bear. The only time Dillon had seen her like this was when someone upset Katie. More accurately, when Dillon had upset her.

Katie Grogan had been attracted to Dillon for years, ever since Dillon's wife and Katie's best friend, Jane, had died. While Katie felt the pairing would be perfect, considering their relationships with Jane, Dillon found it unnatural and avoided Katie's advances, which often left Katie upset. Renee, who secretly had feelings for Katie, sided with Katie.

That had been months ago, so this outburst made little sense.

Dillon sized Renee up before speaking. She preferred to be direct, but she couldn't afford a misstep that might splinter the Commission. Especially now. "Renee, do you care to tell us what's bothering you?"

"Sure. I'd be glad to." Renee stared down Dillon. "I know how this is going to go." She glanced at the others. "Who everyone will blame."

Duh. Why hadn't she seen it? Even before Renee began dating Katie, she'd been protective of her. "Ah, I understand what you're getting at, but my mind hadn't even gone toward Katie."

"Until now," Jake added.

Not helpful. Dillon braced for Renee's outburst.

"Seriously? You suspect her?" Renee sat up taller.

She gave Cynthia a pleading glance, afraid to

agitate Renee any further. At the first sign of trouble, Dillon tended to rely on Cynthia. Even though they'd only met the day of the crisis, she'd become one of Dillon's closest friends. Someone she trusted completely. Cynthia gave her a nearly imperceptible nod.

"I'm sure that's not what Jake meant." Cynthia shot him a look reserved for a child misbehaving in public. "But we have to look at everyone. No matter how hard it might be on all of us. Not to accuse anyone but to get to the bottom of it."

"Maybe I missed something, but I don't recall us taking a vote on how we were going to proceed with this." Renee's voice dripped with sarcasm. "Obviously, you've decided to take the word of that psycho Alaina since we *all* know her so *well*."

"That's out of line." A vein throbbed in Cynthia's neck. "Don't shoot the messenger. She's trying to help."

Renee snorted. "Who's she trying to help? Us? Herself?" Renee raised her eyebrows a couple of times. "*Or you?*"

Crap. This was going downhill fast. Renee's defense of Katie might be chivalrous, but it certainly wasn't helpful. "I think we've jumped way ahead of ourselves," Dillon said. "Let's finish the original logic exercise." She smiled, hoping to lighten the mood, but the only one who returned her smile was Karen. "Let's talk about what happens if we decide Alaina is lying to us and choose to do nothing."

"No way," Jake shouted and pounded his fist onto the table. "As the head of defense, that's not an option. I'd never vote for something so stupid."

"Put your testosterone back in your pants, Jake," Dillon said and winked at him.

"Uh, sorry." His face reddened, and he sheepishly looked down at the table. "It's just not a responsible choice."

"Objection noted." Dillon turned to Karen. "Since you gave us the potential consequence of taking Alaina's accusation seriously, what is the consequence of not doing so?"

"Death," Karen said.

So much for Karen's calm demeanor. She was right, though. The outcome could be catastrophic. "Anyone else have anything to add?"

Heads shook around the table, even Renee's. She didn't look happy but would be hard pressed to make a case against proceeding with an investigation.

"Should we take a vote?" Cynthia asked. She'd always kept the Commission organized and on point. "All in favor of developing a plan to address the potential breach in our group say aye."

A chorus of ayes rang out.

"Opposed?"

Silence.

"Motion carries." Cynthia turned to Dillon. "Would you like to lead the discussion on how we move forward?"

No. "Sure."

⁕ ⁕ ⁕ ⁕ ⁕

Cynthia twisted in her chair, stretching her back. They'd been at it for two hours, and her body felt the effects of sitting. The discussion at times had been lively, even contentious, but Dillon rose to the challenge.

She smiled to herself. *Dillon.* Cynthia couldn't

imagine living through this horror without her. Despite a rocky start to their friendship, Dillon was the person she relied on the most. She sat back and admired Dillon's confidence and the strong set of her jaw as she summarized their decisions.

"So we're all in agreement that we don't share any of this information with anyone outside this room. Not our friends or lovers."

"With the exception of CJ," Karen added.

It had been one of the many points of disagreement. At first, Renee and Jake had objected since CJ McCormick was Karen's wife and Dillon's longtime best friend, but soon, logic prevailed. As the computer guru, CJ would be invaluable.

"Yes, of course," Dillon said. "We'll bring CJ up to speed on the situation after this meeting. She should be able to begin diagnostics on her computer system to pinpoint when and how often the breach might have occurred. I cannot stress enough that under no circumstances should you reveal to anyone what we've discussed here."

Cynthia's heart went out to Dillon. She suspected it would give Dillon many sleepless nights having to keep this from her partner Skylar Lange, but she also believed Dillon would keep her word to the Commission.

While Dillon had kept her feelings to herself, Renee had loudly voiced her displeasure with the rule in light of her recent relationship with Katie. In the end, Renee had joined the others in voting to keep the information among the Commission members only.

"I want to be very clear." Dillon's voice went up an octave. "That we are not conducting a witch hunt. These are our friends. Our family. We are simply collecting information. Alaina's information could be erroneous."

"Or an outright lie," Renee said under her breath but loud enough for the others to hear.

Cynthia bristled but remained silent.

Dillon didn't even turn to look in her direction before continuing. "And if it does turn out to be accurate, it doesn't necessarily mean the individual was purposefully trying to cause harm."

Unlikely. But if Dillon needed to believe it, Cynthia wouldn't take away her lifeline. They all could use some hope.

"I also must stress that even though we discussed several names today, nobody is currently a suspect." Dillon paused and gazed around the room, letting the message sink in. "We need to keep our minds open, or we could inadvertently miss an important clue. Our investigation must be not only methodical, but subtle. We don't want to tip our hand to our possible traitor, nor do we want to create panic. I'd like to review our assignments." Her eyes narrowed as she squinted at her notebook.

Cynthia shook her head. "Do you have any idea what you even wrote?"

Dillon's brow furrowed. She glared at Cynthia, but the slight quiver at the corner of her mouth gave her away. "Just give me a minute."

Cynthia held up her own notebook. Her neat block printing filled the page. She'd taken notes complete with bullet points and different colored ink for the various topics. "Want me to help you out?"

"Fine." Dillon dropped her journal to the table. "It's all in there. Some of us just aren't as anal as others."

Cynthia chuckled as did the others. The last couple of hours had been heavy, so a light-hearted moment felt good.

Cynthia cleared her throat. "Karen, you will assist CJ with collecting data on when the breach may have occurred."

"Got it," Karen said.

"Renee, you come in contact with the most people on a daily basis," Cynthia said.

"Feeding people makes me popular." Renee smiled.

Good. She'd been worried about Renee, but the joke alleviated some of her concern. It was true that Renee was popular. Having owned five-star restaurants in Los Angeles, Renee had been the obvious choice to head food services at the estate.

"Your job is to snoop around." Cynthia smiled. "Eavesdrop on conversations. Ask questions. Get people talking."

Renee returned the smile. "It's in my wheelhouse. I'll see what I can dig up."

"Jake, your assignment is to up your communication with Braxton Babcock's people."

Jake groaned.

"I know you hate it, but he only knows you and CJ."

"And the traitor." Jake rubbed his chin. "I'll take one for the team. But those guys give me the creeps any time I talk to them."

"Thank you." Cynthia smiled at Jake before she turned to Dillon. "And you'll reach out to our allies. We need to build a defense against Babcock. Convince the others that we need to meet face to face. Have a summit."

"I'll work on it." Dillon pointed to her journal. "I've got it noted right here."

Jake chuckled. "Look on the bright side. If Dillon's notes ever fall into enemy hands, it won't be a big deal. Nobody will be able to read them, anyway."

Dillon pulled her notebook to her chest. "You'll be sorry for teasing me. I have some valuable information here."

"You just keep gathering it." Cynthia smirked. "And under the pretense of building medical records, something I should have done a long time ago, I'll be collecting information for our investigation." She ran her finger down the page. "My focus will be on discovering if anyone grew up in an evangelical household. Crisis can turn people back to their roots. And determine if we can trace the name Bertie. Possibly a middle name or a parent's. That about sums it up."

"I think we're ready to adjourn," Dillon said.

"Next meeting?" Karen asked.

"Um, I don't think we decided. I think we discussed around two or three days."

"Let's go with two," Renee said. "We can always push it back if we have nothing."

"I'm good with that," Dillon said.

Everyone nodded.

"Meeting adjourned.

Chapter Three

Dillon pretended to fumble with her belongings. She wanted to get Cynthia alone. *Stupid.* It wasn't as if the others would be suspicious, so why was she putting on this charade? Even though the meeting had gone well, after the rocky start, she hadn't been able to shake her edginess.

Cynthia's brow, creased in concentration, was partially covered by her long brown hair. She made no move to leave as she flipped through the pages of her notebook, occasionally making notations in the margins. When the last Commission member exited, she gazed up at Dillon and said, "I thought they'd never leave."

Dillon smiled. "You knew I was waiting to get you alone?"

"You're clumsy but not that clumsy. I doubt anyone bought it. I think dropping your pen and then kicking it under the table was my favorite move."

Dillon groaned. "I was that transparent?"

"Afraid so. Are you okay?"

Dillon dropped her head into her hands. "I don't know."

"What's going on in that head of yours?" Cynthia asked.

"Nothing. I'm just being silly." Dillon shoved her journal and pen into her bag.

"Seriously?" Cynthia sighed. "It's been a long day for all of us. Don't make me pull it out of you."

For the first time today, Dillon really looked at Cynthia. Heavy bags underlined her warm brown eyes, which took away some of their spark. Worry lines creased her forehead, and her complexion was pallid. "Whoa. I just got a good look at you. Maybe I should be asking you if you're okay."

Cynthia gave her a half smile. "It's been a rough couple of weeks, but I know we have to keep on living."

"I'm so sorry." Dillon put her hand on Cynthia's. "I hate it when I get like this. Fixated. I don't see anything outside of my tunnel vision. Turns me into an insensitive jerk."

"I never said you were insensitive." A mischievous spark returned to Cynthia's eyes.

"Thanks." Dillon smirked. "Seriously, so much has happened that sometimes it feels like Tiffany died months ago."

"I understand." Cynthia's eyes filled with tears. "I loved her. I know she could be impossible, but I wish you would have met the Tiffany I knew in college, before she let her father's judgment destroy her. She had so much artistic potential, but Stanton Daniels III wouldn't hear of his sole heir wasting her time with such frivolity. He crushed her spirit, and she became someone I didn't know."

Dillon's heart ached for Cynthia. "I think I was starting to see a glimpse." Tiffany had begun to turn her life around. With Cynthia's help, she'd rediscovered her first love—painting. In the atrium, they had a beautiful, almost finished mural of the crisis to prove it. Dillon doubted anyone would have the heart to finish it, but maybe someday.

"Nothing makes sense." Cynthia frowned. "Why her? Why now?"

Dillon picked up her bag. "Come on, let's walk."

"I think a little fresh air might do me some good," Cynthia said as she gathered up her stuff.

They made small talk until they were outside on the path leading from the mansion to the hotel. The once pristine grounds of the estate showed the effects of being untended. While the foliage was still beautiful, it was starting to look overgrown.

"I'm not sure we can always answer why things happen," Dillon said, returning to the earlier conversation. "Sometimes, they just do."

"Are we being punished?"

Dillon hoped her surprise didn't show. *Strange.* In all these months, they'd never talked about it. Maybe because they were too busy surviving, but Dillon suspected it went deeper. "Are you asking if God had something to do with this?"

Cynthia shrugged and waved her hand. "Never mind. I'm being stupid."

"No. Don't be embarrassed." Dillon picked up a large branch blocking their path. Cynthia grabbed the other end and helped her heave it out of the way. "I'm sure we've all had those thoughts."

"Why haven't you and I talked about it? We talk about everything else."

"Good question." Dillon let her gaze follow the flight of a goldfinch as she considered her answer. "Probably because our group is highly educated. Scientific."

Cynthia narrowed her eyes and cocked her head. "What's that have to do with it?"

They rounded the bend and were bathed in

sunlight. The forest provided shade on the first part of their walk, but they'd emerged into a grassy area with few trees, so the sun smiled down on them.

Dillon shielded her eyes from the glare. "Religion and science haven't mixed well in recent years."

"Probably because of idiots like Babcock."

"Exactly my point. I know…um…knew educated people who would rather have been caught picking their nose in public than admit they believed in God."

Cynthia pursed her lips. "Afraid people would think they're ignorant?"

"Peer pressure is real, and adults can be the worst." How many times had she remained silent when someone made a crack about religion? More times than she'd care to admit.

"It was rampant in college. Everyone wanted to prove how intelligent they were. Atheism was all the rage." Cynthia met Dillon's gaze. "Isn't there an old saying, there are no atheists in foxholes?"

Dillon nodded. "I think it's something along those lines."

"Have you had any epiphanies? Changes of heart?"

They took several steps before Dillon responded. "I've never believed in the God that Braxton Babcock is selling." Dillon picked up a stick and began peeling off the bark.

"Is this conversation making you uncomfortable?" Cynthia asked.

Why should talking about religion with one of her best friends make her feel so vulnerable? "I guess I internalized more of the messages than I thought. I don't want you to think I'm ignorant."

"You just lobbed up a watermelon for me to

knock out of the park." Cynthia smiled. "But I'll be kind."

"Gee, thanks." Dillon returned the smile, happy that Cynthia knew when to lighten the mood. "There's so many unanswered questions, but I don't see the biblical God in the sky pulling puppet strings. But I'm not arrogant enough to say it's impossible." Dillon smiled again. "I guess you could say that I'm smart enough to admit I'm ignorant."

"I like that." Cynthia nodded. "I really do. It's the reason I'm agnostic, not atheist. I can tell you more of what I don't believe than what I do. Before all this... whatever happened, I used to say the Universe put something in my path or was sending me a message. But I can't figure out what kind of communique this is supposed to be."

"Communique? Sounds sophisticated."

"I was going to say missive, but I think that has to be in writing." Cynthia grinned. "Whatever's going on is bigger than a simple message. Carrier pigeons bring messages. You get messages in your inbox. This is like a freaking flashing neon billboard." Cynthia raised her hands over her head and waved them around, scaring a group of birds that had landed on a nearby bush. "This is shit falling from the sky. Literally."

Dillon couldn't help but smirk at Cynthia's animated display. It was one more thing she loved about her normally controlled friend. Every now and then, she'd let loose like this. "Tell me how you really feel."

Cynthia reddened. "Um, I guess I got a little passionate."

"Just a tad."

"I can't think about this, or my head might explode." Cynthia clenched her head between her hands and pretended to squeeze, dramatizing her words. "Besides, I don't think you stuck around after the meeting to have a theological discussion with me."

"I've enjoyed it, but I wanted your thoughts on the traitor. The meeting got pretty intense, so with everyone walking on eggshells, I didn't feel like we could be completely open."

Cynthia's eyebrows shot up. "You think Katie might be the one?"

Dillon adamantly shook her head. "No. I don't believe... I can't believe it. But I can understand why she'd be a suspect. What do you think?"

"I'm not sure. She was pissed at you, not the rest of us."

Dillon cringed at the truth. For years, Katie had been trying in vain for a romantic relationship with Dillon. When Dillon began dating Skylar, the tensions boiled over. It culminated in Katie's ugly confrontation with Skylar, which ironically brought Dillon and Skylar closer. The memory flashed in Dillon's mind, and her heart raced. It had been the first time Dillon told Skylar she loved her.

Cynthia waved her hand. "What's that look for?"

"Um, sorry. Just thinking." Heat crawled up Dillon's neck. She quickly moved on. "We're in agreement that Katie is unlikely?"

"Yeah. Any other likely suspects on your radar?"

They arrived at the end of the path, which opened into the hotel's parking lot. Weeds had begun to grow in some of the cracks, and the overgrown bushes that once served as a privacy block spilled onto the pavement. "We should turn around," Dillon said, letting her gaze land anywhere but on Cynthia.

"Nice try," Cynthia said. "Spill!"

"Do you think maybe Tiffany could have had anything to do with it?" Dillon drew her shoulders in and waited for Cynthia's reaction.

"I know that's what everyone was thinking. Who wanted to be the one to speak ill of the dead?"

Dillon flinched.

"Oh, God," Cynthia said and grabbed Dillon's arm. "That wasn't directed at you. Trust me. When I first heard about the traitor, Tiff's name was on my short list. But I've had time to think about it, and I'd put money on her innocence. It wasn't her style to be sneaky. Loud and brazen, yes. Sneaky, no."

The pressure on Dillon's chest eased, and she nodded. "Very true. Nobody ever would have accused Tiffany of being subtle."

A sad smile crossed Cynthia's lips. "Besides, she would have confessed before she died. She'd never leave Anne in danger."

"Or you."

"Or me," Cynthia agreed. Her eyes misted over. "We've eliminated two, but it doesn't get us much closer to who it might be."

"I hate this." Dillon threw her hands in the air. "I don't want to believe anyone here could do such a thing."

"Maybe we're approaching it backwards. If we figure out the motive, it would be easier to find the culprit."

"Is there any other motive other than betrayal?"

"Spoken like a true loyalist." Cynthia smiled. "People do odd things when they're scared. We just have to keep our eyes open and watch out for anything that seems suspicious."

"Do you know how terrible this is going to be? Looking at our friends like they're common criminals."

"Just because everyone looks to you for answers doesn't mean you have to shoulder it all."

"But isn't that what a leader does? Carries everyone?"

"No!" Cynthia said. "You'll crash and burn if you try to take responsibility for everything. You have to learn to let go. Rely on us. Lean on us sometimes."

"I hate this." Dillon kicked a rock off the path for emphasis.

"Was that your exclamation point?" Cynthia winked. "Not Oscar-worthy, but still, I like your flair for the dramatic."

"Fine." Dillon laughed. "That was a little drama queenish, wasn't it?"

Cynthia smiled and nodded. "We can drive ourselves crazy speculating, or we can wait until CJ comes up with a little more data. I for one don't want to toss around names like they're glitter. It makes me feel dirty and dishonorable."

"The double D's."

Cynthia turned her nose up and frowned. "What do boobs have to do with this?"

Dillon burst out laughing. "Seriously? I meant the double D's, dirty and dishonorable. Not big boobs."

"Oh." Cynthia's cheeks turned crimson.

"But now that you mention boobs."

"I didn't mention boobs." Cynthia playfully slapped Dillon's arm. "You did."

"Oh, yeah." Dillon flashed Cynthia a cheesy grin. They always found a way to laugh, even during the darkest times. "So, speaking of boobs, what's going on with you and the mysterious hottie?"

"You did not just use the word hottie, did you? Are you thirteen?"

"On a good day." Dillon winked. "Answer the question. I saw heat bouncing off the two of you earlier." They'd nearly arrived back at the mansion, but Dillon wasn't done quizzing Cynthia, so she slowed her pace.

Cynthia fiddled with the seam at the bottom of her shirt and wouldn't meet Dillon's gaze. "I'm not sure what you thought you saw."

"I saw you hanging on Alaina's every word."

"Everyone was. She was telling us about a traitor." Cynthia picked up the pace that Dillon had just slowed. "That doesn't prove anything."

"So I have to prove it, instead of my friend just telling me the truth?"

"No fair." Cynthia scowled but turned her gaze back to Dillon. "Fine. I find her interesting."

"Interesting enough to want to sleep with her?"

"I knew you'd jump to that conclusion."

"So you're not sleeping with her?"

"No!"

"Do you want to be?"

"Damn it, Dillon." Cynthia's blush lit up the tips of her ears. "Talking about religion caused you to practically crawl out of your skin, but now you're perfectly okay quizzing me about my sex life."

"Yep, about sums it up." Dillon chuckled.

"You're impossible." Cynthia huffed.

"And you're stalling." Dillon huffed back at her.

"I find her very attractive in myriad ways."

"Oh, a myriad. Sounds serious."

"I will not continue having this conversation if you insist on behaving like a juvenile."

Dillon stifled a laugh. "Would you care to share the *myriad* ways that she interests you?" Dillon made sure to put a sleazy emphasis on myriad.

"For fuck's sake. Stop saying myriad like you'd say nipple."

Dillon pointed and laughed, intentionally sinking to a new low. "You said nipple."

Cynthia rolled her eyes and shook her head, but the slight upturn of her mouth gave her away. Her now ruddy complexion and the twinkle in her eye erased the earlier evidence of her fatigue. "Are you done?"

Dillon scratched her chin and pretended to think. "For now." She gave Cynthia a warm smile. "Seriously, tell me about Alaina."

"I like her," Cynthia said with a goofy grin. "But I've only known her for a couple weeks, so I don't know her well enough to say much more."

"Skylar and I fell pretty fast. In crazy times like these, I don't think the old rules apply anymore."

"True. Who needs a U-Haul when we all live together already?"

Dillon laughed. "See. Easy. Plus, she can't ghost you."

"Good point." Cynthia smiled. "I just want to see where this might lead. She's a mysterious puzzle wrapped in an enigma. Isn't that a line from a movie?"

Dillon squinted and searched her mind. "I think it was a politician. Roosevelt? No, I think maybe Churchill."

"What was he referring to?"

"No clue, but it's a great line."

"Why do we always end up going off on tangents

when we talk?" Cynthia put on her best scowl.

"Because you're a squirrel."

"Sure. That's it. Anyway, I hope to get to know her better, but she might decide to return to Amarillo. In that case, it'll be short-lived."

"Has she given any sign of what she plans to do?"

"Not really. To be honest, we haven't really talked about it."

"Too busy having sex?"

"Dillon Mitchell. I told you we have not had sex."

Score. She loved it when she could get a Dillon Mitchell out of Cynthia. "Too busy kissing then?" Cynthia's face immediately turned crimson. Dillon pointed. "I knew it. You kissed her."

"I will remind you once again that you are not a teenage boy. Can you possibly react to this like an adult?"

Dillon shrugged. "I'll try."

They'd stopped on the patio outside the Athens Room, and Cynthia glanced at her watch. "Skylar is going to wonder what happened to you."

"Changing the subject?"

"Maybe."

Dillon didn't want to address the elephant in the room when Cynthia seemed so enthralled. The possibility still existed that Alaina was playing them and lying about there being a traitor, but that was a conversation for another day. Or better, a conversation they'd never have to have. "I'll let you off the hook. For now."

"How generous of you."

Chapter Four

Skylar yawned and stretched out on the sofa. Her book laid on her chest. *Shit.* She must have fallen asleep. Everything looked blurry, so she blinked a couple of times to clear her vision.

The sun filtered through the oversized patio doors into the Athens Room. It hung much lower in the sky than she'd last remembered. Apparently, she'd been out for longer than she thought. She'd been looking forward to spending time alone with Dillon, but the likelihood of that dimmed with the fading light.

Since the attack, they'd gotten little privacy. With Dillon being a Commission member and one of the most influential leaders on the estate, the others sought her out. Mostly, they sought reassurance, which Dillon offered freely.

Skylar wished they could slip away and pretend none of the horrors that had befallen the group was real. *Escape.* Even if it were just for a couple of hours. She longed for intimacy with Dillon. They hadn't made love since the attack, both exhausted when they fell into bed at the end of the evening. She'd planned on changing that today. The longer the meeting dragged on, the more she doubted it would happen.

Earlier, her hopes had risen when Alaina breezed into the room. She'd abruptly stopped when her gaze landed on Skylar. A veil descended, and she mumbled something Skylar couldn't make out before she fluttered away.

Skylar's thoughts drifted back to the awkward encounter with Alaina. Her natural beauty was unmistakable. She had long dark hair, penetrating blue eyes, and cheekbones that any model would kill for. Even though it was a cliché, she had a body that turned heads. Skylar had witnessed several women at the estate nearly get whiplash when she passed by.

It went beyond the physical, though. Her presence was immediately evident by the electric energy that accompanied her. As conspicuous as she was, she seemed to desire the opposite. Like a ghost, she disappeared when anyone paid attention to her. Cynthia seemed to be the only one Alaina allowed in her sphere for long.

Lately, Cynthia had been elusive, and Dillon had been worried. It concerned Skylar, too, but since the beginning, Dillon had a protective streak when it came to Cynthia.

Skylar closed her eyes, arched her back, and threw her hands over her head, stretching as far as she could reach. She let out a groan when her back cracked.

"Holy shit," a voice said.

The voice startled Skylar, and she abruptly sat up.

"Sorry," Cynthia said. "I thought you'd broken in half with that sound."

"Aren't doctors supposed to be able to handle these things?"

Cynthia's eyes widened in mock horror. "Not when we're not expecting it."

Skylar chuckled.

Dillon made her way across the spacious floor and bent to kiss Skylar. The kiss was over before Skylar had a chance to respond. Probably for the best since desire lingered just under the surface. She'd love to pull Dillon to the couch and ravage her. *What the hell?* Where had that come from?

Lately, her reactions confused her. Never had she allowed herself to want—or more accurately need—someone like she did Dillon. Those emotions laid her wide open, and the vulnerability left her uneasy.

She gazed into Dillon's eyes, expecting to see the same longing. Skylar flinched at the distance she found there. Something seemed off. After searching Dillon's face, Skylar turned to Cynthia. The hard set of Cynthia's jaw confirmed her suspicions. One didn't grow up in foster care or live on the streets without the ability to quickly size up those around her.

Skylar weighed her words, but before she could speak, Cynthia clapped her hands together. "Well, I should leave you two alone and track down Alaina." She bent and gave Skylar a one-armed hug before she slipped out the patio door.

What the hell was that? If there had been any doubt that the two weren't right, Cynthia's abrupt departure confirmed it. She wavered between addressing it head on or pretending not to notice. She settled on the former. Skylar slid her hand into Dillon's and guided her onto the couch next to her. "What's wrong?"

Dillon shrugged and squirmed in her seat. "Tough Commission meeting."

"Did you guys fight?"

The creases in Dillon's forehead deepened, and

a vein throbbed near her temple. Skylar expected she was gauging her words. "It got a bit contentious, but everyone came around in the end." Dillon smiled, but it didn't reach her eyes.

"Care to share the topic?"

Dillon's face fell, and her gaze shifted toward the bank of windows where the sun continued to creep toward the horizon. She shook her head. "I can't."

Skylar's heart raced. Dillon was always so open with her, which sometimes made her comfortable enough to do the same, but now Dillon was shutting her out. Despite her deep inhalation, Skylar struggled to get enough oxygen to prevent the suffocating feeling.

Dillon squeezed her hand. "I'm sorry. Not being able to talk to you about this feels so wrong."

"We've always talked about everything." Skylar paused. She couldn't lie to Dillon. There were still things Skylar wasn't ready to talk about, and Dillon knew it. "I mean...um...we always talk about the current stuff going on."

"I've told you it's okay, and I mean it." Dillon gazed into Skylar's eyes and gently put her hand against her cheek. "You'll tell me about your past when you're ready. No pressure. I love you regardless of whether you tell me tomorrow, next year, or never."

Warmth spread across Skylar's chest. How had she gotten so lucky? Dillon seemed to know when Skylar needed reassurance. She suspected Dillon wanted to know more of what made her tick, but she would never push for answers.

Skylar laid her head against Dillon's shoulder. "Thank you. You've never pressed me to talk about things I don't want to, so I'll return the courtesy."

"You know I trust you. It's not that."

Skylar put her finger against Dillon's lips. "Shh. You don't need to explain or defend yourself." Dillon's soft lips trembled under her finger, so Skylar slowly ran it around Dillon's mouth.

Dillon moaned and closed her eyes. On the second pass around her lips, Dillon sucked Skylar's finger into her mouth. The sensation ran through her and ended at her center. She gasped. *Lightweight.* It had been too long, and her body vibrated with the need to be touched.

Dillon continued to tease Skylar's finger, sucking harder and then running her tongue the length of it. If she didn't stop Dillon soon, Skylar feared she wouldn't be able to. She wanted Dillon to take her here on the couch, but the possibility of others wandering in was too great.

Skylar pulled back. Her face burned, but it was nothing compared to the heat coming from between her legs. *Maybe just one more kiss.* She leaned in, and her lips met Dillon's with a heightened urgency.

Their lips pressed together, and Dillon's tongue gently pushed through Skylar's. Dillon's tongue withdrew only to thrust back inside a fraction of a second later.

Skylar moaned, and her back arched. She squirmed, trying to take away some of the pressure throbbing between her legs. "God, Dillon. You can't do that to me here. It's been too long. I might burst."

Dillon responded by running her hand along the inside of Skylar's thigh but stopped inches from her target. "What do you say we go somewhere more *private*?"

Skylar glanced at the bank of windows. "It's almost

dinnertime."

"Even better." Dillon smirked. "We'll have the suite to ourselves."

Skylar returned the smile. "I like the way you think, Dillon Mitchell." She rose to her feet.

Dillon continued to smirk as Skylar offered a hand to help her up. "That way, you can be as loud as you want."

Skylar pulled back her hand and glared in mock outrage. "I am *not* loud."

"Sure, whatever you say."

"You're a bit cocky today, aren't you? Maybe I'll just demurely lay there and let you have your way with me. You won't hear a peep."

"So Victorian of you." Dillon ran her hand up Skylar's leg, but this time, she didn't stop inches from her destination.

Skylar shuddered and stepped back. "You did that on purpose."

"Me?" Dillon put her hand to her chest, and her mouth dropped open. "I didn't think your demure self would even notice."

Skylar gazed into Dillon's dark brown eyes. *God, she's sexy.* "Smartass." She held out her hand and pulled Dillon to her feet. "After that move, no dinner for you until you take care of a few things."

"I think I'm hungrier for something other than food." Dillon squeezed her hand. "Let's get out of here."

Gladly. Skylar smiled. A thought pinged in her mind about Dillon's earlier strange behavior, but her ache caused her to quickly push the thought away.

Dillon didn't know how long she'd been staring at the ceiling, but her focus shifted when Skylar whimpered in her sleep. After sleeping in the same bed for nearly six months, Dillon had become accustomed to Skylar's nightmares, but they still broke her heart.

By trial and error, she'd discovered what worked when it came to comforting the sleeping Skylar. She'd learned the hard way that doing anything that made Skylar feel trapped was a recipe for disaster.

Dillon gently pulled Skylar closer but left plenty of room for her to move. She lightly rubbed her back and whispered, "It's okay, Sky. You're safe."

Skylar murmured and pressed tighter against Dillon. Her breathing became regular as Dillon continued to softly talk to her. *Who hurt you so badly?* Dillon wondered if she'd ever find out. It seemed Skylar wanted to keep it in the past, especially since their lives would never return to what they were before.

Once Skylar settled back into sleep, Dillon returned her gaze to the ceiling. She hadn't known how much she'd needed a release until they'd arrived back at the suite. Both were fully clothed when the first orgasm rocked them. After the first, they were able to leisurely explore each other's bodies until they were both satiated.

They should probably wander down to see if there was any dinner left, but food could wait. Now that she was alone with her thoughts, the Commission meeting weighed heavily. She didn't want to believe anyone from the estate would betray the group, but there was only one alternative. *Alaina.* As mysterious as Alaina was, something told Dillon she was being truthful. She shuddered. Lying here thinking about this wasn't good for her.

She gently nudged Skylar. "Hey, Sky, I think we should go grab some dinner." Skylar stirred, and her beautiful gray eyes flickered open. Dillon's chest filled. She could get lost in the depth she found there.

"What time is it?" Skylar said, her sleep-filled voice even huskier than usual.

Dillon shrugged. "Don't know. Half past a stomach grumble."

"Didn't I fill you up enough earlier?" Skylar teased and ran her fingers across Dillon's breast.

"Oh, god, we're never going to make it to dinner, are we?"

"Do you want to?" Skylar slid off Dillon's shoulder and flicked her tongue against Dillon's nipple.

"Um, not if you're going to keep doing that." Dillon laughed. "Take me, I'm yours."

"Music to my ears," Skylar said before devouring Dillon's erect nipple.

Chapter Five

CJ draped her arm over Karen's shoulders as they walked through the atrium toward CJ's makeshift computer center. In order for Karen to keep up, CJ shortened her long stride, allowing them to stroll slowly across the large area.

Never would CJ take these moments for granted again. The two days after the crisis, when she feared Karen might be dead, were the longest of her life. She gazed down at the woman who still, after fifteen years, made her heart race. Karen's shoulder-length brown hair had recently begun to show signs of gray, which CJ surprisingly found sexy. She wondered if Karen would have started going gray if it weren't for the crisis.

"What are you thinking about?" Karen asked.

Not wanting to broach the subject of Karen's graying hair, CJ said, "Where the hell do you think Dillon and Skylar were?"

Karen rolled her eyes. "Do you really have to ask?"

CJ made a gagging sound. "Stop." She crinkled her nose. "I don't want to think of my best friend in the throes of passion."

"You should be happy for her." Karen leaned into CJ.

"I am, but it's still gross." CJ smiled. "And I plan on letting her know it when she finally crawls out from under the sheets."

Karen chuckled. "You two are impossible. But seriously, it's nice to see her so enthralled with Skylar."

"I don't think I completely understood how messed up she was after Jane died, until you went missing." A lump caught in CJ's throat. "I feel guilty now."

"Don't. You always empathized even if you couldn't fully relate. It doesn't make you a bad person. You were there for her. And when she's not giving you shit, she'd tell you that you kept her going on her worst days."

"Never. You'd have to torture her to get her to admit it." CJ laughed.

"True. But she's told me plenty of times."

"See. She's an ass." CJ smiled. "And I'm so going to razz her about missing dinner."

"I'm sure you will."

They arrived at the computer station. *Good.* The surrounding area was empty. She didn't want an audience. After Karen had filled her in on the Commission meeting, they'd decided to wait until after dinner to investigate. They feared someone might catch them while they researched the breach. They were probably being paranoid since CJ often worked during the evening, but they didn't want to tip their hand to the traitor.

"Just don't act suspicious," Karen said. "Don't go rambling on making up an elaborate story for why we're here. The traitor will figure you out in a heartbeat."

CJ's palms began to sweat. She hadn't thought of that. "But I created a brilliant story. I thought I'd start by saying—"

Karen held up her hand and shook her head. "I have a better idea. Everyone knows you get obsessed when you're working on your computer." Karen picked up a novel off the stack that Anne kept in the area. "I'll be sitting here with a book like I'm just hanging out while you're doing your thing. If anyone approaches, I'll do the talking. You grunt and huff like you normally do when you're preoccupied."

"Hmph. I don't do that."

Karen gave her a big smile. "Sure you don't, darlin'."

"No fair, you're pulling out all the stops," CJ whined.

"Whatever do you mean, darlin'?" Karen stifled a grin.

CJ pointed. "You did it again." Karen knew CJ couldn't resist when she said *darling* in her Texas drawl.

Karen winked and nodded toward a chair a couple of feet away. "I'm going over there to read. I know you hate when I look over your shoulder when you're geeking out."

CJ glowered. "You've been hanging around Dillon too much. I don't geek out."

"Anything you say." Karen bent and kissed her forehead before retiring to the chair.

CJ had been at it for nearly half an hour when she isolated the data she was looking for. She could have accessed it immediately, but she'd wanted to hide her tracks. She couldn't be too careful. If the traitor had been able to trick them all these months, it was hard telling what else she may be able to do.

"I'm almost ready for you to take a look," CJ said to Karen.

"Is it wrong that I'm nervous?" Karen asked as she stood. "Silly, I know. It's not like the computer is going to give us a name."

"Afraid not. It's only going to tell us the dates and times of contact." CJ focused her attention on the computer again. With a few mouse clicks, the screen filled with dates and times.

Karen leaned over her shoulder. "Holy shit. That's a lot of times."

CJ shook her head. "Not really. Every time Jake and I communicated with them is on the list, too." CJ pointed to the first column. "Almost all of these, I would bet, were us."

"How will you know for sure?"

"Jake and I were pretty consistent with our communication times. Plus we kept the calls short."

CJ studied the list. *Holy hell.* One of the entries showed sixty-eight minutes. She highlighted the final time and sat back in her chair, studying the entries.

"Interesting." Karen pointed at the screen. "It seems to have stopped a couple months ago."

CJ narrowed her eyes. *Why?* What would make the traitor abruptly stop? "Guilt? Change of heart?"

"Or she found another way to communicate with them."

"Oh, god, you're right." CJ's heart sank. She'd been so focused on the computer aspect that she'd missed the obvious. "This isn't going to tell us shit." CJ crossed her arms over her chest.

"Not so fast." Karen rubbed CJ's shoulders. I think there might be a lot we can glean from it.

CJ counted silently to herself. "There are thirteen contacts. If one were superstitious..."

"But neither of us is." Karen's voice was firm.

"Maybe you should print it out, so we can study it away from here." Karen's gaze darted around the dimly lit atrium.

"Excellent idea." CJ's gaze followed Karen's. The lower lighting that she'd previously considered ambiance, suddenly seemed ominous. Her eyes narrowed as she tried to see into the shadows. Had something moved? She blinked twice but didn't catch any movement. The dark must have been playing tricks on her. *Sure. That was it.*

Karen leaned farther over CJ's shoulder and put her mouth near CJ's ear. "Are you getting a creepy vibe, too?"

CJ nodded. "Yes. Look at all this data I've kept on your supply runs." CJ pointed at the screen and hoped Karen would understand. "I've kept it all in one place. I'll print a couple reports out so you can do an updated inventory."

"Huh?"

CJ patted Karen's hand and then squeezed tighter than normal. "I know computers confuse you. But if you give yourself a chance, you'll understand." CJ squeezed her hand again on the word *understand*.

"Ah," Karen said. "But you know I'm no good with computers. Why can't you keep doing it for me?"

CJ let out the breath she hadn't realized she'd been holding. *Karen understood.* She hit print and selected four copies. "We can take these sheets back to the suite, and I'll explain how you can use them."

Karen snorted. "Fine. If I have to." She snatched the pages off the printer, folded them, and stuffed them into her front pocket.

With a couple of mouse clicks, all evidence of the data disappeared from the screen. CJ breathed a sigh of relief. *What was wrong with them?* They'd been spooked and needed to get out of here.

CJ logged off and stood. She fought the urge to grab Karen's hand and run from the room. Casually, she held out her elbow and hoped it didn't shake too badly. "Shall we?"

Karen latched on to her arm but didn't speak.

CJ started out faster than she had earlier, knowing Karen would have to practically jog to keep up. A shiver ran down her spine. Maybe she was being ridiculous, but she didn't care. She wanted to get Karen out of here.

They made small talk about nothing as they hurried toward the stairwell. Their footsteps echoed loudly in the empty chamber. At least CJ hoped it was empty. Every shadow drew her gaze, but it was impossible to focus due to the speed they were moving. She strained to see into the depths of the darkness. Her heart raced as she searched for any sign of movement. *Nothing.* Perhaps they'd allowed the situation to get the best of them.

When they reached the stairway, CJ ripped open the door and motioned Karen inside. CJ slipped through behind Karen. She tugged on the handle and fought against the resistance of the door closer. *Damn it.* Despite her strength, the door didn't shut as quickly as she would have liked.

A vision of a black and white thriller flashed across her mind. Her parents had loved old movies and played them often. The heroine would run toward a door as the music swelled. She'd arrive, slip inside, and slam the door shut. The music would hit its crescendo when a foot slid across the threshold, stopping its closure.

Involuntarily, CJ glanced toward the ground, half expecting to see a foot jut inside. The latch clanked. She fell against the door and let out a large exhale.

Karen did the same. "Are we nuts?"

CJ contemplated her answer. After their near sprint across the atrium, she felt a little crazy. How had she allowed herself to get so freaked out? She sighed. "If Dillon saw us nearly running across the atrium, she'd tell me I wasn't being logical."

"Jesus, that was pathetic." Karen laughed.

"No doubt. But didn't it feel creepy?"

Karen's gaze darted around again. "Maybe we should keep moving and have this conversation as we walk."

"Yeah." CJ took Karen's hand. "Let's get back to the room. Then we can look at the printouts."

They'd only climbed a couple of steps when Karen stopped, nearly pulling CJ off balance. "Shit. We can't."

"Whoa." CJ grabbed the handrail and righted herself. "Why not?"

"Skylar." Karen sighed. "We can't talk in front of her. Commission orders."

"Ugh, this is so stupid. Nobody would suspect Skylar."

"I know, but we have to follow the rules. If we tell her, then who's next?"

CJ groaned. "Maria, Tasha, Leslie, Katie..."

"Exactly." Karen gripped CJ's hand tighter. "It sucks, but we have to do it this way. What if it's some-one we know and love?"

CJ's jaw clenched. "I refuse to believe it."

"Ya know what Dillon would say, don't you?"

"I could guess." CJ rolled her eyes.

"She'd tell you that you need to be logical and look at the data impartially."

"Yeah, I get your point. The evidence is the evidence."

"You and Dillon need to go over it, maybe I can get Skylar out of the room for a bit."

"No!" CJ's voice rose. "After what happened in the atrium, I don't want you running around on your own."

Karen put her hand against CJ's cheek. "My protector. But I don't think I need one. What is the likelihood that the traitor suddenly became suspicious and started tracking us the day we uncovered the truth? Sounds pretty coincidental."

A door banged below, and CJ flinched. "Let's get back to the room."

❦ ❦ ❦ ❦

"I love your hair," Skylar said as she twirled one of Dillon's curls around her finger.

"I've always hated it. It's a wiry hot mess," Dillon said. The sensation of Skylar's hand as she moved it in a circular motion felt good. "It's way too long."

Skylar extended the curl to its full length and laughed. "A whole two inches. What a disgrace."

Dillon playfully swatted at Skylar. They'd managed to get dressed and made it to the suite's common area. For the last half hour, they'd been lounging on the couch but hadn't gotten any farther. Dillon's stomach rumbled, reminding her that they'd missed dinner.

"Getting hungry?" Skylar licked her lips.

"That's exactly what got me into trouble the first time." Dillon pointed. "I won't let you lure me in again. Or at least my stomach won't."

"Does any other part of your body have a say?" Skylar's mischievous gray eyes held Dillon's gaze. "I know some that might have a different vote."

Before Dillon could respond, the door swung open. Karen entered first followed by CJ, who grinned broadly when she saw the pair. "Well, what do we have here? Did you two forget something, or were you just preoccupied?"

Dillon's cheeks blazed. *Damn it.* She didn't need to give CJ any more ammunition to harass her. "What?" Dillon put on a confused look. "We've just been hanging out talking."

"Ah, talking. Is that what you're calling it nowadays?" CJ turned to Karen. "Can we *talk* later?"

"I'd love to spend all evening *talking* with you," Karen responded.

Dillon turned to Skylar. "Are you going to let them abuse me like this?"

"Afraid so." Skylar got to her feet. "I'm too famished to fight."

"Really? Didn't you just say a few minutes ago that food could wait?" Warmth spread up Dillon's neck. Did she just say that out loud?

"Priceless." CJ pointed at Dillon. "You just embarrassed yourself."

"Did not." Dillon tried for a menacing scowl but feared it came out looking more like she was constipated.

"So you guys haven't eaten?" Karen asked.

Weird. That seemed like an abrupt change of topic. She studied Karen. "Nope. We're famished."

"Renee outdid herself tonight. She used vegetables from the garden in the stir fry, and it was heavenly."

"Superb." CJ brought her fingers to her lips and did a chef's kiss. "I think there's leftovers."

"We should go get some," Skylar said. "Let these two lovebirds have the nest to themselves."

"No." Karen's response was immediate and loud. "I mean...now that Cynthia and Anne have moved back into the suite with Diana, we don't lack for privacy."

Dillon had no doubt Karen and CJ were up to something. Normally, she could read CJ, so she shifted her gaze. CJ made an almost imperceptible movement with her head, motioning toward the door. *Ah.* She wanted to get Dillon alone.

"Karen," CJ said. "Would you mind taking Skylar on a quest for food? I need to talk to Dillon about that new building project she's been working on. The CAD program is giving me trouble again."

"I thought you fixed that last week." Skylar narrowed her eyes and looked at CJ suspiciously.

"We did." CJ shrugged. "Seems like we have a gremlin. It stopped working again. I think it has something to do with the cross vectors or the triangulation of the trusses that's causing the problem."

Dillon stifled a groan. Did she think Skylar would fall for her mumbo jumbo?

"Oh." Skylar flicked her wrist at CJ. "Above my pay grade. I have no idea what you just said nor do I care to learn."

Dillon snapped her mouth shut to keep her jaw from falling open. She couldn't believe the streetwise Skylar fell for such a load of bullshit. It was almost too simple.

Karen grabbed her sweatshirt that hung from the back of the chair. "Are we ready?"

Skylar stood and offered her hand to Dillon. "As soon as I hug this luscious woman goodbye, I'm all yours."

"Oh, you wanted to hug me?" CJ said.

Dillon shot her a look but decided no response was the best response. Skylar fell into her arms and hugged her tightly.

"Don't think for a minute I fell for that triangulation crap," Skylar whispered in her ear before breaking the hug.

"I love you, too, sweetheart," Dillon said with a smile.

When the door clicked shut behind Karen and Skylar, Dillon turned to CJ. "You two won't win any acting awards."

CJ slung the back of her hand against her forehead and pretended to swoon. "Whatever do you mean?" she said in her best Scarlett O'Hara voice.

"Nice try." Dillon slid into a chair at the table. "So lay it on me. What do you have? I saw Karen slip you those folded-up papers."

"We didn't even do that exchange believably?"

"Afraid not."

CJ plopped into the chair across from Dillon and dropped the printout onto the table. "Records of when someone called Babcock. The yellow highlighted ones are the ones you want to look at. The other ones are mine or Jake's."

Dillon pulled the page closer to her and studied it. Silently, she counted the highlighted entries. *Shit.* Thirteen times. She scanned the document. "It looks like they started a couple weeks after shit hit the fan."

CJ reached out and ran her finger down the first column. "The greatest concentration seems to span about a month. They start to taper off around mid-July."

Dillon pointed to the final date. "It looks like the last date is shortly after the attack on Amarillo."

"We didn't get a chance to study them before we came back to the suite." CJ squinted and leaned over the paper. Her long blond hair cascaded toward the table and blocked Dillon's view.

"Do you mind tossing back those locks, Rapunzel? I can't see anything."

In one fluid motion, CJ pulled a hair band off her wrist and had her hair reined into a ponytail within seconds. "Better, crybaby?"

Dillon smiled to herself. After Jane's death and before the crisis, she'd spent little time with CJ. To keep her demons at bay, she'd isolated herself. Until recently, she hadn't realized how much she'd missed her best friend.

"Are you listening to me?" CJ said in a loud voice.
"Huh?"

"I knew it. You weren't." CJ scowled and crossed her arms over her chest. "I was making a brilliant observation, and you missed it."

"CJ. Brilliant." Dillon held her hands out in front of her, palms up. She moved them up and down as if she were weighing something. "Nope, they don't balance out."

"Whatever, smartass. What I was saying is...." CJ's nostrils flared. "Shit, now I can't remember what I was saying."

Dillon threw her head back and laughed.

"Would you shut up and focus?" The corner of CJ's mouth quivered. She put one hand over it while she pushed the printout closer to Dillon. "What do you think?"

Dillon flashed a cheesy smile before she bent over the page. Teasing CJ was one of her favorite pastimes. "How can you be so sure that you and Jake didn't do these? Did you keep records?"

"No, but check out the times." CJ pointed at several items.

The pattern became clearer. All the calls took place between eleven p.m. and one a.m. "Our traitor is a night owl."

"It makes sense. Most times, I'm working on the computer during the day, and people are in and out. It would raise suspicion if someone were messing with my equipment."

"Do you remember anyone lingering around your computers? Or maybe saw them wandering around the atrium later at night?"

CJ looked toward the ceiling. "I've been searching my brain, but no, I can't think of anyone. Every now and then when I worked late, I'd see someone walk through, but I never registered anything suspicious. Like, I never thought, *Odd, I keep seeing that person here all the time.* Or nobody acting strangely."

Dillon's gaze returned to the paper. *What the hell?* She did a double take before she put her finger on one of the entries and slid it to another. "They talked for over an hour here and here."

"Yeah, it looked like they had a few lengthy calls early on." CJ moved her finger to a date in late June. "The calls start to dwindle here. Less frequent and much shorter."

Dillon nodded. "Strange how abruptly the pattern changed. Any clue what event might have caused it?"

"That would have been shortly after Anne caught Tiffany in bed with Willa and KC."

Dillon's skin crawled. What a terrible time it had been. "And when Tiffany was a one-man wrecking ball at the Commission meeting."

CJ groaned. "I almost forgot about that."

"I didn't. You weren't one of the lucky ones to get eviscerated." Dillon closed her eyes, seeing the scene play out in her mind,

"True. I remember Karen was a wreck."

"No doubt." Dillon shook her head. "Tiffany all but insinuated that Leslie was going to kill herself, and it would be all Karen's fault."

CJ wore a pinched expression. "That tore her up."

"Several of us were torn up that day."

"Do you think it has anything to do with the reason the traitor stopped?" CJ picked up the page from the table and held it out in front of her.

"It could be. My odds-on bet is still Willa. The timing would work. Maybe she'd turned remorseful after sleeping with Tiffany and broke off contact."

"It's possible." CJ didn't sound convinced. "But what if they just went underground?"

Dillon had been following CJ's logic until that point, but now she narrowed her eyes in confusion. "Into the bunker?"

"No, not literally. I mean they found a more secure way of contacting Babcock."

Dillon rested her forehead against her palms. "So the traitor could still be contacting him?"

"It would make sense."

"No," Dillon practically shouted. "That would mean we are in serious danger."

"I hate to break it to you," CJ said and put her hand on Dillon's arm. "We already are regardless of whether they're still talking to Babcock."

"I hate this." Dillon tossed the paper onto the table and leaned back against her chair. "All of us will be looking over our shoulders at our friends. It won't matter if Babcock comes or not. The suspicion will continue to erode our tenuous group. One bad conflict and who knows if we'll stay together."

"You're just full of optimism today, aren't you?"

Dillon ran her hand through her hair. "Sorry, this is just so frustrating."

"I know." CJ gathered the papers, folded them into a neat package, and held them out to Dillon. "Here, we better not have these laying around in case the girls get back."

Dillon started to tuck the papers into her pocket but stopped. "No, you need to give these to Karen. God, I hate this."

"What?"

"Now I'm hiding shit from Skylar. I don't want my relationship with her to be tainted by lies." Dillon rubbed her chest to alleviate the pressure building there.

"You make it sound like you've got some clandestine plot you're hiding." The creases in CJ's forehead deepened as she spoke. "It's not like you're meeting up with a secret lover."

"That's how it feels."

"Now you're just being a drama queen. You need to stop it, or you'll drive yourself crazy. More importantly, you'll drive me crazy."

Dillon laughed. "Stupid of me. I should have known this would turn out to be all about you."

"Yep." CJ grinned. "How about we put this away for now and have ourselves a beer?"

"I'm in."

Chapter Six

Cynthia ran her finger down the list for the third time, but nothing jumped out at her. Either she was missing something, or it was too big of a long shot. Guilt nibbled at her. As the only physician in the group, she should have recorded this medical information earlier. It had been an unacceptable oversight on her part. She put her hand against her forehead and rubbed, hoping to relieve the pressure.

"This doesn't look good," Alaina said. Even without looking, Cynthia would recognize the low silky voice anywhere.

Cynthia dropped her hand from her forehead and smiled at Alaina. Her heartbeat quickened. Alaina's tight black jeans hugged her in all the right places, and her loose button-down shirt showed a hint of cleavage. But it was her face that captivated Cynthia, or more accurately, her eyes. *Cerulean blue.* Wasn't that the color that was all the rage? She wasn't sure if they were cerulean or not, but they held a depth and intensity that entranced Cynthia. Made her want to discover everything that lay behind those eyes.

What was wrong with her? In the midst of discovering she'd been negligent in her duties, her body was reacting like a hormonal teenager. "Hi. I didn't hear you come in."

Alaina held up a bag. "I missed you at lunch. I

thought you might be hungry since it's nearly three."

"Damn. How did it get to be that late already?" Cynthia motioned to the seat in front of her desk. "Join me?"

"Certainly. I think there might be an extra cookie or two in the bag." Alaina pulled the chair closer to the desk as she sat.

"Who says I'm not going to eat them all?" Cynthia smiled. "After all, I missed lunch."

Alaina smirked. "I guess I'll have to go in search of my own then." She made as if she were about to stand.

"Fine. I'll share." Cynthia pulled the bag toward her.

"I thought you'd see it my way."

"Wow. This is a feast," Cynthia said as she peeked inside.

"When I told Renee I wanted to bring you lunch, she went to work. Said she'd make sure it was extra special."

Cynthia's mouth watered as she pulled out a sandwich made of her favorite sourdough bread. She lifted the top, and her eyes widened. "Did you see what's on this?"

Alaina leaned forward. "It certainly isn't what the rest of us got for lunch. Is that goat cheese?

"Goat cheese and pesto. And veggies out of the community garden." Cynthia brought the sandwich up to her nose, inhaled deeply, and let the aroma wash over her. "Cheese is becoming a sacred commodity."

"I can't believe you still have any." Alaina's gaze lingered on the sandwich.

"I'm sure we're nearing the end of the stash they grabbed in LA. Katie and Renee have been experimenting with making their own. The results have been mixed." Cynthia crinkled her nose at the thought of their earlier failed attempt. "The last one tasted more like earwax than cheese."

"Eww. They have to figure it out. What kind of world is it without cheese?" Alaina's smile held a hint of melancholy.

"Exactly." Cynthia replaced the top bread and bit into the sandwich. The mixture of goat cheese, garlic, sage, and olive oil exploded in her mouth, and she moaned. When she remembered where she was, she muttered, "Um, sorry."

Alaina laughed. "If that's your reaction to a sandwich, I can only imagine how you'd respond to other pleasures." Alaina raised her eyebrows.

Heat rushed up Cynthia's neck. The room suddenly felt extremely warm. "Um, I, ah…" She didn't want Alaina to see her so flustered, so she needed a comeback. "I'm not sure that's a topic we should be discussing during lunch." *Lame.* But it was the best she could come up with.

Alaina's eyes twinkled as she put her hand to her chest. "Are you talking about what I think you are?"

"I don't know. What other pleasures are you referring to?"

With a deadpan expression, Alaina said, "Ice cream."

Cynthia laughed, and the heat in the room came down a notch. Thankfully, because she needed to eat her lunch and complete her data analysis before the Commission meeting tomorrow. "Would you like to share?" She held the sandwich out to Alaina.

Alaina eyed it longingly before she held up her hands. "No, it's yours. Besides, I already ate."

"There's plenty for both of us." As Alaina wavered, Cynthia thrust the food out farther. "I insist."

"Doctor's orders?"

"Definitely. Doctor's orders."

Alaina grasped the sandwich in both hands. Her long fingers curved around the bread, and the veins in the back of her hands stood out. Cynthia gaped as she brought the sandwich to her thin lips.

Once Cynthia realized she was staring, she busied herself with the bag, sifting through the goodies inside. She pulled out a container of Renee's specialty garlic potato salad. She pulled off the lid, and her senses were assaulted by the heavy aroma of garlic. "Apparently, Renee wants to keep the vampires away."

"Or me," Alaina said as she set the sandwich back on the napkin spread out on the desk.

"You?"

"Garlic and kissing aren't a good combination." Alaina's gaze locked on Cynthia's.

"Oh." Without thinking, Cynthia straightened and leaned hard against the back of her chair. More than likely, she looked like a deer in headlights. "I didn't know there was any kissing planned." God, she sounded like a dork. For someone so sure in her profession, why did she have to sound so awkward?

"You didn't get the memo?" Alaina winked.

"Um, ah..." *Damn it.* Why didn't she know how to flirt like a normal person? Bantering with Dillon came so easy, but Alaina left her all sorts of flustered.

"God, you're adorable when you're rattled."

"They make toothbrushes," Cynthia blurted out. She did not just say that. Her already hot cheeks turned into an inferno.

Alaina pushed the sandwich toward Cynthia. "I'll stop or you won't be able to eat."

"It might be too late." Cynthia fanned her face with her hand.

"Nope. We can't let vintage goat cheese go to waste."

"True." Cynthia nodded. "In our new world, that would be like throwing the Hope Diamond into the ocean. But you're going to have to help me." Cynthia held up the sandwich. "This thing is enormous."

"You twisted my arm."

The conversation shifted to safer topics as they shared Cynthia's lunch. Every time they talked, Alaina proved to be quite the conversationalist. She could intelligently discuss many topics, so the conversation never lagged. Today they'd fallen into a debate on which was better, Shakespeare's comedies or tragedies.

Not wanting to miss any of the creamy garlic, Cynthia licked the spoon after she'd taken the last bite of the potato salad. To ensure she'd gotten it all, she ran her tongue around the spoon one last time. When she glanced up, Alaina's gaze was locked on her. Cynthia pulled the spoon from her mouth and slapped it onto the desk harder than she'd intended.

A flicker of mischief danced in Alaina's eyes, but then they softened. "Geesh, it's not the spoon's fault that there's no more potato salad left."

Thank you. Cynthia was relieved that Alaina chose not to take the conversation down a sexual path. "I can still blame it, anyway."

Alaina nodded toward the list Cynthia had pushed off to the side. "You weren't having any luck?"

"Why do you say that?" She took a stack of cookies out of the bag, then stuffed the garbage into the now empty sack, before sliding the papers in front of her.

"When I walked in, you didn't look happy. I distracted you with lunch, but I'm afraid you'll be back to brooding soon."

"I don't brood." Cynthia drew her eyebrows in, hoping to look menacing.

"Sure you don't. So anyway, did you discover anything with your research?"

"Yeah, I suck as a doctor."

"Really? And how did you figure that out while simply getting a medical history on your patients?"

"Because I should have done this months ago. A good physician would already have had all this info at her fingertips."

"I see." The corners of Alaina's mouth quivered but didn't rise. "Do you think there might have been a couple of other things on your mind? Like, um, I don't know. Maybe like...the end of the world."

Cynthia's shoulders relaxed. She knew Alaina had a point, but she still felt negligent. "Well, there is that."

"That's better. Now that we've established beating yourself up isn't a good thing, did you discover anything from your research?"

Cynthia let out a long breath. "I've been poring over the list, but I've found nothing. A couple fathers named Robert, but that seems like a big stretch. Robert to Bert to Bertie? I don't know."

"You've gotta cover all your bases. Maybe one of the other Commission members will see something you don't."

"This sucks. I don't want anyone to be the traitor."

"I know you don't." Alaina's eyes softened. "But you can't let that get in the way. It could put everyone in danger."

"God, I know." Cynthia rubbed her chest. "I feel like a horse kicked me. My chest has never felt this tight."

"Scary times we're living in." Alaina leaned across the desk and put her hand on Cynthia's. "It's okay to be scared."

Scared? What the hell was Alaina talking about? She'd faced everything that had been thrown at her and survived.

"Did I say something to upset you?" Alaina asked.

"Funny, but my first reaction was to adamantly deny it." Cynthia's shoulders slumped. "But then I realized I'm not scared for me per se. But...."

"But everyone here has become your family. The people you love. And it terrifies you what could happen to them."

Tears welled in Cynthia's eyes. She'd already lost Tiffany. Who would be next? She nodded, unable to speak.

"I'm sorry. I shouldn't have brought it up." Alaina squeezed her hand. "You've been through a lot the last couple of weeks."

"Me?" Cynthia's mouth dropped open. "I can't believe you're comforting me after everything you've endured."

A veil descended, and Alaina's face lost all expression. She dismissively waved her hand. "That's all in the past."

Cynthia studied Alaina. As they'd gotten to know each other the last few weeks, she'd seen this reaction before. Alaina refused to talk about what happened while on the road with her captors. She also declined to comment on her escape from Braxton Babcock's compound. There had to be a boatload of pain buried inside her, but it didn't seem she had any intentions of sharing it. "Sorry. I won't pry." Even though she sensed it would make Alaina uncomfortable, she couldn't resist adding, "but I'm here if you ever need someone to talk to."

Cynthia waited for Alaina's usual drawback, but she didn't close herself off like normal. *Progress?* Cynthia would take it as such.

Alaina sighed. "Thanks. You've been a good friend."

Friend? Yes, they had become friends, but Cynthia couldn't deny she'd like more. "And I can say the same for you. I'm glad you're here." Another awkward moment. Saying she was glad Alaina was here might be the most insensitive thing she'd ever said, considering she'd been forcefully dragged across the country. As she searched for a way to recover the situation, Alaina stood.

"Quit looking like you're going to vomit." Alaina walked around the side of the desk. "That would be a huge waste of goat cheese, and Renee wouldn't stand for it."

Cynthia smiled, feeling only slightly better.

Alaina stood next to Cynthia. "Get up. Let's hug it out."

Happy to oblige, Cynthia leapt to her feet. Alaina stepped into Cynthia's embrace, and the rest of the world faded away. Their bodies melded into each other. *Perfect fit.* Cynthia fought the urge to inhale Alaina's scent but lost the battle. She always smelled like a combination of sandalwood and sage. Strange combination? Possibly, but it worked.

Cynthia closed her eyes and felt the stress leave her body.

"Is there something else bothering you?" Alaina asked when they separated.

Cynthia stiffened. Her growing attraction to Alaina was definitely bothering her, but she had no intention of telling Alaina. "Um, why do you ask?"

"I'm cheating." Alaina smiled.

Oh, god, what did that mean? Cheating on Cynthia? Was that even possible when they weren't dating? Cynthia ran through the list of possible candidates who might have caught Alaina's eye. She needed to come up with a response since Alaina was looking at her with a puzzled expression. "Care to elaborate?"

"I saw Dillon and some of the others heading out on ATVs when I was walking here. I thought maybe you were feeling…um, well…" Alaina waved her hand. "Never mind. They were probably going to work on the garden or something."

"You thought my friends went out to play without me." Cynthia chuckled. "And that I might be sad about it."

Alaina put her hand against her forehead. "God, when you put it like that, I feel ridiculous. Forget I even said anything." Her cheeks reddened as she spoke.

Cynthia's heart fluttered. As if Alaina wasn't attractive enough, her blush was adorable. "I get why you thought that. I would've been sad if I wasn't invited." Cynthia picked up the paper from her desk. "I needed to get this done for the Commission meeting tomorrow, so I told Dillon I couldn't go."

"Ahh, good. Well, not good that you couldn't go, but I'm happy you weren't left out." Alaina nodded toward Cynthia's desk. "I better let you get your work done, or you'll miss dinner, too."

Cynthia sighed. "Yeah, I still have a little more to finish. But thank you so much for bringing me lunch."

"It was my pleasure." Alaina turned to leave but stopped and turned back. "Will I see you at dinner?"

"Definitely."

"Good," Alaina said with a smile that Cynthia couldn't read. Before Cynthia could respond, Alaina left the room.

Cynthia flopped onto her desk chair but didn't reach for her papers. Her thoughts were still occupied by the fascinating woman who had just exited. Another side of the normally reserved Alaina was revealed today. A less guarded, softer side. Her blush had taken Cynthia completely off guard. She wished she'd gotten a picture of it, although the image still danced in her head. It had been so sweet. Vulnerable.

"Alaina Renato, who are you?" Cynthia said to no one.

She glanced down at her papers and sighed. Thinking about Alaina would have to wait. Reluctantly, she picked up her pen.

Chapter Seven

Dillon threw her headset onto the desk and grabbed her short hair with both hands. The call with the New York group had left her unsettled. They'd reported more defections, and their group had fallen into a conflict, which threatened to separate them into two factions.

"That reaction doesn't exactly instill confidence," CJ said.

Dillon shifted her gaze to CJ. "We've gotta figure out a way to get everyone together before everything falls to shit. They found another group in upstate New York. They'd been in talks to join forces until they discovered the insanely harsh punishment being doled out for the slightest transgression."

"What do you mean?"

"They've built stockades and are publicly whipping offenders."

"Are you serious?" CJ's eyes widened. "What is wrong with people?"

Dillon's gaze met CJ's. "Does it really surprise you? Our world had already been going down the wrong path before this happened. Without laws, the ugly side of people has taken over."

"You're just tired." CJ's brow furrowed.

"What the hell does my sleep patterns have to do with the shitty state of people?"

CJ pointed her finger at Dillon. "No. We can't have you being all doom and gloom. You're our cheerleader. The one that tells us everything will be all right. So we need to snap you out of this."

Dillon groaned and flopped against the back of her chair. "Ugh, I know. I hate being Debbie downer." She turned to CJ. "And you're right, Mom. I need a nap."

CJ glanced at her watch. "Don't you have a Commission meeting in ten minutes?"

Dillon groaned and stood. "I guess it'll have to be a power nap."

❧ ❧ ❧ ❧

Judging by the volume in the meeting room, one might think it was a packed house. Dillon's gaze circled the faces of the other Commission members. Nope, only five people, including her. She'd remained silent for the last ten minutes as the voices rose. Someone needed to get control of the meeting before it spiraled any further out of control, and apparently, it would have to be her.

Dillon cleared her throat, but nobody turned to look in her direction. She'd need to be more forceful. "Guys," she said in a normal tone. No reaction. She let out a deep sigh and stood. "Guys," she said in a louder voice. Conversation stopped, and all gazes turned toward her. "This is *not* getting us anywhere. Tearing each other apart and pointing fingers isn't helpful."

There were some general mutters from the others, but nobody said anything comprehensible.

"Now that I have your attention," Dillon said as she sat. "We need to have this discussion in a respectful and orderly way."

"What did you have in mind?" Karen said with an edge to her voice.

"Funny you should ask." Dillon smiled, hoping it would defuse some of the tension. She held up the notebook sitting in front of her. "I've taken the opportunity, while you were otherwise engaged, to make a few notes. One might call it an agenda."

Cynthia craned her neck to see the list. "Care to enlighten us with what you have in mind?"

Dillon held up three fingers. "I'm thinking we have three major areas of discussion. First, and the most controversial, is discussing possible suspects. We can't sit around and yell at one another and defend our friends."

"Somebody has to," Jake said, his face still red from the earlier argument. "Especially when people are being disrespectful of our loved ones." His gaze fell on Renee as he said it.

"Disrespectful, let's talk disrespectful." Renee's voice rose.

"This is exactly what Dillon is talking about," Cynthia spoke loudly to be heard over the raised voices. "This isn't getting us anywhere."

Jake and Renee fell silent while Karen continued to sit with her arms crossed, glaring at the others.

Dillon shot a pleading look at Karen, who was normally the calm, sensible one, but she'd become defensive when the others had questioned why CJ had been so sloppy to let this kind of breach happen. Karen's gaze softened, but her jaw remained tight.

"What's the second point?" Cynthia asked.

"We need to make a plan of action to further *investigate* them."

"What if we pick the wrong suspects, and the real culprit walks around undetected?" Karen asked.

"That's a possibility," Dillon said. "And one I don't think we can avoid. There's only five of us, so we don't have the manpower to cover everyone."

"I say we just tell the group there's a traitor and flush them out," Renee said. "I hate all this secretive espionage bullshit."

"That's a sure way to get us all killed," Jake said. "As the defense specialist, I object."

Dillon nodded and met Renee's gaze. "I have to agree with Jake on this one."

Renee snorted and leaned back in her chair. "Of course you do."

Dillon fought against reacting out of frustration and instead held Renee's gaze. "I understand your frustration. But if the traitor knows we're on to her, then it could get dangerous. It could trigger an all-out blitz from Babcock's group."

Renee nodded. "You've got a point."

Jake threw up his hands. "For Christ's sake, that's what I've been trying to say for the last twenty minutes."

Dillon glared at Jake until he sheepishly dropped his head and stared at the table.

"And the last item?" Cynthia asked.

"We have to make plans to take the Amarillo women home, which might coincide with a summit with the other groups."

Renee's eyes widened. "They want to meet?"

"Yes, I'd wanted to save discussing that until after we got our first two agenda items out of the way," Dillon said.

"Maybe we should talk about it first," Jake said.

Dillon shook her head. "No, I think everything ties together. We need to determine who our top suspects are, so we make sure to strategically pick our team."

"Fair enough," Jake said.

"Okay then, I need two commitments from each of you." Dillon studied the faces of the others before she continued. Everyone appeared receptive. "First, you remain respectful and open-minded when another member is discussing someone dear to you. We have to be as objective as possible." Dillon held up an empty water bottle. "If we can't do that, then I propose using this water bottle."

"What are you gonna do?" Renee smirked. "Fill it with water and throw it at us if we misbehave?"

"Hmm, I hadn't thought of that." Dillon smiled. She hoped a little humor would lighten the heaviness in the room. "Actually, it's an old method I used to use in disputes between my workers. Only the person with the bottle would be allowed to speak. Everyone else would have to listen until they were passed the bottle."

"I think we can control ourselves," Jake said.

"But I'd keep the bottle on standby just in case." Karen grinned. "You know how out of control Dillon can get."

The others laughed, further lessening the tensions.

"The other might be even harder. I ask that you look at those around you with an objective eye and be honest about anything suspicious you may have seen. We need to look at them from two angles. First, think back to their state of mind at the time of the event. Obviously, everyone has changed a lot since then, but we need to think of them then."

Dillon opened her folder and distributed the papers inside. "These are copies of the logs that CJ printed. You'll note the time frame that the individual was most active."

"It looks like it's stopped the last couple of months," Renee said.

"Yes. And we figure that could mean two things." Dillon paused while the others studied the sheets. "Either the person stopped communications with Babcock, or she's found another means. Depending, we're looking at two completely different motives."

"I agree," Cynthia said. "We either have someone that thought better of the interaction with Babcock and cut it off, or we have someone who's even more entrenched with him and is trying to hide it. Found her own equipment. A ham radio. A satellite phone. You name it."

"Let's do it then," Renee said.

Cynthia pulled paper from her folder. "Here is a roster of everyone at the estate, so we can go name by name." She handed the papers out.

"Alaina's not on the list." Karen looked at Cynthia and gave her a wry smile. "Sorry, Cynthia, but I think we need to discuss her, too."

Cynthia nodded. "Agreed."

Dillon smiled to herself. Excellent role modeling. Now if they could only continue the civility. "Okay, let's take a few minutes to independently go through the list. Write your notes and choose the people you think we need to discuss."

Everyone bent over their sheets, studying them intently. Dillon glanced at the others out of the corner of her eye as she marked her own page. Renee decisively went down the columns without hesitation and finished first. Jake went through almost as fast, but then the scratching of his pen against the paper filled the air as he scribbled out several and changed his answer. Cynthia took the longest. She studied the sheet for several seconds between people before she put her pen to paper. When she did, her motion was quick and decisive.

They chose to start with the women none of the Commission members were close to and made it through over half the list with little debate. From this, they put three names on the suspect list.

"The next name is Willa Andrews," Dillon said.

The loud reaction told Dillon everything she needed to know. "Apparently, there are some strong opinions of Ms. Andrews," Dillon said. She'd been a thorn in many sides, especially early on when she'd hung on Tiffany's every word. She made her living as an independent filmmaker and enjoyed creating a stir. Her pink hair and flamboyant personality spoke to that.

"I've got a star next to her name as one of my top candidates," Karen said. "She's a shit stirrer that loves drama. Sometimes, I feel like we're all unwitting participants in a sick documentary she's creating."

"Oh, my god, that is so true," Renee said. "I swear she says and does things just to get a reaction."

"Does everyone agree?" Dillon asked.

Everyone nodded.

Dillon wrote Willa's name in the column labeled suspects. "Now shall we go on to the harder people?"

Cynthia raised her hand. "I'll start. Since I only knew three people when I arrived, and Tiff is gone, I probably have the least number of original connections. So let's discuss my two."

Jake cleared his throat. "No disrespect, but do you think we should at least discuss Tiffany?"

Cynthia's eyes clouded with pain, and she shifted her gaze to the table. "Whatever the group decides."

Dillon put her hand on Cynthia's back. "I personally think it's unnecessary. Even if we decided she was a suspect, it's not like we can investigate her."

"I'm going to have to disagree," Karen said. "I hate to say this, but someone could go through her things to see if there's any evidence."

Cynthia's hands clenched into fists, but she remained silent.

"Do you really think if she were responsible that she'd leave any trace?" Renee asked. "I think it's a stretch."

"Tiffany may have been a lot of things," Cynthia began. "But not sneaky. If she was pissed about something, she'd come at us with both barrels."

"True," Jake said. "I'm still scarred from the meeting she ripped us to shreds."

"I believe Cynthia should look through her things," Karen said.

Dillon's chest constricted. The tension pouring off Cynthia was palpable. How horrible to have to discuss one of her closest friends, who'd been dead for less than a month. Dillon's heart went out to her. "Let's give Cynthia a little space on this one. We can circle back later."

Cynthia's shoulders relaxed, and she shot Dillon a thankful look.

"What about Cynthia's other two? Diana and Anne?"

The group quickly dismissed Anne as a suspect

but had a livelier debate concerning Diana. They finally agreed that in the beginning she'd been drunk or passed out more times than not, and it would have been unlikely she could have pulled it off.

"Before we move on," Jake said, "we need to talk about Alaina. There's the possibility she made the whole thing up to sow discord."

Dillon kept her gaze on Cynthia. She felt sorry for her but knew they'd all have their turn in the hot seat. "Cynthia?" Dillon said. "What do you think?"

"For the record, I want to say that I don't believe she's lying." Cynthia blew out her breath and pursed her lips. "But it would be negligent for us not to explore that possibility." Cynthia looked down at the table. "I think she needs to go on the list."

The others readily agreed.

They moved on to Jake, who also only had two candidates. From the earlier argument, Dillon knew the discussion concerning Nancy could turn contentious. Nobody likely suspected Lily, Jake's wife, but Nancy was a different story.

They made quick work of dismissing Lily before Cynthia said, "I think Nancy has to be considered as a candidate."

Jake crossed his arms over his chest. "And here we go. Nancy gets to be the target just because she's different."

Cynthia bit her lip. "I'm going to pretend you didn't just say that. Playing the discrimination card doesn't suit you." Cynthia's tone was sharp and her words biting.

Dillon contemplated a response. While technically Cynthia was abiding by the rules, she walked a fine line of hostility. Likely the discussion of Tiffany put her on edge.

Before Dillon could think of something to say, Jake spoke up. "I'm sorry, Cynthia." He gazed around the room. "I apologize to everyone. I'm just a little defensive when it comes to Nancy." He held up the paper with the call log. "I can say, beyond a shadow of a doubt, she couldn't have made all these calls."

Of course. It was no secret, at least not anymore, that Jake and Lily had developed a polyamorous relationship with Nancy. Tiffany had revealed it during one of her rampages at the Commission meeting.

Dillon cleared her throat. "What I hear you saying is you can supply her with an alibi on some of these occasions?"

"Yes." Jake's cheeks flushed, and he avoided eye contact with the others.

"Anyone have any objection to removing Nancy from the list of potentials?"

Nobody did, so they moved on.

Renee put up her hand. "I might as well go next and get this over with. I came with my posse, my three besties." Renee glanced at Cynthia. "And I lost Dee in the battle. I'll go through her stuff if it'll make everyone happy, but no way do I suspect her."

Dillon nodded. "Thanks. That would be great. Let's talk about the other two, Sid and Tina."

After a short discussion, the group agreed to dismiss them from the list. They had no motive nor had they exhibited any suspicious behavior.

"So shall we talk about the elephant in the room?" Renee's eyes narrowed.

"I'm assuming you mean Katie," Cynthia said.

Thank you, Dillon thought. She dreaded this conversation. While she and Renee had made peace concerning Katie, it was still a topic best avoided.

"None of us want to believe Katie would do something like this." Karen looked toward Renee. "She's been a friend of mine for years, but we have to have the tough conversations."

Renee rubbed her temple. "I know. But for the record, this feels horrible."

Dillon smiled at Renee. "Something we can agree on."

Renee returned the smile. "Let's get it over with."

Dillon sat back, hoping the others would say the things she didn't want to.

"In the beginning, she was angry." Karen glanced at Dillon. "Beyond pissed off at you. We know she did and said some things she regrets."

Renee rested her forehead in her hand and wouldn't look at the others. "So that makes her a suspect?"

"I'm afraid it does," Cynthia said. "As hard as it is on you, I don't think you're the only one struggling with it. Dillon, you look like you want to vomit."

Perceptive. Dillon's stomach had been roiling from the moment Katie's name was spoken. "I don't want to believe it, either, but I know I'm too close to the situation to be objective. Despite everything, I love that woman. She was Jane's best friend and has become a good friend of mine, too. Yes, she had a motive, but I've seen no signs of anything since we cleared the air."

"Unfortunately, that plays into one of the theories," Jake said. "The calls stopped shortly after you guys made up." He shifted his gaze to Renee. "And you started dating."

Dillon groaned, and her stomach clenched.

She raised her hands over her head. "I have to recuse myself. I cannot be objective when it comes to Katie."

"Me either," Renee added.

"I'm willing to abide by what the other three Commission members decide, but I would like permission for Renee and me to abstain."

"Fair enough." Cynthia turned to Renee. "Do you agree?"

Renee nodded.

"I'm sorry, but I think she has to be a potential suspect," Cynthia said. "What do you say, Jake?"

"Sorry, I agree." He wouldn't look at Dillon or Renee as he spoke.

A sharp pain, as if she'd been stabbed by a knife, spread across Dillon's chest.

"I'm afraid I'm with the other two," Karen said with her soft Texas twang.

The juxtaposition of her soothing voice and her vote almost made it seem worse somehow. "Okay." Dillon wrote Katie's name on the list of potential suspects. "Shall we continue?"

The energy in the room felt heavier now and the silence more ominous.

"Karen and Dillon, you guys are the only ones left," Cynthia said. "Since all your friends are mutual, how do you want to do this?"

Dillon turned to Karen. "Let's just go down our list. Anyone a definite no for you?"

Karen nodded. "I'd like to believe they all are, but my definite nos are CJ and Leslie."

Dillon's back stiffened. Karen hadn't mentioned Skylar. Her grip on her pen tightened, but she hoped nobody noticed. She'd agreed to be objective. "I have to add Skylar to the list, for the same reason that Jake included Nancy. Since we've been here, I've become a light sleeper. No way could she have snuck out of our bed that many times without me noticing it."

"I agree," Karen said quickly.

Dillon pushed down her ire. "Do we all agree with Karen's assessment? Can we eliminate CJ, Leslie, and Skylar?"

"Not so fast," Cynthia said.

Dillon's heart raced, and her anger returned. "You have something to add?" She tried not to glare at Cynthia, but she suspected she wasn't entirely successful.

Cynthia smiled at her. "I'm good with CJ and Skylar, but I think we need to discuss Leslie a bit."

"Leslie?" Karen said. "She was practically comatose with grief. I can't see her being a suspect."

"That's exactly why I think we need to talk about her. Grief can make people do strange things," Cynthia said.

Renee raised her hand. "I can attest to that, but if we use that logic, then everyone is a suspect."

Jake nodded. "Renee has a point. But let's at least do the exercise of considering Leslie."

After several minutes of discussion, it was put to a vote. All five members of the Commission agreed to leave Leslie off the suspect list.

"That leaves Maria and Tasha," Cynthia said. She shifted her gaze between Karen and Dillon.

The color drained from Karen's face. "This is awful. I've known Maria for a long time." Karen put her arm across her stomach and held it there as if she were in pain.

Dillon understood the feeling well. Her stomach continued to gurgle. "I'm gonna need a shower after this meeting. I'm not sure I'll ever be able to wash the proverbial stench off."

Jake gave her a sympathetic nod. "I know it seems disloyal, which smacks in the face of all we stand for. But this is bigger than us."

Dillon closed her eyes and nodded. "Thank you, Jake. I know it is. We must think of the group first, or we could all end up dead. It's just so hard."

"Karen, would you care to tell us why you've brought Maria's name up?" Cynthia asked.

"I wouldn't have thought of her, except for yesterday." Karen turned to Dillon. "You were there. Was it me or was she more aggressive than usual?"

Dillon inhaled and held her breath. She knew Karen was right. Slowly, she let out the breath. "I noticed it, too."

"What happened?" Cynthia asked.

Dillon waited for Karen to speak since she'd put Maria's name on the table. When Dillon glanced in Karen's direction, she realized it was up to her. Karen had wilted against the back of her chair and appeared to have no bones.

Cynthia must have noticed, as well, because she turned to Dillon. "Would you like to explain?"

Dillon took a sip of water and cleared her throat. "Yesterday, Maria was more intense than usual. I felt like she was grilling us on Commission business. Wanting to know why we were being so secretive. She wouldn't let it be."

"Oh," Renee said. "Maria can be a spitfire, but you're saying it seemed over the top?"

Dillon ran her hand through her hair. "I don't know. I thought maybe I was just being hypervigilant, but since Karen saw it, too, maybe not." Dillon shook her head a couple of times as if to clear her racing thoughts. "I don't want to believe Maria could be involved. Besides, what would her motive be?"

"She lost the election," Jake said, his voice barely over a whisper. "I think she really wanted to be a Commission member."

"No," Dillon said louder than she intended. "Nobody would do that over a lousy election. Would they?"

"I'm sorry, Karen and Dillon. We know this is hard on you," Cynthia said. "But as an attorney, she's used to winning."

Dillon put her head on the table. "Ugh. Do we have to keep talking about her like this?"

"Do you want to put it to a vote?" Cynthia glanced around the table. She was met with nods. "Show of hands, who thinks Maria should go on the list?"

Jake and Renee's hands went up immediately, followed by Cynthia's. Reluctantly, Dillon raised her hand at the same time Karen did.

Dillon swallowed down bile. She wrote Maria's name on the list right below Katie's. This couldn't be what they'd come to, suspecting their friends. But she knew Jake was right, there was something bigger than themselves to protect.

"What do you say we take five before we talk about the summit?" Cynthia said with her gaze locked on Dillon.

Everyone rose and headed for the door.

"Dillon," Cynthia said, stopping Dillon in her tracks.

Dillon turned back. They were the only two left in the room.

"Are you okay?" Cynthia asked.

"I don't know if I'll ever be okay again. What have we become? Did you ever read *The Lord of the Flies*?"

"God, that's an oldie. I was thinking more like the *Hunger Games*." Cynthia draped her arm over Dillon's shoulders and squeezed. "We're doing the right thing. Don't forget we were elected because the others believed we would do the hard things."

Dillon put her arm around Cynthia's waist. "Nobody said it would be *this* hard."

"I expect it might get harder."

"Aren't you a ray of sunshine?" Dillon tried to put a hint of mirth in her voice.

Cynthia laughed. "Just keeping it real."

☙ ☙ ❧ ❧

The mood was somber when the others filtered back in. Cynthia wanted the meeting to be over, but she knew they had more to do. She'd prefer to sneak off somewhere on her own to recharge her batteries, but it wasn't in the cards. They had to reach a decision about the summit. It was already late October, and if groups from around the country were going to meet, they'd need to travel before winter arrived.

Dillon was the last to return. Although she tried to conjure her normal playfulness, the strain around her eyes gave her away. She joked with Jake and complimented Renee on last night's meal, but it didn't fool Cynthia. Over the past several months, she'd come to know Dillon well. In fact, she considered Dillon her closest friend.

While secrecy was necessary, it also took its toll

on Dillon. She'd always been a straightforward leader who believed in transparency. How they'd been forced to handle the mole went against everything Dillon believed in. Truly, what they all believed in, but Cynthia knew it affected her in a much deeper way.

Dillon sat beside Cynthia and gave her a sad smile. Cynthia patted her leg, not knowing any other way to reassure her friend.

"I'm hoping this discussion will come much easier than the last," Dillon said. "I've had quite a few conversations with Caleb. He's from the group in New York. They, along with several others, are interested in sending delegates to a summit. But with winter coming on, they'd like to have it within the next month."

"Shit," Renee said. "That doesn't give us much time."

"I know." Dillon flipped open her notebook, the one where she kept records of the various groups they'd made contact with. "At last count, there are over thirty-five groups we know of. Some are relatively small and are in negotiations to join with other groups. But as of yesterday, there are fifteen contingents that are interested in coming to the summit. I expect this could grow."

"Are we sure we can trust all of them?" Renee asked.

"Excellent question." Dillon pursed her lips. "I wish I could tell you that without a doubt it was safe, but I can't promise anything. I feel comfortable with most of the groups and hope they can be strong allies."

"But the danger is there," Jake said as a statement, not a question. "We're in a damned if we do and damned if we don't situation."

"Care to explain?" Renee asked.

"If the last few weeks has taught us anything, it's we're vulnerable. The right, or I guess I should say wrong, people could come in here and wipe us all out."

Cynthia's heart raced. Even though she knew the truth, hearing Jake speak the words was an unpleasant eye opener. It had been closer to utopia for them, in their secluded hideaway, compared to the dystopia some of the other factions reported.

"You okay?" Dillon put her hand on Cynthia's arm.

"Huh?" Cynthia felt the heat rise in her cheeks. How much had she missed?

"Jake asked for our thoughts on whether we thought Las Vegas would be a suitable location for a meeting."

"The others are willing to travel that far?" Cynthia said.

"Yeah, some of the groups in the north are contemplating relocating as winter comes. Possibly becoming nomadic, or at least moving to a location with a more temperate climate."

"And they think Vegas is the answer?" Karen's mouth dropped open. "Have they never been there in July?"

Jake smiled. "They don't want to be there in the summer, but they could head north in the warmer months. Or even to California or Colorado."

"We can't let anyone in here," Renee said in a raised voice.

Jake sighed. "Trust me. I don't want to, either, but we got lucky the last time and still lost three. Doing the math, that was nearly ten percent of our population.”

Jake’s words stopped Cynthia cold. Her swallow caught in her throat. She’d never done the math before, but ten percent ran chills through her body.

“And don’t forget our most immediate threat. Babcock,” Dillon said. “The man’s insane. He wants to turn the country into a theocracy, with him at the helm. I have no illusions that he won’t attack us once he’s sure he has a large enough army.”

“And if he’s still in contact with our traitor...” Karen paused and took a deep breath. “He could be biding his time.”

Renee held her hand out. “Let me get this straight. You’re saying we *must* go to the summit. There really is no choice.”

Dillon nodded. “Yes. I think it’s a foregone conclusion. We need to have a seat at the table.”

“And don’t forget,” Cynthia began, finally finding her voice. “We’ve got the ladies from Amarillo that need to be reunited with their families, so we already have to venture out since we don’t want to bring them here.”

“With a show of hands, who thinks we should attend the summit?” Dillon said.

Everyone’s hand shot up.

“Okay,” Dillon nodded, seemingly pleased with the vote. “The next thing that has to be decided is who goes. We obviously should have representation from the Commission, but I don’t recommend all of us going. We’ll need a presence here, too.”

“I want to go with you, Dillon,” Cynthia said before anyone else could speak up.

“And who said I was volunteering?” Dillon said.

Cynthia’s head whipped around, and her gaze

met Dillon's. She opened her mouth to express her surprise when she noticed Dillon's smirk. "Asshole. You had me going for a second."

Dillon chuckled.

"Priceless," Renee said. "You should have seen your face."

"Now that we've established that Dillon and Cynthia want to go," Jake said. "I want to be the final member of the Commission to go."

"What about Lily?" Cynthia asked.

"She'll understand why I need to. She'd insist on coming, too, if it weren't for the kids."

"Sacrifices of a parent," Karen said. "But is it smart to send all three of you?"

"It makes practical sense. It will be much more dangerous out there, so the defense guy should go," Jake said.

"And the doctor," Cynthia added. She didn't want to admit her real reason for volunteering. *Alaina.* She still hoped Alaina would agree to stay permanently, but if Alaina decided to return to Amarillo, Cynthia wanted the opportunity to say goodbye. "Besides, Lily and Skylar have gotten damned good at what they do and can cover for me."

Karen snorted. "Do you really think Skylar is going to stay back and let Dillon go off on her own?"

Dillon sighed. "She's right. As much as I want to keep her safe, she'll insist on coming along."

"What if I want to go?" Karen asked.

Dillon shook her head. "Nope. CJ has to stay and man the computers, and I can guarantee she'll never let you out of her sight again nor would you want to be. There would be a revolt if Renee tried to leave."

Renee laughed. "Yeah, we don't want to move

their food bowl."

"Then it's settled. Cynthia, Jake, and I will be the representatives from the Commission."

Cynthia put her hands in her lap, in hopes that nobody would see how much they trembled. "I think we should have in mind who we'd like to join us, not just leave it to chance."

"This might sound crazy, but I think we need to take some of our potential traitors with us," Dillon said.

"Are you nuts? You need people you can trust with your life," Renee said.

Dillon raised her hand palm out. "Hear me out. We'll be in tighter quarters out there. The estate is huge with more people, so the traitor will have more of an opportunity to communicate with Babcock without us ever knowing. This way, we might be able to catch them."

"But they'll know where you are and where you're going," Karen said. Her voice grew louder as she spoke. "They could lead you into a trap."

"Already have a plan." Dillon kept her voice calm and level. "We tell everyone that's not in this room, except for CJ, a false destination. The leaders from the other communities are worried, too, so they plan on doing the same."

"Apparently, you've put a lot of thought into this," Cynthia said. Her stomach knotted further as she considered the suggestion.

Dillon nodded. "Most are worried about Babcock building an army against us."

Cynthia debated whether to speak. Part of her knew that her comment might not be well received, but she needed to say it. "I think Dillon is right. From everything Alaina has told me about Babcock, he is more ruthless than we realize."

"More reason to gather our forces," Jake said. "Where are we telling the others we're going?"

"Salt Lake City," Dillon said. "We'd go through Vegas to get there, so nobody will suspect."

"Is Sin City the best destination?" Jake asked. "There's likely to be dead bodies all over the casinos."

"Already thought of that," Dillon answered. "They were building a new casino that was set to open in June. Right before *it* happened."

"Oh, right." Renee snapped her fingers. "The Mayan."

"That's the one," Dillon said. "It should be relatively free of people while hopefully being ready for habitation."

"Sounds like the best plan," Renee said. "Who else on our list of *suspects* do you want to take?" It wasn't lost on Cynthia her venomous tone when she said suspects. "I reluctantly agreed to putting Katie on the list, but I won't vote to send her on the mission. No way." Renee crossed her arms over her chest.

"I don't think Katie should go," Dillon said before anyone else could speak. "For several reasons. First, I think it would look suspicious if we asked her while Renee stayed back. And second, I will say again, I don't believe she's the traitor."

"Hear! Hear!" Renee smiled at Dillon. "Thank you."

Cynthia nodded in agreement. It wasn't a battle worth fighting. "Who else should we target?" She inwardly groaned at her use of the word *target*.

"For me, Willa's our number one suspect," Jake said. "We have to figure out a way to get her to go along."

"I've got it." Karen snapped her fingers. "We play to her vanity. Tell her we want to film the journey for posterity. It would be the first record of a newly formed coalition. The rebuilding of our way of life. Something that future generations would turn to, just like the Constitution. With her background and ego, I don't see any way she'd refuse."

The others readily agreed.

"Who else?" Dillon asked.

"As much as I feel like a scumbag saying it, I think Maria would make sense," Karen said. "We could use Tasha on the trip since she's our mechanical wizard. Keeping vehicles running is going to be the key. Win-win."

"Brilliant," Cynthia said. "Maria would naturally want to go with Tasha, so it wouldn't seem suspicious." Out of the corner of her eye, Cynthia saw Dillon slump in her chair.

"Betrayal," Dillon muttered and dropped her gaze to the table.

"I know it feels like betrayal." Cynthia wanted to reach out and offer a reassuring gesture but held back. "But the bottom line is that someone here may be guilty of a much larger betrayal. We have to do what we have to do."

"I'll keep telling myself that until I believe it." Dillon's voice was somber. "But what about Tasha's arm?"

"She's doing great," Cynthia said. "It wasn't near as bad as first thought."

"Seemed pretty messed up to me," Jake said.

"In the midst of a battle, that's pretty common," Cynthia said. "Luckily, the bullet went clean through.

Missed the bone. She's still healing but should be fine to go. Besides, if any complications arise, I'd rather her be with me."

"Good point," Dillon said. "Who else do we want to include?"

"With only three of you in the know, I don't think it's safe to take more." Karen cleared her throat. "I do have one other recommendation. Actually, a request. Leslie would like to go."

Cynthia noted the surprised looks around the table that matched her own.

Jake spoke first. "Leslie? That's interesting. Not someone I would have added to my short list of volunteers. Did she say why?"

"She feels guilty," Karen said. "Feels like she let everyone down during the first few months."

"She was mourning, for fuck's sake," Renee said. "I hope you told her no one feels that way about her."

"I did." Karen smiled.

"I think we have enough," Dillon said.

Cynthia nodded at Dillon's notebook. "Could you read them to us?"

"Sure. Me. Skylar. Cynthia. Jake. Willa. Tasha. Maria. Alaina. And Leslie."

"Don't forget we have to take the ladies from Amarillo," Karen said.

"Uh, yeah." Dillon scratched their names onto the list.

"Are we ready to put it to a vote?" Cynthia asked.

Despite the somber faces, the list passed unanimously.

Chapter Eight

The next two weeks were a flurry of activity as the entire group planned the departure of their contingent. Dillon had little time to think of anything other than the preparations, which suited her fine. She didn't want to dwell on the secrets she was keeping from Skylar and the suspicions that swirled around everyone.

The final dinner, or as CJ called it, the Last Supper, had been consumed. The affair had been subdued without the normal levity they tried to bring to their dire situation. Dillon had talked with many of the women, and they were scared. Rightfully so. Both groups would be smaller, which would make them both more vulnerable.

The dishes had long been cleaned up, and various women had stopped by their table to wish them well on their journey. Most of the exchanges had been quick and awkward, nobody knowing what to say in a situation like this.

Jake and Lily had slipped away early, probably wanting a little time alone before he left. Nancy had stayed back with the children to give them privacy.

Maria had hammed it up and held court as the stream of well-wishers cycled through. Dillon wasn't fooled. She'd known Maria a long time, and Maria used her flamboyant act to hide her fears. But it had the perfect effect on the others, who responded to her infectious energy.

Now the party was winding down, and the room was beginning to clear out. For the past fifteen minutes, CJ lingered around the perimeter. Whenever Dillon glanced in her direction, she was staring.

Dillon leaned over toward Skylar and whispered in her ear. "I'm going to go see what CJ wants."

Skylar smiled. "I noticed. Poor thing. I think she's freaking out."

"Yeah. It's sweet, but I'll never tell her." Dillon chuckled.

"That's what best friends are for." Skylar patted Dillon's knee. "Come get me when you're done. I want to say goodbye, too, since we're sneaking out at the butt crack of dawn."

Dillon stood and meandered toward CJ, who pretended not to notice her approach. "Hey, stalker. I couldn't help but notice your beady eyes all over me."

CJ put her hand against her chest. "*Moi*? I don't know what you're talking about. I was just hanging out over here stretching my legs."

"Sure. I'll let you go with that." Dillon frowned. "Scared?"

CJ shrugged. She started to speak, but tears filled her eyes.

"Dude, it's okay." Dillon hated when her Spock-like friend became emotional.

"Just promise you'll be safe."

"Always." Dillon smiled.

"Come here and give me a hug." CJ opened her arms. "Then I'm going to walk out of here and not look back."

Dillon stepped into CJ's tight embrace. "You

have to go tell Skylar goodbye, or she'll never forgive either of us."

Once they separated, CJ held out an envelope. "I had to make this for you."

Dillon started to take it, but CJ pulled it back.

"No, you can't read it until I've left." CJ smiled. "Unfortunately, Hallmark doesn't have a section for good luck on your apocalyptic journey, so I had to make my own."

Dillon chuckled. "Did you look? Never underestimate the power of Hallmark."

"I checked the museum gift shop." CJ smirked. "No luck. Besides, the nearest Hallmark is a bit far, so you'll have to accept the card I'm giving you."

"I'm sure I'll love it." Dillon blinked back tears. "I love you, too, CJ."

"Goddamn it. Why did you have to go and say that?" Tears streamed down CJ's face. "I love you, too." CJ pointed at Dillon. "Just come back in one piece, or I'll never forgive you."

Before Dillon could respond, CJ turned on her heels and walked away.

Dillon walked in the opposite direction, farther from the group. She stared down at the envelope in her hand. CJ hadn't sealed it, which made Dillon chuckle. She knew if she had Dillon would have torn the shit out of it, which would have made CJ crazy.

She slid the card from the envelope and laughed. CJ had made a picture collage of the two of them together. In her neat script, she'd written, *I love you, just don't tell anyone, or I'll deny it.*

As Dillon studied the card, she heard her name being called. She shoved the card into the envelope and slid it into her pocket.

Cynthia and Alaina walked toward her.

"Hey," Cynthia said. "I just wanted to...." Cynthia must have seen the tears in Dillon's eyes or the look on her face. "Are you okay?" Cynthia put her arm over Dillon's shoulder.

Dillon smiled to herself. How had she gotten two best friends that were so different? While CJ was awkward when it came to emotions and affection, Cynthia showed her feelings with ease. "I just said goodbye to CJ. It was harder than I thought."

"Aw, I'm sorry." Cynthia pulled her into a sideways hug.

"Even Spock was struggling with it."

Alaina, who stood several feet away, sported a puzzled expression. "Spock?"

Dillon grinned.

Cynthia shook her head. "That's what she calls CJ. The two of them love to annoy each other. You'd think they were sisters."

Alaina smiled. "I see. Do you have...um, I mean, did you have any sisters?" Alaina's normally reserved expression showed signs of discomfort at her question.

"It's okay," Dillon said. "Yes, I did have sisters. We had nothing in common, but I loved them."

"I'm sorry." Alaina's cool mask was back in place. "I wasn't thinking. I apologize."

"No need to apologize." Dillon held out her hand. "I'm sure we've all lost people."

Alaina nodded but didn't speak.

"I suppose we should be getting to bed," Cynthia said, jumping in to quell the discomfort. "We leave at first light."

Dillon stretched and yawned. "Yeah, I'm hoping to be able to fall asleep."

"Doubtful," Cynthia said.

Cynthia and Alaina walked in silence as they made their way toward their rooms. They arrived at the stairway where they would need to split to go to their respective wings. Cynthia stopped and gazed at Alaina. "Can I walk you to your room?"

Alaina smiled. "I had something different in mind."

Cynthia's mouth went dry. Was Alaina flirting? She hoped her voice would come out steady. Cool. "And what would that be?" She tried for a smirk but feared it came out as a grimace.

"Anne and Diana are still in the atrium. Looked like they were talking with Leslie." Alaina lightly brushed Cynthia's arm. "I think they might be awhile."

Yep. Mentioning that Cynthia's suitemates weren't going to be in the suite had to mean something. Cynthia's heart raced. The words smoky and sultry must have been created to describe Alaina. *Crap.* Alaina was staring. She needed to say something or risk looking like more of an idiot than she felt. "Um...I'd like that."

"Good." As if in slow motion, Alaina's tongue wet her lips. She weaved her arm through Cynthia's. "Lead the way."

Cynthia didn't remember the walk to the room. Her blood pulsed in her ears, making it hard to hear. It had been too long since she'd slept with a woman. Was that what Alaina was suggesting?

As if on cue, Alaina said, "Are you okay with this?"

Cynthia nodded, afraid that her voice would betray her. They'd stopped just outside the room, but Cynthia made no move to open the door.

"What's wrong then?"

"It's been a while," Cynthia admitted. "Long before the crisis happened. I'd been single." She wasn't sure why she'd added the last part. She'd already told Alaina that she had been.

"I see." Alaina took her hand and rubbed her thumb gently over Cynthia's wrist.

Cynthia shivered and resisted the urge to pull away. The sensation wasn't unpleasant, far from it. The throbbing between her legs told her that. Cynthia's face flushed. "I'm sorry. I feel like an inexperienced virgin."

"With all these ladies around, you never?"

Cynthia shook her head and diverted her gaze from Alaina's. "No. I can't believe I'm going to tell you this." Cynthia took in a deep breath. "I let the others…Dillon…think I was sneaking around with other women." Cynthia abruptly stopped. "I never lied to them. I just let them believe what they wanted and didn't correct them." *God, why was she rambling?* Alaina would think she was a bumbling fool.

Alaina squeezed her hand. "It's okay, Cynthia. Just relax."

Cynthia's gaze met Alaina's ice blue eyes that held a surprising warmth with a hint of amusement. "You must think I'm a moron."

"Not at all. I think you're sweet. It's endearing to see someone with your…." Alaina took a step back, and her gaze ran the length of Cynthia's body until she arrived at her face. "Your beauty and intelligence be self-conscious. Most women with those attributes would be arrogant."

The heat rose up Cynthia's neck. "What about you?" *Oh, god.* She hadn't meant to say that.

The corners of Alaina's mouth twitched, but she pursed her lips. The amusement dancing in her eyes couldn't be so easily hidden. "What about me?"

Damn it. She wasn't going to make it easy. "Um. Well, you were at Babcock's place. I can't...um...think that they would approve of...well, you know...."

"Lesbian sex?" Alaina said with the twinkle still in her eyes.

Cynthia fumbled with the hem of her shirt. "Yeah. Is that why you...why you left?"

"Talking about Babcock is a surefire way to throw cold water on what I'd like to do with you." Alaina stepped forward and touched Cynthia's cheek. "I want to spend a couple hours with you and forget all that. Is that wrong?"

Alaina's fingertips on her cheek made it hard for Cynthia to think. "No, it's not wrong." Cynthia looked away and stared at the painting at the end of the hall. "I just want to know what this is about. I don't want either of us to be confused." She stared at Alaina's mouth since she was afraid to look in her eyes. "It's horrible when two people have different interpretations of an event. When one person thinks it's one thing, but the other person thinks it's something entirely different, it can really mess things up." *Shut up.* She needed to stop rambling or Alaina would call the whole thing off, and her body would never forgive her.

"God, you're adorable." Alaina ran her fingertip across Cynthia's lip.

Cynthia fought the urge to suck Alaina's finger into her mouth.

"If I said that I just needed to feel close to someone, to get a release before we leave in the morning, would you still want to take me inside?" When Cynthia didn't answer, Alaina continued. "Or if I told you that you've intrigued me since the first time we met, and it's only grown stronger these past few weeks?" She gently tapped her own chest. "Something that's chipped a tiny hole in the armor that I thought was impenetrable, then would you say yes?"

"Yes to both." Cynthia's gaze finally met Alaina's. "I'd just like to know what I'm agreeing to."

"Would it make a difference in how you behave in bed?"

Cynthia swallowed hard. She couldn't believe they were having this conversation while their bodies raged with desire. The easy answer would be to say *no*, so they could get on with what Cynthia wanted so badly, but she wouldn't lie to Alaina. "It would." Cynthia lowered her gaze.

"How so?"

Shit. She didn't want to answer the question, but it wouldn't be fair not to. She wouldn't tell Alaina that she'd never had a one-night stand before, but she could still be honest. "If it were deeper than just...just sex, I would be more nervous. I know that sounds stupid and backwards." *Stop.* She didn't need to go into another ramble.

Alaina smiled. "Okay then. What do you say that we *pretend* it's just sex?"

Cynthia forced herself to breathe. Did Alaina just say that it was more than just sex? She wanted to come up with a witty line, but her body was making it hard to concentrate on anything but touching the woman in front of her. Afraid of what she might say, she lowered her face to Alaina's.

Their lips met, and Cynthia's mind went blank. Alaina's soft lips brushed against Cynthia's, but instead of pressing in harder, Alaina broke contact before moving in with a feathery touch. Cynthia fought the desire to devour Alaina; instead, she gently tickled Alaina's lips with her own.

Alaina let out a satisfied moan. They continued to tease each other with tiny kisses. The sensations were almost too much for Cynthia. Her mouth searched out Alaina, wanting to taste her again and again.

Alaina pulled back. Why did she break their connection? Cynthia opened her eyes and tried to focus. Alaina's ice blue eyes were only inches from hers and held an intensity that made Cynthia shutter.

"Why did you stop?" Cynthia asked.

Alaina smiled and gestured to their surroundings. "Don't you think we should go inside?"

Cynthia cringed. "Oh, god, I forgot where we were." She fumbled for the doorknob.

"Let me get it." Alaina reached around her and pushed open the door.

"Thanks," Cynthia muttered, still embarrassed she'd nearly lost control in the hallway. Luckily, none of the others were around.

As soon as the door clicked shut, she wanted to kiss Alaina again but stopped herself. She took two steps back. If they started kissing, she couldn't guarantee they'd make it to the bedroom.

Alaina chuckled. "Afraid we won't be able to control ourselves?"

"Uh-huh." Cynthia smiled. Her gaze locked on Alaina's lips. "I'd prefer my roommates not discover us in a compromising position in the middle of the common area."

Alaina took a step toward Cynthia. "Then you better get me somewhere private. Quick. Or I can't promise what your roommates might see."

Cynthia's pulse raced. She took Alaina's warm hand in hers. It was soft, but her grip was strong. Firm. Without speaking, Cynthia led her to her bedroom. *Crap.* She hadn't made her bed this morning, but it was too late to worry about it now.

Once inside, Cynthia took the time to lock the door. She didn't want Anne or Diana to wander in unannounced. She wasn't ready for anyone to discover whatever it was she was doing with Alaina. Not even Dillon. For now, she wanted it to be something only between the two of them.

Suddenly, Cynthia was nervous. She was back inside her head, thinking too much. Something that always got in her way. Her gaze shot around the room in a panic. Should she shut the lights off or leave them on? What underwear did she have on?

"Hey," Alaina said. "Why the look of terror?"

Cynthia wanted to crawl under the bed. She'd been fine in the hallway, but now her doubts were back. "Sorry. I don't want to disappoint you."

Alaina moved closer. "If that kiss was a preview of what's to come, I'm not worried about being disappointed."

Cynthia took a deep breath, hoping a blast of oxygen would clear her head. The temperature in the room was stifling, or maybe the heat radiated from her. Even though she'd never been confident of her sexual prowess, this felt different. She needed to speak, but the words weren't coming.

Alaina brushed Cynthia's hair away from her face. The touch sent shock waves through Cynthia's body. "Maybe you need to think less and kiss more," Alaina said.

"Um, you might be right. My mind went blank after the last kiss."

"Good. Let's see if I can clear your mind again." Alaina put her palm against Cynthia's cheek and gently drew Cynthia's mouth to hers.

The kiss began tentatively, but as it intensified, all of Cynthia's doubts disappeared. When Alaina ran her tongue over Cynthia's lips, Cynthia moaned and sucked Alaina's tongue into her mouth.

Alaina returned the moan and pressed her body against Cynthia's. Several minutes passed as their lips met, retreated, and met again. Every nerve ending in Cynthia's body fired as they continued to kiss.

Cynthia wasn't sure who broke the kiss first, but they were both breathless when they parted. Her heart raced when their gazes met. A look of pain flashed in Alaina's eyes but was gone as quickly as it came. Maybe Cynthia had imagined it, but something told her she hadn't.

"Are you sure you want to do this?" Alaina asked. "When I can't make any promises about what happens next?"

"You mean whether you're going to stay or go back to Amarillo?" Cynthia asked.

"That, among other things."

"I'm afraid I'm not following." Cynthia gave her a puzzled look. Between her heightened arousal and Alaina's cryptic message, Cynthia struggled to understand.

"I can't promise you anything but tonight."

Alaina cupped Cynthia's chin and ran her thumb over her lips. "Will that be enough?"

Alaina's thumb moving across her lips made it hard for Cynthia to concentrate, but she did her best to focus on Alaina's words. "Something tells me it will be more than enough and never enough."

"Poetic." Alaina's thumb parted Cynthia's lips. "But I think I know what you mean."

Cynthia sucked Alaina's thumb into her mouth.

"Oh, god." Alaina tilted her head back and moaned.

A tiny vein throbbed in her exposed throat. The need to put her mouth on Alaina's long slender neck was overpowering. She ran her tongue around Alaina's thumb one last time before she lowered her mouth to Alaina's throat. With a gasp, Alaina threw her head back farther, giving Cynthia full access.

Cynthia's tongue flicked against Alaina's neck with feathery precision. From this position, Cynthia caught a whiff of Alaina's intoxicating scent. Sandalwood and sage. She continued exploring Alaina's neck, careful not to leave a mark.

Alaina ran her hand slowly down the length of Cynthia's body. Her hand stopped at Cynthia's hip and continued around to her backside. Alaina kneaded Cynthia's firm buttocks before she pulled Cynthia's body against hers.

Pressed against Alaina, it took all Cynthia's willpower not to grind into her. She didn't want Alaina to think tonight was simply about animalistic lust. Though her body would be okay with that. The throbbing between her legs was becoming almost unbearable. All she would need to do is slide over a few inches and straddle Alaina's leg.

As Cynthia continued to run her tongue the length of Alaina's neck, she unbuttoned Alaina's shirt starting with the top button. Cynthia moved to slide Alaina's shirt off.

Alaina gripped Cynthia's hand and shook her head. "Please, leave it on. I'm a bit chilled."

Strange. Everywhere Cynthia touched on Alaina's body felt warm, almost hot. Cynthia nodded. "Okay. Can we remove your bra?"

Alaina smiled, unclasped the front, and slipped out of it. Cynthia gaped at her perfect breasts. They were larger than Cynthia expected. Alaina's minimizing bras concealed the treat she now feasted her eyes on.

Cynthia licked her lips at the thought of tasting Alaina's breast. She couldn't wait any longer. Her kisses trailed down Alaina's neck, past her collarbone to her erect nipple. She wanted to savor the experience, so she licked around it. With each pass, she got closer to her goal. Alaina writhed and pushed toward Cynthia's mouth. When Cynthia finally conceded and let her tongue brush the hardened tip, an unexpected sensation coursed through her body. It was almost as if Alaina's tongue was on her, as well. She glanced down. It was no miracle. Alaina had found Cynthia's nipple through her shirt and rolled it between her fingers.

Cynthia threw off her shirt and bra, wanting Alaina's hands on her bare skin. At the first touch, Cynthia trembled. Nothing else mattered except for the woman in front of her. She explored Alaina's body, wanting to touch every part, while Alaina did the same. The sensations nearly overwhelmed her. Her senses were heightened. The soft sounds of Alaina's moans filled the room like an orchestra while it felt as if Alaina touched dozens of places on Cynthia's body at once.

They fell onto the bed, and their bodies intertwined.

❧❧❧❧

Cynthia wondered if her heart rate would ever slow. She smiled to herself. If she weren't a doctor, she might be concerned.

Alaina lay beside her, still trying to catch her breath. Her dark hair splayed out over her pillow in an unruly mop. Her breasts were partially covered by the shirt she still wore, but the tease made her body even more alluring. Her long tanned legs still quivered around her thighs. Cynthia had never seen anyone more gorgeous with an after-sex glow.

"Are you staring?" Alaina asked with a smirk.

"Maybe." Cynthia returned the smile.

"I might be taking a peek myself." Alaina's gaze traveled the length of Cynthia's naked body before returning to Cynthia's face.

"Like what you see?" Cynthia nearly gasped. *Where did that come from?* Apparently, she had post-orgasmic confidence.

"Mm-hmm." Alaina licked her lips. "I like what I felt even more."

Cynthia ran her hand across Alaina's flat stomach. "I want to see all of you." She pushed back Alaina's shirt and started to remove it.

Alaina pulled her shirt together and began buttoning it. "No. I'm chilled again."

Cynthia studied Alaina's face. "But you're

covered in sweat."

Alaina's gaze shifted away from Cynthia. "Yeah...um...you know how cold it gets when your sweat dries." She finished buttoning the last of her buttons.

Cynthia tried to hide her disappointment or, more accurately, her fear. Was Alaina shutting her out? *No.* She shouldn't read anything into it and let her insecurities run rampant.

"Come here and keep me warm." Alaina opened her arms.

All doubt faded as she snuggled against Alaina's chest, her scent intoxicating. "Mmm... this is nice," Cynthia said as she nestled in.

"Very." Alaina hugged her tighter. "What you did to me before was even nicer. I lost track of how many times I came."

"Six."

Alaina laughed. "Apparently, you didn't."

Cynthia's cheeks warmed. She was glad that Alaina couldn't see her embarrassment.

Alaina kissed the top of her head. "It's okay. I think it's adorable that you kept count."

"Don't you mean dorky?"

"That too. But I'm partial to dorks."

Cynthia relaxed further against Alaina's chest. "That's good because I doubt if I'll ever shake my awkwardness."

"When you get between the sheets, there's nothing awkward about you." Alaina slowly ran her hand through Cynthia's hair.

"I'm not sure what happened. I swear something took over my body."

"Are you telling me that you're usually not that...

um, skilled?"

Cynthia squirmed and pulled the blanket over her. "Are we really having this conversation?"

"Yep, so answer the question."

"I don't think anyone would exactly describe me as skilled when it comes to this. To sex."

"Let me be the first to tell you that you have some mad skills. It's not often that I have *six* orgasms."

"Stop." Cynthia pulled the covers over her head.

Alaina peeked her head under the blanket. "You can't hide from me that easily." She put her hand under Cynthia's chin and gently tilted her head upward. Their gazes met and held. "You may never know how much I needed that, so please stop devaluing yourself."

Cynthia stiffened. Her mind exploded with thoughts. Images more than anything. Rescuing Alaina from the kidnappers. The state all the women were in when she'd first examined them. "Oh, god. I'm such an idiot."

"No." Alaina swept Cynthia's hair off her forehead. "That look in your eyes is killing me."

What look was she showing? Pity? Horror? Disgust? Guilt? "I'm so sorry. I'm not sure what look you're seeing."

"Tell me what you're thinking," Alaina said, skillfully avoiding the question.

"I got lost in us. In this. And I totally forgot what happened to you. I'm so embarrassed. I'm such a clod." In that moment, Cynthia hated herself for her insensitivity.

"Don't you see, it was perfect? I was afraid you'd treat me like a glass doll. Breakable. But instead, you treated me like a whole woman. A desirable woman."

"How could I not?" Cynthia gazed into Alaina's

eyes, which held a mixture of pain and conviction. "Despite what happened, I still see you as strong and capable. Certainly not a glass doll."

Alaina closed her eyes and let her head drop against the pillow. "Thank you." Tears pooled on her eyelashes, but none fell.

Cynthia moved up and kissed her eyelids. "I'm so sorry for whatever those men did to you. But I've never met anyone that epitomizes the term grace under fire better than you."

Alaina squeezed her eyes shut tighter. "Stop. You're going to make me cry."

"Maybe that's not a bad thing." Cynthia shifted and put her arm behind Alaina's back, so she now held Alaina.

"Let's just say I learned the fine art of disassociation from Babcock and his ministry."

Cynthia's chest tightened. The reason for Alaina's cool exterior became clearer and explained the complex woman she'd been getting to know the last several weeks. Anger surged inside her, but she knew Alaina didn't need her rage. "I'm a good listener if you ever need to talk."

Alaina squeezed Cynthia, but her eyes remained dry. "I don't want to talk about that right now. I want to bask in this. In you. Please."

The word *please* cut into Cynthia like a dull shard of glass. "I'll never ask you to talk about something you don't want to. Ever."

"Thanks." Alaina's shoulders relaxed, and she snuggled against Cynthia. "I suppose I should get back to my room. Sunrise will be here before we know it."

"Don't you want to try for seven?" Cynthia asked.

"Seven?" Alaina shifted her head and met

Cynthia's gaze. "I thought we were leaving at dawn."

Cynthia smirked. "I mean lucky number seven."

Alaina laughed. "I've never been a big fan of the number seven. I'm partial to eight or nine."

"Done." Cynthia brought her lips to Alaina's. As soon as they met, she had no doubt they would achieve number eight or nine.

Chapter Nine

Dillon clasped Skylar's hand in one hand and her duffel in the other. They descended the stairs in silence, not wanting to wake any of the others. Their caravan had been packed the night before with the group's supplies, so they only needed a small bag. Before they reached the bottom of the staircase, Dillon paused and unzipped her pack.

"You've only checked for it three times now." Skylar bumped her hip against Dillon's and grinned. "I doubt if it's disappeared."

Dillon smiled, thankful for the woman beside her. After Jane's death, she didn't think she could ever love that deeply again. She was wrong. Skylar made the last several months bearable. More than bearable. Despite everything, Dillon was happy for the first time in years. She wondered how much longer that happiness would last.

"Gremlins. Haven't you heard of gremlins?" Dillon shuffled through her belongings until her hand touched the hard plastic of the satellite phone. It would be their lifeline to the estate, so she couldn't be too careful.

"Yep. Gotta be wary of those sat phone-loving gremlins."

Dillon faked a sneer as she zipped her bag. She took Skylar's hand again as they traversed the last of the stairs. They pushed through the door into the empty atrium. Their footsteps echoed heavily in the cavernous expanse.

"I used to love the quiet," Skylar said. "But this is just creepy."

Dillon tightened her hold on Skylar's hand. She surveyed the empty space. "Do you think we're early or late?"

"My guess is late since you had to check your bag two dozen times."

"I'm telling everyone it's your fault." Dillon smirked.

"I'm sure you will. Make like I was glued to the mirror primping?"

"Nah, nobody will believe that."

"Hey." Skylar fluffed her hair. "I think I clean up okay."

"You clean up more than okay. What I meant to say is everyone knows how beautiful you are with or without primping."

"Good save."

"Seriously, Sky. I mean it. You're beautiful."

"Would you stop it? You're gonna make me blush."

"Flushed cheeks make you even more attractive." Dillon grinned. "Especially when they're flushed for other reasons."

"Damn it, Dillon." Skylar stopped and put her hand on her hip. "You can't say things like that. We're going to be in tight quarters for I don't know how long, so there will be no flushed cheeks in your near future."

A mischievous smile lit Dillon's face. "We're probably already late." Dillon jokingly pulled Skylar toward the nearby bathroom instead of making their way to the exit. "We better get in one last quickie."

Skylar slapped at Dillon's arm. "You're impossible. I won't show up late with the afterglow of sex written all over my face." Skylar pulled Dillon toward the exit.

"Buzzkill."

"Besides, you can't put down your precious cargo, or the gremlins might get it."

Dillon raised her eyebrow. "I've got one hand... and..." She ran her tongue over her lips. "Mouth."

Skylar pulled her hand out of Dillon's. "That's it. You're not allowed to touch me until after we've settled into our vehicle."

"Hey, that's right. We have our own truck. Nobody will be able to see what kind of action's going on during the drive."

"What is wrong with you?" Skylar tried to sound offended, but her gray eyes twinkled.

It was her eyes that Dillon noticed first and had captivated her since. They were deep, wise but still retained a playful joy. "It's your fault."

"I see a pattern here." Skylar kept walking, so Dillon was forced to hurry to catch up.

"What sort of pattern?" Dillon asked when she pulled up next to Skylar.

"Blame everything on me."

"Cool, thanks." Dillon couldn't resist teasing Skylar.

"That wasn't giving permission." Skylar glared at her from the corner of her eye.

"Sheesh, I guess you shouldn't say it if you don't mean it." Dillon knew they were playing this game to avoid the seriousness of the journey they were about to take. They both used humor to make even the worst situations bearable. One more item to put in the column of why she loved Skylar so much.

Skylar pushed through the door and gasped. "Apparently, nobody followed the rules."

Dillon peered around her at the crowd huddled around their caravan of vehicles. "Shit. It looks like everyone woke up to see us off."

"Appears that way." Skylar looked down at the gathering below. "Shall we go?"

Dillon hooked her arm through Skylar's. "Let's."

They scurried down the long set of stairs to join the others.

⁂

Cynthia still couldn't believe the turnout for their departure. She'd expected one or two people might get up to see them off, but a quick headcount said it was nearly everyone.

A lump formed in her throat. They'd truly become a close-knit community, and the thought that one of them might be a traitor made her stomach churn. She and Alaina had been two of the first to arrive, but soon others had poured in, offering words of encouragement and small gifts to take on the journey. Renee had slipped her a couple of packages of her favorite cookies that they were running dangerously low on. She giggled to herself. She doubted it was appropriate to consider being low on cookies a tragedy.

Movement at the top of the stairs caught her eye. Skylar and Dillon scampered down the stairs. Her face grew hot. *Crap.* She didn't want to see Dillon today. Would what she and Alaina did last night be written all over her face? Dillon might miss it, but Skylar picked up everything. *Shit.* She needed to busy herself.

She plunged into the nearest group and soon became part of their conversation. Dillon and Skylar were swallowed up by the crowd, as well, so she began to relax.

She glanced around, and her gaze landed on Leslie and Anne talking quietly away from the others. She wanted to say goodbye to Anne but didn't want to interrupt the two, who seemed deep in conversation.

Leslie had been wonderful with Anne since Tiffany's death. Having experienced the loss of Denise, she seemed better equipped to handle Anne's grief. While the loss of Tiffany tore Cynthia's heart out, she doubted it was anything close to Anne's grief.

Anne and Leslie were huddled close together, talking softly. Engrossed in their conversation, they didn't see her approach, which gave her time to study the pair. They'd make an attractive couple. *Where the hell had that come from?* Guilt washed over her. Tiffany had been gone for a month, and already Cynthia was trying to find a partner for Anne.

She pushed back against the voices in her head that chastised her. The uncertainty of the world made love more important than ever. Anne and Tiffany's relationship had been tumultuous for years, and only the last couple of months had they begun to right the ship.

Anne must have heard Cynthia's footsteps because she looked up and smiled. Subtly, she let go of Leslie's hand without drawing attention to it. "Cynthia, I was just about to come looking for you."

Anne's eyes were red and swollen. Her usual perfectly tended hair was mussed while her clothes hung on her tiny frame. How had Cynthia missed her weight loss? Regardless, a stranger would deem her elegant, but for Anne, she looked disheveled. Cynthia hoped her surprise didn't show on her face.

"I wouldn't have left without saying... seeing you," Cynthia said.

Leslie smiled. "I can leave you two alone."

"No," Cynthia and Anne said at the same time.

"I guess I've been voted on the island," Leslie said with a chuckle.

Cynthia suspected she wanted to break the tension that swirled in the air. She'd known Anne for a long time, so this awkwardness confused her. Although, they'd never faced circumstances like this before.

"How have you been?" Cynthia said and groaned inwardly. Maybe she could make it even more awkward.

"I've been good," Anne said.

Anne's stilted response increased the level of discomfort. Now all she'd have to do is mention the weather to complete the trifecta.

"Looks like we're going to have a perfect day for travel," Leslie said.

Leslie for the win. She couldn't leave on such an odd note. *Screw it.* "Oh, Anne, I'm so sorry for everything. I haven't known what to say to you. What to do." The words tumbled out, and she couldn't stop them. "I was afraid to show my grief around you, but then I was afraid not to, either. I didn't want you to think I wasn't missing Tiff. I hid. I cried by myself and wanted to come to you so many times, but I didn't.

I was a coward." Cynthia took a deep breath and stepped back, mortified by her outburst.

"Nonsense." Anne waved her hand at Cynthia and scowled. "I avoided you, too. Every time I looked at you, I saw Tiffany. You two could have been sisters."

Cynthia knew it was true. Over the years, people had mistaken them for sisters, although she didn't think they looked that much alike other than their build and long thick hair. "Remember what they used to call us in college?"

"The tower twins." Anne laughed.

"Not terribly original, huh?" Cynthia shook her head and smiled.

"It's not every day you see two six-foot women strolling around together."

"I'm only five-eleven," Cynthia said. It was her standard joke whenever anyone commented on her height. "Tiffany was the tall one." She took in a sharp breath when she realized she'd used the word was.

"Yes, she *was*," Anne said in a voice barely louder than a whisper. "God, I miss her."

"Me too."

Leslie stood a few feet away. Anne reached out her hand. "Don't try and sneak away."

Leslie gazed at Anne with obvious affection. It was clear the two had grown close. Bonded over the last few weeks. "I didn't want to intrude."

"Nonsense." Anne held Leslie's hand and took Cynthia's with her other. "I can't believe you're both going. I'm gonna be lost."

"Dillon said we'd be back in a week to ten days. If everything goes as planned," Leslie said. "The time will go quick."

Sure. What could go wrong traveling during an

apocalypse? Cynthia knew Dillon would find the dark humor funny, but this wasn't the right audience, so she kept her sarcasm to herself.

"Leslie's been my rock these past few weeks," Anne said to Cynthia. She turned to Leslie. "I still can't believe you volunteered to go."

"I know." Leslie's shoulders hunched, and she glanced at the ground. "It was the hardest decision I've ever made. I just—"

"No," Anne interrupted, "I'm being selfish. It's not your job to babysit me. I've got to stand on my own eventually. You've just been such a comfort. All the times you sat with me and let me talk. Let me cry. Let me be angry at the world. At God. You never judged. You listened. You offered encouragement, and you prayed with me."

Leslie's cheeks reddened. Cynthia glanced around at the nearby groups, feeling as if she should extract herself from Anne and Leslie's private conversation.

"You got me through some of my darkest days," Anne said.

"But there will be more days like that, and I'm leaving." Leslie bit her lip. "What was I thinking? I never should have volunteered."

"Maybe we could talk to Dillon and Jake," Cynthia said.

"No." Anne stood to her full height, which always made Cynthia smile. Despite her short stature, when she struck that pose, Tiffany knew to step away slowly. "As much as this journey frightens me for all of you, I won't be that woman. Leslie, I know you need to do this for yourself to heal, so I won't stand in your way."

"Leslie, I've seen that pose many times. Surrender now because you won't win," Cynthia said. "Walk away slowly from the tiny woman with fire in her eyes, and nobody gets hurt."

Leslie laughed. Her genuine smile transformed her face. "Okay. I know when I'm defeated."

"Smart woman." Cynthia winked. "I'm going to leave you two to finish up, just in case Anne wants to chew you out a little more."

"I do not chew people out." Anne glowered. "I simply point out the obvious."

Cynthia looked at Leslie and raised her eyebrows. "Ah, that's what she's calling it."

"Get over here and give me a hug," Anne said. "Then get your butt out of here."

Cynthia's chest expanded. She'd almost forgotten how familiar it felt in Anne's presence, like family. Anne and Diana were the only two people she'd known before the crisis. She held on tightly and didn't let go for several beats. "I love you."

"I love you, too," Anne said. "Just please come back safe."

"I'll do my best."

Chapter Ten

Dillon leaned against the pickup and sighed. Most of the well-wishers had left, leaving the group to finish preparations before they pulled out. An eerie quiet had fallen over the estate, or maybe it was just her imagination.

The sun had climbed well above the horizon with the promise of a beautiful day. If they'd truly been going all the way to Salt Lake City, Dillon would be edgy with such a late start. They needed to stop in Primm, Nevada, to check out the solar farm but should still arrive at the summit by midafternoon.

"Whatcha thinking about?" Skylar asked as she sidled next to Dillon.

"Solar power."

Skylar groaned. "You need some work in the romance department. The correct answer would have been me."

Dillon grinned. "Now I'm thinking about you. Have I mentioned you've got the most gorgeous eyes I've ever seen?"

"Good save." Skylar gave her a quick peck on the lips. "Jake loaded up a bunch of gas cans in the back of the truck, but I think he messed up. I can't see it getting us all the way to Salt Lake City."

Guilt washed over Dillon. She pointed to the cab. "I've got a siphoning hose in the back, and I'm sure Jake has one in the van, too."

Skylar nodded. "Then I think we're about ready to head out. I just need to go pick up our weapons from Jake."

Dillon no longer outwardly cringed at the mention of weapons, but her insides still churned. "Let's go."

When they arrived at Jake's cargo van, he was nodding as Willa yammered at him. Dillon stifled a giggle. It was clear he was only half listening, at best, but Willa didn't seem to notice. Several bags of Willa's camera equipment laid open. *Smart.* Jake must have asked her about the equipment, so he could get a look inside the bags to ensure she wasn't smuggling in a sat phone or any other means of communication. She didn't appear to be hiding anything. Still, Willa remained Dillon's prime suspect.

"Hey," Jake said as they approached. "About time you picked up your guns."

"We're the last ones?" Dillon asked.

"Yup." Jake shot a glance toward Skylar and then motioned Dillon with his head. "Come on around back."

Willa had snagged Skylar, who patiently studied the camera Willa held out to her.

As soon as they were out of earshot, Jake leaned in. "Her bags are clean."

"Yeah, I noticed she wasn't trying to hide anything." Dillon raised her eyebrows. "Or maybe she's trying to throw us off her trail."

"Way ahead of you. I've already gone down that rabbit hole. Jumping at my own shadow." Jake rubbed his chin, which didn't appear to have been shaved this morning. "Just the other day, I started following Kelly around because she seemed a little suspicious."

Dillon laughed. "Investigating a ten-year-old seems a bit harsh."

Jake's eyes twinkled with mischief. "You laugh, but can you think of a better disguise to throw us off the track? Who'd suspect such a sweet little girl?"

"Lily won't be happy if you put your daughter under house arrest."

He shrugged. "She can be so unreasonable. So, are we ready for this?"

"You know I am. As much as I love our little corner of the world, we need to work with the other groups if we're going to survive. Rebuild."

Jake held out his hand, which had a slight tremble. "It's been doing this for the last two days. I'm a combination of terrified and excited. I love that we found you." He swept his hand through the air. "Everyone. My family couldn't have asked for a better group to end up with. But..."

"But you want your kids to be able to find partners and have children of their own."

Jake averted his gaze to the ground. "That's not offensive, is it?"

Dillon pushed him in the shoulder. "You breeders are all the same."

He looked up in horror until he saw her smirk. "Jackass. Here I was trying to have a serious conversation with you, and you pull your shit." His boyish grin spread across his face.

"You know I love you." Dillon put her arm around him. "And no offense taken. Your kids need the opportunity to fall in love and start a family, which might be a bit hard in a colony of lesbians."

"Ah, when did you become a colony?"

"Always been one, we just didn't let the straight people in on the secret."

"I'm honored."

"You shouldn't be. I'm afraid now I'm gonna have to kill you," Dillon deadpanned.

They both doubled up in laughter, calling each other names between their snorts.

"What the hell are you two up to?" Skylar came around to the back of the van.

"Dillon was just threatening to kill me."

"Again?" Skylar said without missing a beat.

Jake's deep laugh rang out. Dillon found so much to be thankful for after the crisis, and Jake was near the top of the list. He was one of the good guys.

"Apparently, you two have been playing instead of getting our weapons together." Skylar narrowed her eyes, trying to put on a stern expression.

Dillon pointed at Skylar. "You look like you're constipated. Trying to push out a big one."

The comment caused another round of laughter from Jake and Dillon.

"You two are impossible." Skylar stood shaking her head.

"Sorry," Jake muttered between chuckles.

Skylar turned to Dillon. "Don't you have something else to do while Jake and I get the weapons together?"

"Apparently, I'm being dismissed." Dillon smirked at Skylar, who unsuccessfully tried to remain stoic.

"Get out of here," Skylar said.

"Fine. I'll go check on the others."

Maria and Tasha's bright blue hybrid car was parked about twenty yards away. As Dillon approached, she couldn't help but notice the sour look on Maria's face.

"Looks like you guys are all ready to roll," Dillon said.

"It doesn't take much to pack up a clown car." Maria crinkled her nose. "Who decided to give us this piece of shit?"

"Come on, Maria," Tasha said and patted the top of the car. "She's a beauty." She turned to Dillon. "I've been trying to tell her that all morning."

Maria glanced at the car out of the corner of her eye with a look of disgust. "Looks like something circus clowns would drive around the big top."

"We chose it especially for you," Dillon said, hoping to turn the conversation around.

"You mean someone thought I'd want this ride?" Maria crossed her arms over her chest.

"Well, actually, it was for Tasha. We've noticed how much she's taken to the electric vehicles."

"Figures." Maria's dark eyes darkened even more.

"I'm sorry. We weren't thinking about you—"

"Seems nobody does," Maria muttered under her breath.

What was up with her? This change in attitude was the biggest reason she'd been put on the suspect list. Her demeanor was doing nothing to lessen suspicion. Normally, Dillon would ask her what was bothering her, but these weren't normal times.

Dillon looked Maria squarely in the eyes. "Well, I for one am happy you're with us." Maria's gaze continued to hold contempt, so Dillon decided a change of tactics might be for the best. "Hey, where's Leslie?"

"Probably doesn't want to be seen in this clown car and stowed away in someone else's vehicle."

Tasha shot Maria a look before she nodded toward the large tree outside the mansion. "Still saying goodbye to Anne."

Dillon followed her gaze. The two were deep in conversation and didn't seem to notice the attention. Anne leaned casually against the tree, nodding intently at whatever Leslie was saying. It was great to see Leslie back in the fold. The chemistry between the two was undeniable.

"Those two have gotten pretty chummy," Maria said. "I just hope Leslie doesn't get her heart broken."

"Anne will need time to heal," Dillon said. "But she couldn't ask for anyone better than Leslie."

"Amen to that," Tasha said. "I believe they might be two of the nicest people I've ever met."

"That's why it won't last," Maria said, her voice dripping with cynicism. "Anne will need to find her another bad girl."

"Ignore this ray of sunshine." Tasha playfully pushed Maria's shoulder. "Cynthia should be the one complaining. Three teenagers and Alaina and Carol in the same van should be lots of fun."

"I doubt if she'll notice anything other than Alaina," Maria said, drawing out Alaina's name. "Cynthia can't keep her eyes in her head any time that woman's around."

Tasha chuckled. "I think I saw her drooling this morning."

Dillon was grateful that Tasha's words elicited a half smile from Maria. "I'll make sure to have a tissue handy when I talk to her."

"Later," Maria said as she opened the car door.

"I need to organize our supplies. Oh, wait, we don't have any. Maybe I'll just take a nap." She plopped into the backseat.

Tasha sighed and shook her head when she met Dillon's gaze.

"Hang in there," Dillon mouthed before she walked away.

Cynthia's was the final vehicle. The Commission had chosen a plush van to comfortably fit Cynthia's five passengers from Amarillo. After what they'd endured before arriving at the estate, it seemed only fitting for them to be delivered back to their group in style. Last week, it had been confirmed that a contingent from Amarillo, including Carol's husband, would be in Vegas waiting for them.

The three teens and Carol were already inside the van, chatting excitedly. The past couple of days were the most animated she'd seen them. Dillon shuddered. They'd endured so much. In situations like these, people should band together and help one another, but the girls were a reminder that evil would always exist.

The girls broke into a fresh round of giggles. Dillon smiled. The resilience of the human spirit astonished her.

Cynthia was rummaging through a large backpack when Dillon walked up. "Looks like you're going to have a lively ride," Dillon said.

"They've been like that all morning." Cynthia smiled. "It's good to hear. I'll take a boisterous ride over the alternative any day."

"Where is Alaina?" Dillon asked.

"She had to run back to the room. She forgot something."

Forgot something? Dillon's mind raced. It would be a convenient way to smuggle in a communication device if Alaina feared the bags had been searched before being loaded.

Cynthia pointed at Dillon. "Get that thought out of your head."

"What?" Dillon tried to appear clueless.

"I see those wheels spinning."

"And yours weren't?" Dillon asked, knowing it was a loaded question. If Cynthia said no, it would put her objectivity into question, but if she said yes, it would be a betrayal to Alaina. A lose-lose situation.

"At first, it seemed suspicious." Cynthia blew out a breath. "But she forgot her mother's necklace. The one she always wears."

"Isn't that a little suspicious?" Dillon narrowed her eyes. "She told us she never takes it off."

"Um...apparently, it fell off." Cynthia shuffled from foot to foot. "Sometime last night."

Dillon studied Cynthia's nervousness. Something was off. She couldn't possibly believe a lame story like that. Necklaces didn't just fall off. A thought erupted in her mind. "Oh, my god. You know how her necklace fell off." Dillon made air quotes when she said *fell off*.

Cynthia's crimson neck answered for her.

Dillon bounced on the balls of her feet and chuckled. She gazed into Cynthia's eyes. "Holy hell. You've got that 'I'll be satiated for weeks' look in your eye. Damn."

"Shut up," Cynthia growled. "You're such a juvenile."

"But you're not denying it." Dillon pointed and circled her finger. "You don't get that look from a quick romp in the sack. That's an all-nighter look if I've ever seen one."

"I am not having this conversation with you." Cynthia put one arm across her chest and grabbed the other.

"Still no denial." Dillon couldn't help herself. Cynthia was so easy to tease. "How was it?"

"How do you think it was?"

"By the look on your face, I'm thinking it wasn't too bad."

"The best *ever*," Cynthia said. "And that's all I'm going to say on the subject. I already said way too much."

"Too much? You call admitting to sleeping with her saying too much? It's not like you gave me any details. Like were there multiple orgasms involved?"

Cynthia's face turned a deeper shade of crimson.

"There were," Dillon said. "What, three? Four? More?"

"I refuse to answer that question."

"Oh, my god, there were more. How many?"

"Would you stop already? I wanted to get your impressions of how everyone is reacting today. Seeing anything suspicious?"

"Other than you and your fifty orgasms?"

Cynthia rolled her eyes. "I got the opportunity to talk to Willa earlier. She seemed jubilant, practically giddy."

"I noticed the same," Dillon said, deciding to let Cynthia off the hook. "Jake got a chance to look in her bags. Nothing suspicious."

"What do you think it means?" Cynthia asked.

Dillon shrugged. "Maybe she wants to throw us off by being cooperative. Or she thinks we don't suspect because we've invited her along. Thinks she's escaped detection."

"Or she's simply excited to be given the opportunity to film the first summit of the new world."

"Or there's that," Dillon admitted. "This sleuthing shit is hard. There's an explanation for everything. Multiple explanations. Enough to make my head spin." Dillon rubbed the top of her head for emphasis.

"What about Maria?"

"What about her?" Dillon said more defensively than she'd intended.

"Whoa." Cynthia put her hands up and took a step back. "Careful, tiger. Who grabbed your tail?"

"Sorry." Dillon sighed. "I just finished talking to her. If anything, her mood is worse than ever. It's getting under my skin."

Cynthia lifted her eyebrow. "Are you starting to think she could be the traitor?"

Dillon raked her hand through her hair. "I don't want to think that, but something is definitely off."

"Have you tried feeling Tasha out?"

"I've thought of that, but it feels so fricking wrong. She's one of my closest friends." Dillon met Cynthia's eyes. "Who have we become?"

"I know it's hard." Cynthia put her hand on Dillon's shoulder. "All of us are struggling with it. Don't you think I'm having a hell of a time trying to balance my feelings for Alaina?" The struggle weighed on Cynthia's face, the bags under her eyes caused by more than a night of passion.

Dillon decided on levity instead of answering Cynthia's question. She slapped her knee. "Damn, that's right, you could be sleeping with the enemy."

Cynthia scowled but then broke into a smile. "That's why I love you. Always so damned supportive."

"I aim to please." Dillon sensed movement out of the corner of her eye. Alaina made her way across the lawn with a purposeful stride. "Speaking of being pleased."

Cynthia pointed her finger at Dillon. "I swear if you do anything to embarrass me, I will never speak to you again."

"Promises, promises." Dillon smirked. "How about sharing some of those cookies with me? I heard Renee slipped you a package."

"Good god. Isn't anything a secret around here? How in the hell could there be a traitor in a group of lesbians? They don't know how to keep their mouths shut."

"I know, right?" Dillon said with a smile. "Alaina," Dillon said as she approached. "Are you all ready to go?"

She held up a bright blue sapphire necklace. "I am now."

"Thank god you found it," Cynthia said. "I was beginning to worry."

"It took a little searching...but I got it."

The sexual tension permeated the air. Dillon wanted so badly to comment on it but knew Cynthia would never forgive her. "We're just about ready to head out."

"Cynthia said we're stopping in Primm?"

"Yeah, we want to check out the solar farm to see what we might be able to scavenge. Plus, there's a casino in case you want to get in a little gambling."

Alaina laughed. "Shoot a few rounds of craps."

"Exactly. Come on lucky seven," Dillon said.

"Seven's never been my number." She glanced at Cynthia and licked her lips. Then she smirked. "I've always been partial to eleven. Especially lately."

Dillon watched the exchange with interest. Cynthia's face immediately colored, and she fumbled with the hem of her shirt. Eleven? *Oh, my god.* She must mean eleven orgasms. *Priceless.* "Eleven, huh?" Dillon said. "Some kind of special significance?"

"You might say that." Alaina met Cynthia's gaze, which caused her to squirm more. The heat between the two was unmistakable.

All right. Warmth spread across Dillon's chest. She adored Cynthia and wanted her to find the love that eluded her. Dillon stifled a giggle when she met Cynthia's gaze. Her look implored Dillon to keep her mouth shut. "Who am I to tell someone what their lucky number should be, but...." She turned to Cynthia with a grin. "I almost forgot. Weren't you going to grab me one of those cookies you promised me?"

Cynthia glared. "Oh, right. I almost forgot, too."

"Where were we?" Dillon said to Alaina.

Alaina's gaze shifted between Cynthia and Dillon. She pursed her lips. "Just discussing the merits of the number eleven."

Cynthia hurried off to the back of the van, leaving them alone.

"Ah, that's right. Have you decided whether you're going back to Amarillo?"

A shadow crossed Alaina's face. She shook her head. "Not yet."

"We'd love to have you," Dillon said.

"After the summit, it's hard telling what the communities will look like, so I'm leaving my options open."

"Very true." Dillon nodded. "I suppose the world as we now know it is about to change again."

Cynthia returned with her box of cookies and handed one to Dillon.

"Thanks." Dillon put on her cheesiest smile. "I'll share it with Skylar."

"Just don't choke on it," Cynthia said, returning the saccharine smile.

Dillon bit back a laugh. "I believe this might turn out to be the sweetest cookie I've ever eaten."

Before Cynthia could respond, Jake called out. "Hey, everyone. We're all ready to go."

"Saved by the bell," Dillon whispered to Cynthia.

Chapter Eleven

They'd made good time from the estate to Santa Clarita. It was a route they'd traveled often. Cynthia remained vigilant, scanning the route for any signs of change. So far, so good.

"You seem a little tense," Alaina said from the passenger seat. She kept her voice low, so Cynthia had to strain to hear her over the conversation in the backseats.

"I just don't want to miss anything. Any signs." She peeked into the rearview mirror to see if the others were listening, but they seemed wrapped up in the guessing game they were playing.

"Anything amiss?"

"Not that I've noticed."

"Good." Alaina sighed. "It's probably for the best we're staying in Vegas tonight. Being on such high alert can be exhausting, so five, six hours behind the wheel is plenty."

"No doubt." Cynthia felt a twinge of guilt for keeping their true destination hidden. She hoped Alaina would forgive her when she discovered the deception.

Alaina put her hand on Cynthia's knee. "Are you going to tell me what you told Dillon?"

Heat rose up Cynthia's neck and covered her cheeks. "Um..."

Alaina laughed. "I knew you wouldn't make a good poker player, but I didn't expect Dillon to be so transparent."

Cynthia suspected that Alaina would wipe up the floor with them if they ever challenged her to a game since Alaina held her cards close to her vest. "I didn't mean to tell her anything."

"Hence my poker comment. I'm sure she saw it written all over your face. Sex can do that to you."

Cynthia shifted her gaze to the mirror. Still good. "Good sex definitely can."

"You're telling me." Alaina's hand resting on Cynthia's knee slowly moved up her thigh.

Cynthia flinched and checked the mirror.

Alaina pulled her hand back and chuckled. "Sorry, I couldn't resist. I figured it was payback for telling her how many orgasms I had."

"I didn't tell her. You did," Cynthia said under her breath. Her gaze bounced from Alaina to the mirror and then the surrounding area. She hoped the others in the caravan were keeping better track because she was struggling to focus.

"I did? By the eleven conversation and cookie incident, I was sure you told her."

"I just told her it was multiple. Not how many."

"So you just walked up to her and said, *Hey, I gave Alaina multiple orgasms last night.*" She bit her lip to keep from smirking.

"Sheesh, will you keep your voice down?" Cynthia motioned toward the mirror with her eyes. "The whole van doesn't need to hear about this. And no, I didn't walk up to her and say that. She guessed."

"Oh, so she walked up to you and said, *Hey, I see you gave Alaina multiple orgasms.*"

Cynthia turned her head and glared at Alaina. "Would you stop saying that word?"

"Which word?"

Damn it. Even while Alaina teased her, she was so damned sexy. "You know which word."

"Orgasm?"

"Stop." Cynthia laughed. "I surrender. I'll answer any of your questions if you stop saying that word."

Alaina twiddled her fingers in front of her like an evil villain. "Ah, now I've found your kryptonite."

Cynthia groaned. "Why do I think that won't bode well for me?"

"Smart woman." Alaina cleared her throat. "Tell me how Dillon discovered the secret of the multiple things that shall not be named?"

Cynthia shook her head and rolled her eyes. "As soon as she looked at me, she knew. Then she started teasing me. Asked me how many we'd had." Cynthia pointed at her cheek. "And as you well know, my face gives me away. Then she started guessing how many I was able to bring you to. I refused to answer. And then you came along spouting off about your favorite number, and she figured it out."

Alaina laughed. "Smart woman."

"It didn't exactly take Sherlock Holmes to figure it out with all your smoky looks and tongue action."

"Did you just say tongue action?" Alaina slowly licked her lips. "I didn't think you'd want to talk about that in front of the children."

Cynthia put her hand against her forehead. "I refuse to have this conversation with you any longer." She leaned forward and peered out the window. "It's amazing how cocky you've become after having those things that can't be named."

"Fine." Alaina smirked. "I'll leave you be...for now." Alaina touched her knee. "I don't want to put us in any danger. But I can't guarantee anything when I get you alone."

Cynthia shuddered. Her sultry voice and light touch awoke something in Cynthia that she thought would be asleep for at least a couple of days.

❧❧❧❧

The trek through the Mojave Desert so far had proven uneventful. They'd driven around the few cars that blocked the road but hadn't had to stop to move any out of the way. Dillon suspected it would be a different story as they got closer to Las Vegas. For now, she allowed herself to enjoy the unencumbered highway.

The desert spanned out around them with no break in sight. Dillon hated the desolation and lack of greenery. At least they weren't driving during the sweltering heat of summer. She'd always hated the drive along Interstate 15, so she insisted on flying whenever they visited Vegas.

She checked her side mirror to ensure their caravan was sticking close together. Even though they'd been driving for nearly three hours with no sign of others, she wasn't willing to take the chance.

Skylar sat in the passenger seat with her gun poised on her lap. Her head moved from side to side as her gaze surveyed the landscape. They'd talked early on, but their conversation tapered off the farther they drove into the desert. The wide-open expanse had them both on edge.

Skylar must have sensed Dillon's gaze on her

because she said, "I forgot to ask you what was up with you and Cynthia and that damned cookie."

Dillon chuckled. "Oh, god. I can't believe I didn't tell you about Cynthia and Alaina."

"Did they finally do the deed?" Skylar asked.

Dillon tilted her head and stared at Skylar but soon needed to turn her attention back to the road. "How did you know?"

"Seriously? The proverbial handwriting has been on the wall for a while."

"Apparently, it was *more* than satisfactory. Cynthia still had that unfocused sex look this morning."

"Good for her."

"Are you sure about that?" Even though Dillon wanted to see Skylar's expression when she answered, she kept her focus on the road. "We don't know much about this woman. There's something different about her. Mysterious. I'm worried about Cynthia getting hurt."

"Ya know the only people that don't get hurt?" Skylar asked.

"No."

"The people that don't put themselves out there. If Cynthia gets hurt, we help pick up the pieces, dust her off, and send her back out again."

"I'd still prefer she not get hurt."

"That's a given. But you can't protect her without clipping her wings. And you never explained the cookie thing."

Dillon chuckled and launched into her story.

They continued talking as they drove when Skylar said, "I know you can't tell me everything, but I'd like to hear more about the summit."

"Okay," Dillon said tentatively. "I'll tell you what

I can."

"I noticed you guys haven't mentioned a date. Depending on how our travels go, it could take three days to get to Salt Lake City, so when is the actual summit scheduled for?"

Dillon leaned forward over the steering wheel and peered into the distance to buy herself some extra time. This wasn't a conversation she wanted to have with Skylar. "I don't need to tell you that travel is much more uncertain, so it's hard to nail down a date."

"But you have a tentative one scheduled?"

"Look." Dillon pointed at two roadrunners scurrying across the desert, thankful to have a diversion from the conversation.

"They are so cool." Skylar watched them with a smile on her face.

"Remember that old cartoon with the roadrunner and coyote?" Dillon said, hoping to divert the conversation further.

It worked. Soon they were on safer ground talking about all their favorite cartoons.

❧❧❧❧

Skylar walked across the parking lot and stood by herself staring out at the miles of flat land. Perfect place to put a solar farm since there was an abundance of sunshine. After they'd eaten lunch, Dillon had led the team to explore the solar panels, but Skylar had stayed back to keep watch over the women from Amarillo.

Being just after noon, the desert had heated up from the morning chill, but still she shivered. Their bathroom stop at the Primm Valley Resort had left her feeling uneasy. They'd only gone inside the lobby to use the facilities, but she couldn't shake the reality the resort was likely a giant coffin to hundreds, if not thousands, of people.

She shuddered and took a sip from her water bottle. If she was this unnerved by a little resort like Primm, how would she handle Vegas? Even though Dillon hadn't admitted it, Skylar suspected the trip was getting to her, too. Since they'd left the estate, Dillon hadn't been herself. Less playful and more guarded. The trip had been exhausting. Although most of the drive was on wide open roads, she'd been on high alert with her weapon in her hands the entire time.

Footsteps pulled her out of her thoughts.

"Solar fields apparently aren't my thing," the voice said.

"Cynthia." Her shoulders relaxed. "You scared the shit out of me."

"Sorry. I thought you heard me coming."

Skylar gazed at Cynthia. While Skylar had dressed comfortably for the trip, Cynthia was dressed in blue jeans and a form-fitting button-down shirt. She'd left her hair down, and it cascaded to her shoulders.

"I didn't get the chance to tell you that you look nice today," Skylar said.

Cynthia unconsciously ran her hand down her shirt as if smoothing out wrinkles. "I just want to look nice when we arrive in Vegas."

Skylar grinned. "Gonna try your hand at the slots while we're there?"

"I know. I'm just being stupid."

"No, I was teasing. Bad joke." Skylar put her hand on Cynthia's arm. "This trip has me on edge."

"I think we all are. We've been in our own little bubble, and soon that'll all change."

"Is it wrong that I'd prefer to stay in our bubble?" Skylar asked.

Cynthia sighed. "Not at all. We've settled into our new way of life, and this has the potential to turn our world upside down again."

"I've had about enough of our world being rocked. Do you think we're up for it this soon?"

"We'll have to be." Cynthia pointed to a nearby bench. "Care to sit down?"

They sat next to each other with their shoulders touching. Normally, Skylar would have moved away, wanting her space, but today, having Cynthia close brought her comfort.

It was several minutes before Cynthia said, "Dillon's carrying a lot on her shoulders."

"I know. She's not been herself lately. I try to be supportive, but at times, I want to shake her. Then I feel bad and want to hug her." Skylar chuckled. "I can never decide which."

Cynthia laughed. "I know the feeling. Like it or not, she's our leader."

"But you're on the Commission, too, and you don't seem to...I don't know...get quite so..."

"Intense," Cynthia said.

"Exactly!"

"It's not really the same for us. While we all have an equal voice, there's no doubt that when push comes to shove, she's our de facto leader. She'll tell you otherwise, but she knows it. Her voice carries the most weight with the group."

Skylar's chest tightened. Cynthia had spoken something she'd known for a long time but tried to push aside. That was why this trip had her so concerned. If anything bad happened, Dillon would put the responsibility squarely on her own shoulders. "She's afraid this could be a mistake, isn't she?"

"I believe so. She doesn't really talk about it. The Commission discussed the possible landmines ad nauseam, but in the end, we knew we didn't have much choice."

"We likely couldn't survive another attack," Skylar said, her voice not much louder than a whisper.

"That's the conclusion we came to. We need allies."

"But the possibility remains that some of the groups at the summit might have different ideas."

Cynthia nodded. "Yep, and that's what keeps Dillon up at night. Even though Babcock's group wasn't invited to the meeting because of the crazy stuff they've been spouting, there's no guarantee that they don't find out about it and show up."

Skylar bit her lip. "I know. That's why I'll be packing plenty of heat."

"And that's why Dillon is freaking out. Hell, I am, too. None of us wants another battle like the last one."

"No, but we have to be prepared to defend ourselves. Our way of life. I think Babcock would like nothing better than to turn the clock back two hundred years and put women in the place they were then."

"Where do you think that would leave lesbians?"

Damn. Cynthia was on a roll today. Saying all the things that nobody wanted to talk about but should.

"I shudder to think. Without the law to protect us, I'm afraid he might resort to more than conversion therapy." Skylar turned to Cynthia. "What's Alaina think? She must have the best insight."

Skylar felt Cynthia stiffen beside her. "She doesn't say much," Cynthia said. "Only enough to let us know that his group is dangerous. She's evasive when I ask her questions. My sense is she experienced something really bad, but she isn't sharing."

"You like her," Skylar said as a statement, not a question.

"I do."

"What are her plans?"

Cynthia shrugged. "She hasn't said."

"So she might rejoin the Amarillo group?"

"Possibly. I'd like her to stay with us."

"Have you told her that?"

Cynthia fidgeted in her seat. "Not exactly."

Skylar bumped her shoulder against Cynthia. "What are you waiting for? Finding a good woman before the crisis was hard enough, now it's a million times worse. Grab her while you can."

"What are the odds?" Cynthia smiled. "Someone I think I could really like shows up like that. But then I start to question myself. Maybe it's just... I dunno."

"Are you thinking you're just attracted because you don't have many options?"

"God, no. Just the opposite." Cynthia's voice came out in a higher pitch. "I know how I feel. She's the most fascinating woman I've ever met. Intelligent. Well read. We've had some amazing philosophical discussions."

"Then what's the problem?"

Cynthia stared out at the horizon. She didn't

answer Skylar's question right away, so Skylar waited. It was one of Skylar's superpowers. The ability to quietly give someone space until they were ready to talk.

After several minutes, Cynthia said, "What if she's just settling for me because the pickings are slim?"

Duh. Why hadn't she realized Cynthia's insecurities had gotten the better of her? Despite everything Cynthia had going for her—looks, intelligence, a sense of humor, the list was long—Cynthia had always doubted herself.

"You are a catch." Skylar patted Cynthia's leg. "Don't you ever forget that. Alaina or any other woman would be lucky to have you."

Cynthia's cheeks colored. "Thanks," she mumbled.

"Don't you think you should tell her how you feel and ask her to stay?"

"Maybe."

"That's all you've got?" Skylar said, hoping to lighten the mood. Her heart went out to Cynthia. Skylar knew how it felt to feel not good enough, and it broke her heart that someone like Cynthia would struggle with those feelings. When Cynthia's only response was a shy smile, Skylar continued. "You know I'm just giving you shit. Trying to light a fire under you."

Cynthia nodded. "I don't want her to go, but I'm afraid I'm gonna blow it."

"The only way you can truly blow it is by not telling her how you feel. That would be the true tragedy here."

There was determination in Cynthia's eyes when

she turned to Skylar. "You're right. You'd think that after all this, I'd have learned the ultimate lesson."

"Which is?"

"Life is too short, and tomorrow isn't promised to any of us."

"Exactly!"

"Thank you." Cynthia put her arm over Skylar's shoulders. "I appreciate your friendship."

Skylar's chest expanded. It still astonished her that she had people in her life for the first time. People she'd kill or die for. "I love you, Cyn. And Alaina will, too, if she has any brains."

"I love you, too." Cynthia held up her trembling hand. "I guess the drive to Vegas just got more interesting."

※ ※ ※ ※

Dillon hit the gas and pulled onto the road leading away from the solar farm. She checked her rearview mirror to ensure the others followed. They'd added another vehicle to the convoy. Tasha had hotwired one of the cars in the parking lot, so the ladies from Amarillo would have their own vehicle in case they wanted to return home instead of staying at the summit.

Dillon stared straight ahead at the road, not wanting to meet Skylar's gaze. The revelation to the group that their true destination was Las Vegas, not Salt Lake City had gone all right. The realization that they were almost to their destination softened the blow of not being told from the beginning.

"Is keeping the location from us why you've been so jumpy?" Skylar asked.

What a loaded question. It would be easy to say yes, but it wouldn't be entirely true. She'd had to keep enough from Skylar as it was, but she'd vowed never to outright lie. "Partially."

Dillon felt Skylar's gaze on her but didn't turn. They drove in silence for some time before Skylar said, "Whatever it is, I hope eventually you trust me enough to tell me."

Ouch. Skylar's words stabbed into her like a dull knife. She took a deep breath before she turned to Skylar. No doubt, her eyes held the pain that radiated through her. "It's not like that, Sky. I made a vow to the Commission, and who would I be if I broke it, even though I trust you with everything?"

The hard set of Skylar's jaw relaxed. "You're right. That was so unfair of me. One of the reasons I love you is because of your trustworthiness, so I'm being a hypocrite wanting you to break it."

Dillon took one hand off the wheel and took Skylar's hand. "Thanks for understanding. If it helps, when the Commission gives the okay, you'll be the first person I tell."

"Deal." Skylar smiled. "Although, you might want to tell Maria first. What is up with her?"

"I don't know. I can't believe how pissed she was. She's a lawyer, for fuck's sake, she should understand the need for secrecy." Maria's over-the-top reaction had Dillon worried on one hand, but on the other, it lessened her concern that Maria could be the traitor. Weren't traitors supposed to stay low key? Maria was being anything but.

"I for one am thrilled that we only have to get to Vegas. It's a long-ass drive to Salt Lake City."

Dillon's heart raced. "Yeah, but it also means

that show time is about to happen."

Skylar squeezed Dillon's hand. "No wonder you're so uptight. You'll have to meet with the other leaders soon."

Dillon nodded. "Tonight, there's a big celebration planned. We'll all get together for dinner." She pointed toward the back. "That's why Renee set us up with the *secret* cooler. It's our offering for the party. Then tomorrow morning, Jake and I will attend the first summit meeting."

"I'd be pissed if I were Cynthia." Skylar frowned. "Seems like we're perpetuating the sexism of the old world."

"Trust me, we had a lengthy discussion about it at the Commission meeting, but it was Cynthia that finally ended the argument. We're not sure who we're dealing with, and she didn't want to risk our contingent not being taken seriously without a male representative."

"Ugh, I hate that."

"We all do. Despite how important female equality is, we decided this wasn't the time to make it the number one agenda item." Dillon groaned. "Politics is hard. I never really thought about it before. Sometimes, we have to make a tradeoff for the greater good. It sucks. But if there's a bright spot, we did put out the request that every group sends one male and one female. Last I heard, about ninety percent of the groups plan on complying."

Skylar nodded. "It's a good start. Are you nervous?"

"I'd be lying if I said no." Dillon shifted her gaze from the road and met Skylar's. "A lot depends on how this goes. This likely could set the whole tone for the rest of our lives and our kids' lives."

Skylar's eyebrows shot up. "Our kids? Is there something you're not telling me?"

"I meant it generically." Dillon smiled. "But I've thought about it."

"With me?"

"No, with CJ." Dillon shook her head. "Of course with you. Obviously, we'd need a donor. I'm still on the fence whether I'd want Jake or a stranger."

"Wow, you have given this some thought."

Dillon's cheeks warmed. "Got a lot of time to think without Netflix and the internet."

"When did you plan on talking to me about it?"

Dillon relaxed. Skylar's tone was playful, not angry. "Certainly not now."

Skylar laughed. "Too late. The cat's out of the bag."

"Can't we shove it back in a little bit longer?"

"Changing your mind?"

"No!" *Damn.* She hoped that didn't come out too strong. "I'd just like to see how things go, so we know what kind of world we'll be living in before we make any big decisions. Is it selfish to bring a child into this?"

"I've thought about that, too. But—"

"Wait." Dillon slapped the steering wheel. "So you've thought about it but let me squirm?"

"Maybe." Skylar shot Dillon an innocent grin.

"Aren't you full of surprises?" Skylar had thrown Dillon for a loop. With Skylar's rough childhood, in and out of foster care, Dillon figured it would be a subject she'd have to broach carefully. Warmth spread over her, knowing that Skylar had been considering it.

"You've changed me, Dillon Mitchell." Skylar

leaned over and kissed Dillon on the cheek. "For the better."

"And you've changed me, too, Skylar Lange. Whatever we're going through has sucked, but I'm grateful you're by my side."

"Stop. You're going to make me blush."

"I suppose the others wouldn't approve if I pulled over to the side of the road, so I could give you a proper kiss."

Skylar laughed. "Probably not. I'll take a rain check that I plan on collecting in Vegas."

"Deal."

❧ ❧ ❧ ❧

Cynthia put her hand on the radio knob but stopped when she realized what she was doing. In her nervousness, she'd hoped for a distraction, forgetting there were no stations left. The drive to Vegas wasn't much more than half an hour, so if she were going to say something to Alaina, now was the time.

"Nervous?" Alaina nodded toward Cynthia's hand that she'd jerked back.

"Yeah."

"Care to elaborate?" Alaina said in her cool tone.

Cynthia was glad to be driving, so she didn't have to look at Alaina, although Alaina's ice blue eyes were etched in Cynthia's mind. She fought the urge to wipe her sweaty palms on her pants. "There's something I want to discuss with you."

When Cynthia didn't continue, Alaina said, "Which is?"

Fuck. She was blowing this. Her heart raced. *Get a grip.*

"Umm, it's just that I kinda wanted to talk about your plans. What you're going to do next." Cynthia hoped Alaina would bail her out, but it wasn't happening, so she forged on. "Have you given it any thought where you'd like to live?"

"Are you asking if I intend on returning to Amarillo?"

Cynthia could swear she heard amusement in Alaina's tone but was too afraid to meet her gaze, so she kept a death grip on the steering wheel and stared straight ahead. "Yeah, I was curious about that. Not that I want to put any pressure on you or anything." *God.* She needed to stop rambling.

"I see. Did you have an opinion?"

Definitely a tone to her voice. Cynthia shot her a sideways glance and made note of Alaina's smirk. "What's that look for?"

"You don't do subtle well," Alaina said with a chuckle. "Care to say what you really mean?"

"Fine." She needed to buck her fear. "I would like you to stay...with me. I've enjoyed getting to know you, and I think maybe...well, maybe we could be good for each other, but if you go, we'll never get the chance to figure it out. And well, life is too short not to at least go for what you want. At least that's what Skylar told me...and..." My god, she just needed to shut up. "But if your heart is set on going back to Amarillo, I'll understand, but of course, I'll be sad. I don't want to pressure you or anything, but I thought you needed to know how I feel and all before you make your decision. Not that you should do something you don't want because of what I want. That would be wrong. That's not what I'm asking—"

"I think you better take a breath before you pass

out from lack of oxygen," Alaina said with a smile.

Cynthia pretended to hit her head on the steering wheel. "Why am I so damned awkward in situations like this?"

"I think it's sweet. Cute."

"You do?" Cynthia hazarded a peek at Alaina. "You don't think I'm a dork?"

Alaina smirked. "I didn't say that. I think you're adorkable."

"That's not even a word."

"It is now."

Cynthia's face burned. In her mind, at least what she'd practiced, she'd say something so poetic and beautiful that Alaina would be reduced to tears, and not because she was laughing so hard at Cynthia's ineptness. "I wish the words came out like they are in my head, instead of this rambling hot mess."

"I think your meaning is pretty clear."

"It is?" Cynthia turned, wide-eyed. "You understood what I just said?"

"Yeah, you said you have the hots for me and would like to get me naked some more, and if I leave, you won't have the opportunity."

"No! I'm so sorry that's how it came out." Cynthia whipped her head around, and as soon as she met Alaina's gaze, she realized her mistake. She lightly slapped Alaina's leg. "You're screwing with me."

"Ya think?" Alaina burst out laughing. "I wasn't kidding when I said you're adorkable."

"Let me try this again." Cynthia took a deep breath. "I've enjoyed our time together and don't want it to end. You are the most fascinating woman I've ever met. I'd like the opportunity to get to know you better because I think there could be something special between us." Cynthia turned her gaze from the road, met Alaina's gaze, and held it. "Alaina, would you consider staying with me at Whitaker Estate instead of returning to Amarillo?"

"Yes."

Cynthia's heart raced. *Yes.* What did that mean? Her face fell. "Did you mean that you'd consider it or that you'd do it? Of course, if you're asking for more time to consider it, I completely understand. Or maybe your yes meant something else."

Alaina held up her hand with her thumb and forefinger nearly touching. "You were this close to pulling this off poetically."

"And then my awkwardness kicked in." Cynthia shook her head and gazed down at the steering wheel. "Damn it."

Alaina put her hand on Cynthia's leg, and electricity shot up it. She needed to focus on the road, not Alaina's hand. She gripped the wheel tighter and stared straight ahead.

"To answer your question. I would love to stay with you at Whitaker Estate and see where this takes us."

"Seriously?" Cynthia turned. She had no doubt that Alaina would see the excitement dancing in her eyes.

Alaina pointed toward the windshield. "Um, you might want to watch the road."

Cynthia jerked the wheel and pulled the van back into her lane. It wasn't as if they'd meet any other traffic, but the others would think she was drunk swerving all over the road. Heat climbed up her neck. "Uh, sorry. I'm just so fricking happy."

Alaina laughed. "I am, too," she said in a quiet

voice.

Cynthia glanced at Alaina but didn't linger this time. The look on Alaina's face nearly took Cynthia's breath away. Her eyes were misty with a mixture of fear and adoration. "Hey, you okay?"

Alaina pursed her lips as if in thought before she responded. "I'm better than okay." She put her hand against her chest. "I'm not sure what you do to me, but I feel you in here. A couple of months ago, I would have told you I'd never feel this way."

Cynthia's pulse quickened. *Alaina felt the same way.* "Can I ask why you thought that?"

"You can ask," Alaina said. "I'm just not ready to answer. *Yet.*"

The word *yet* was music to her ears. Alaina became guarded any time Cynthia asked about her life before Amarillo. Normally, she'd change the subject and on a couple of occasions even became defensive. "That's fair enough. Thanks for giving me hope that one day you'll let me in on everything."

Alaina smiled. "I want to make sure you're good and hooked before I let you in on the train wreck of my past."

"If that's all you're waiting for, then you'll be telling your story soon." Cynthia's eyes widened. Did she just say that out loud? What had gotten into her?

"Something tells me that you might be right, but for now, can we talk about what happens when we get to Vegas? The world is going to turn on its ear again."

"But I want to bask in the glow of this conversation." Cynthia couldn't keep the goofy grin off her face, but she didn't care. She wanted to shout from the rooftops that Alaina was staying. The thought of telling Dillon and Skylar made her smile bigger.

Chapter Twelve

Dillon slowed. Several trucks blocked the road ahead. From this distance, it appeared they were stationed by the famous Las Vegas sign. Her stomach clenched. Nobody had mentioned blocking the route into the city.

"Did you know about this?" Skylar asked.

Dillon shook her head. "Nope."

As they drew closer, she could make out a group gathered around the trucks. A bearded man with a clipboard stood near the road while the others stood at attention with assault weapons at the ready.

Skylar gripped her weapon tighter. "What are you going to do?"

"It has to be people for the summit. Maybe they had a scare and wanted to put in an extra layer of security."

Dillon pulled to a stop, and the dark-haired man with a bushy beard approached. He wore faded blue jeans and a plaid shirt and carried a clipboard.

"Stay here," Dillon said. "Keep your eyes open." Before Skylar could react, Dillon jumped from the truck.

The man approached with a large smile. "Hello," he said. "Welcome to the summit."

Dillon's shoulders relaxed slightly, but she remained on guard. "Hello." She feared it came out more formal than she'd wanted it to.

He glanced down at his clipboard. "I'd like to check you in. May I ask where you're from?"

"California," she answered.

"Oh, my god, Dillon?" He raced toward her. "I've been waiting for you to arrive." He must have seen the puzzled look on her face. He laughed. "It's Caleb. From New York."

"Caleb! Holy shit." Dillon smiled broadly and reached out her hand.

"Oh, no." He took her hand and pulled her toward him. "I said the first time I laid eyes on you, I was going to hug the stuffing out of you."

She laughed and returned his hug. "Damn, it's so good to finally meet you."

He pounded her on the back and laughed. "We're doing this. After six months alone, we are fucking doing this."

She and CJ had spent many hours in conversation with Caleb's group from New York. Despite being on opposite coasts, they'd become their closest allies. "I know, unbelievable right?"

"When you talk to CJ, you tell her it'll take a long time before I forgive her." He squeezed her one last time, nearly taking her breath away, before he released her.

"Oof." Dillon exaggerated the sound of the breath being squished out of her. "She didn't want the stuffing squeezed out of her," Dillon teased. "Although, you would have had a harder time with her."

Caleb gave her a puzzled look.

"She's six-foot-four," Dillon said.

His eyes widened. "Why didn't I know that?"

"Same reason we didn't know you had a lumber-jack beard."

Caleb's eyes twinkled, and he turned from side to side. "You like it? I've been growing it since the crisis." He leaned in. "The wife hates it. Says I look like a wild man."

"It suits you." Dillon smirked. "I've always thought you were a wild man."

He grinned. "I still can't believe the angel-voiced CJ is six-four."

"Oh, my god, wait until I tell her you said she had an angel voice." Dillon shook her head. "On second thought, I don't need to see her puff up about her angel voice."

The others began to pour out of the vehicles and approach the pair. Caleb's eyes lit up. He nodded toward Skylar and then met Dillon's gaze. "I'm guessing that's your lady, Skylar."

"Yep."

He extended his hand and shook. "Pleased to meet you. Dillon talks about you all the time."

Heat rose in Dillon's cheeks.

"She does, does she?" Skylar said.

"Only good things." Caleb leaned in. "I think she's smitten."

Skylar grinned. "I'm pretty smitten with her, too."

Jake joined the group, and he and Caleb clasped hands and enthusiastically pumped each other's arms. Caleb called the guards over and introduced them, as well.

With everyone milling around and talking, Dillon already felt more at ease. The atmosphere was festive.

Willa made a beeline to the *Welcome to Fabulous Las Vegas* sign and snapped pictures from every angle. Dillon gazed at the iconic sign. It looked much the same as she'd remembered it, except the grounds around it were no longer immaculately tended. Instead, weeds and grass grew up around the blue legs. The sign, designed in the late nineteen fifties, didn't have the same level of lights and glitz that most in Vegas did. She could almost imagine that nothing had changed looking at it.

Dillon turned to Skylar, whose entire attention was on Willa's photo shoot. "Surreal, isn't it?" Dillon asked.

"Yeah. I'm not sure what I expected to see."

"It almost appears normal. Which in some ways is even creepier. If that makes any sense."

Skylar nodded. "I had visions of it tipped over and decaying. I guess that doesn't happen in six months." She pointed. "The white looks a little dingier, or maybe it's my imagination, but the red lettering looks the same."

"Do you think the others would be willing to take a picture with the sign? Or will they think I've lost my mind?" Skylar asked.

"If you want a picture, go for it. If they grumble, they grumble."

Skylar smiled and gazed around the group. "By the looks on their faces, they're feeling as nostalgic as I am."

It didn't take any persuasion to get their clan lined up near the sign for a picture. Caleb snapped a few photos before Dillon insisted he join them. One of the guards took the camera from him, and Caleb squeezed between Dillon and Skylar, causing the entire group to laugh. It soon turned into musical chair picture taking as different pairings rotated through.

Dillon smiled when Caleb asked for a picture of just the two of them. His mischievous eyes danced when he said, "That'll make CJ jealous."

In the moment, they forgot themselves and the situation. They could have been a group of tourists, enjoying their visit to Vegas. Dillon hoped the cheerful atmosphere carried over into the actual summit. Even Maria's surly mood had improved. She and Tasha were in the middle of a goofy pose when the roar of an engine brought them out of their celebration.

A pickup tore down the road, coming from the Strip. Dillon's eyes widened. It seemed to be coming fast.

Skylar reacted first and ran back to their vehicle, returning with a machine gun slung across her front.

"Whoa. I'm not sure we need that much firepower," Dillon said.

Skylar glanced down at the weapon in her hand. "Uh, yeah. Maybe I should've just stuffed a handgun in my belt." She headed back to the vehicle with Jake in tow.

Dillon's pulse quickened. Even though she knew it was practical to have a weapon at the ready, it still made her uneasy. Caleb's guards moved into action, as well. They stood on each side of the trucks that blocked the road.

The pickup roared up to the barricades and slammed on the brakes. The guards pointed their guns at the truck.

Caleb waved his arms. "Hold up," he shouted. "Stand down. We know them."

Dillon's shoulders relaxed when the men lowered their weapons.

The pickup door flew open, and Dillon heard a scream from behind her. She nearly jumped out of her skin until she realized what was happening.

Carol screamed as she ran down the road. The large man who emerged from the truck smiled broadly before he ran, his cowboy boots slapping off the pavement. It reminded Dillon of the old movies where people would run across the beach to each other. She smiled to herself; this was just a little less athletic. She hoped the man wouldn't sprain his ankle running in those boots.

Skylar took Dillon's hand. "Isn't that sweet? It must be Carol's husband."

Warmth spread across Dillon's chest. Maybe she should look away and give the couple privacy, but her gaze remained riveted to the two. When Dillon glanced at the others, she discovered everyone else was also watching the pair, even Alaina. Despite Alaina's contentious relationship with Carol, Alaina's eyes glistened in the sun. Cynthia put her arm around Alaina and pulled her closer.

The teenagers' parents also arrived, and the joyful reunion continued. The festive feeling of earlier became a full-fledged party. Dillon almost wanted to pull out a bottle of champagne to cap the celebration.

The festivities were interrupted again as a caravan of eight vans approached from the other direction. The guards quickly got into position and ordered the group off the road.

The lead van pulled up behind their vehicles and killed the engine. The rest did the same.

A large man tumbled out of the van, sporting a

huge smile. "Howdy," he said and waved.

Dillon surveyed the situation. All the passengers remained inside their vehicles. Dillon's shoulders tensed.

Caleb moved forward with his infectious smile while Dillon moved up alongside Jake.

Caleb stuck out his hand. "Welcome. I'm Caleb from New York." He glanced over his shoulder. "And this is Dillon and Jake."

"Dillon and Jake. You're CJ's friends." The man smiled. "Love that girl."

Dillon nodded. She didn't want to be rude, but she couldn't help but study this bear of a man. He stood well over six foot, and the buttons on his shirt strained against his chest. "Yes, we are," Dillon said. "And you are?"

"Oh, shoot, where are my manners? I'm Gus."

The tension in Dillon dissipated. "*The* Gus from Georgia?"

"Yes, ma'am." He smiled, which made his baby face look even younger, but Dillon suspected he was nearly fifty.

"CJ will be so jealous we met you," Jake said.

"Wait. We need to get a picture with you." Dillon smiled. "Gift for CJ."

"I'd be happy to get a picture for the little lady," Gus said.

Dillon chuckled. "You might want to rethink that. CJ's as tall as you."

Gus's mouth dropped open. "No way, you're shitting me."

Dillon stifled a chuckle. If he called CJ an angel, too, Dillon wasn't sure she could hold it together. "It's the truth."

"Well, I'll be damned. You tell her I want to meet her one day, so we can have our picture taken side by side. That way, I can see for myself."

"Deal," Dillon said. Her buoyant mood surprised her, but Gus had a larger-than-life energy that put her at ease. CJ had made contact with their group early on, so she felt as if she knew them. Maybe her fears were unfounded, if all the contingents turned out as friendly as Caleb and Gus.

"I wasn't expecting a welcome wagon," Gus said.

"We just got here ourselves," Dillon said and nodded at Caleb. "He's checking everyone in. Shit, I don't think we even finished, did we?"

Caleb laughed. "No, ma'am. We got sidetracked. I best stop shirking my duty and get my records in order." He held up his clipboard. "I need to get a count and names from each group. I better start with Dillon. How many do you have?

Dillon frowned. "Depends on how you want to count us."

Caleb looked up from his clipboard, a puzzled look on his face.

Dillon pointed at the boisterous reunion. "We brought the four women back to their loved ones, so I'm thinking they should be counted with Amarillo."

Caleb gazed at his clipboard, back to Dillon, and then his clipboard again. "Says here that you should have five from Amarillo."

"We have a fifth." Dillon pointed to where Alaina stood deep in conversation with Cynthia. "But she's not sure if she's going to return to Amarillo or stay with us."

Caleb's eyes twinkled when his gaze landed on the pair. "How many do you have without her?"

"Eight," Dillon said.

"I'll put down nine," he said with a chuckle.

"I think you're right." Apparently, it wasn't just her who could see the chemistry oozing off of Alaina and Cynthia.

Caleb made a note on his clipboard. He took out a separate piece of paper and handed it to Dillon. If you'd have someone write down everyone's names, I'd appreciate it." He then turned to Gus. "Let's get you checked in."

"That's a bit of a problem. We have a few more than we'd intended." Gus smiled and shifted his gaze to the ground.

Caleb studied his clipboard. "I show you were bringing eight." Caleb glanced at the vans. "Unless you're each driving separately, it looks like you have a few more."

Gus nodded. "Yes, sir. We only have twenty-four people total. It's quite the trek from Georgia to here, so we decided not to separate."

Caleb's eyes widened. "You have all twenty-four with you?"

"And some." Gus pointed his thumb over his shoulder. "We picked up a van load in Oklahoma that were just wandering, and then picked up a couple about ten miles down the road. Said they'd been making their way toward the West Coast."

Caleb's eyes darkened. "I see. I'd like to record those individuals separate from your group." He shot Dillon a concerned look. "Mind if I get the names of everyone in your vehicles?"

"Be my guest. I told them to stay inside until I got further instructions. Do you prefer them to stay where they are until you've taken their names?"

"That would be perfect."

Jake stepped up beside Caleb. "I'll help you."

Once Caleb and Jake made their way toward the vans, a sad smile crossed Gus's face as he stared at the sign. "Doesn't seem possible, does it? The casinos are going to be creepy without the sounds of the slots going off 24/7."

"Vegas as a ghost town gives me the creeps," Dillon said. "But it's better now that the life of the party is here."

Gus blushed, and he swatted his hand at Dillon. "Now hush. My wife is in the van, and I reckon she's not gonna let me party."

"I'd guess a party naturally follows you."

It startled Dillon when he let out a loud belly laugh. He must have noticed because he put his hand on her shoulder. "Sorry about that. My wife also says my laugh is too loud. Gauging by your reaction, she might be right."

Once everyone had been counted, a guard moved one of the trucks that blocked the road to let them pass. Dillon said a quick goodbye to Caleb, promising to meet up at the party before she climbed back into her truck. They'd planned on quietly making their entrance into Vegas, but she doubted that would be possible since they'd grown to a caravan of fifteen. They slowly made their way up Las Vegas Boulevard, heading toward the Strip. Soon, they'd know what it looked like with no neon and no people.

Chapter Thirteen

The floodlights lit the street outside of the Mayan Casino. It was an impressive sight. Enormous. Like the Luxor, it was shaped like a pyramid except it was flat on top. It was also nearly twice as big. Dillon had been a builder in her previous life, so the structure fascinated her. Unlike the Luxor that was black and shiny, the architects had managed to capture the imperfect shape of the stone structure. If she didn't know better, she would have sworn they were at Chichen Itza in Mexico.

Music filled the street. Dillon leaned against the construction fence and groaned. She and Skylar had slipped away and found a deserted corner where they didn't have to interact with anyone. She'd met so many people that she doubted she'd remember half the names by morning.

They'd had a feast that would rival the most elaborate Thanksgiving meal. In a way, it felt like the first Thanksgiving in the new world. The crowd was happy, almost giddy. After six months of isolation, there was something hopeful, seeing evidence that they were not alone in the world.

Dillon couldn't believe the quality of the food. Each group had brought a regional dish, making it feel as if she'd taken a trip around the country. Renee's food had been a hit and disappeared quickly. Dillon's favorites had been the tamales from Albuquerque. She must have eaten half a dozen.

They'd anticipated about a hundred participants, but at last count, Caleb tallied one hundred eighty-four. Based on the noise level coming from the partygoers, she'd have guessed at least triple that number.

As exciting as it was, to Dillon, it also held an element of uncertainty. Of the twenty-three groups gathered, theirs and the group from Missouri were the only ones that hadn't taken on new citizens after the first wave. Most were expanding their numbers regularly while the estate being isolated had not grown.

Of further concern, theirs was one of the smaller groups, which left them vulnerable to attack. Dillon knew they would eventually have to join another group or invite more people into the estate. She shook her head, not wanting to think of such things in the middle of the celebration.

"What's got you so deep in thought?" Skylar asked.

"Um, sorry. Just thinking," Dillon said, hoping Skylar didn't realize that she'd not answered the question.

Skylar pointed toward the street where a makeshift dance floor was in full swing. "It's nice to see Cynthia so happy."

Dillon smiled. Cynthia and Alaina had been on the dance floor more than they'd sat. "I'd never imagine that someone who can trip over a piece of lint could dance like that."

"No doubt, but she's got some moves."

"Alaina's no slouch, either."

Dillon nodded in the direction of a few men standing at the edge of the dance area. "I think there's a few guys that are liking what they see."

Skylar sat up straighter, and her jaw clenched. "Maybe we should get them to come sit down."

"Why?" Dillon looked at her puzzled.

"There isn't a police force to break things up if the guys decide to take what they want."

She'd been swept away by the joyful atmosphere and hadn't considered the possible dangers here. "Shit. Why didn't I think of that?" She pushed off the fence she'd been leaning against and scanned the crowd. "Maybe we should get a little closer, so we can keep an eye on things."

"I'm not trying to freak you out. I have a little more practice than you at spotting danger. Where I came from, it's all about survival. I can smell trouble a mile away."

While Skylar's skills were an asset, the fact she had them broke Dillon's heart. "What are you sensing from the group? Should I go get them off the dance floor?"

Skylar shook her head. She gestured toward the men she'd mentioned earlier. "No, we just need to watch those boys."

Dillon noted she called them boys. The group of six couldn't be much over twenty-one. "Bad vibes?"

"Nothing like that. But the alcohol is flowing, and everyone is in a relaxed mood. We don't want it to turn into a horny free-for-all."

"Gotcha. Any vibes from any of the other groups?" Dillon had made her own assessments but was curious to hear Skylar's thoughts.

"For the most part, I think everyone is excited to be here and just letting down their hair."

"For the most part?" Dillon raised her eyebrows

and met Skylar's gaze.

"The group from Washington aren't your average Joes." Skylar's eyes narrowed, and she gazed at the table where most sat.

"Agreed. It wasn't an accident that they survived."

Skylar smiled. "The blue jeans and T-shirts aren't working for them. I'm sure most of them would be more comfortable in a black suit."

"Or full military dress. Do you think they'll let us in on who they really are tomorrow? Or will they continue to play the role?"

"If they don't reveal the truth, be very cautious of them." Skylar grabbed Dillon's hand. "I'm serious. They could be our biggest allies or our biggest threat. How they play it out tomorrow says a lot about their intentions."

Dillon shivered, even though the night was still warm. She wished Skylar could be in the meeting room with her. Skylar picked up things she feared she'd miss. "Let's hope they come clean. We don't need to start things out with a military takeover."

Skylar cuddled up next to Dillon. "Don't even say something like that, even if you're joking."

Who's joking? Dillon thought but decided against saying it. "I suppose we should join the others. Looks like Maria's mood has improved." Dillon pointed toward the dance floor. Maria, Tasha, and Leslie had joined a conga line that was weaving between the tables and other dancers. Jake and Willa were at the back of the line, enjoying the fun. So far, Willa had not just been pleasant, but useful. She'd been snapping pictures and taking videos all day to memorialize the occasion. No doubt, she was in her element.

"You should talk to her. Find out what's bothering her. No offense, but she seems the tensest when you're around."

"You noticed that, too."

Gus, who led the line, must have seen them staring because the line made a beeline to where Dillon and Skylar hid.

"Uh-oh," Skylar said. "It looks like we've been spotted."

By the time the line arrived in front of them, it was at least twenty-five deep.

"Come on," Maria yelled with a smile.

Dillon returned the smile, happy to have Maria acting more like herself. "Only if you show me a few moves."

Maria let go of Leslie's shoulders. "You two jump in front of me, and I'll show you how to move those hips." Maria smiled. "Well, Skylar could probably teach me a move or two, but I've seen you dance, Dillon. You need serious help."

"I've got some mad dance skills, don't I, babe?" Dillon said to Skylar as she stepped into the line.

"No comment," Skylar said over her shoulder as she stepped in front of Dillon and put her hands on Leslie's waist.

"Ha!" Maria said. "This should be fun."

Once they'd entered the fray, the line sped up and careened back toward the dance floor. Everyone in line whooped and motioned for others to join. It didn't take long before everyone on the dance floor filed in. It took a few more passes through the tables to pick up the stragglers, but in the end, the line must have been a hundred fifty deep. Even the group from

Washington stepped into the mix.

Dillon laughed so hard tears streamed down her face as Maria kept grabbing her waist to get Dillon to move more seductively.

Happy to be joking with Maria, Dillon exaggerated shaking her butt, wildly swinging her hips from side to side.

"Whoa," Maria said through her laughter, "you're going to dislocate a hip."

"And it will be all your fault," Dillon called over her shoulder.

Tasha yelled from behind Maria. "Now those hips don't lie."

"What are they telling you?" Maria asked.

"That Dillon can't dance to save her life," Tasha responded.

The group laughed and continued their carefree trek through the tables.

Dillon wasn't sure how long they'd danced the streets of Vegas, but by the time they stopped, sweat poured from her forehead, and she panted for breath. The experience was cathartic, all her earlier trepidation forgotten. Hope rose in her chest. Maybe they could all come together and create a new world. One with less violence and more dancing.

❧❦❧❦

Cynthia and Alaina returned to their table loaded down with beers for everyone. Cynthia had one beer dangling from her mouth and the others precariously grasped against her chest. She hoped she wouldn't chip a tooth. Her dentist would have frowned on this.

"You should have let me go with Alaina," Skylar

said to Cynthia. "She looks like a natural, but you're one step from disaster."

"Don't let her drop our beer," Jake said.

Skylar gently removed the bottle from Cynthia's teeth and grabbed two others that had nearly slipped through her fingers.

"This one's for you, Jake." Skylar held up the beer she'd pulled from Cynthia's mouth.

"Um, if you don't mind, I'll take one without the spit string." He snatched one of the bottles from Skylar's hand.

"Honey," Alaina said. "I'm afraid I have to agree with Skylar. Next time, leave it to the pros."

"I accept my inferiority." Cynthia bent at the waist. "And I bow to your skills." She turned to Alaina. "You used to be a server?"

"That's how I paid my way through college." Alaina smiled. "My parents didn't think a woman needed an education, so I put myself through."

"Amen." Skylar raised her bottle. "Nobody can keep a good woman from an education."

Alaina and Skylar tapped bottles and took a large gulp of their beer.

Cynthia flopped down on a nearby chair. Her feet felt the effects of dancing. Otherwise, it made her feel alive. Free. If she closed her eyes and didn't think about it, she could almost believe the world was normal.

When they'd first arrived, she'd made the mistake of looking down the Strip. She didn't do it a second time. It had been jarring seeing Vegas without the neon and lights. Now as the sun had nearly set, she stared down the Strip, and her eyes played tricks on her. Any time she'd been in Vegas, the streets teemed with people regardless of the time of day or night, so her mind had imagined movement. The first time she thought she'd seen something, she almost shouted to the rest of the group, but when she blinked again, the movement was gone. *Wishful thinking.*

She tuned back into the conversation.

Maria stood and raised her bottle over her head. "Here's to new beginnings."

They cheered and were joined by several people at surrounding tables. Soon the chant circled the area, and everyone yelled out, "New beginnings." Once the cheers died down, Maria called out again. "To new beginnings."

This time, the group responded back. "New beginnings."

Alaina snaked her fingers between Cynthia's and smiled. She slid her chair closer and held up her bottle. "To our new beginning," she said so only Cynthia could hear.

"Definitely." Cynthia clinked her bottle against Cynthia's. "To our new beginning."

After they took a drink, Cynthia leaned in, and her lips met Alaina's.

The surroundings faded away as Alaina's soft lips pressed against Cynthia's. She wanted nothing more than to deepen the kiss, but Alaina pulled back.

Alaina's face was flushed. "Probably better hold that until we're in private."

Cynthia wasn't sure if she'd ever stop grinning now that Alaina had agreed to stay. She leaned over and whispered in Alaina's ear. "Do you mind if I tell the others you're coming back to the estate with us?"

"Go ahead."

Cynthia cleared her throat and stood. "I have

something I want to tell you." She had to call out a couple of times because Dillon and Jake were in the middle of a playful disagreement.

"Sorry," Dillon said sheepishly when she finally noticed everyone else had stopped talking.

Cynthia shook her head and gave Dillon a disapproving look.

Dillon winked at her.

"I have an announcement I'd like to make," Cynthia said. Everyone's gaze was on her now. She normally wasn't one for dramatic effect—she left that to Dillon and Skylar—but today felt different. She wanted to shout her news from the rooftops. "I want to share that today we are adding one more person to our clan at Whitaker Estate."

She was greeted by several blank stares until Skylar jumped from the table and rushed toward Cynthia. "Oh, my god. Alaina's staying?"

Cynthia's head bobbed up and down, and she suspected she had a goofy grin on her face.

Skylar wrapped Cynthia in a hug and pulled Alaina to her feet to join them. The rest of the group crowded around and joined in on the hug.

Cynthia laughed as tears streamed down her face. She didn't care that several other groups were staring. This was her moment of joy, and she wanted to share it with her friends.

Chapter Fourteen

What an incredible evening," Dillon said to Skylar as they walked toward the Mayan Resort. It was after midnight when the group decided to call it a day. They'd met so many incredible people that gave her hope for tomorrow's meeting, and Cynthia's news was the cherry on top. Even though Dillon still wasn't one hundred percent sure of the mysterious Alaina, her heart soared seeing Cynthia so happy.

Caleb and his clan from New York had become the unofficial hosts. They'd arrived in Vegas two days early since the trip across the country had taken them less time than they'd anticipated. Being there early, they'd set up all the rooms for the visitors. Now, Caleb and his wife, Janis, led the way into the hotel.

The Mayan had been only weeks from opening when the crisis struck, so the rooms were all but complete without having to worry about finding dead guests inside. When they'd arrived this morning, they'd staked out their block of rooms and dropped their bags off.

Dillon was thankful for that now. All the stress, the food and drinks, and dancing had caught up to her. She just wanted to fall into bed and sleep. She glanced over at Skylar. *Nope.* Not even her beauty could convince Dillon she wanted anything other than a firm mattress and a soft pillow.

Ahead of them, the group pushed into the lobby. A few seconds later, a murmur rose from the crowd. Dillon strained to see what created the reaction, but she couldn't make out anything. The line stopped, and no one else entered the building. Something was wrong.

"Jake," Dillon said. "Should we go see what's up?"

He pushed past the others as he made his way to Dillon. His brow furrowed, and he unconsciously touched the holster under his shirt. Skylar had already drawn her weapon.

Caleb called out from the front of the line. "There seems to be a little problem inside. Can I have the two representatives from each group come inside?"

"Do you want this?" Skylar pulled up her shirt to reveal the gun tucked into her waistband.

Dillon shook her head. "Jake's got his. You keep it." She bent and pecked Skylar on the lips before she turned to Jake.

They walked quickly toward the Mayan, resisting the urge to break into a jog. The volume grew amongst the crowd. Dillon picked up snippets of conversation as they passed, then wished she hadn't. Panic can burn like a wildfire, but she hoped it wouldn't be the case.

They'd almost reached the front when the sound of running footsteps drew her attention. Obviously, someone else hadn't been able to keep their composure. She turned. Her eyes widened. *Shit.*

Willa pushed through the crowd. She held her camera in the air as she weaved through the tightly packed mob. "I need to record whatever's going on."

Dillon hesitated. If she were the traitor, was

this a good idea? On the other hand, having a record of things made sense. She shot a look at Jake, who shrugged and gave her a half smile.

Dillon sighed and motioned Willa forward. At the front of the line, a guard blocked the door. He was one who had been at the Vegas sign. His friendly smile told her he'd remembered her from earlier. She quickly explained why there were three not two as Caleb had ordered. He studied Willa for a beat and then nodded before he let them pass.

Half the representatives were already inside and gathered around the gigantic replica of the steep Mayan stairs. Even though Dillon had read that each side of the pyramid only had ninety-one stairs, they were seemingly without end.

Halfway across the lobby, Dillon noticed the paint on the stairs.

LEAVE! NOW!

The words were at least ten feet tall. The lettering was painted in red and dripped down the stairs. She suspected to emulate the appearance of blood.

"What the fuck?" Jake said.

Willa moved into action, snapping pictures from multiple angles.

Dillon and Jake edged up to Caleb and Janis. "What's going on?"

Caleb shook his head. "No clue. It wasn't here earlier. Someone must have snuck in and done it."

"But we were all outside," Janis said. "No way could someone have disappeared that long to do something like this." She gestured toward the graffiti.

Jake's face paled, and his gaze darted around the room. "Do you think Babcock's group is here?"

Dillon moved toward the stairs and put her

finger against the paint. It had already dried. It looked to be spray paint. She studied the precision of the letters and the choice of colors. "Unless they have a graffiti artist in their midst, I'd say no. Look at this."

The others drew closer and had to push past those who milled around talking in hushed tones.

Caleb's brow furrowed as he studied the letters. "Being a New Yorker, I know good graffiti from bad, and this took some talent to do on a flight of stairs." He pointed. "See how artistic and uniform the letters are? And the dripping effect wasn't done by accident. They wanted to make it look like blood."

"Who's they?" Janis said.

"That I don't know," Caleb said. "But I'm afraid we aren't alone."

The euphoria from earlier drained from the room. It was replaced by fear and suspicion.

"I think whoever it is wants to scare us," Dillon said.

"It worked," Jake said.

Dillon shot him an annoyed look before she continued. "We need to figure out why."

A tall man and woman, with a purposeful stride, walked toward them. She'd met so many at the party, but Dillon was almost sure they belonged to the Washington contingent.

The woman held herself with an air of authority. Her black hair was pulled back into a tight ponytail, and her dark brown eyes were intelligent. She held out her hand to Dillon. "We met earlier. Sylvia Garcia, and this is Brent Underwood. We're from Washington."

Brent extended his hand. His white-blond hair was so short he looked bald from a distance. He had a lean face with hollow cheeks. Dillon suspected he was a runner or spent a lot of time outside.

After handshakes all around, Dillon asked, "What's your take on this?"

"We're not prepared to say," Sylvia said. "But usually when someone plans an ambush, they don't leave a calling card."

"Agreed," Dillon said. "But we still need to take the threat seriously."

"Definitely," Brent said. He rubbed his five o'clock shadow, and his eyes narrowed. "Our group will volunteer to stand guard tonight."

Caleb stepped up. "While generous, we'd like to have more than one group representing us on protection duty."

"Understood." Sylvia nodded. "Makes practical sense. Although, none of the guests left the party long enough to do this."

Dillon snapped her fingers. "But that doesn't mean that a group didn't bring someone we don't know about."

Brent nodded. "Yes, that's one of our theories."

"I think this just made the summit meeting even more interesting," Caleb said.

They talked a while longer before they agreed to let the guests in. Standing around without sleep wouldn't do anyone any good. Caleb made a quick announcement about the threat and the actions being taken to keep everyone safe.

Much to Dillon's chagrin, Skylar would be taking the three a.m. watch with Leslie. The collective had voted against allowing summit representatives to take watch since they needed to be fresh for the meeting. Dillon would likely get no sleep while Skylar was gone, anyway. At each watch, there would be two individuals from four different groups to ensure diverse representation.

The lively camaraderie had turned to mistrust and suspicion with two simple words. *LEAVE! NOW!*

❧❧❧❧

Skylar held Dillon's hand as they made their way to their room. Everyone was abuzz, speculating on the situation, but Dillon was the only person Skylar focused on. She'd come to know the hard line in Dillon's jaw. It was her biggest tell. Dillon would likely be able to crack a walnut in her teeth, just like the wooden nutcracker soldiers.

Skylar bit her lip. Wrong time for her to be amused by her own analogy. She considered sharing the joke with Dillon but thought better after another glance. Dillon's mood oozed off her. An image of green slime seeping out of Dillon's pores flashed in her mind.

She tried to stifle her giggle but hadn't been successful. What was wrong with her? Apparently, her tiredness was making her slap happy. She glanced around wide-eyed and realized her friends had heard since several sets of eyes were on her.

"Uh, sorry. It was nothing," Skylar said, hoping to recover from her faux pas.

"I'm glad you find the situation funny," Dillon snapped. Her eyes blazed, but Skylar saw the fear behind the anger.

"Oh, babe. It's not funny, but we've overcome worse." Skylar stopped walking and turned to face Dillon.

"And how do you know how bad this is?" Dillon

asked.

Their friends politely continued to walk, likely deciding not to get in the middle of the couple's squabble.

Skylar shrugged. "I don't. But logic dictates it can't be any worse than whatever wiped out ninety-nine percent of the population on the planet."

Dillon glared without speaking for several beats before her mouth twitched. "Damn you. You're going to pull the apocalypse card on me, huh?"

"Afraid so." Skylar smiled, knowing she'd broken through to the Dillon she knew and loved. "It's only up from here, baby."

Dillon pulled her close. "How dare you defuse me so quickly when I'm busy pouting?"

Skylar put her hand against Dillon's cheek and gazed into her eyes. "I love you more than anything in this world, but you can't keep treating me like I'm precious china that might break."

Several other groups brushed past them on the way to their rooms. "Do you think maybe we should have this conversation in private?" Skylar shifted her gaze between Dillon and the others streaming past.

"Um, yeah. Probably." Dillon smirked. "Nobody else in the world exists when you're around, babe."

Skylar laughed, took Dillon's hand, and began walking again. "Do you think your corny attempt at charming me is going to work after all the brooding you were doing?"

"Hopefully." Dillon gave her an innocent smile and puppy dog eyes.

"You're pulling out all the stops. You must think you're in some big trouble."

Dillon's expression turned serious. "I feel bad

when I upset you."

"You didn't upset me. It's more like you frustrate me."

They arrived at their room, and Dillon pushed open the door. Thankfully, the room was as they'd left it. She'd feared the vandals might have ransacked their rooms, too.

As they readied themselves for bed, there was minimal conversation. Skylar was exhausted and suspected Dillon was, too. Their preparations didn't take long. They remained dressed in their clothes, so they would be ready should they need to react quickly. After throwing off their bras, brushing their teeth, and washing their faces, they climbed into bed.

Skylar snuggled against Dillon and rested her head on Dillon's shoulder before she spoke. "Was there anything more you wanted to say?"

"About?"

Skylar flopped onto her back. "Never mind. I have to be up in a couple hours." She double checked her alarm to make sure she'd set it for the right time.

"Sky, please, come back." Dillon held up her arm, so Skylar could return to her shoulder.

"Are we sleeping or talking?"

"Both," Dillon said. "I don't want to keep you up much longer, but we need to talk about why I frustrate you."

Skylar rolled back into place in Dillon's arms. "Frustrate was probably too harsh. I don't always know how to handle it when you get overprotective."

"But I love you," Dillon protested. "And I don't want anything to happen to you."

"Sometimes, I think we're a bad combination."

Dillon stiffened, and her breath caught. Skylar

felt her swallow hard. She put her hand on Dillon's chest and gazed into her eyes. A mist covered them, and she blinked several times.

"That came out way wrong," Skylar said. "It's not what I meant."

"Can I ask what you did mean?" Dillon said in a measured tone.

"I've never been taken care of in my entire life. Never. Well, maybe until I was three, but even that's debatable. This is foreign as hell to me. To be honest, it makes me feel better than I ever have in my life, but at other times, it freaks me out."

"I know that about you," Dillon said. "And I try not to overwhelm you, but isn't that something you need to work on? Letting me protect you?"

"To a point, but sometimes, you push that point further than need be." Skylar rubbed Dillon's chest. "I know you have a huge heart and want to protect everyone, but it can be a bit misguided."

"How's that?"

"Take tonight, for instance." Skylar rested her chin on Dillon's shoulder, so she could see her eyes. "You're not happy that it's me doing watch duty instead of you."

"True."

"And that's why you were quiet on the walk back."

"Possibly."

"I'll take that as a yes." Skylar continued to gaze into Dillon's eyes. "Let's just play a little game for a second."

Dillon's eyes narrowed.

"Humor me," Skylar said.

"And the game would be?"

"Truth."

"Just truth, no dare?"

"Nope, just truth."

"Okay." Dillon nodded. "Hit me with it."

"Who would make a better guard, you or me?"

Dillon averted her gaze. Skylar put her hand on Dillon's chin and gently turned her head, so their gazes met again. Dillon stared into her eyes for several seconds before she said, "You."

Skylar leaned forward. "I'm sorry, I didn't quite hear you. What did you say?"

"You, smartass," Dillon said in a louder voice.

"So you admit that my street smarts and experience with a weapon make me a better candidate."

"That's what I said." Dillon pressed her lips together.

"Okay, then. Now that we've established that. On what planet does it make sense for you to pout because I'm doing the job that I'm better suited for?"

"Ugh." Dillon pressed her head against her pillow and closed her eyes. "Stop being logical. It's not fair."

Skylar chuckled. "Don't you think I get scared sometimes? Hell, the summit meeting isn't exactly safe. We don't know most of these people. Any of the groups could have a hidden agenda, and it could get dangerous. You put yourself out there every day as our leader, and sometimes, I want to stamp my foot and say no. You're the first person in my life that I've given all of myself to. And the thought of losing you terrifies me, but...."

"But you don't clip my wings." Dillon finished her sentence.

"Exactly."

"So I should stop clipping yours." Dillon sighed.

Skylar tapped her finger against Dillon's nose. "Smart cookie. Now I know why we made you our leader."

Dillon smiled. "God, I love you."

"Remember the first time you said that to me?"

"Remember? How could I forget? You were so pissed off at me."

The memory flashed in Skylar's mind. Dillon had just discovered Skylar had practically prostituted herself with Tiffany to pay her fees for nursing school. She'd felt so ashamed and dirty, sure that Dillon would find her disgusting and break things off. "In the middle of my rant, you told me you loved me."

"I thought you were going to slug me or at least throw something at me."

"I wasn't that bad, was I?"

"I think your first reaction was to ask me *what the fuck* I just said."

Skylar winced.

"Followed by, *You can't say that kind of shit to me.*"

"And yet here we are." Skylar averted her gaze. "I'll never forget what you said to me next. Do you recall?"

Dillon nodded. "What better time for me to say it than when you really need to hear it?"

"Yes." Warmth spread across Skylar's chest. "I need something else from you now."

"Anything."

"Even though you'd love to wrap me in bubble wrap, I need you to let me put myself out there and contribute."

Dillon groaned and covered her face in mock

distress. "Can't you give me something easier?"

"Afraid not. I promise, I'll be careful because I want to spend a lifetime loving you. I won't take unnecessary risks."

Dillon peeked out from under her arm. "Promise?"

"Promise."

"Can I protect you a little?"

"Of course." Skylar squeezed Dillon. "I love that you want to protect me. First time in my life, and it feels good. Just tone it down a bit. Let me feel competent and capable, not like a delicate flower that will wilt or blow away."

"How about I treat you like a precious gem instead? Something that needs to be cherished."

"Precious gem?" Skylar nodded and bit her lip. She put her hand against Dillon's chest. "I still struggle to understand how you could possibly see me that way when most of my life I've felt like an insignificant pebble on a good day."

Dillon scowled. "To me, you're a gem. Is that okay?"

"Yeah, as long as you don't hide your gem away in a safe somewhere and not let it see the light of day."

"Deal." Dillon smirked. "You remember what happened after the first time I told you I loved you?"

"Hmm, vaguely."

"Just vaguely?"

"I might have recalled more." Skylar met Dillon's gaze. "It was the first time in my life that I let someone *make love* to me not just have sex."

"Care for a re-enactment?"

"I thought you'd never ask." Skylar rolled on top of Dillon, and their lips met.

❧❧❧❧

Skylar tiptoed to the bathroom, carrying her shoes and bag, hoping she'd satiated Dillon enough she wouldn't wake when Skylar left for watch duty. She flipped on the lantern and peered at herself in the mirror. *Yep.* No doubt, Leslie would be able to tell what she'd been up to.

After running a brush through her tangled hair, she gave up and pulled it into a ponytail. The cool water was refreshing, so she splashed more onto her face and let it cascade into the sink. It felt good on her burning eyes, too. She was thankful she'd gotten an earlier shift, so she would have time to come back to bed and get a few more hours of sleep.

She yawned and stretched. Her body was still asleep, at least some parts. A smile crossed her lips as she remembered how tenderly Dillon had made love to her. *Nope.* That was the last thing she should be thinking about while on duty. It would surely distract her from the task at hand.

She unzipped her pack and peered inside. Probably shouldn't arrive with a semi-automatic weapon, so she pulled out her Glock instead. As she went to set the bag on the ground, she had second thoughts. It wouldn't hurt to take the extra ammo with her, just in case. She shouldered the bag and peeked in at the sleeping Dillon one last time. If it wouldn't wake her, she wanted to kiss Dillon on the forehead before she left but thought better of it.

"I love you," she whispered into the dark before she slipped from the room.

Leslie stood at the end of the hall waiting. Even

in the dim lighting from Leslie's lantern, Skylar could make out her red hair.

"Are you ready to do this?" Skylar asked.

"I think. Although, I'm used to guard duty in the tower, so this will be a little different."

After Dillon and her construction crew had built the watchtower, Leslie had immediately volunteered. At first, everyone was surprised since she'd gone into such a funk after Denise's death, but she'd taken to the task. It was as if the job gave her purpose again, and she'd slowly become the person that Dillon and the others said she was before Denise's death. Recently, Skylar had been getting to know her better and enjoyed Leslie's quick wit.

She nodded toward the bag in Leslie's hand. "Got your weapons?"

"Yeah. It still sounds weird when I say it." Leslie held up the bag and smiled. "I can't even imagine what Denise would say about the new me." Leslie chuckled. "She'd probably tell me I should wear an ammo belt and nothing else."

Skylar laughed. "I'm glad you guys talk about Denise now," Skylar said. "I never got the chance to know her, but when you tell stories about her, it makes me feel as if I did."

"She was one of a kind." Leslie smiled. "With a wicked sense of humor. You would have liked her."

"No doubt. The stories crack me up." They began walking toward the stairs that would take them to the lobby.

"I just want to apologize," Leslie said.

Skylar shot her a glance. "For what?"

"For the first few months. I was a mess. I didn't think I was going to survive."

"Give yourself a break, you were grieving."

"But we all were, weren't we?" Leslie sighed. "I acted like I was the only one that lost someone. I'm embarrassed for everything I did."

"No! Nobody thinks that way but you." Skylar put her hand on Leslie's back. "Trust me. I know how it feels to think you screwed up. But you can't let it keep you down."

They arrived at the stairs and began their descent. "I guess all I can do is make amends and try my hardest to be a valued member of the group," Leslie said.

"You already are." Skylar's heart went out to Leslie. The excessive guilt she carried had to be horrible. "We all manage grief differently, so please, stop beating yourself up."

Sadness crossed Leslie's face before she smiled. "I'm trying. Every day I wake, vowing to do better than I did the day before."

"That's the spirit." Skylar debated on whether she should ask Leslie the question that had been on her mind. Times were different now, so why not? "Can I ask, how did you change your mindset? It's like you did a one-eighty."

"Good question." They walked in silence before Leslie continued. "I can attribute it to a couple of things. Of course, my faith normally carries me through everything, so I leaned on that. But really, it was something Cynthia said to me that began to set me free."

When Leslie didn't elaborate, Skylar said, "Would it be too forward to ask what that was?"

"Oh, god, sorry." Leslie patted Skylar's arm. "I was lost in my thoughts. She told me that allowing myself to grieve didn't mean that I had to forget Denise and move on."

Skylar narrowed her eyes, trying to unpack the meaning.

Leslie grinned. "By that look, I'm guessing that was as clear as mud. It's like this." Leslie took a deep breath. "I thought when people grieved, the goal was to forget the person. Put all their memories in a box and set it on the shelf and maybe bring out that box a few times a year. Their birthday, the anniversary of their death, and maybe the holidays. That was it."

Skylar nodded as she began to understand.

"But for the most part treat it as if they never existed. Hell, that's what we did the first few months. Nobody would even say Denise's name in my presence. I should have been saying her name to everyone, so she could live on. Denise Roberta Freeman. It's freeing. I'll likely miss her until the day I die, but a little part of her will always be with me. And not in a creepy, I'll never move on way, but as a tribute to the amazing woman she was."

"I like that." Skylar touched Leslie's shoulder. "No, I love it. What a positive way of looking at things."

They exited the stairway. The enormous lobby was bathed in shadows, despite the large floodlights that had been installed near the graffiti.

"Holy hell," Leslie said. "Do we need to see that message in all its glory?"

"We are in Vegas. Be thankful it's not in neon."

"True, very true." Leslie grabbed Skylar's hand and stopped walking. "Before we join the watch detail," she nodded at the crew milling around as the shift changed, "I wanted to thank you for the talk."

"Thank you," Skylar said and genuinely meant it. "I'm enjoying getting to know you better."

"Same here." Leslie wrapped Skylar in a quick hug. When they broke, she said, "Are we ready to report for duty?"

Skylar waved her hand in front of them. "After you."

The previous watchers gave a brief report. Real brief. Nothing happened. After they trudged off to bed, their crew introduced themselves. The others on duty with them were from Chicago, Amarillo, and New Orleans. They were the only all-female group, and only the pair from New Orleans had another woman. Skylar hoped the men didn't treat them as if they couldn't do the job.

The shift turned out better than she'd expected. All their co-watchers were pleasant and engaging, not once making their gender an issue. Skylar was shocked when the four a.m. crew filtered in. The time went fast, and thankfully nothing had happened on their shift, either.

Chapter Fifteen

Dillon checked her hair in the mirror for the third time. It had gotten a little long for her liking. Maybe she should have Skylar give her a trim before she left for the summit meeting.

"Are you primping again?" Skylar asked from the bedroom.

"Maybe."

"You look dapper today, so stop."

Dillon studied herself. She'd replaced her normal T-shirt with a button-down shirt and a new pair of dark blue jeans for the occasion. She turned sideways and examined herself. With all the physical labor after the crisis, she'd gotten her muscular physique back. One positive of an apocalypse, she figured.

She stepped from the bathroom. "Okay. Are you going to escort me?" Dillon offered her arm.

"Of course."

Skylar looked amazing today. She'd put on a touch of makeup and wore a scoop-necked green shirt. The makeup and the color made her gray eyes pop. Her black slacks hugged her hips and accented her perfect buttocks.

"You look beautiful," Dillon said. "Maybe I should skip this meeting and take you out on the town. Hit a casino or two."

"Nice try." Skylar smiled. "You'll be fine. Nothing

to be nervous about."

"Who says I'm nervous?"

"I do. And so do the grooves in your forehead. You don't want the other members to think you have a permanent frown."

Dillon scowled harder. "It'll make me look more serious."

Skylar rolled her eyes. "Fine. Scowl away."

They left the room and began their walk. The hallway was teeming with people. They waved and said hi to those they'd met last night. Dillon scolded herself for only remembering a handful of names while Skylar addressed everyone they'd met by name.

Once they were alone in the stairwell, Dillon asked, "How the hell do you remember all those names?"

"I was a bartender. I was paid to remember people. It was the difference between a mediocre tip and a good one, which translated into whether I'd have to eat ramen noodles for every meal or not."

"Now I don't feel quite so bad." Dillon smiled. "What are your plans for the day while I'm in the meeting?"

"I think we're going to look around a bit. Willa wanted to get a few pictures of the Strip."

"Is that a good idea, in light of the message?"

"I'm prepared." Skylar patted her waist. "Plus, we won't go as far as we intended."

"Be safe," Dillon said, remembering their conversation last night. She vowed she'd try harder not to be so overprotective and respect that Skylar could take care of herself.

"I will. I've been protecting myself for a lot of years." Skylar squeezed Dillon's linked arm. "The summit didn't change their mind on weapons after last night, did they?"

"Not that I've heard. Caleb told me at breakfast the order is still the same. No weapons. No exceptions. Which, quite frankly, suits me fine."

"I volunteered to take a shift to guard the conference room, but they weren't using anyone who took a stint last night. I guess it makes sense, but I would've liked to help."

"Oh, so you're wanting to protect me now?" Dillon smiled and bumped her hip into Skylar's.

"Damned sure." Skylar playfully put her arm around Dillon's waist and squeezed. "I want to protect my woman."

"I don't even know how to respond to that." Dillon shook her head and laughed. "I'm happy nothing eventful happened last night. It still creeps me out to know someone is out there. Or that someone in here is fucking with us."

They arrived at the lobby where over two-thirds of the attendees were already gathered. Dillon expected it to be louder. The crowd was likely subdued because of last night's threat. When she glanced around, she realized her error. The conversations were animated and loud, but the sound didn't overpower. She smiled as she surveyed the structure. The architects had done a brilliant job of dampening the noise levels.

She'd not taken time yesterday to marvel at the interior construction of the newest, and possibly the last, offering to the Vegas Strip. She could only imagine what it would look like with all the lighting and sounds that should have been piped in.

The place would have put the Rainforest Café to shame. She'd read they'd planned to have actual jungle birds flying free throughout one area of the resort. Over time, all the artificial trees would be taken over by local birds once they found a way in.

Skylar shook her arm. "Admiring the architecture?"

"How'd you guess?"

"That dreamy look in your eyes. The one I thought you reserved only for me."

Dillon turned and fixed Skylar with her best smoldering gaze. "I don't think you have anything to worry about."

Skylar's face reddened. "Stop it." She glanced around. "We're in a room full of people."

Dillon chuckled. She enjoyed being able to rattle the normally unflappable Skylar. Who knew a little public flirtation would do the trick?

Skylar pulled her arm away from Dillon's and made her best effort to scowl, even though her lip betrayed her and curled upward. "You're enjoying my discomfort a bit too much."

Dillon shrugged and gave her best innocent look.

Skylar shook her head. "You're a shit. Lucky for you, the others are gathered over there." She pointed toward the front of the lobby near the large glass doors.

❧ ❧ ❧ ❧

Cynthia smiled when Dillon and Skylar approached. By the set of Dillon's shoulders, she was nervous about the upcoming meeting, but Cynthia doubted she'd admit it to the group. She needed to get Dillon alone, so she'd quiz her then.

"Hey," Jake said as they got nearer. "We've

been waiting for you." He glanced at his watch. "Only fifteen minutes until show time." He unconsciously wiped his palm on his pants leg.

Sweaty palms, Cynthia guessed. Part of her was disappointed she couldn't be in the meeting, but gauging the reaction of her friends, she was likely the fortunate one.

Willa bounced up to Skylar. "We've been waiting for you. I'm ready to get some shots of the Strip."

"Whoa." Cynthia held up her hand. "I need to have a word with Dillon and Jake before the meeting. Then we can head out."

"Where are Maria and Tasha?" Skylar turned to Leslie. "Aren't they coming with us?"

"Maria isn't feeling the best." Leslie grinned. "She said it's been a while since she's had tequila, and those margaritas packed a wallop last night."

"That'll teach her." Dillon chuckled. "She was giving me grief after I took one drink and refused to touch it again. That shit was strong."

Cynthia stood back and listened to the banter; her mind raced. Suspicious? In the months Cynthia had known Maria, she'd never been one to overindulge. It was a convenient way to split off from the crowd. *Damn it.* She hated this. Being watchful of every move her friends made was uncomfortable and exhausting. She wished CJ and Karen would come up with something soon. The last word Dillon had gotten from CJ was they'd searched Willa's room but came up with nothing.

"Hey," Dillon said, waving her hand in front of Cynthia's face. "What's got you so preoccupied? I've been trying to get your attention."

Cynthia tuned back into the conversation. "Sorry."

"We should have a quick meeting before we go our separate ways," Dillon said.

"Are you breaking up with me?" Cynthia laughed at her own joke.

Dillon's eyes narrowed, then realization hit, and she laughed. "I guess 'going our separate ways' does sound a little dramatic. How about 'do our own thing'?"

"Better." Cynthia followed Dillon and Jake outside. A couple of other groups had gathered near the entrance of the building, so they walked about twenty yards down a path to find privacy. They stopped under a gigantic palm tree.

"Are you two nervous?" Cynthia asked.

Dillon shook her head. "Nah, I...." She must have noted Cynthia's skeptical look because she stopped and said, "Fine. Nervous as fuck. Make you feel better?"

Cynthia put her hand on Dillon's shoulder. "I'm happy you're telling the truth but not happy you're nervous. What about you, Jake?"

Jake had been exceptionally quiet all morning, which was unusual for him. He ran his hand through his dark wavy hair. He hadn't shaved for a couple of days, so his stubble was beginning to look as if he were trying to grow a beard. Unfortunately, it was at the stage where it made him appear unkempt.

He held out his hand that tremored slightly. "I'd say I'm a bit nervous."

Dillon gave him a one-armed hug. "We're quite the pair. Maybe they chose the wrong reps."

"Nah," Cynthia said. "I'd be concerned if you weren't nervous. A healthy dose of apprehension keeps people on their toes."

"Then I'm definitely on my toes." Jake turned to Dillon. "Did you want to go over last-minute strategies?"

"No."

He looked at her puzzled. "Then why did you drag us out here?"

"Actually, I wanted to get Cynthia alone but didn't want to arouse suspicion. I'm more worried about her day than ours."

"Mine?"

"Yeah, you could be spending the day with the traitor. Plus, whoever vandalized the place last night could be out there watching. Do you really think it's the best idea to wander around the Strip when you aren't certain?"

"We can't stay locked in our rooms forever." Cynthia patted her hip. "Besides, I'm packing." She groaned. "My god, when did I become someone who would say that?"

Dillon and Jake laughed.

Jake's eyes twinkled and he said, "But you say it with such finesse."

Cynthia rolled her eyes. "Thanks, I guess."

Dillon sighed. "Skylar reassured me earlier that you'd be okay. But promise you'll be careful."

"Of course. Plus, I have Alaina, who can help watch for the traitor. I just wish we could tell Skylar. It would be nice to have another set of eyes."

"I think we should," Jake said. "I've been thinking about it. She's smart and observant. She might see something we miss. And with the stakes higher since there's another threat, I think we should clue her in."

"But the Commission voted that we wouldn't," Dillon said.

Cynthia recognized the look of hope in Dillon's eyes. Keeping the secret had been rough on her. "But there's new information." Cynthia motioned among the three of them. "We have three of our five members here. I think Karen and Renee would understand if we voted to do something different."

"But won't it look like we only did it because of our relationship?" Dillon asked.

"It's a chance we'll have to take," Jake said. "No offense, but if there's anyone in the group that I'd want on my side in a battle, it's Skylar."

"I second that," Cynthia said. "We're wasting one of our best assets, and I know I'd feel much more secure today if I knew she had my back."

Dillon's shoulders relaxed, and relief washed over her face. "You know where my vote lies. Should we take a formal vote?"

"Sure," Cynthia said. "All in favor." She was met with a chorus of ayes. "The ayes have it."

"Shit." Dillon slapped her hand against her forehead. "I'm not going to have time to tell her. We need to get into the meeting."

"I'm going to have to be the one," Cynthia said. "I know you want to, but time is of the essence."

"But—" Dillon started to say.

Cynthia held up her hand. "I'll make sure to explain everything. Especially how torn up you've been about it. She's a good woman. She'll understand."

Dillon smiled. "I know she will. But I hate it just the same. I wanted to be the one who told her."

"Your sole focus needs to be on this meeting," Cynthia said.

"I second that," Jake added with a grin.

"Okay." Dillon nodded, but her expression

was strained. "I trust you, but please make sure she understands I was obeying my oath to the Commission."

"Trust me, it'll be fine." Cynthia put her arm over Dillon's shoulder.

Chapter Sixteen

Whoever thought using the Tzolk'in Room, named after the Mayan calendar, was a good idea had seriously miscalculated. Dillon assumed they'd wanted to make the first summit meeting grand, but the effect had been just the opposite. With only forty-six people, representing the twenty-three groups, they were dwarfed in the enormous conference room. The capacity had to be in the thousands. Instead of giving a feeling of grandeur, it made Dillon feel insignificant. She doubted the planners wanted insignificant to be the first word that came to mind when describing the event.

The meeting had gotten off to a rocky start when they'd found another note. It was hand-written and stuck to the table by a knife plunged through it. Another calling card, Dillon assumed.

It read:

Beware- Snippers on the roof.
Your in danger!
This is a trap. Your in there spider web
Escape while you still can

Despite the poor spelling, the message was ominous. The representatives from Chicago and Florida insisted the note wasn't there the night before. They'd checked the conference room after finding the message on the stairs, which meant someone had gotten in later under the guards' noses, or someone inside the hotel was the culprit.

Their reason for the summit, which was to discuss the establishment of a new government and determine whether some groups should merge, was put on hold with the new threat.

Introductions took nearly two hours, a large part of it taken up by Sylvia and Brent from Washington. Dillon was both relieved and concerned. They admitted that the bulk of their community consisted of military and special ops personnel. They'd skirted several questions from the others, but by Dillon's calculations, they most likely were in an underground compound in the Pentagon when the crisis struck.

After the others cajoled them, they revealed they'd been in contact with operatives from around the globe. Everywhere was as decimated as the United States. The excitement of finding others was overshadowed by the thought of the entire world being down to such a small population. Could they survive?

Dillon pushed the thought out of her head, wanting to focus on what Sylvia had to share.

The group, thirsty for information, peppered her with questions. She'd graciously answered all, although Dillon suspected that she held back some information.

The conversation turned to how and why the crisis occurred. All attention was on Sylvia as she stood at the podium with her posture still perfect.

Sylvia cleared her throat before speaking. "We

believe a pulse encircled the globe. It only lasted for a short period, likely less than a couple minutes. It acted to accelerate the heart rate, which in some species, including humans, resulted in a heart attack. Many animal species survived, especially those with higher heart rates. It seems that most healthy people who were underground were spared. In most cases, the deeper the better. Those at a high enough altitude also lived."

Dillon nodded. It was consistent with what Cynthia had discovered.

Several members shouted out, wanting Sylvia to clue them in on how it happened.

Sylvia held up her hand for quiet. "There are many theories, but we have yet to isolate the origin."

"Was it the Russians or Chinese?" someone called out.

"Or maybe it was our own government," an angry woman yelled, causing the room to erupt in side conversations.

Sylvia waited several minutes for the others to quiet until she continued. "It could have been a natural event. An emission from the earth's core or possibly something in our solar system." She paused and took a drink before continuing. "There is some indication that it may have been man-made; however, scientists will be poring through the available data for some time. If it were man-made, we suspect something went horribly wrong, and the intention wasn't to cause such dire consequences. But with limited scientists who survived and sparse data, it could take years to discover the origin."

The speculation and side conversations began in earnest. The members from the Seattle and Minnesota groups continued to pepper Sylvia with questions. She patiently answered, but her standard answer continued to be *the data is being reviewed at this time.*

After nearly fifteen minutes, Dillon waved her hand. "I'm not sure that speculating about what happened is the best use of our time. It's not going to solve the problem at hand. Someone has made it clear they want us to leave. We need to focus our energy on the immediate threat."

Sylvia grabbed on to Dillon's interruption. "Yes. I agree. While the previous conversation is important, I believe we should table it. For the sake of democracy, we should take a vote."

The vote passed with three dissenters.

Sylvia moved from behind the podium and took her seat. *Interesting.* The Washington group was going out of their way to allow the group to lead themselves. Dillon understood their thinking but wondered how long a leaderless group could function. Likely, officers would need to be elected, but until the group knew one another better, this chaotic model would continue.

They'd been discussing, or more accurately arguing, about the course for some time when the woman from Chicago pounded the table. "For God's sake, this is getting us nowhere. Why don't we talk about the elephant in the room? Or more accurately, the elephant that's not in the room. I'm sure I'm not the only one wondering if Braxton Babcock and his crazies are behind this."

Finally. They'd been dancing around the topic for the last half hour. Human nature was funny, even though they'd all agreed not to invite Babcock's group, nobody seemed to want to broach the topic in the larger forum. Dillon had considered it but, considering their traitor, had decided against it.

"It's about time someone brought that up. Thank you," the man from Seattle said and nodded to the woman who'd spoken. "They'd be the most likely candidate."

Multiple conversations branched off, and Babcock's name filled the room.

Jake leaned over and said into her ear, "Mention Babcock, and it turns into a free-for-all."

"It's giving me a headache," Dillon said. "Let's see if we can get some order."

Dillon stood and cleared her throat. When the conversations persisted, she called out, "Everyone, can I have your attention?" It took two more attempts, but eventually, the group quieted. "I'm certainly no fan of Babcock's, but this isn't adding up." She pointed to the note still lying on the table. "He doesn't seem like the kinda guy who would warn us before striking." Dillon shrugged. "At least to my way of thinking."

Others voiced their agreement. Babcock's M.O. would be sneaky. To strike when nobody was ready for it, but now they were on high alert.

The woman from Georgia grabbed the note and held it up. "I've been thinking about this. If you really read it and the message on the stairs, it's not a threat, but more like a warning."

"Or is it just meant to scare us, so we get the hell out of here?" the Minnesota man said.

"If we assume snipper really means sniper," the Georgia woman said, still holding the paper, "that seems more like they're warning us against someone else."

"Babcock?" several people said at once.

The man from Minnesota waved his hand.

"Nonsense. Whoever it is wants us to believe there's a threat, so we leave."

Dillon snapped her fingers. "What if another group lives here? We suspect there's likely more people out there, just not with the same technology we all have. Maybe we're invading their home, and they want us gone."

"Excellent theory," Sylvia said. "But that leaves us with a lot of questions."

The room erupted again into side conversations. Dillon put her hand against her forehead. At this rate, the debate could go on for hours.

Janis, Caleb's wife, stood. "This is wonderful that we have so many opinions, but I feel we might be spinning our wheels. And I'm concerned that all our energy is focused on this."

A few grumbles came from the crowd.

She held up her hand. "Don't get me wrong. This is an important concern that can't be ignored. We just need to be more strategic. Divide and conquer, so to speak. I used to lead large teams and found breaking into manageable subgroups got the work done much quicker and more efficiently."

"What are you recommending?" someone called out.

"We could break into subcommittees. The bulk of the group can continue with the work that we came here to do, which is to discuss the future. What kind of government we want to form and whether we should consolidate groups."

"But we all need to be at the table for those decisions," the man from Amarillo said.

"Definitely," Janis said. "But the preliminary work could be done in committee. Because nothing's going to get done with forty-six people throwing out ideas."

"Besides," Dillon said. "We aren't going to solve all these things at once. It will likely take months to do. How long did it take to write the Constitution?"

The nerdy man in glasses from Philadelphia said, "The Constitutional Convention began on May 14, 1787, and ended on September 17 the same year."

"See." Dillon counted on her fingers. "It took them four months, so we'll be at this for a while."

"Yeah, if somebody doesn't kill us first," someone called out.

Brent, Sylvia's sidekick from Washington, stood. "I think that is a brilliant idea. I would like to offer our group's expertise in managing the immediate problem. With our experience, I think we are well suited to the mission and would like to lead the group."

After another twenty minutes of debate, the committees were formed, and the full meeting adjourned.

❧ ❧ ❧ ❧

With her signature confident stride, Sylvia approached Jake and Dillon. She reached out her hand. "Welcome to our committee."

Dillon's hand was practically crushed by Sylvia's vise-like grip. It was probably a necessity for her in what still was a man's world. "We're glad to be of help."

"Brent is talking with the group from New York. We'd like to convene the full committee at fourteen hundred hours."

Dillon did the math in her head. Two o'clock.

"It surprises me that you don't want to get on this right away. That's nearly an hour from now."

Sylvia's head bobbed as Dillon talked. "I understand. We have a couple reasons for the delay. First, we think everyone needs a break and to eat something. To tackle this, we need fresh thinking." Sylvia leaned in. "And between you and I, that meeting was exhausting."

Dillon smiled.

"And second, with the committee's permission, we'd like to bring a couple from our rank into the meeting. They are experts in the field and will have much to offer, but they'll need to be briefed."

Dillon glanced at Jake, who met her gaze.

Sylvia held up her hand. "Let me step away for a few minutes while you discuss this."

"Uh, no offense," Jake said.

She smiled. "No offense taken. I'd actually be disappointed if you'd agreed without discussing it." She turned on her heels and made a beeline toward Brent.

Dillon noted that Caleb and Janis were huddled while Brent moved away from them. Dillon's gaze met Caleb's. They nodded in agreement.

"Let's go talk this out with Caleb and Janis," Dillon said. "Get their take on it."

Caleb and Janis were already making their way across the floor, so Jake and Dillon walked toward them. Out of the corner of her eye, she saw Sylvia smile.

As soon as they met, Caleb said, "What do you think?"

"They know a hell of a lot more than we do about this kind of stuff," Dillon said. "I think we almost have to trust them."

Jake nodded as she spoke.

"I agree," Janis said. "We've watched too many movies. Washington and the military are always suspect in situations like these."

"Which is a shame," Caleb added. "If we're going to survive, we're going to need them."

"Or they could have lied to us," Jake said.

"I'm sure they aren't telling us everything," Dillon said.

"True." Caleb nodded. "More than likely, they're closer to discovering what caused this than they're letting on. But at least they're here and seem to want to work with everyone instead of just taking over."

Jake smirked. "But that's what they do in all the movies. They come in with their planes and tanks and take over. They aren't following the script."

Dillon shook her head. "I'm having a talk with Lily when we get home. Who knew you were so paranoid?"

"You say paranoid. I say cautious." Jake glowered.

"Our prejudices aside," Janis said. "Is anyone picking up bad vibes from them?"

Everyone shook their head.

"Then we're in agreement?" Caleb asked. "We allow them to bring in their buddies?"

Dillon's heart raced. Why suddenly did this seem like a monumental decision? For the first time since the crisis, they would be putting their trust in someone else's hands. She hadn't realized until that moment how much they'd circled their wagons at Whitaker Estate, only truly trusting the people in their midst.

Her heart sank. But now even that was in question

since there was still a traitor. *Shit.* Would they have to reveal that when they met?

Jake's eyes narrowed. "What's going on, Dillon?"

"We'll have to tell them about our traitor." She turned to Caleb. "And your defectors."

"Oh, god." Jake ran his hand through his hair. "I hadn't even thought of that."

"Fuck," Dillon said. "We still say yes to Sylvia."

They all nodded.

Chapter Seventeen

Dillon found the group drinking a beer while they sat outside under an awning. If she didn't know better, she could almost believe they were vacationing in Vegas by the jovial atmosphere. She put on a smile. Just because her morning had been anything but relaxing, she didn't want to take that away from the others.

Skylar held up her beer and smiled. "Cheers."

Dillon let out her breath, not realizing she'd been holding it. She bent down and kissed Skylar, who enthusiastically returned it. *Thank god.* Dillon was sure it was Skylar's way of saying that she wasn't angry about keeping the traitor from her. The others, not knowing the situation, let out catcalls. She let her gaze drift to Cynthia, who gave her a slight nod and a smile.

"When did you guys get back?" Dillon asked.

"About half an hour ago," Skylar answered.

Dillon shifted her gaze to Maria, who wore a large straw hat and a pair of sunglasses. "Still not feeling well?" Dillon said with a laugh.

"Shut up, *chica*, or I'm gonna kick your ass when I feel better."

Tasha giggled. "She won't be drinking tequila again any time soon."

"Ugh, don't even say that word. From now on,

it's demon fire."

"Want some bacon and runny eggs?" Dillon asked just to rub it in further.

Maria pointed. "Keep it up. I know where you live, and I will hunt you down."

Everyone laughed. It was good to have Maria back. No way could she be the traitor; she couldn't fake her ashen coloring.

Dillon chatted with the group for a while before she was able to get Skylar and Cynthia alone. They slipped back inside the resort to an out-of-the-way nook just inside the door, and Dillon filled them in on the meeting.

"Where'd Jake go?" Skylar asked.

"He went to grab us some food. He should be along shortly. I need to know what happened while you guys were out. Did you see anything unusual? Any more thoughts on our traitor?"

Skylar took Dillon's hand. "Thanks for trusting me."

"I always did." Dillon hoped her words didn't come out as defensive as she felt. "You know—"

"That came out wrong." Skylar squeezed her hand. "I don't blame you for not telling me. It was honorable. But to answer your question, we didn't see anything that would make us think traitor, but Willa was acting strange."

"Strange how?"

Skylar turned to Cynthia. "Artsy? Hell, that's not the right word."

Dillon's gaze moved between Cynthia and Skylar. What the hell did artsy mean? And why would Skylar label it suspicious?

"It was the artsy shots she took," Cynthia said.

"She took some of the hotels, but then she kept finding these gutters to take pictures of."

"Gutters? On the buildings?"

"No." Cynthia shook her head. "Maybe gutters is the wrong word."

"Yeah," Skylar jumped in. "They're like concrete tunnels outside the hotels. And then she took shots from the street, looking down into the grating."

"You mean storm drains?" Dillon asked.

"Yes!" Cynthia said. "It looks like water probably runs through them sometimes. They're kinda creepy. Lots of debris around them and graffiti."

"Graffiti?" Dillon's mind churned. "Like what was on the stairs?"

"We thought of that," Skylar said. "So we asked her. She just shrugged and said she likes to capture a place from the highest to the lowest. Then she kept on shooting."

"Did anything else with her seem off?"

"Not really," Cynthia said. "She seemed giddy about taking the pictures. It wasn't like she tried to slip away from us or anything."

Dillon nodded. It didn't sound like she'd get any more insight on Willa. "So, Sky. Do you have any theories on the traitor?"

"Before we talk about that," Cynthia said. "We need to tell you the weird thing we discovered on our photo excursion."

Dillon raised her eyebrows. Maybe Cynthia would have something they could take to their meeting.

"There were no bodies on the streets. None," Cynthia said. "We were so stupid. It took us nearly an hour before we realized it."

"Even if the crisis happened after midnight,"

Skylar said, "we're in Vegas. No way could everyone have been in bed. The streets should have been full of people and cars. But there isn't either."

Dillon frowned. "There went my theory. I thought maybe animals got them."

"Our first thought, too," Cynthia said. "But animals wouldn't eat the clothes. And I doubt if they'd drive off with someone's car."

"Then somebody's been here before," Dillon said. "Possibly still are. But wouldn't they have come out last night once they saw we were just having a good time? Introduce themselves."

"Maybe they've had a bad experience with another group," Skylar said. "Besides, I'm not sure we'd come out if this many people invaded the estate."

"True. There are so many casinos. They could be hiding anywhere." Dillon ran her hand through her hair in frustration. It would be like finding a needle in a haystack.

"Maybe not," Cynthia said. "There weren't any bodies in the lobby or casino at Caesar's Palace or the Bellagio, either."

"And the other hotels?" Dillon asked.

"Yep, dead people everywhere."

"This is great info to have for our meeting."

"What is?" Jake walked up carrying two lunch bags. He handed one to Dillon.

Jake ate his sandwich while they filled him in. He scowled as they talked. When they finished, he said, "This is getting stranger and stranger."

Dillon glanced at her watch. "We don't have much time," she said between bites of her lunch. "I still want to hear Skylar's take on the traitor."

Skylar bit her lower lip. "I hate thinking anyone

could be a traitor. It makes me want to throw up."

"Now you see why I've been so edgy," Dillon said, relieved that Skylar would understand her moodiness.

"Completely. My head's been spinning all day, trying to figure it out. But I've got nothing. I don't want to believe anyone could betray us this way, not even Willa."

"I keep thinking we're missing something," Cynthia said. "But for the life of me, I can't figure it out." She turned to Dillon. "Have you talked to CJ today? Maybe they've come up with something."

"Nope, I haven't. But she'd call if they did." Dillon shoved the last bite of sandwich into her mouth. "I suppose we should get to the meeting. You guys be careful," she said, her gaze shifting between Skylar and Cynthia.

"Always," Skylar said and wrapped Dillon in a hug.

⚜ ⚜ ⚜ ⚜

Ever since Dillon and Jake had left for the meeting, Cynthia felt unsettled. She and Skylar had returned to the group and taken their place back under the awning, but she could no longer concentrate on what the others were saying.

She knew Alaina had been watching her, but she pretended not to notice, nervous that she'd recognize the fear in Cynthia's eyes.

Now that Maria was feeling better, she was in her element and charmed all the visitors who dropped by their table. She'd become the Whitaker Estate ambassador. Before they left, she wouldn't know a stranger.

Willa had disappeared shortly after they'd come back to the table and had yet to return. Cynthia played the photo-taking excursion over and over in her mind. Maybe if she thought hard enough, an answer would come to her. As if on cue, Willa marched toward them. Gauging by her gait, she was on a mission. She slipped between Cynthia and Alaina's chairs and leaned down.

With her mouth inches from Cynthia's ear she said, "I need to talk to you. Alone. It's important."

Cynthia glanced up into Willa's eyes. They were a bit unfocused, but she couldn't tell if it was excitement or agitation. Cynthia nodded and answered quietly. "Meet me inside in five minutes."

Without a word, Willa turned and walked toward the casino.

The rest of the table, except for Alaina and Skylar, didn't notice and continued their conversations. Cynthia made eye contact with Alaina and then Skylar, motioning for them to follow her lead.

Cynthia stood. "I need to stretch my legs. Alaina and Skylar, care to join me?"

Both leapt to their feet and followed. Once they were out of earshot of the others, Cynthia filled Alaina and Skylar in on Willa's request.

"You can't meet her alone," Alaina said. "If she's the traitor, she could be dangerous."

"But if I don't meet her, we may never know what she wants to talk about. Maybe she'll tell us something we need to know." Cynthia turned to Skylar. "Looks like you're the tie breaker."

"Whoa." Skylar put her hands up and took a couple of steps back. "Don't put this on me."

"You're right, sorry," Cynthia said. "That wasn't fair."

Skylar turned to Alaina. "As much as I hate it, she probably needs to see what Willa wants. I can't see that it would be dangerous meeting inside." Skylar pointed at Cynthia. "But you have to promise that you won't let her talk you into going somewhere else."

"I have a better idea," Alaina said. "Why don't we show up with you? Surely, she'll be okay with it."

"It could spook her and then she won't talk," Cynthia said. "We can't risk it."

"I'm afraid she has a point," Skylar said.

"Okay." Alaina crossed her arms over her chest. "But I want it noted that I'm not happy about this."

Alaina's reaction warmed Cynthia's heart. Under the circumstances, it probably shouldn't make her feel so good, but it did. Cynthia took her hand. "Thank you for looking out for me. I promise I'll be careful."

Cynthia decided the casual approach was best, so she strolled into the building with an air of calm. She took in the large expanse when she entered and immediately spotted Willa standing in front of the stairs. To give herself time to study Willa's demeanor, Cynthia further slowed her pace. Willa's gaze shifted between her camera and the stairs. The deep lines in her forehead conveyed her concentration.

"What did you want to see me about?" Cynthia asked.

Willa jumped. "Shit, you scared me."

"I thought you heard me coming up. What are you looking at?"

"I think I know who did it." Willa pointed to the stairs. "Who painted it."

Cynthia's mind raced. This wasn't what she'd expected Willa to say. "Okay" was all she managed in response.

Willa moved closer to Cynthia and held out her camera. "Take a look at this one and then go forward eight."

Tentatively, Cynthia took the camera, her mind still in overdrive. Was Willa trying to trick her, but for what endgame? She wasn't sure what she expected to see in Willa's pictures, but this wasn't it. One of the many shots Willa took of the storm drain filled the screen. She flipped back eight pictures as Willa instructed only to be met by a different storm drain.

After studying the pictures, Cynthia held the camera back out to Willa. "I'm afraid I don't understand. What am I supposed to see?"

Willa held the camera out in front of her and moved closer to Cynthia. Was she trying to lure her? Sure, Willa was going to overpower her, throw a hood over her head, and drag her away in front of at least twenty people lounging in the lobby.

Willa, apparently, hadn't picked up on Cynthia's distress since she continued to move closer. "Look, right here." Willa put her finger on the upper left-hand corner of the screen. "See the shape of these letters? Especially the e's."

Cynthia's gaze darted back and forth between the graffiti on the wall and the photos. Realization started to dawn. "Flip back to the other picture," Cynthia said. Her pulse quickened.

When the second image came up, Cynthia gasped. She stared down at the words that appeared to have blood dripping from them. "Holy shit. How did you know?" As soon as the words were out of her mouth, fear bubbled inside her. Had Willa truly discovered something or was this a trick?

"I wasn't sure," Willa said. "But something kept tickling my brain." She motioned toward the stairs. "Whoever did this had some experience. They didn't just pick up a spray can yesterday and crank this out. This takes talent."

"The same level of talent in some of the pictures you took today."

"Yes! I think this was done by the same person or at least someone that's emulating the original artist."

Cynthia glanced at Willa out of the corner of her eye. "I'm taking it you have more theories."

Willa bounced on the balls of her feet like an enthusiastic five-year-old. "I think it's the mole people."

"Mole people?" Cynthia crinkled her nose. "What are you talking about?"

"The people that live in the storm drains."

"Um, they live where?"

"The storm drains. I should have thought of it sooner." Willa smiled. "One of my buddies did a film about them. He went down into the tunnels and talked to them. It's where some of the homeless people live."

Homeless. Of course, the picture was becoming clearer to Cynthia. Her nervousness receded. "You mean actual people lived down there?"

"Yep. His documentary was fascinating. They were mostly druggies and gamblers down on their luck, but the storm drains kept them out of the brutal desert heat. Gave them shelter."

"But what about the water, isn't that where all the runoff goes?"

Willa nodded. "Yeah. Many of them have their belongings up on pallets, so they don't get wet." Willa frowned. "But every once in a while, it would sweep all their stuff away, and they'd have to start over."

"Oh, my god," Cynthia said louder than she'd planned. Several people turned and stared at them. Cynthia put her hand over her mouth and gave them a sheepish expression until they turned back to what they were doing. "If they were in the tunnels, most likely they would have survived just like we did."

"Yes. That's why I'm so excited. I think I solved it." The normally hardened Willa beamed. "I solved this thing when all the best brains haven't figured it out yet."

"We've invaded their home."

"Exactly, and they want us to go away."

"And the hotels that were cleaned out. They've probably moved out of the drains and into the luxury suites."

"That's what I figure."

"But aren't they dangerous?"

"Good question. I'd like to say no, but we're living in a different world, so I can't say for sure. I remember in his film he talked about the heroin and the meth addicts hating each other. Both groups thought they were better than the other, so they lived in separate tunnels."

"Hence Caesar's and the Bellagio?"

"I'm thinking."

"You're a genius." Cynthia's mind raced. "We need to tell Dillon right away."

"That's why I came to you. I didn't think they'd listen to me if I barged into their meeting."

"We need to get Alaina and Skylar now." Cynthia turned and headed across the lot. She soon realized Willa wasn't following and stopped. "Hey, aren't you coming?"

Willa shrugged. "I gave you the info. I doubt if

they'll want me for anything."

It suddenly hit Cynthia, beneath all of Willa's wild colored hair and bravado was a woman who didn't feel as if she belonged. Cynthia walked back toward Willa with a reassuring smile. "This is your discovery. You need to be there. They'll probably have questions that I won't be able to answer."

"Seriously? You want me to come with you?" Willa's shy smile made her look ten years younger.

"Of course." Cynthia put her hand on Willa's arm and urged her to come with.

As they walked across the lobby, Cynthia hoped that Willa's insecurities and not feeling that she belonged hadn't caused her to get in bed, so to speak, with Babcock's group, but now wasn't the time to worry about that.

❧❧❧❧

Dillon listened as one of the guests from Washington talked about securing the perimeter of Vegas and how they could best accomplish it. They hadn't decided on a course of action yet but were laying out all the possible scenarios. She wasn't sold on the method they were discussing. It seemed like overkill until they knew what they were dealing with, but then again, she had no experience in such matters, so she needed to keep an open mind.

A rap on the door stopped the speaker. Everyone stared but made no move to respond. A louder rap occurred, which set Sylvia in motion. She went to the door and opened it halfway. From where Dillon sat, she couldn't see who was on the other side, but if Sylvia's frown was any indication, it couldn't be positive.

Sylvia nodded, and her look of irritation turned to one of curiosity. She pushed open the door farther and turned back to the room. "Dillon and Jake, these ladies say they're with you."

Skylar, Cynthia, Alaina, and Willa stood just outside the door. *What the hell?* They certainly wouldn't interrupt a meeting of this magnitude without reason. But with Willa? "Yes, they are," Dillon said.

"They say they have information that might be valuable to our proceedings here," Sylvia said. "Should we have them come in?"

Dillon jumped to her feet. "Of course, let me pull up some chairs."

Jake and another member of the committee joined her in retrieving additional chairs.

Dillon gave Skylar and Cynthia a questioning gaze. Skylar widened her eyes, indicating to Dillon that the information was interesting. Cynthia nodded, giving Dillon the same impression.

Once they were all seated, Cynthia was the first to speak. "I want to turn this over to Willa, who made the discovery." She swept her hand in Willa's direction.

Willa started out in a quiet voice, so the members had to strain to hear her. As she got into her tale, she forgot her nerves and probably that anyone else was in the room since she'd locked her gaze on Dillon and spoke directly to her. Willa soon hit her stride, and the story came out with authority. She shared the pictures with the group and outlined her theory about the mole people.

Once she stopped speaking, everyone's gaze traveled around the room. It seemed no one wanted to be the first to speak.

"Wow," Jake finally said. "So mole people are really a thing?"

"They are," Caleb said. "I didn't realize Vegas had them, but we've had them in New York City for a long time. They live in the subways."

Brent nodded. "It makes sense why it seemed like more of a warning than a threat. In our experience, most homeless people aren't dangerous. Although there are some, they're usually just lost and abandoned."

"Many have mental health or addiction problems," Willa said. "That would be my only concern. Are they still on drugs? If so, where are they getting them?"

"We also need to consider that the mole people before the crisis could be very different from who we might be dealing with," Sylvia said.

"Meaning?" Dillon asked.

Sylvia rubbed her chin and looked to the ceiling. "Before the crisis, these were people down on their luck, but they were kept in check by law enforcement. Now there is nobody to control them."

"Maybe that's a good thing," Willa shot back. "They were marginalized and probably treated less than human. But now they get the chance to start over with something better."

Out of the corner of her eye, Dillon caught Skylar vigorously nodding. A wave of sadness washed over Dillon as she realized how much Skylar could relate.

"All right," Brent said. "I'm willing to concede that we can't stereotype this group until we know more about their motives and who they are."

"What about the sniper comment?" Janis asked. "That's a bit concerning."

Willa's eyebrows shot up. "Sniper? Where did that come from?"

Duh. Willa hadn't been privy to the note they'd found on the table. "Sylvia," Dillon said. "Do you have the note we got this morning?"

Sylvia pulled it out of her pocket and passed it down the table to Dillon, who in turn gave it to Willa.

Willa silently read it and nodded. She must have read it a couple of times because she didn't look up right away. "I don't see this as a threat. I think they're trying to warn us about something else."

"That's what I thought, too," Dillon said. "Snipers don't announce themselves, and people trying to cause harm don't, either. They strike without warning."

"Since we know where they are," the tactician from Washington said, "we hit Caesar's and the Bellagio and bring them in."

"No!" Willa practically yelled, causing Dillon to jump. "I mean..." Willa looked down at her hands. "This is their home. We are the invaders. It's not fair to pull them from their homes." She pointed at the group from Washington. "Would you take kindly to someone showing up and doing that to you?"

"She has a point," Jake said. "They've not attacked us."

"Oh, so we wait until they do, then do something about it?" the imposing man with a rigid posture said. "Really smart."

Brent scowled at him. "No, John. We have to think different. We don't just walk in, kick ass, and ask questions later."

John glowered. "It's worked for thousands of years, so why change now?"

Ugh. Dillon wanted to scream. They needed to be better than before and not make the same mistakes of the past. "Shouldn't we at least try and talk to them first?"

John rolled his eyes. "And how do you intend on talking to them until you round them up?" His voice dripped with disdain.

Dillon noticed Brent and Sylvia exchange glances. Where did they stand in all this? Would they side with John, their brethren, when all was said and done?

Caleb leaned forward and put his elbows on the table. "I think we have to be better than we were before. And this is our test."

"Great way to annihilate the rest of the planet," John said. "Why are we discussing a bunch of hold hands and sing concepts?" He gazed at Willa with a look of contempt. "We're going to let a freak like Pinkie here set our strategy?" He crossed his arms over his chest. "Well, count me out."

Brent stood. "Okay, John." He walked over to another two of their team and put his hand on one of their shoulders. "Timothy and Jason, would you mind taking John out of here? And please inform General Morgan of the situation."

"My pleasure," Timothy said as he rose, followed closely by Jason.

Once they left the room, Brent turned to Willa. "I apologize for my colleague."

Willa nodded. "Accepted."

"General?" Dillon said. "Who's General Morgan?"

Sylvia went on to explain what they'd not revealed earlier. Their entire special ops unit had been undergoing rigorous training in the bowels of the Pentagon when the crisis hit. All thirty-eight members of their unit survived, with General Morgan at the helm.

"Why didn't you tell us that earlier?" Caleb asked. His face was a mixture of suspicion and anger.

"It was probably a mistake," Sylvia said. "We've watched the same end of the world movies you have. The military is always the bad guy, so we didn't want everyone being suspicious of us right out of the gate."

"So you left us to be suspicious later on when we found out you were lying?" Caleb said.

"Withholding information," Brent corrected. "In hindsight, maybe not our best strategy."

Dillon sighed. This had the potential to spiral out of control. "You know what. We can't be fighting amongst ourselves." She nodded toward the Washington group. "You obviously see why candor is important. However..." She turned to Caleb. "We can't let their error in judgment make us forget what our priorities are."

Caleb nodded and gave her a half smile. "Fair enough." He pointed at Brent. "But we want the truth out of you from now on."

Brent nodded. "Okay. I think we established that we don't want to go after the...the homeless...um..."

"Mole people," Sylvia said.

"Yeah, the mole people. That we would like to have a conversation with them. How do we do it? We can't drive up and down the Strip with a bullhorn asking them to come out."

Willa raised her hand but didn't speak. Probably gun shy from being unloaded on earlier.

"Willa, you have a suggestion?" Sylvia said.

"I do. They know how to move around undetected. My guess is they still travel the tunnels to get from place to place." She pointed at the note sitting on the table. "Evidenced by their ability to get into the conference room while we have people on guard duty. I have no doubt they are watching us pretty carefully to see what we do next."

Dillon shuddered and looked around the room. Her gaze locked on an overhead vent. They could be listening in now. *Stop.* She was just being paranoid, wasn't she?

"We just sit here and discuss wanting to talk to them in the belief," Sylvia glanced at the ceiling before continuing, "that they're listening in?"

Willa smiled. "No. They left us a calling card. We give them one back. We write a note asking them to meet us."

"You think they'll really come back looking for a note?" Sylvia narrowed her eyes and crinkled her nose.

"No," Willa said. "We leave it at their house." She glanced around the table. "We leave one in the lobby of Caesar's and another in the Bellagio."

Dillon smiled at Willa. *Brilliant.* Dillon's stomach dropped, but what if Willa was the traitor? Before they agreed on a plan, she and Jake had to come clean about their traitor, and they had to talk about Babcock, but they couldn't do that with Willa in the room.

"I like it," Brent said.

Skylar stood. "I want to thank everyone here for listening to our concerns, and of course Willa for bringing them to light, but I think we should excuse ourselves so you can finish preparations."

"Nonsense," Janis said. "You've been so much help, why would we want you to go?"

"I think Skylar's right." Cynthia pointed at each member of Whitaker Estate. "There are six of us here, and I'm worried about the appearance it may give the others not on this committee. It might look as if we are exerting undue influence."

"And, um," Cynthia looked sheepish and met Willa's gaze. "And in case it doesn't work or something goes wrong, I would prefer not to be blamed and ostracized."

Willa's eyes widened. Cynthia's comments obviously hit the mark. "Yeah, I think we've shared everything we need to." She met Sylvia's gaze. "If you want someone to talk to the people or deliver the note, I would like to volunteer." She ran her hair through her colorful hair. "They might respond better to me than GI John."

Sylvia smiled. "Thank you. We will take that under advisement. Once again, on behalf of this group, I would like to thank you for your contribution."

Everyone remained silent as they stood to leave. Dillon's heart warmed as she watched them make their way out of the room. After the door clicked shut, she said, "I think we need to explore the sniper comment a little more. If these mole people are benevolent—"

"If is the key word," Brent interrupted.

"Yes, if," Dillon continued. "Then Babcock's group may be here and truly on the rooftops. We would be crazy not to consider that."

Brent sighed. "We did consider it, but why didn't they strike right away? We were sitting ducks the night of the party. They could have wiped us all out."

"Maybe they don't want to wipe us out," one of the men from Washington said. "We're treating them like the enemy, but who made that determination?" He held up his hand. "Don't get me wrong. I find their version of religion way off base, but that doesn't mean they're assassins."

Dillon met Caleb's gaze. He knew about the traitor and Alaina, but he wasn't going to give them away. That was for Dillon to do. She raised her hand. "I have something I need to say before we can continue this conversation."

All eyes turned to her. She'd certainly gotten everyone's attention.

She took a deep breath and glanced at Jake before she began. "We have more insight on Babcock, as well as a potential problem. Alaina, the quiet dark-haired woman that was here earlier, came from Babcock's compound."

Their gazes burned into her. She wished someone would say something, but no one did. "She escaped from their compound after the crisis. She ended up in Amarillo. That's where she was taken, along with five others, by the gang that attacked our community." Dillon looked around the table. "The group from Amarillo is not aware of where she'd come from. And I ask that this information remain confidential unless there's good reason to reveal it."

"But why did she tell you when she didn't tell the other group?" Sylvia asked.

"That's the other part of the story. She told us because she wanted to let us know that we have a traitor in our midst."

Audible gasps came from around the table. "What the hell? You all have a traitor, and we're just now hearing about this?" Brent said.

Caleb waved his hand. "We've had three people disappear who we suspect left and joined Babcock's ministry. I know of three other groups that have experienced the same. There are probably more."

"The problem is," Dillon said. "We haven't been able to determine who our traitor is. She's out there somewhere. Either here with us or back home. Either way, we've had to be careful what we say."

"How do you know that Alaina isn't a plant?" Brent asked.

"We don't for sure." Dillon put her hand against her forehead. "It's horrible knowing we have someone that we're close to that might be working against us. It's the ultimate betrayal."

"In other words, someone from your group could have tipped Babcock off," Sylvia said.

Dillon's back stiffened.

"Or from another group," Jake said, entering the conversation. "Because we know we have a traitor, we were extra careful on what information we shared. Only a handful of us knew that Vegas was our destination. Communities without that worry would probably have been much looser with it, even though we asked that it be kept quiet."

"I'm afraid we have more potential leaks than the Titanic," Caleb said.

Dillon sat back in her chair and took a deep breath. A weight lifted off her shoulders, knowing she'd revealed their secret. She'd never forgive herself if their traitor caused harm to anyone at the summit.

Brent stood. "There's a lot of moving parts here. I think our best bet is to make contact with the mole people. That way, we can find out what the sniper comment truly means. But we can't discard the idea that Babcock may have an army here, which puts everyone in grave danger. Until we know for certain, we must take actions as if they are here. All agree?"

"Agreed," Dillon said along with the others.

"I would like to offer our expertise in securing this building until we get a handle on what's going on," Sylvia said.

"As long as John isn't a part of it," Caleb said.

"I'm sure General Morgan will not be using him for anything we're doing here," Sylvia said. "To summarize, our two immediate goals are to get a note to the mole people and secure our location. I would ask that Dillon and Jake's group work on the note. We, of course, will provide protection in delivering it while the Washington group works on security."

"I'd like to offer my services to you," Jake said. "I am very comfortable with weapons and think I could be of value. I would also like to recommend that you recruit other volunteers like me from other clans. Just like we didn't want our community to be blamed if something goes wrong with the mole people, I don't think it's wise for the Washington group to have sole responsibility for security. If something should go wrong, your reputation in this new world could be tarnished."

"Good point," Brent said. "We would love to have your help, Jake."

Chapter Eighteen

Greetings:

We believe you left messages for us. If we are not mistaken, you likely survived the crisis by being in the storm drains when it occurred.

We believe that there are two groups, one living in Caesar's Palace and the other at the Bellagio.

We mean you no harm. We were not aware that you were here. We come from all around the country. There are 23 groups in all. We met here to discuss how we move forward as a society. We would like to talk to you.

We suspect that you may be warning us of a threat. If so, we need more information to keep everyone safe.

We would like to meet with you. Tomorrow at 9 a.m., four of our delegates will be in the lobby of Treasure Island. We request that you send delegates, as well.

Thank you.

The note had been delivered. While they'd never win a Pulitzer, Cynthia thought it hit the high points. Now it was a waiting game. As much as they wanted to meet as soon as possible, they'd decided to set the meeting for the morning. Nobody wanted to be creeping around empty buildings in the dark.

The room held none of the festive tone from yesterday. The mood, dampened by the turn of events, had grown somber. Tonight, the meal would be served indoors since the Washington group determined it was too dangerous to be outside. They'd been herded into the conference area for protection, but to Cynthia, it felt like a prison.

Armed guards patrolled the perimeter, and most of the guests openly carried their weapons. It was likely everyone was armed yesterday, as well, but none of the guns had been visible. The show of force unnerved Cynthia, even though she suspected the heavy firepower was meant to put them at ease.

Small groups assembled throughout the large room, talking in hushed tones. The time dragged, and it was still a couple of hours until dinner. She just wanted to eat, so they could return to their rooms. Her friends made small talk, but she didn't even make a show of listening.

Skylar sat to Cynthia's right but hadn't spoken in over a half an hour. She shifted in her seat but never took her gaze off the doors. Dillon, along with Willa, Brent, and Caleb, were chosen to attend the meeting with the mole people, so she'd been whisked away to a preparatory meeting.

Cynthia leaned over toward Skylar. "How are you doing?"

Skylar put her hand in front of her and shook it back and forth, communicating so-so. She didn't seem to want to talk, so Cynthia returned her attention to the others.

A loud crash came from behind Cynthia. She flinched and spun around in her chair to see a red-faced man apologetically picking up the chair he'd knocked over. Her heart pounded in her chest. *Damn it.* She was crawling out of her skin, but she had no idea how to alleviate the anxiety building inside her.

She hoped Dillon returned soon. Somehow, she always had a way about her that put her and the others at ease.

Alaina had been quiet today, too. Something was on her mind, but Cynthia hadn't been able to get it out of her. Cynthia fought against the seed of doubt that lingered in her thoughts. She hated the feeling. She trusted Alaina. She couldn't be playing them, but Alaina's silence made Cynthia uneasy.

Without warning, Skylar leapt from the table, banging her leg against it in her haste. Dillon must have arrived for Skylar to react that way. Cynthia's head snapped around toward the door where Dillon had just entered.

Cynthia sighed and got to her feet. She needed to talk to Dillon away from the others. By the time Cynthia reached Dillon, Skylar had Dillon in a bear hug.

Dillon laughed. "Holy hell. Maybe I should volunteer for more missions if this is how I'm greeted."

Skylar playfully punched her in the upper arm. "Don't even think about it."

Dillon shot Skylar a grin before she turned to Cynthia. "And you practically sprinted across the room. Why all the attention?"

"We need to talk." Cynthia glanced around at the group closest to them. "But not where anyone can hear. I've got a bad feeling."

Dillon's brow furrowed. "Why? What happened?"

"Nothing," Cynthia admitted. "I've just felt edgy

all afternoon.”

Skylar put her hand on Cynthia’s shoulder. “We all have. I think it’s natural.”

“Maybe.” Cynthia shook her arms. “It feels like I have bugs crawling under my skin.” She brusquely rubbed her arms, hoping to alleviate the uncomfortable sensation. “It’s driving me nuts.”

“No doubt,” Dillon said. “Is there anything we can do to help?”

“I’m not going to be right until we figure out who the traitor is. What if they’re working against us, and we don’t know it? I don’t think it’s Willa, which means it’s someone else. We’re being played, but by who?” The more she talked, the more she wanted to crawl out of her skin. It was uncharacteristic for her to get so panicky, but she had little control over the feelings bubbling inside. She took in a deep breath. She didn’t want to embarrass herself but probably already had.

Skylar took her elbow and motioned to a table away from the crowd. “Why don’t we sit? We need our levelheaded Cynthia.”

Cynthia allowed herself to be led to the table. Her face warmed. It wasn’t like her to overreact. Was she having a panic attack? Her heart raced. “I’m sorry,” she said as she sat. “You have enough on your plates. You shouldn’t have to worry about my meltdown.”

“Stop.” Dillon put her hand on top of Cynthia’s. “Something’s bothering you, and we want to help.”

“I feel like we’re driving through fog. We have no idea what’s in front of us or whether a truck is bearing down.”

“I get that,” Skylar said. “The uncertainty sucks. Can I ask you something?”

"Always," Cynthia said.

"First, let me tell you since you told me about the traitor, my chest feels like an elephant is sitting on it. I was convinced it was Willa. But I'm not anymore, so that leaves the door wide open."

Cynthia nodded.

"The thought that it could be one of our friends makes me want to throw up," Skylar said. "Are you afraid it's someone you're close to?"

Cynthia's eyes filled with tears. She angrily swept them away. "I don't want it to be, and I feel so disloyal. But now Maria and..." Cynthia put her head in her hands.

"And Alaina," Dillon said.

Tightness gripped Cynthia's chest. She kept her head in her hands but nodded.

"You've fallen for her, haven't you?" Skylar asked.

"Fuck me," Cynthia said with venom.

"Whoa, okay," Dillon said.

Cynthia inhaled deeply. She had to be freaking out her friend. Hell, she was freaking herself out. "I guess falling in love makes me swear like a sailor. Oh, fuck me again. Did I just say I'm falling in love?"

"I'm pretty sure that's what I heard," Dillon said.

Cynthia removed her hands from her face and met Dillon's gaze. Light danced in Dillon's eyes, and she was trying hard not to laugh. Cynthia laughed instead. "It's okay. You can laugh. I must seem ridiculous."

Dillon and Skylar both laughed. "We're just not used to you using the F-bomb," Dillon said.

"Yeah," Skylar said. "That's Dillon's favorite word, not yours."

"I know." Cynthia slapped her hand against her forehead with exaggeration. "I'm a hot mess."

"We all are in our own way." Skylar patted Cynthia's arm.

"Let's stop sitting around waiting for something to happen." With authority, Dillon slapped her hand onto the table. "We have more than an hour until dinner, so let's work on the problem. It's time I talk to Maria. Maybe she'll have insight that we haven't thought of. Why don't you two give CJ and Karen a call and see if they've come up with anything? There's the real possibility that the traitor is still at the estate."

"Plus, we should fill them in on what's going on here," Skylar said.

Cynthia straightened her back and wiped the last tears from her eyes. "Thanks. I think I can hold it together now. But if there's a God, I pray that Alaina is who she says she is. I'm not sure my heart can take it if she's not."

Dillon stood and put her hand on Cynthia's shoulder. "I want to believe she's for real, but on the off chance that she's not, you've got us."

Skylar stood and wrapped her arms around Cynthia's neck. The hug felt good, just what Cynthia needed. "And we'll pick up any pieces," Skylar said. "Believe everything will work out as it need be, but if the worst happens, you won't be alone."

Cynthia swallowed down the lump in her throat. "You guys are the best. Thanks."

*　*　*

As soon as they joined the others, Dillon filled them in on the latest information. When she announced that she and Willa were on the team assigned to meet with the mole people, a shadow crossed Maria's face before she righted it with a fake smile. It only reinforced to Dillon that she needed to get Maria alone.

Once she'd finished and side conversations began in earnest, Dillon motioned to Maria. When she met her gaze, Dillon asked, "Can we talk?"

Maria nodded but didn't smile.

Dillon rose from the table, and Maria followed. They walked to the far side of the room before Dillon said, "I wanted to talk to you alone. Get your take on the situation."

Maria crossed her arms over her chest. "Really? Now you want my opinion."

Dillon recognized that it wasn't a question. Maria's hostility had returned. She didn't have time for games or beating around the bush, so she said, "What's going on with you? Lately, you seem pissed off at me half the time."

"Try three-quarters."

Ouch. It hadn't been her imagination. "All right. It's good that we've established that. Mind telling me why?"

Maria's dark brown eyes filled with fire. "Do you really want to know?" She put her fist on her hip.

Dillon bit her lip. Her patience was low, but getting into a pissing match with Maria wouldn't help anyone. She silently counted to ten before she responded. "Yes, I would." She tried to keep her voice steady.

"Fine. I'll tell you." Maria threw her hands around as she spoke. "I've been sitting on my ass doing nothing. Before we left the estate, you guys holed up in meetings for hours. Top secret shit that I obviously wasn't good enough to be included in."

Maria's voice had grown louder, and several people turned to look. Maria must have noticed, too, because she moved closer to Dillon and said between clenched teeth, "Then when I was invited to attend this little summit, do you remember what you said when you asked us?"

Dillon searched her mind. She couldn't remember. The battle. The deaths. And then finding out about the traitor had overwhelmed her. "I'm sorry I don't."

Maria's eyes flashed. "Well, I remember every word. You said Tasha needed to come along because you needed a mechanic." Maria shook her head, and her jaw clenched. "I'm a fucking civil rights and constitutional law attorney who's argued cases in front of the Supreme Court, and we came here to set up a government. And nobody said shit to me. Didn't ask me for one goddamned piece of advice." Maria poked her finger into Dillon's chest. "And then today fucking Willa was asked to help. Willa! So fuck you, Dillon. I deserved better."

Shit. How had she missed it and been so insensitive? Dillon's gaze dropped to the floor. She couldn't bear to look Maria in the eye. What an asshole she'd been. Maria was right, she'd been so consumed that she'd lost sight of everything. They all had.

Maria poked her again. "Don't you have anything to say to me?"

Dillon looked up and stared into Maria's angry eyes. "You're right." She should say more, but she didn't know what.

Maria's shoulders slumped as if all the air was let out of her. If she'd been expecting Dillon to fight back, she hadn't. The anger was replaced by pain. "But why?"

Dillon considered the question. How did she answer? She was tired of the cloak and dagger. In the moment, all she felt was defeat. Dillon shook her head. "Fuck it. I'm done. I can't do this anymore."

Maria's eyes narrowed.

"This has been the most fucked-up situation," Dillon said. "I have no excuse for not considering your talents. If I were in your shoes, I'd be pissed, too. In hindsight, I'm not sure the Commission made the right decision. I'm not sure if we're making the right decision on anything." Dillon met Maria's gaze. "I was trying to do the best that I could. We all were, but looking at you, one of my closest friends in the world, we were stupid."

Maria's gaze softened. "What's going on? You haven't been yourself, either. It's not just me."

"You're right." Dillon took a deep breath. Things had to be different. "Hell, I don't know if I should do this or not, but it feels right in here." Dillon patted her chest. "There's more to what's going on than you know. Than just about everyone knows."

Maria fixed Dillon with her intense gaze.

"We were all still reeling from the battle and the lost lives when Alaina dropped a bombshell on us. She originally came from Babcock's ministry before she escaped and ended up in Amarillo."

Maria's mouth dropped open. "Holy shit!"

"That's not the half of it." Dillon swallowed hard. She was about to break her oath to the Commission. They'd done it earlier today with Skylar, but she'd had the blessing of Jake and Cynthia. Now she'd be making the decision on her own. She plunged on. "There's a traitor in our group."

Maria crinkled her nose and cocked her head. "A traitor?"

"Yes. A snitch. Someone who's been talking to Babcock's crew."

Maria shook her head. "No, I can't believe that. How do you know?"

"Alaina told us."

"Seriously? We've known her for a minute." Maria glanced over her shoulder. "Why would you accept her word?"

"CJ pulled up the communication records. Someone's been talking to Babcock."

A deep furrow creased Maria's brow. "And you suspect me? Is that why you didn't tell me?" Her eyes flashed angry again.

"We didn't tell anyone. That's the pact we made as a Commission."

"You told CJ."

"She's the only one and only because none of us knew how to access the computer records without her."

"You didn't tell Skylar?" Maria's voice was accusatory.

"Nope, not until today."

Maria studied Dillon for a couple of beats before her face relaxed. "Nobody?"

"Nope. Jake couldn't tell Lily. Renee couldn't tell Katie, and I couldn't tell Skylar. I kept my oath. We only told Skylar after Jake and Cynthia agreed Cynthia needed another set of eyes to keep track of Willa today."

"Do Jake and Cynthia know you're telling me?"

Dillon shook her head and averted her gaze to the floor. "Nope. I did this one on my own." Dillon ran her hand through her hair.

"Why now?"

"It's been the longest month of my life keeping a secret like this. Watching everything everyone did, trying to figure out who might be the betrayer, and then feeling guilty for it. I put a wall around myself and everyone else. I thought it would make it easier. And then I saw the pain on your face. The pain I caused, and I just couldn't do it anymore." Dillon sighed. "They can kick me off the Commission if they want, but this isn't working. We're no closer to figuring out who the traitor is, and now we have mole people to contend with and possibly Babcock's people." Dillon met Maria's gaze. "And I need my friends."

Maria surprised Dillon when she stepped up and wrapped her arms around her. Tears welled in Dillon's eyes and soon rolled down her cheeks. She tried to blink them back, not wanting a room full of people to see her cry.

"Let it out, my friend," Maria said as she held Dillon. "You're a pressure cooker that was bound to blow. No shame in that. We're all in this together."

⚜⚜⚜⚜

Skylar flopped back onto the bed as she hung up the satellite phone. "Ugh," she said to Cynthia. "Do you think Dillon's gonna be pissed at Renee?"

Cynthia slumped in the chair in Skylar and Dillon's room. They'd just finished their call with CJ and Karen with no progress on the search for the traitor. Cynthia massaged her scalp, hoping to rid herself of the headache that had been threatening all day. "I hope she's not pissed. After all, we told you."

"True." Skylar dropped the phone onto the bed and lay still.

"You worried about her?" Cynthia asked.

"Yeah. She's been wound so tight these last few weeks. At least now I know why. She's always been the steady one. The one we can rely on."

"I know." Cynthia continued to rub her temples. "It worried me more when CJ said she's never seen her like this."

"Yeah, what's her problem?" Skylar said. "You'd think she could handle a small thing like an apocalypse a little better."

Cynthia laughed. It was probably the best thing for her tension headache. "Thanks, I needed that."

Skylar smiled. "I'm keeping my fingers crossed they figure something out tomorrow. Maybe Katie will bring a fresh set of eyes to the situation."

A knock on the door startled Cynthia. She looked at Skylar. "Are you expecting anyone?"

Skylar shook her head and pulled out her pistol. She slowly walked to the door. "Who is it?"

"Dillon."

"Jesus. You scared the shit out of us." Skylar threw back the deadbolt. "Why didn't you just come in?"

"Because I hoped you had everything locked up tight, and I figured you might have your weapon out," Dillon said as she entered the room and re-engaged the locks.

"Oh, yeah." Skylar smiled, but her smile faded when she studied Dillon. "This may be the oddest comment I've ever made. You look like hell, but you look better, too."

Cynthia studied Dillon after hearing Skylar's

words. "Strangely, she's right." While Dillon appeared to be wrung out, the tension that had become permanently etched on her face had disappeared.

"I told Maria," Dillon said and flopped onto the bed next to Skylar. "I couldn't do it anymore."

"Then it probably won't bother you that Renee told Katie." Skylar laid her head on Dillon's shoulder.

Dillon wrapped her arm around Skylar. "I don't blame her. Did CJ have anything brilliant to share?"

"Tomorrow, Renee and Katie, and CJ and Karen are going over CJ's notes together," Cynthia said.

"Maybe the new sets of eyes will find something CJ missed," Skylar said.

"CJ's the smartest person I know." Dillon pointed at Cynthia and then Skylar. "And don't either of you tell her. If she hasn't been able to figure it out, I'm not holding much hope they'll come up with anything."

"It can't hurt," Skylar said. "They're still convinced that Willa is our culprit, but I'm not buying it."

"Did you notice how she lit up when she talked about the mole people? It was almost like she considered them kindred spirits," Cynthia said.

"They're mine." Skylar put her hand against her heart.

"I forgot," Cynthia said. It was easy to forget that Skylar had been homeless before being noticed by a social worker who helped get her off the streets.

"It's not something I go around advertising." Skylar smiled. "But I'm sure the mole people will touch me in a way that most won't be able to understand."

"What do you think will go down tomorrow?" Dillon asked.

"I'm not sure, but I'd trust them a million times

more than I would Babcock. There's a code on the street. I saw more ethical behavior on the streets than I did in college."

"Seriously?" Dillon asked.

"Yep. Don't get me wrong, there were some bad actors on the street, but we usually policed our own, and they didn't stick around. In college, I saw so many people cheating, being cutthroat with each other. My street family would never have thrown me under the bus, but my college classmates would have in a heartbeat if it meant something better for them."

Cynthia smiled to herself as Dillon subtly pulled Skylar closer. There was no doubt how much Dillon loved Skylar, but she walked a fine line of empathizing with her past without pitying her.

"I'll keep that in mind when we meet tomorrow. Do you think they'll show?"

"Yup," Skylar said without hesitation. "They left their calling card, so no doubt they'll accept the invitation."

Dillon closed her eyes. "I'd just like to fall asleep right now and sleep until morning."

"It's almost dinnertime," Skylar said. "What say we get a little food in you and call it an early night?"

"I don't think anyone will be partying tonight," Cynthia said. "It's a shame with how hopeful everything felt when we first arrived."

"And it will be again." Skylar sat up in bed. "Come on, guys. We can't let Babcock, if it's even him, bring us down. This very well could be the moment in history that we form a brand-new society." She put her legs over the side of the bed. "Let's go."

Dillon smiled and turned her gaze to Cynthia. "And that's why I love her so damned much."

Chapter Nineteen

Cynthia swore as she shoved her arm into her T-shirt. It had gotten twisted, and she'd tried three times to put it on with no luck. They needed to get down to the lobby where they would gather before Dillon and the others went to meet the mole people.

Alaina put her hand on Cynthia's arm. "Stop." She straightened the sleeve. "Okay, now try."

Cynthia smiled. "Thanks."

"I know you're worried about today."

"What gave me away? The wrestling match with my T-shirt?"

"That was the cherry on top." Alaina rubbed her back. "I can feel the agitation radiating off you."

"I've felt like this since yesterday. I can't shake this feeling...of...what's the word? Foreboding? I know that sounds ominous, but I've just felt wired inside. And I hate it." Cynthia pulled on her jeans and tucked in her shirt.

"I understand. You know it's okay to feel what you're feeling."

"I'm supposed to be the calm one." She sat on the bed and pulled on her shoes. "I was a doctor, for god's sake."

"You still are."

"Right." Cynthia smiled as she rifled through her bag, making sure she had everything she needed.

"See how rattled I am."

"Would it be wrong to tell you that I'm honored? Honored that you're willing to share all sides of you. Even when you don't think you're at your best."

Cynthia stopped her frenetic preparation and dropped her bag onto the bed. She took a step toward Alaina and met her gaze. "I hadn't even thought of that, but you're right. I feel comfortable with you. Like you don't expect me to be perfect and won't judge me for being human."

"I've been subjected to too much judgment in my life, so I never want to do it to you." Alaina put her hand on Cynthia's cheek. "You're perfect just the way you are."

"Thanks." Cynthia paused and gazed deep into Alaina's eyes. "Why can't you accept that about yourself?"

Alaina shrugged and looked away. "Years of conditioning." She hurried across the room and picked up her shoes.

"Why do you do that?" Cynthia asked.

"What?" Alaina said but didn't turn toward Cynthia.

"You accept me and seem to like it when I'm open with you, but whenever your past comes up, you do this." Cynthia moved her hand in a circle to show Alaina's avoidance tactics. Realizing her gesture wouldn't help since Alaina wasn't looking at her, she said, "I mean you either change the subject or suddenly get busy. Don't you want to share with me? I sometimes feel like I let everything hang out, but you're...um..."

"Guarded?" Alaina's shoulders dropped, and she sighed. With her back still to Cynthia, she said,

"There's some ugly things. Painful, dark things."

Cynthia moved closer to Alaina but held back from touching her, not sure if Alaina wanted her to. "They don't scare me."

"I believe that. But they scare me." Alaina turned and stepped forward. She took Cynthia's hand in hers. "What if I promise when we get home…" Alaina smiled. "Home. I like the way that sounds. When we get home, I'll start letting you in on some of those things. Slowly. It'll take me time, but now isn't the time or place."

Cynthia's heart soared when Alaina spoke of home. She wanted to go *home* with Cynthia. She fought the urge to wrap Alaina in her arms in celebration, but she suspected it would make Alaina uncomfortable if she made too big of a deal of it.

Cynthia smiled. "I like the sound of that." She brushed an errant strand of hair off Alaina's face. "I want to hear all your stories. Know what makes you tick. What in your life has defined you. Made you the woman that I'm enjoying so much." Cynthia held back from saying "the woman I'm falling in love with," afraid it was too soon and might scare Alaina.

A pained look crossed Alaina's face, and she put her hand on her chest. "That hurt. Most of what's defined me is negative. What does that say about me?"

Cynthia narrowed her eyes and studied Alaina, trying to decipher the meaning. "I'm not sure I fully understand."

"Most people have positive life events that define them. The time they went to the circus when they were five. A kindly grandma who they baked cookies with. Movie night with Mom, eating popcorn and watching romcoms. Aren't those the type of moments that you had?"

Cynthia shifted her weight from one foot to the other. Alaina was right. "I won't lie. They are. I used to feel guilty about it until Skylar told me to knock it off. My life was a cakewalk compared to hers, so I found that I wouldn't share my experiences because I didn't want to come off as bragging. She reminded me that my experiences were my experiences, and I never judged her for hers, so why would she judge me for mine."

"Wise woman. And I feel the same way." Alaina looked down at the floor. "Truth be told, I'm afraid once I start telling you everything that the bloom will fall off this rose. Quickly."

"No!" Cynthia lifted Alaina's chin so their eyes met. "Whatever experiences shaped you, I like what I see. More importantly, what I feel. My guess is you've tried to become everything the negative in your life wasn't."

"Very perceptive. I fought like hell not to become everything that I hated. I've tried to build a life that's the opposite." Sadness filled Alaina's eyes. "But I haven't always been successful."

"We're all works in progress."

Alaina leaned in, and her lips met Cynthia's. Alaina's kiss always made Cynthia forget everything, and today was no exception. It started out light as they explored each other's mouths, but it soon turned more urgent. More passionate.

Several minutes later, out of breath, Cynthia pulled back. "We have to stop, or I won't be responsible for my actions."

Alaina blinked a few times, erasing her unfocused gaze. "I hate that you're right." She smiled.

"Rain check?"

"Rain check. Is it wrong that I just want to get home? Back to the estate in our own little bubble."

"It's not wrong at all. Life will change after the summit, but I want to believe we can still hold on to our community. It just might get bigger."

Cynthia nodded. "By the way, thanks. You distracted me from my jitters."

"My diabolical plan worked." Alaina pretended to twirl a mustache. She took Cynthia's hand. "Let's go support Dillon and Skylar."

"And Willa," Cynthia said.

"And Willa."

⁂

All Skylar wanted to do was pace, but she couldn't. She didn't want Dillon to see how nervous she was. Dillon, on the other hand, seemed calm, almost Zen-like. Skylar was still debating with herself whether it was a good or bad thing.

A steady stream of people from other communities had stopped by to wish Dillon well. Pride welled in Skylar as she watched Dillon confidently greet everyone with a smile and reassured them that things would work out okay.

Nearby, Willa, Caleb, and Brent chatted about the mission with their well-wishers. Skylar grinned. Willa had become a bit of a celebrity with the younger, edgier crowd. What they lacked in numbers, they made up for with their enthusiasm.

Leslie slid up next to Skylar. "How are you holding up?"

Since their guard duty together, Leslie sought

her out. Previously, they'd not gotten much of a chance to get to know each other, even though she was a part of Dillon's crowd. When they lived in the same suite, Leslie was so deeply consumed by her grief they'd not talked much.

"I'm doing okay." She nodded toward Dillon. "She's been fine all morning. Calm and cool as they come."

Leslie put her arm over Skylar's shoulders. "That's Dillon for you. I'm sure she's nervous under the surface."

"A little. But not as bad as you'd expect. She believes that the mole people are friendly, and this will go fine. She's either blindly optimistic or has a bead on the situation."

"Let's hope it's the latter."

"No doubt."

Dillon made her way through the throngs of people to where they stood. "Hey, Leslie. How's it going?"

"Shouldn't I be asking you that?"

Dillon shrugged. "I'm good." She glanced at her watch. "I'm just ready to get this show on the road. Waiting around is the hardest part."

"Only about five more minutes," Skylar said and then frowned. "Has anyone seen Cynthia and Alaina yet?" She couldn't believe Cynthia wouldn't be here to see Dillon off unless she was so uptight that she couldn't bring herself to do it. Still that would be so unlike her.

"I haven't seen her." Leslie scanned the crowd. "Wait, I think she and Alaina just got here."

"About time," Dillon said. "I'm gonna have to give her shit for this."

"You'd give her shit if she turned up early, on time, or late," Skylar said.

Dillon laughed. "True."

They walked up holding hands. Skylar took in Cynthia. She didn't seem to be crawling out of her skin like yesterday, but Skylar still recognized the fear in her eyes.

Cynthia grabbed Dillon and gave her a huge hug. When they parted, Cynthia said, "I'm getting that out of the way now. I won't be able to when you go to leave."

Dillon put her hand on Cynthia's arm. "Don't be nervous. My gut tells me we're going to find allies today."

Sylvia and three other men from Washington entered the room. Sylvia raised her voice to be heard over the crowd. "May I have your attention, please?"

It took several attempts before the crowd obeyed.

"We have the transport van out front." They'd decided not to walk since Treasure Island was on the other end of the Strip. Sylvia and the other three men, Jake being one, would remain in the vehicle. They'd be heavily armed but would stay out of sight unless an emergency occurred. "Would our four volunteers please meet in front of the lobby doors?"

The crowd moved aside, giving the volunteers a clear lane. Unconsciously, they'd formed a human tunnel.

Dillon leaned over and whispered in Skylar's ear. "Looks like I'm running the gauntlet."

Skylar smiled, knowing Dillon was trying to put her at ease before she left. Skylar put her hand on Dillon's cheek and gazed into her eyes. "I love you, Dillon Mitchell. Do not do anything foolish. And be careful."

Dillon put her hand against her chest and said, "Me do something foolish? Never."

Skylar rolled her eyes. "Sure. Give me a hug and a kiss and get out of here. I can't take much more of this."

Dillon drew Skylar against her. She'd always fit in Dillon's arms perfectly since their first dance. *What the hell?* Why was she thinking about their first dance now? Dillon would be back.

Dillon held her without speaking.

Do not cry, she repeated to herself for what must have been the hundredth time in the past hour. She steeled herself and put on her best smile as they separated.

"I love you, Sky," Dillon said. "I'll be back before you know it."

Then Dillon turned and walked through the tunnel of people. She shook hands and high-fived the entire way.

Skylar turned away before Dillon exited the building.

Chapter Twenty

The atmosphere in the van was more like a party bus than a special ops mission. Everyone was upbeat and optimistic about the meeting. Dillon hoped it wouldn't turn into a letdown if the mole people didn't show. *No.* She couldn't think that way.

This had to work. They needed the mole people as their allies. She'd not mentioned it to anyone, not even Skylar, but she'd begun to sense Babcock's presence. There'd been nothing to confirm those suspicions except for the sniper comment in the note.

When they rolled up in front of Treasure Island, it was eight minutes until meeting time. Would the mole people show up early? Dillon doubted they'd come out right away. Likely, they'd observe for a bit before they showed themselves.

"Shall we go in there now?" Brent said. "Let them assess the situation and size us up."

"Let's do it." Caleb put his hand into the center of the group like a football huddle.

They all put their hands in. Willa beamed the entire time. Dillon had no doubt she was having the time of her life. She just hoped Willa was right about the people they were about to meet and that Willa wasn't a mole of a different kind.

As they walked to the entrance of Treasure

Island, Dillon glanced at the ship that once sank at regular intervals. She knew it was silly, but she loved the whole show. She'd normally stop and watch every time she walked past. The ship sitting empty gave her a chill.

They walked into the casino first. Without the bells and dings coming from the slots, the hotel held an eerie vibe. Like Caesar's Palace and the Bellagio, there were no signs of any dead.

Willa swung her camera around, snapping pictures as they walked. Maybe one day, people would look at her photojournalism to know what it was like after the crisis. Would there still be people to see it? Dillon shoved the thought from her mind.

She needed to be on high alert, prepared for anything. She scanned the area and noted that Caleb and Brent were doing the same. Nothing seemed amiss, except for a large pile of boxes in front of the check-in counter. *Odd.*

They approached the boxes carefully, afraid of what they might discover. Upon further inspection, it was only a pile of canned goods and packaged food. Even odder.

Willa held up a piece of paper that she'd picked up from behind the counter. "Looks like we have a message."

We are waiting for you at Senor Frogs.

Brent took the note and studied it. "I don't like this."

"Why did they want to change locations?" Caleb asked.

"To show us who's in charge," Dillon said. "Take

control of the situation."

"Do we let them?" Caleb asked.

"I don't see that we have any choice," Dillon said.

Brent stood, obviously thinking, but said nothing. This changed their backup safety plan should something go wrong.

"We can't abort now," Dillon said, hoping to persuade Brent, who she knew held the most weight.

"I'm not making the call on my own," Brent said. "The situation has become potentially more dangerous. I won't direct anyone to continue on." He paused for several beats. "But I intend on complying with their request."

Almost in unison, Willa, Caleb, and Dillon agreed.

They walked in silence, more hyper-alert than they'd been when they'd arrived. The short walk proved uneventful. The restaurant still had all the tables and barstools but no patrons, dead or alive.

Dillon scanned the room, and her gaze fell on a table with a large ornate centerpiece that looked out of place in the casual atmosphere. She pointed. "I think that's where we're meant to go."

Her pulse quickened. This could be a trap, and the gaudy centerpiece could be the last thing she ever laid eyes on. *Stop.* She couldn't think that way. Sweat dripped down her back; her deodorant wasn't keeping up with her fear.

"What the hell is that?" Caleb asked.

Willa snapped a few pictures as they approached.

Dillon smiled to herself. There were six place settings at the table with a bottle of beer next to each. She put her hand on the closest beer. "They're cold."

"Which means someone's nearby," Brent said, surveying the area. He began to say more when his words caught in his throat as soft chamber music began to play.

"What the hell?" Dillon said.

Willa smiled and continued to snap pictures. "How cool. They're welcoming us."

"Welcoming?" Caleb said. "It's creeping me out."

Dillon pointed to a sign on the table they'd missed. "It says have a seat."

Caleb's eyes widened. "How the hell are we supposed to run if we're sitting? I don't like it."

"I doubt if they'll come out until we sit," Willa said and plopped into a chair.

Dillon shrugged. "She's probably right." She sat next to Willa.

Brent and Caleb exchanged glances before both reluctantly sat. The music abruptly changed to a more upbeat march. Then two men walked into the room. Dillon stared. She wasn't sure what she expected, but this wasn't it. She'd pictured grubby street people who didn't look like they'd bathed in months, but both men were dressed in crisp white shirts and black pants. They resembled maître d's or waiters.

Of course, they weren't homeless anymore. Instead, they were living in two of the most luxurious hotels in Vegas. Likely, they had access to more clothes than they'd ever be able to wear in a lifetime.

Other than their choice of clothing, the two were a study in opposites. The tiny white man looked to be in his sixties, his hair white and his skin leathery. His companion was a mountain of a man with dark brown skin. He limped slightly as he walked. Both had an air of formality to them as they made their way to the table.

Dillon and the others stood as they approached.

The white man smiled, revealing a mouth with several missing teeth. "Welcome," he said. "My name is Skeeter, and this here is Bobby."

Bobby smiled, his teeth all intact and beautiful white against his dark skin. They shook hands and introduced themselves.

Bobby motioned to the chairs. "Please, have a seat."

Now was the moment, Dillon thought. Did she trust these two? For some reason, she did. Had they lulled her with their pomp and circumstance, or was it real? There was something welcoming in their preparations. If they wanted to cause them harm, surely they wouldn't have gone to such elaborate preparations.

Dillon made her decision and sat. The others followed suit.

"We hope you like Coors Lite," Skeeter said. "We talked about serving some of those fancier beers, but sometimes, people don't like those, so we went with the safer bet. We hope that's okay."

Surreal. Were they actually about to have a drink with people who once lived in the storm drains?

"Coors Lite is perfect," Willa said.

At least Willa had manners, Dillon thought as the rest of their party gaped. She needed to stop overthinking and engage in the moment. "I love Coors Lite."

Bobby snatched the beer in front of her and with a quick twist removed the cap. Skeeter joined him, and they'd removed all the caps before anyone spoke.

Skeeter pointed at the glasses. "We put glasses on the table in case you wanted them, but we prefer drinking out of the bottle."

"Bottle is great," Caleb said, holding his in the air. "Here's to meeting new friends."

They clinked bottles before drinking. The moment kept getting stranger.

Brent cleared his throat. "I suppose we should get on with the reason we asked you to meet us."

Skeeter and Bobby nodded.

"We're assuming it was you that left the message on the stairs and the note," Brent said.

Skeeter grinned. "It were." He turned to Willa. "And Picasso, that's what we call him, wants me to tell you that you have a good eye."

Willa smiled. "How so?"

"We reckon you tied his work in the drains to what he did on the stairs by the pictures you were taking."

Willa slapped her hand on the table. "So I was right."

"Yes, ma'am. He said it took a real artist to see it. Especially since he was disappointed in his work on the stairs. Can't expect perfection, being on a time crunch."

"Tell him I thought it was superb," Willa said.

Dillon was running out of words for bizarre and surreal. This would have been an interesting dinner party if the stakes weren't so high.

Brent cleared his throat. "Um, back to our reason for this meeting."

"Oh, yeah," Skeeter said. "Bobby, tell them what you seen."

Bobby sat up straighter in his chair and took a drink of his beer before he spoke. "I'm the head of security here in Vegas. My boys have lookout spots throughout town. We've had a couple groups come through, and we normally just stay out of sight until they leave 'cause we don't want no trouble. Ya understand?"

He paused and gazed around the table. He waited for everyone to nod before he continued. "About a week ago, four big old military vehicles rolled up. We all split but kept our eye on them. They carried a bunch of stuff into the Mayan. We weren't sure what they were up to. Then they started checking out the rooftops around there, too."

"Is that what you meant by snipers?" Brent asked.

"Yes, sir. Looked like they had big firepower. They'd get on top of the hotels around the Mayan. It was like they was doing drills or something. Then they left."

Dillon took note of the puzzled looks on the faces of the others around the table. Would the crew from Washington have done reconnaissance before the others arrived? If they had, why hadn't they mentioned it?

"Then the next day, you all started showing up." Bobby shook his head. "We thought the others would return with y'all, but they didn't."

Obviously, it wasn't the Washington team then unless there were others that were stationed elsewhere. Dillon motioned with her hand before she spoke. "Do you know where the other people went?"

"Well, aren't you a smartie?" Skeeter cackled. "We just might have staked them out. They're camped out at Lake Las Vegas, about twenty-five miles from here. They've got a few people still on the Strip, but they seemed to retreat to the lake after your party. Was the strangest thing."

"Anyway," Bobby said. "Getting back to the story.

You guys started showing up. We reckon there are twenty-one or twenty-two groups.”

“Twenty-three,” Brent said.

“Damn,” Skeeter said. “I lost that bet.”

Bobby shot him a look before continuing. “The night of the party, the snipers flooded the roof. Me and some of the boys were trying to figure out what to do. We thought you’d likely shoot us, or the snipers would if we just walked up on you. But you seemed like such a happy lot, with all the music and dancin’, so we wanted to help.”

Skeeter slapped Bobby’s arm. “Don’t be modest. He had a regular army out. They had a bead on the shooters should they try anything. Those boys were all so cocky they didn’t have a clue we were around, so they walked around here like they owned the place. Not being quiet about their plans.”

“So why did you decide we were okay? That you wanted to help us?” Willa said.

Bobby chuckled. “You guys were a bit full of yourselves, too, but harmless. We had people listening in on you, too.” He pointed toward the floor, “You’d be surprised what you can hear from the grates in the streets.” Then he pointed at the ceiling. “And the air ducts.”

“You determined we were okay and the others weren’t?” Caleb asked.

“That about sums it up,” Skeeter said. “You all seem like decent enough people, at least as a whole. Those others are bad news.”

Dillon studied Skeeter and Bobby. She sensed there was something they weren’t saying. “Do you know who those other people are?”

“Hot damn.” Skeeter slapped the table. “I told

you she was a smartie with her probing questions. We believe we do, but we're not sure if you'll believe us."

"Braxton Babcock Ministries," Dillon said.

Skeeter shot a look at Bobby, then grinned. "Aren't you full of surprises? You know about that scumbag?"

Dillon nodded. "Yeah, we know all about him."

"Bobby here knows them firsthand." Skeeter motioned to Bobby. "Tell 'em."

"When I got let go from the military after I got injured, I was pretty lost. Ended up here on the streets. I was at a low point in my life. Babcock's people had a presence here, trying to reform the homeless. They trolled the streets looking for converts. Well, I thought what the hell, my life can't get any worse, so why not see what they have to offer." Bobby shook his head. "At first, they seemed real nice. Giving me food and clothes and a place to live. Then they started teachin' me the Bible. It weren't anything like the Bible I learned about in Sunday school. There weren't much love in any of their teachings. So I left. They sent the cops after me, telling them I touched one of their women in a wrong way. I had to hide out in the storm drains for months until the cops stopped looking for me."

"Lots of our friends had similar stories. A few joined them. That was over ten years ago. Don't know what ever happened to them," Skeeter said.

"What happened to the snipers?" Caleb asked.

"It were strange. We were in position to take them out," Bobby said. "Then their radios started blowing up, telling them to stand down. We couldn't make out exactly why. Just heard the calls to abort. They packed it all up and headed out."

Dillon narrowed her eyes. This story wasn't making any sense. Why would they have aborted at the last second? "Wait, you're saying they were on the roof and gonna shoot us, but then poof they just stopped?"

Bobby and Skeeter nodded.

"But they wouldn't have gotten us all," Dillon said. "Some of us would have been able to get inside the building. Were they planning on raiding us during the chaos?"

Bobby gazed down at his large hand and picked at his fingernail. "That's where I messed up. We didn't check things out good enough the first time. We missed the explosives."

"What?" Dillon and at least two others at the table said.

"When they were leaving, one of my boys heard the crew ask if they were going to be able to detonate the bombs. So we snuck in, same time we put the note on the table, and had a look around underneath. There's enough explosives sitting under there to take out the Empire State Building."

Dillon's hands went cold as she tried to wrap her thoughts around what they were saying.

Caleb jumped up. "We've got to get everyone out."

"Sit down." Brent grabbed his arm. "We can't go pouring out, or they could light us up. We need to think."

"We've already done that for you." Skeeter grinned. "Bobby and the boys have a plan. Tell 'em."

Bobby smiled, but it didn't reach his eyes. "I want to apologize to you folks for not being on top of things. I should've known about the explosives, so you wouldn't be in so much danger."

Willa put her hand on top of his. It barely covered half. "No, you can't think that way. You're helping us now."

"That's mighty kind of you to say, ma'am."

"About the plan," Brent said. The veins in his neck stood out, but Dillon suspected he was trying to appear patient.

"Oh, yeah, we take you all out through the storm drains. There's one that runs under the Mayan. We can access it through the basement. That's how we got in and out."

"Perfect," Caleb said, the strain on his face lessening.

"There's only one problem," Dillon said. "We have a traitor. At least one, and we don't know who it is."

Willa's mouth dropped open. Unless she was a world-class actress, it wasn't her. "We? Like in the group as a whole or our group?"

"Our group for sure," Dillon said. Willa's face drained of color. "But we believe there might be some from the other groups, too."

"And you don't know who it is?" Willa said.

Dillon shook her head. "We've been trying to figure it out, but we've come up empty. All our leads have gone nowhere."

Willa narrowed her eyes and frowned. At that moment, Dillon was sure she knew she was a suspect. "Do you think the traitor is here in Vegas or back at the estate?"

Dillon let out a deep breath. "Originally, we thought she was with us, but now we're not sure." Dillon didn't want to say the next line, but this was no time to censor. "But now we've ruled out all the people we suspected." *Except for one.* Alaina's face flashed across Dillon's mind. She didn't want to think this way. It would kill Cynthia, but the stakes were higher than ever. "One more thing I need to put on the table. Recently, a group from Amarillo was kidnapped and ended up with us. We brought them back to Vegas, and they have rejoined their clan, except for one. She's decided to stay on with us. She's the one that told us about the mole. She escaped Babcock's compound before joining the group from Amarillo."

"So let me get this straight," Skeeter said. "A strange woman wanders in and tells you about a traitor and admits she once was part of Babcock's crazies?"

Dillon's back stiffened. "It's not like that. She was kidnapped. Beaten and raped, so it's not like she could have set something like that up."

Willa nodded. "It's true. No way was she sent to infiltrate us."

"But she could have been sent into Amarillo," Bobby said.

Dillon's shoulders sagged. That thought had run through her mind multiple times, but she'd never voiced it. Hearing it said out loud unsettled her. "Anything is possible, but I don't want to believe it. She's become a part of our community."

"Yeah, because she's sleeping with Cynthia." Willa crossed her arms over her chest and glared.

Bobby and Skeeter's eyebrows shot up, but they quickly put on poker faces. Bobby tapped his finger on the table and looked skyward. "This creates a bit more of a challenge, but I think we can still make it work. Any other surprises?"

"We just need to be clear," Brent said. "We suspect that there could potentially be more traitors than just the one from their group."

"Do you Washington boys believe you have any?" Skeeter asked. "Military traitors can be some of the worst. Just think of Benedict Arnold."

Brent's mouth dropped open. "What...how..." he stammered.

Skeeter cackled. "Like we told you. It weren't just Babcock's crew we were listening in on."

"I hate to break up this party." Bobby glanced around the table. "It's been a pleasure talking to you all, but if Babcock's guys are watching, they're gonna start getting suspicious since you've been in here so long and left the others in the van."

Damn. These guys didn't miss a thing.

"We need to get you out of here, so we can start evacuating the Mayan," Skeeter said.

Willa's gaze darted around the room. "Won't they be on high alert when we cruise out of here?"

"We got you covered," Skeeter said. "Did you see the boxes up front when you came in?"

Willa nodded.

"Make it look like you came looking for supplies," Bobby said. "They'll think you were looking for food for a feast. They'll be none the wiser."

Dillon sat back in her chair and stared at the two men with admiration. "I have to ask you, did you clean up all the bodies?"

The lines in Skeeter's forehead deepened. "Of course we did. We wanted our place to look nice. Just 'cause we was homeless doesn't mean we liked living that way."

"I'm sorry." Dillon held up her hands. "I didn't mean any offense. I'm just marveling at how good everything looks."

"Apology accepted," Skeeter said.

"One further question, if I may," Brent said.

Skeeter nodded. "Go ahead."

"How many people are here?"

"I wondered when you were planning on asking that," Skeeter smiled. "We have one hundred and thirteen at Caesar's. Used to have a couple more, but they broke the rules, so they're gone."

Dillon cringed. She hoped nobody asked what happened to them.

"And we have one hundred thirty-eight at the Bellagio," Bobby said.

"That's 'cause there was more meth heads," Skeeter countered.

"Better than heroin," Bobby responded. "But we ain't got time to debate that right now."

Dillon wondered if the groups still did drugs. Bobby and Skeeter seemed clean, but she couldn't be certain, and right now, it was the least of their worries.

"There's over one hundred fifty people we need to evacuate," Brent said. "But we have to do it in such a way that if there is a traitor, they can't tip anyone off, or they might decide to blow the building sky high."

"I still don't understand why they didn't before," Caleb said.

"Somehow, I think before this all ends, we'll know the answer," Brent said. "I think it would be best to take each community out together but have someone watching them. Not let them sneak off and contact anyone."

"Good plan," Bobby said. "I'm sure between our team and yours," he nodded in Brent's direction, "we've got enough military training that we can assign a couple to each group. We just need to get them out."

"Do you plan on keeping everyone in the tunnels?" Caleb asked.

Skeeter shook his head. "I'm afraid it would freak some of your people out. We'll take you through the tunnels and come out into one of the hotels."

"We aren't going to tell you which one, so there's no way your traitor will be able to squeal."

Brent puffed out his chest and looked like he was about to protest but instead he deflated and said nothing.

The short drive back was quiet, each lost in their own thoughts. It was decided that the four who'd been on the mission would help lead the groups to safety. They agreed not to tell the others why they were evacuating, to quell the panic. Brent planned on enlisting the security team to help on the mission, which meant Jake would be involved. His involvement put Dillon at ease.

Who their traitor could be still nagged at her. She feared when they found the traitor, she'd unleash her stress in a fit of rage against whomever put them through this torture.

Brent had called ahead, so when they arrived, they were spirited off to a room where the security forces milled around. Dillon's gaze met Jake's, and he smiled. She wanted nothing more than to rush across the room and wrap him in a hug, but she didn't want to seem weak, so she simply returned his smile.

Jake didn't seem to have such reservations. He pushed through the group and enveloped her in a hug. She let her head rest against his chest and held him tight. He'd become like a brother to her, and his steady presence made what they were about to embark on less terrifying.

When they separated, his eyes twinkled, and he said, "God, I needed that."

Dillon grinned. Obviously, Jake was secure in his masculinity. "I did, too, but I wasn't going to let on."

"You butch women are all the same," he said with a smirk. "Your estrogen makes you so macho."

Dillon laughed. God, it felt good. Several of the others around the room shot them looks, but she didn't care. "You're such an idiot," she said.

He gave her a cheesy grin. "I know."

General Morgan and Sylvia walked to the front of the room where a white board had been set up. Each of the twenty-three groups was listed, with the number of attendees present.

General Morgan tapped the board. "As you can see, our biggest issue is the group from Georgia. All twenty-four of them made the trip, and there is reason to suspect that they may have a traitor in their midst. Getting them out will prove more challenging."

"We should leave them until last," Jake said. "Get everyone else out first."

"We agree," General Morgan said. "We also have the issue with John. He has been detained. We have concerns about his mental health. He will have to be evacuated separately and possibly to a different location."

Dillon glanced around the room and silently counted those present. Only ten of the thirteen from Washington were here, likely the other two were guarding John, which weakened their forces. Jake and one member of Caleb's crew were also here. "Will anyone else be helping with the evacuation?" Dillon asked.

General Morgan shook his head. "No. We believe sixteen is plenty. Once we get to the tunnels, Skeeter," his nose crinkled as he said the name, "and Bobby's crew will take over." He pointed at the board again. With only twenty-one groups, I'm not counting Washington and Georgia, we should be able to move rather quickly." He nodded to Caleb and Jake. "The groups from New York and California can also be taken out of the equation for now. Which leaves nineteen groups. We should be able to do it in three rounds."

Bile churned in her stomach. She wanted her loved ones to get out as soon as possible, but it sounded as if the general had other plans.

Chapter Twenty-one

Jake approached Dillon and Willa after the meeting. He was astonished by Willa's transformation. She'd not been one of his favorites with her outrageous hair and even more over-the-top personality. An attention seeker whose outlandish behavior screamed of insecurity.

"Are we ready to do this?" Jake asked.

Dillon nodded. The set of her jaw gave away her nerves, despite wanting to appear calm. At any time, if something went wrong, Babcock could blow the entire building, killing everyone. With the Whitaker Estate crew being one of the last to be evacuated, they were at the most risk.

Willa put her hand on Dillon's arm. "I think you should be the one to round up the Whitaker gang while Jake and I help get the others out. The quicker we do that, the sooner it will be our turn."

"But I should help, too. We're all in this together." Dillon's protest was half-hearted.

"I agree with Willa," Jake said. "You're the most logical. They'll respond best to you and will be less likely to panic or demand answers that we can't give."

"I know you're right, but I feel like I'm shirking my duty."

"Nonsense," Willa said. "We're a team, and getting everyone out, including our people, is what's important."

"Besides, one of them still could be the traitor, so you're certainly not getting the easy assignment," Jake said.

"Okay." Dillon nodded. "I know you don't have time to argue about this. Sylvia just left."

"Yeah, we should be going," Jake said. "We've got New Orleans, Chicago, and Missouri, and they're in the first wave."

Dillon nodded. "Go. And be safe."

Jake hugged Dillon and was surprised when Willa followed suit. They left Dillon standing in the situation room.

Jake and Willa jogged across the lobby. Sylvia had just entered the conference room, and they needed to be there when she made the announcement. They'd decided lying was the only course of action.

When they entered, Skylar waved at him. Her brow furrowed when she noticed Dillon wasn't with them. She motioned him over.

He shook his head but gave her a thumbs-up and mouthed, "Dillon."

Skylar relaxed against the back of her chair, but her face still showed concern.

Jake hated that he couldn't talk to her but knew there was no time. Plus, it was too risky that someone might overhear their plans, including someone who might be sitting at their table. The thought made his stomach churn.

Sylvia did a headcount of her escorts and nodded. She stepped up to the podium near the front of the room and called for everyone's attention. It didn't take long to get it since the room had quieted when they'd all burst onto the scene.

"Thank you," Sylvia said. "We've discovered an unfortunate situation. Some of the items in our rooms have come up missing. We know that we've already suffered vandalism to the stairs and now fear that theft may have also occurred."

A murmur went up from the crowd.

Sylvia held up her hand. "Please," she said in a louder voice. "So far, nothing of value has been taken, no weapons, but we still want to check it out." She pointed to the first group of escorts. "We have volunteers who will accompany you to your suites while you check your items. They'll make note if anything is missing."

A couple of people stood from their tables.

"Please, sit," Sylvia said. "We want to do this in an orderly fashion. We ask for your patience as we take a few groups at a time to do this."

"That's bullshit," someone from the Georgia group called out. "We don't need babysitters. We can report our missing items on our own."

"Of course you can. But with us knowing that someone has been in the hotel, we want to make sure you have escorts who are also members of the security team."

That seemed to appease the man who sat down, but he continued to grumble to the woman next to him. Jake avoided looking at his friends while Sylvia talked. He feared that Skylar and Cynthia would be staring holes in him, not believing a word that Sylvia said.

He hazarded a glance in their direction. Skylar's gaze was fixed on him, but he realized Cynthia wasn't at the table. He did a quick glance around the room but couldn't find her. Maybe she was in the bathroom.

He didn't have time to consider it when Sylvia called his name and asked the groups from Chicago, New Orleans, and Missouri to come to the front of the room.

He met Skylar's skeptical gaze once more before he turned. His heart raced. He hoped he'd see her face again soon.

❧❧❧❧

Skylar turned to Maria as soon as Jake left. "What the fuck was that about?"

Maria shook her head. "Something is seriously wrong. And where the hell is Dillon?"

"Jake gave me a thumbs-up and said her name, so I'm taking it as a positive. But it's weird that she didn't come herself."

Skylar wished Cynthia was here. She had to be careful not to slip up and say something she shouldn't.

"That was about the lamest excuse for pulling people out of here that I've ever heard," Tasha said.

"Definitely," Leslie said. "Maybe they think someone in one of the groups wrote the graffiti, and they took them out to interrogate them."

"Who knows?" Tasha said. "But it's weirding me out."

Skylar's gaze landed on Alaina. She had a faraway look, and Skylar doubted she heard much of what was being said. No doubt, something was bothering her.

"Do you think we should go get Cynthia?" Skylar said. When Alaina didn't react, she said it again.

"Um, I was just thinking the same thing." Alaina motioned to the two imposing men standing by the door. "Somehow, I don't think they'll let us. I've been trying to figure out an excuse that might get me past them."

"Periods usually work," Skylar said.

Alaina gave her a blank stare.

"Tell them you need to change your tampon."

"Oh, god, that's good."

"Maybe give it a few more minutes to see if Dillon shows first."

Alaina nodded.

※ ※ ※ ※

The people Willa and Jake were responsible for gathered around them in the casino area.

Willa waved her hand. "Can I please have your attention? I have an announcement." The group quieted.

"First, we would like to apologize to you. We lied to you in the conference room, there has not been any stolen goods."

Jake marveled at how calm she was addressing the crowd. He'd gladly agreed to let her do it when she'd volunteered. She was a natural.

"There has been a breach in security, and we need to evacuate the building."

A murmur rose, and panic crossed several faces.

"I know that sounds scary, but I assure you that we are taking every measure to ensure everyone's safety." Her voice remained steady, even with the knowledge they were sitting on a ton of explosives.

Jake studied the group. His job was to watch for any signs of trouble. Anyone suspicious who could potentially be tied to Babcock. He also needed to look for anyone who could cause problems, either through belligerence or fear. So far, no one worried him.

"We will be moving toward the kitchen area shortly. Which is where we will exit the building."

"Why don't we just go out to the parking garage where our vehicles are?" someone called.

"As you know, someone broke in and defaced the stairs in the lobby. We believe someone may be watching the parking lot. We need to change our location as quietly as possible."

Sylvia stepped into the room and waved to Jake. They were up. He gave Willa a thumbs-up.

"I would love to answer all your questions and will eventually, but Jake just gave me the sign that it's our turn to evacuate. Please stay close together, we will be going in some darker areas and do not want anyone to get lost."

The murmurs grew louder. Several people voiced their displeasure. It could easily grow if they didn't get moving.

"Let's go," Jake said and took off at a trot. He glanced over his shoulder to ensure the others followed. *Good start.* They all filed in behind him, and Willa took up the rear. He hoped not giving them much time to think would keep them moving along.

They made good time to the kitchen, which was where they would descend into the basement level through a service elevator shaft. Two of the Washington crew were there to greet them.

The female crew member stepped up. "Hello," she said with a bright smile. It would have been welcoming had she been a server, but it was almost off-putting in this situation.

"We're going to help everyone into the basement," the smiling woman said. "You'll need to climb down the ladder that will take you to the top of the elevator. Then another ladder will take you inside the elevator itself, which has been permanently stopped on the basement floor. Any questions?"

"What if we're afraid of heights?" a large man said.

"I assure you, the distance isn't far, and we'll all be here to help you." She smiled again. "We need to keep moving because another group will be along behind you soon."

Jake scampered down the ladder first, followed by the woman with the bright smile. Her companion and Willa stayed in the kitchen. One by one, the first five people climbed down to the first level.

The woman with the smile went down to the next level, and the others followed. As the last person was going down the second ladder, Willa sent the next batch of five. Everyone moved quickly and efficiently, even though the man who was afraid of heights took a little extra coaxing.

Willa was the last to climb through. The next group had already arrived at the kitchen. Jake followed Willa into the basement. When he emerged from the elevator, his gaze darted around the large expanse, looking for signs of the explosives he knew were there.

He shook his head. Now wasn't the time to think about that. His job was to watch for any suspicious activity from the group. Several people scanned their surroundings, but it was human nature with this unexpected flight from the hotel.

The next challenge would occur when they met up with the mole people and moved into the tunnels. Jake expected they might be met with resistance. Maybe not as much, if the other mole people dressed like Skeeter and Bobby. Jake hoped they would. It was best that the group didn't know they were being led by former homeless drug addicts.

Willa pointed at the floor where arrows had been drawn on the surface. Jake smiled to himself. *Skeeter and Bobby were efficient.*

"Follow me," Willa said.

This time, Jake took up the rear. Willa started out at a fast walk that soon turned into a trot. They made it across the large span and rounded a blind corner.

A thin Hispanic man stood by a set of concrete stairs. He was dressed in a polo shirt and a nice pair of blue jeans. He put his finger to his lips.

Where in the hell did they have to go next? Jake wondered. Daylight came from outside. Did that mean they would have to go outside and risk potential exposure? His chest tightened. This didn't seem safe. Would Babcock's people blow the building if they saw them streaming out, trying to escape? Jake wiped his palms on his pants. Dillon and the others were still inside.

Everyone remained quiet as the man continued to hold his finger over his lips. He motioned for everyone to gather around him, and he leaned in. "I'm gonna need you guys to listen carefully," he said in a near whisper. "I'm gonna ask you to follow me up these stairs. There is a tarp draped over some garbage cans. The space isn't very wide, and you won't be able to stand up. But we don't want to cause the tarps to move much, so you're gonna have to stay low on your bellies."

Someone started to protest, but he shook his head violently and scowled. "There might be bad people watching the building, so we can't let them know you're here. Just follow me and you'll all be just fine." The authority in his voice stopped all questioning.

He crouched and climbed the stairs. One by one, their charges followed suit. Jake assumed the rear. He hadn't been able to see what they faced until he got to the top of the stairs. *Brilliant.* In the back of the building, construction had still been underway. The area was littered with scaffolding and other construction materials. Several tarps hung loosely off the scaffolds. Two looked as if they'd fallen to the ground but instead were a cleverly disguised tunnel that led to a large hole in the ground. The grill that once covered the hole was off to the side.

Jake looked up at the tarp that was no more than three feet off the ground in places. Nobody would see them through it unless someone bumped it excessively. He watched the group as they commando crawled through the obstacle. This would be the time when a traitor would try to move the tarp to alert Babcock's crew to their escape.

Jake slid up next to Willa, who'd been the first up after their guide. She'd been smart enough to stop, so she could observe the others. She gave Jake a thumbs-up but didn't speak.

With only about a thirty-foot distance, many had already disappeared into the hole. Jake gestured for Willa to follow the last escapee, and he fell in behind her, pulling himself along with his elbows.

Jake slipped into the hole and landed in a cavernous storm drain. About twenty yards to the right, the tunnel opened to the outside. Two of Skeeter and Bobby's men waved at them but motioned for quiet. The man who'd helped them to this point turned and headed back to the Mayan.

Four from their party had taken steps toward the sunny exit, but Jake doubted that was their escape route, judging by the large flashlights in the two men's hands. Jake jogged around those who were headed for the exit and shook his head. He pointed them toward the tunnel.

One of the women scowled at him but finally turned back. The men with the flashlights motioned for them to put their hands on the shoulders of the person in front of them. After some commotion, they managed to get into a line.

Jake's heart raced. They were almost home free with this group. He longed to let Willa go ahead and hurry back to help Dillon, but he knew he had to see this through to the end. He'd never forgive himself if someone turned out to be a traitor and he'd not been there to watch for it.

His grip tightened on Willa's shoulders. She must have sensed his mood because she patted his hand before she returned it to the person in front of her.

Once lined up, one of the men joined Jake at the back. The line began to move like a slow train. The tunnel was dank and at least fifteen degrees cooler than above. He shivered; he could use a coat. As they moved farther into the tunnel, they walked through shallow puddles of water that splashed against his shoes.

In spots, the walls were covered in graffiti; there were even a few pictures hanging from the sides of the tunnel. The leader warned them to watch out for the debris on the ground. They walked past what appeared to have once been someone's home. A now saturated mattress was laid out on several pallets. Other belongings littered their walk. Clothes. Shoes. Shopping carts. Hypodermic needles. Even a few televisions.

Jake lost all sense of direction and time. They could have been walking for ten minutes or half an hour, he wasn't sure. Finally, the leader stopped and called out into the darkness. A light bobbed in the distance.

"Billy, you ready for us?" their guide called out.

"I'm here, boss," Billy said.

Their guide turned to the group. "It's been our pleasure serving you." He bowed. "You are in the capable hands of Billy here."

Before anyone could respond, he and his companion took off at a run back down the tunnel.

"We're just about there, folks," Billy said. "If you follow me, we'll have you as our guests in the incomparable Caesar's Palace."

※ ※ ※ ※

Dillon dug her fingernails into the palm of her hand. Waiting was excruciating. She'd been making small talk with Caleb but couldn't have repeated what they'd talked about. She doubted he could, either. Sylvia had returned and was briefing the second group.

Skylar and Cynthia would surely have seen through their ruse. She wondered if Jake got the chance to talk to them. Doubtful. Even if he'd had the opportunity, he likely would have avoided it for fear of giving something away.

She took a deep cleansing breath. Her heart raced, and she felt light-headed. Was this what an anxiety attack felt like? After everything they'd been through, somehow this moment made her the most nervous.

Probably because she was separated from her people, surrounded by near strangers. Soon she'd be back with her group, so she needed to hold it together for a little longer. The last thing she wanted was to be in this state when they were reunited. Her job would be to put the others at ease, not send them into a panic.

Sylvia walked past her as she was leaving with the next group. She touched Dillon on the shoulder. "Hang in there. Everything will be okay."

Dillon smiled. *Great.* Obviously, she was a hot mess if Sylvia noticed. She would *not* let the others down. She breathed in deeply. Counted to ten and exhaled. In. Out. In. Out. She could do this.

⁂

Skylar felt like throwing up. Sylvia had just finished speaking, and more of the groups were taken from the room. Still no Dillon. The only people left were the group from New York and the large contingent from Georgia. After Sylvia's first announcement, people had begun to mingle and speculate on what might be happening. Skylar hadn't been in a talkative mood but had done her best to make small talk, even though it had been exhausting.

Alaina hadn't even tried. She sat on the floor against the wall with her chin on her knees. Maria and Skylar took turns checking on her, but it was evident that she preferred not to have any company, so they'd quickly moved along.

When someone tapped on her shoulder, Skylar

turned. She was surprised to see Alaina standing behind her.

"I can't do it anymore," Alaina said. "I'm crawling out of my skin. Something doesn't feel right. I thought Cynthia would be back by now."

Skylar nodded. "It's strange. It's been well over two hours. I thought she'd take a little nap and come back." Skylar's chest tightened. "I would have thought she'd be wanting to know what happened with Dillon."

"I know," Alaina said, her ice blue eyes full of concern. "She ended up with a tension headache since she was so worried. It's not making sense that she wouldn't be crawling out of her skin wanting to know."

"Maybe she's with Dillon." Skylar's hope rose. "Yeah, maybe they ran into each other, and Dillon's filling her in on what's going on."

Alaina's eyes brightened. "I hadn't thought of that. But do you really think Dillon would leave the rest of us waiting and just fill in Cynthia?"

Skylar's shoulders sagged. "It would be doubtful, but who knows what's happening out there? This is making me crazy."

"I'm going to use your tampon trick. I can't stay here any longer."

Dillon walked into the room. Her heart soared when she saw Skylar across the way. Skylar looked in her direction, and her eyes widened.

Much to Dillon's surprise, Skylar ran across the floor. Before Dillon could react, Skylar was in her arms. Dillon hugged her with all her might, and their lips met. Dillon didn't care who was watching, she needed Skylar.

Emotions welled inside of Dillon. Fear. Pain. Relief. Love. If they'd been alone, she would have broken down into tears, but she wouldn't here.

Skylar pulled back enough to look into Dillon's eyes. "Are you okay, baby?"

"I'm better now." Dillon's gaze shifted from Skylar when she realized their friends had encircled them. Reluctantly, she let go of Skylar and stepped back.

"What the hell is going on?" Maria said. "This is crazy."

"We just need to gather our group together." Dillon's gaze shot around the room, and her jaw tightened. "Where are Cynthia and Alaina?"

"Cynthia had a bad headache," Skylar said. "She's been in her room since you left. It's weird, but she never came back. Alaina went looking for her a few minutes ago."

Dillon's heart raced. "You mean nobody has seen her for the last couple of hours?" Dillon ran her hand over the top of her head. "Fuck."

"What's the matter?" Leslie asked.

"It's time..." Dillon started to say.

"Time for what?" Maria asked.

Dillon glanced around and saw Caleb leading the New Yorkers out. The group from Georgia was the only one left. A couple from the group stood apart, talking in whispers and staring at Dillon. They looked away quickly when she met their gaze. Something wasn't right with the pair.

Sylvia. She needed to let her know. "I need to talk to Sylvia." Dillon said. "I'll be right back."

Alaina rushed into the room before Dillon reached Sylvia. "Thank god, you're here. Cynthia's gone!"

Dillon stared. It sounded like Alaina had said Cynthia was gone, but that couldn't be possible.

"Dillon." Alaina shook her by the shoulders. "Did you hear me?"

Skylar arrived at Dillon's side. She took Alaina's hand. "What do you mean, gone?"

Alaina held out a note. "Read it for yourself." And then she burst into tears.

Chapter Twenty-two

Would you sit down already?" Karen said.

CJ had been pacing around the Athens Room, impatiently waiting for Katie and Renee's arrival. She'd pored over her notes one last time but couldn't find anything. She hated they were so far away from Vegas and could do nothing to help. The one assignment she'd been given she'd failed. "Where are they?"

"Probably on their way. They aren't due for another ten minutes. I told you we didn't need to get here so early."

CJ plopped into the chair, causing the entire table to shake.

"Do you feel better after that dramatic landing?"

CJ grinned. "A little."

"I know you're worried sick about Dillon. I am, too, but we have to do what we can."

"Why haven't they called?"

"I'm sure they have a lot going on. They'll call when they can." Karen put her hand on CJ's. "Didn't Dillon say it might be later this afternoon since they'll likely be in meetings afterwards?"

"No news is good news is what she said." CJ sighed. "I think she just said it to get me off her back."

"Whose back are you on?" Katie said from behind them.

CJ jumped up from her seat. Katie and Renee strolled across the room holding hands. Both looked rested and didn't show any of the strain that CJ knew was etched on her own face, but then again, she hadn't told them of Dillon's mission. "You're here."

Renee held up her wrist. "Five minutes early."

Karen was right, she needed to chill out. "Thanks for coming. I've got everything laid out." She pointed to the table.

Katie held up a folder. "Lily gave us a copy of the citizen roster that they've kept at Cynthia's clinic."

"I've got that, too. Haven't been able to find anything, though."

"Remember," Karen said. "We're wanting a new set of eyes, so you need to sit back and keep your mouth zipped. I know it'll be hard."

CJ glared. "But I don't want them to waste their time on trivial things."

Karen gave her an exasperated look. "Remember, a new set of eyes. What you might find trivial could be the key to unlocking this." She put her hand on CJ's arm. "Sit down, and we can get started."

"Who twisted your undies this morning?" Katie said as she sat down.

They'd decided not to tell Katie and Renee about Dillon's mission. It would only create anxiety and make it less likely they could concentrate on the task at hand. "Just anxious to get started and figure out who it might be."

"Is Willa still everyone's prime suspect?" Renee asked.

CJ sighed. "Not according to Dillon. Apparently, she's been extremely valuable in Vegas."

"Even more reason to suspect her in my book,"

Katie said. "When a leopard changes their spots, you have to ask why."

CJ nodded. "Good point."

"My bet is still on Alaina, though. That dark mysterious act is just strange," Katie said.

"I still can't figure out what Cynthia sees in her," CJ said.

"Seriously?" Renee said. "She's gorgeous."

Katie playfully slapped Renee on the arm. "You better check yourself."

Renee gave Katie a sheepish smile. "Sorry. You know I have a thing for beautiful women."

"Good save." Katie gave her a peck on the cheek. "Let's get this party started."

CJ had all the documents laid out with a label next to each. "I'm not sure where you'd like to start."

"I'd like to see the call log," Katie said. "Get an idea of the time frame of when they were made."

CJ pushed a folder toward her. "I've highlighted all the calls that I can't account for."

Katie opened the folder and set it between her and Renee.

CJ started to explain more, but Karen squeezed her knee. She leaned back in her chair. Saying nothing was going to be harder than she thought.

"CJ has been instructed to let you guys look at things and not speak," Karen said. "She will, however, answer any questions you have."

Katie giggled. "This is almost too fun. Wait until I tell Dillon about this."

CJ glared and crossed her arms over her chest. "You guys are so funny." She closed her eyes. "I'll be over here taking a nap if you need me."

As soon as she heard pages rustling, she couldn't

bear not to see what they were examining. Karen winked at her when she opened her eyes. She scowled but winked back.

Katie's finger trailed down the list. "The mystery calls started a couple weeks after the crisis and ended a couple months ago."

"That we know of," CJ said. "At least they stopped using my equipment."

Katie nodded. "Oh, so you think they could still be in contact but have their own means?"

"Anything is possible."

Katie and Renee went back to studying the printout. After nearly five minutes, Katie looked up and put her finger on the page. "Why isn't this one highlighted?"

CJ leaned over. "It's during the day, so I likely made it."

"That would be a feat," Katie said.

CJ narrowed her eyes. "Why?"

Katie pushed her finger onto the page harder. "This is the day we went into LA to pick up supplies. You couldn't have done it."

Fuck. How had she missed it? "Are you sure?"

"It was my mom's birthday," Katie said. "I always remember that date."

Dumbass. How had she been so stupid? She grabbed the page and turned it toward her. There it was in black and white, and she'd overlooked it a hundred times.

Karen put her hand on CJ's back. "That's why we asked for another set of eyes, honey. It's okay."

"No, it's not. My incompetence missed a vital piece of information. Fuck."

"That takes Willa off the hook," Renee said. "She

was a thorn in my side the entire time we were in LA."

"Maria and Tasha are cleared, too," Karen said. "This narrows the field."

CJ pulled out her list of everyone at the estate and began crossing off names. Katie opened her folder with the list she'd gotten from Lily and began to do the same.

Renee looked over Katie's shoulder, and her eyes narrowed. "Almost all our potential candidates have been ruled out."

"Including me," Katie said with a bite to her voice.

CJ remained silent. She knew it would take time to repair the damage with anyone who'd been suggested as a possible suspect. Katie's own actions had been the cause of their suspicions, but CJ didn't think now would be a good time to bring it up.

As they continued to tick off names, Renee said, "Maybe there never was a traitor. Alaina is looking more and more like our culprit."

Katie finished and slowly ran her finger down the page. As her finger neared the bottom of the page, she stopped and gasped.

"What is it?" CJ asked.

"Alaina said the only name she ever heard mentioned was Bertie, right?"

"Yep, but I've looked at everyone's name a million times." She pulled out another sheet from her folder. "I even have most everyone's parents and siblings." She held out the paper.

Katie continued to stare at her list, so Renee took it from CJ. When Renee tried to put it in front of Katie, she waved it off. "No, I don't need that." She finally looked up, her eyes wide. She turned her list around and pushed it toward CJ and Karen. "Look at the name. The fifth from the bottom."

CJ looked down. "Fifth from the bottom is Tad Stein." CJ shook her head. "Tad was in LA, too."

"No, look at mine." Katie pushed the paper farther across the table.

Karen grabbed it and gasped. Her face went white. "No. It can't be. Never. That's just a weird coincidence."

"She didn't go to LA," Renee said.

"What are you guys going on about?" CJ looked up from her page, annoyed by their theatrics. "Tad's the fifth name."

"CJ, look at this one," Karen said. "You don't have a list with the deceased."

CJ shook her head. "I already checked out the three that died during the ambush."

"But you didn't look at the ones that died before that," Karen said.

CJ took the page from Karen. "How the hell could someone who died before become a suspect?"

"For God's sake, CJ. Just look at the damned paper," Katie said.

CJ's gaze shifted to the bottom of the page and moved upward. She stared at the name. Denise Roberta Freeman. CJ spun around toward Karen, and her gaze met Karen's pained eyes. "Leslie?"

Katie put her finger on the printout with the listing of calls. "The calls stopped right around the time she pulled out of her funk."

Karen put her head in her hands. "It can't be. We've been best friends for over a decade. I won't believe it." Karen pushed the papers away. "Fucking thin evidence. Nobody would convict her on this."

"We're not trying to convict anyone, just figure out who's behind it," CJ said and gently put her hand on Karen's back.

"She would never betray us. Me." Karen twisted so CJ's hand was no longer on her back.

Ouch. Karen had never brushed her off before.

"She wasn't herself after Denise died," Katie said. "We have to at least consider it."

"The others could be in danger," Renee said. "I don't believe anyone has ever mentioned Leslie as a candidate. She's likely flying under the radar, being a confidante."

"Listen to you guys." Karen pushed off from the table and stood. "Guilty without a trial."

"Damn it, Karen," Katie said and got to her feet. "You need to think clearly. We don't know what we're dealing with, but if the others are in potential danger, they need to know what we've found. Do you want something to happen to Dillon, Maria, or any of them?"

Karen's lip trembled, and her eyes filled with tears. CJ rose from her chair and slowly approached Karen. "I know this hurts. It might be nothing, but we owe it to the others to at least let Dillon know. Since she trusts Leslie, she might be letting her in on information she shouldn't."

Karen walked into CJ's embrace and buried her head against CJ's chest. She held the woman she loved as her heart broke. "Don't give up hope," CJ said. "There may be another explanation. You're right, it's circumstantial. Don't lose faith."

Karen stepped back and swiped at her eyes. "Let's call Dillon."

Chapter Twenty-three

Dillon rested her head in her hands. She needed to think, but all the activity in the situation room, as they'd named it, made it difficult. They were now in a small conference room in Caesars Palace. Despite her protests, Sylvia and General Morgan insisted they continue their evacuation despite Cynthia's disappearance. They'd been right, but she'd been too overcome by emotion to see it at the time.

The others in the room were giving her a wide berth. The general had called a meeting for two p.m., which was only minutes away. She needed to get it together before it started. The evacuation through the tunnels had been a blur. She remembered crawling under the tarps and the debris scattered everywhere in the tunnels, but her mind had been elsewhere.

After the evacuation, they'd detained the couple from Georgia, a man from Denver, and two from Florida on suspicion that they might be operatives working against the group. No headway was made in uncovering the traitor from Whitaker Estate.

Could it be Alaina? Was the note and Cynthia's kidnapping another ruse to throw them off the trail? If she was the traitor, she deserved an Oscar. After her meltdown, she'd been nearly comatose, not saying anything to anyone. Since the crisis began, Dillon had witnessed the reactions of many women who were overcome by the situation, but Alaina's response still surprised Dillon. The woman who seemed to have ice water running through her veins had fallen apart. After everything Alaina had already survived, Dillon couldn't understand what had spiraled her to this level.

Her chest tightened. Skylar had been tasked with staying with Alaina. What if Alaina was the traitor? Wouldn't that put Skylar in jeopardy?

Dillon took a deep breath. She was overreacting. There were numerous people with Skylar, she'd be okay. Before they'd parted, Dillon had made Skylar promise that no matter what Alaina said, Skylar would not go anywhere alone with Alaina nor would she leave the safety of the group.

General Morgan pushed through the door with Sylvia and Brent on his heels. He glanced around the room. "I believe we're all here, so let's get started."

Jake sat on one side of Dillon and Sylvia the other. Caleb, General Morgan, Brent, Skeeter, Bobby, and two others from Washington rounded out the group.

"We have a situation." General Morgan nodded toward Dillon. "You have lost one of your people."

Dillon nodded but didn't trust her voice to speak.

"May we see the note again?" he asked.

Dillon pushed the note toward him. It was now wrinkled from her clutching it so tightly.

We have your friend. If you want to see her alive, you will meet us for a prisoner exchange behind the Tropicana at 4 p.m.

One member of your team should bring the

woman you know as Alaina Renato to that location where we will exchange prisoners. Your friend's life depends on it.

"What do you make of this, Dillon?" General Morgan asked.

Dillon shook her head. "I don't know. My head is a jumbled mess. This doesn't make any sense. If Alaina is the traitor, why would they go to such an elaborate ruse to get her out? Couldn't she have snuck out in the middle of the night to return to them? Why take Cynthia?"

Jake blew out a breath. "That's what's driving me crazy. We're missing a piece somewhere. Why do they want Alaina? What's their endgame?"

"And why did they call off the strike? We were sitting ducks outside at the party. They could have wiped a lot of us out," Brent said.

"We've been talkin' bout that," Skeeter said. "Maybe they didn't know Alaina was with you, but someone spotted her that night. If she ran away like she said, they might want her back."

Dillon perked up. He had a point. "So maybe she's not the traitor?"

"Hard to say for sure," Bobby said. "But I agree with Jake, there's a piece of this puzzle we still don't have, but I'd bet Alaina has it."

Sylvia nodded. "I believe you're right, but somehow I don't think she's going to tell us anything." She turned to Dillon. "And what about your traitor? Still nothing?"

Dillon shook her head. "Our friends back home have been trying to figure it out, with no luck. Who knows, it could have been someone that died in the raid, and we've been driving ourselves crazy for nothing. Chasing a ghost. This is so fucked up. I just want to get Cynthia back." Dillon fought back tears. She wouldn't cry here. "If they hurt her, I will hunt down every one of those sons of bitches."

Jake put his hand on Dillon's arm. "I know you're upset, but we need you. We need you to keep your calm."

Dillon inhaled. Jake was right. The best way to help Cynthia was to think clearly, which meant keeping her emotions in check. "You're right."

"Speculating has gotten us nowhere," Brent said. "We need to focus on the four o'clock meeting."

"Agreed," General Morgan said. "A decision needs to be made."

Dillon swallowed bile that rose into her mouth. "We can't do it." The words cut her like a knife. They would be words she suspected would haunt her the rest of her life.

Jake looked at her with a stunned expression. "Can't do what?"

"We can't take Alaina to them." Dillon's gaze fell to the table. She couldn't make eye contact with anyone in the room.

"Of course, Dillon is right," General Morgan said. "We don't negotiate with terrorists."

"And Cynthia would never forgive me," Dillon said. She finally looked up. "If you traded Skylar, Cynthia, or anyone I loved for me, I'd hate you all for the rest of my life. I know what Cynthia would want us to do." Dillon put her hand over her face. "I barely know Alaina, and I so badly want to say do it. But I can't. I could never look Cynthia in the eye again." A lump caught in her throat. "And I may never get that opportunity, but I can't do the wrong thing."

The speech took all Dillon's energy. She slumped against the back of her chair and stared at the table in front of her. The conversation went on around her.

After several minutes of discussion, General Morgan cleared his throat. "Yesterday, we contacted Washington. We have flown two fighter planes and a cargo carrier to Utah. There are seventy-five troops standing by. We did not want to alert Babcock's people by flying into Nellis Air Force Base, but we have troops in place there now. We are more than ready to take out any threat that may exist."

Dillon sat up straighter in her chair. "You've had this capability all along?"

General Morgan nodded.

"Why the hell didn't we know sooner?" Dillon's voice raised.

"We came here to form a government, not flex our military strength." General Morgan looked her directly in the eye. "You yourself have said that in every movie the military is always the bad guys. We didn't want to exert undue influence on the group. I would think you'd understand the wisdom of that."

"Holy hell," Caleb said, finally joining the conversation. "This is a game changer. It means we have some force to push back against Babcock."

"Exactly," Sylvia said.

"Why haven't you just taken them out already?" Jake asked.

General Morgan smiled. "That would be what they did in the movies, but we had to be sure that Babcock's people were indeed a threat. Just because we don't like his politics or religion is no reason to take them out, as you so eloquently put it."

"And now?" Jake said.

"And now, the evidence is mounting against them," General Morgan said. "We were in place to storm their camp after meeting with Skeeter and Bobby. But the taking of your friend has forced us to change tactics."

"You can't go in guns blazing, or Cynthia surely dies," Dillon said. "What are her odds?"

Once again, General Morgan met her gaze. "Honestly, not the best, but we want to give her every chance before we have to move in."

Dillon rubbed her head and felt that she might vomit. Could she voice what was on her mind? "This might sound crass," she put her hand against her chest, "but this puts me at some peace. As terrible as it is, I can take the thought of Cynthia dying. What has haunted me since this meeting started was the thought of her living."

Jake did a double take and looked at her as if she were insane.

Sylvia put her hand on top of Dillon's. "There are things much worse than dying. I know. I was captured and held for two months in Iraq."

Dillon squeezed her hand. "I'm so sorry."

"We won't let that happen to your friend," Sylvia said with conviction.

Dillon's heart ached. After the raid on Whitaker Estate, she wondered if she'd ever be the same, but now she was certain she wouldn't.

"But that doesn't mean we give up," Brent said. "We can still make a counteroffer to Babcock to get Cynthia back."

"You're right." Dillon settled her gaze on the general. "Is your team working on a plan to extract her?"

"That might be in the works," General Morgan said with a half-smile. "But we need to know as much about Cynthia as we can."

As they asked Dillon questions, a loud commotion came from outside the door. One of the sentries peeked his head inside. "Sir, we have a woman here insisting she speak to Dillon."

"We are in the middle of a briefing," General Morgan said with a wave of his hand.

A frantic voice drifted in from the hallway, calling Dillon's name. *Alaina.*

"General Morgan, I believe that's Alaina. I think we should hear what she has to say," Dillon said.

He glanced at his watch. "We still have time. Very well, let her in."

The man held her arm firmly as he guided her into the room. His grip would surely leave bruises, but Alaina didn't appear to notice. Her gaze darted around the room at all the faces.

Dillon's heart went out to her. She looked a mess, her normally cool demeanor replaced by a frantic unfocused aura.

"What can we do for you?" General Morgan said to her.

Alaina shook her head, and her gaze bounced from person to person. "No. I just want to speak to Dillon."

"I'm afraid that isn't possible," General Morgan said. "Please state your business."

Alaina's attention fell on Dillon, and their gazes locked. Dillon saw desperation and pain in the ice blue of her eyes. "Please, Dillon. What I have to say I can't with all these people. I love Cynthia. You have to know that."

Dillon felt every word she said. Either she was a great actress, or every ounce of pain was real. Dillon stood. "General, I would like to speak to Alaina alone."

He met her gaze. "Very well. I can't stop you, but remember time is of the essence."

"Skeeter," Dillon said. "Is there another room we could use?"

"Certainly." He leapt to his feet. "Right through this door is an office. You're welcome to use it."

Alaina and Dillon made their way to the next room in silence. It wasn't until they sat in chairs across from each other and heard Skeeter's footsteps walking away that Dillon finally spoke. "What did you want to talk to me about?"

"I know you probably blame me. I blame me, but it isn't what you think," Alaina said.

Dillon stiffened, wondering where Alaina was going with this. "What is it you believe I'm thinking?"

"The same thing I would be. That I'm the traitor. But I'm not." Alaina took a deep breath. "You have to convince them to trade me."

Dillon hoped surprise didn't show on her face. She wasn't sure what she expected Alaina to say, but this wasn't it. Dillon shook her head. "You know how much I love Cynthia, but we can't do that."

"I'm begging you. Please."

"We'd be leading you to the slaughter. We can't in good faith do that."

"Leaving Cynthia there is the same thing. Just let me do this." Alaina pounded her fist on the table. "It's my life. I should get the say. Not you or the military. Or anyone else."

"What about Cynthia?"

Alaina's face dropped, and tears streaked down her cheeks. She put her hand against her chest and rubbed. "Damn it, Dillon. That was a low blow."

"No, it's just the truth. What would Cynthia tell me to do?"

Alaina rose to her feet and towered over Dillon. "Please. You have to let me."

Dillon strained her neck to look up at Alaina, who continued to invade her space. "Are you trying to intimidate me?"

"No." Alaina dropped to her knees and let her head fall into Dillon's lap. Her body shook as she was wracked by sobs.

Dillon stared. She didn't know what to do. This wasn't the reaction she'd expected from the dark mysterious woman. Dillon put her hand gently on Alaina's head and ran her hand the length of her hair. Alaina's pain seemed to come from her core. Dillon didn't speak but instead rubbed Alaina's back as she cried.

Eventually, Alaina rose to her feet and returned to her chair. While still beautiful, she was a shell of the woman she'd first laid eyes on during the raid. Despite the situation, there had been a fire burning while the other women had the vacant stare of defeat. Something had broken Alaina, and Dillon still wasn't sure what. She didn't strike Dillon as a hopeless romantic. As much as Dillon loved Cynthia and the situation ripped her heart out, Alaina's complete meltdown shocked Dillon. It seemed so out of place. Was it guilt? Had she been the traitor all along and was now consumed by guilt? There was still something she was missing.

Dillon flinched at the loud pounding on the

door. What the hell was going on? Her nerves were already frayed, now someone else was demanding something. "Who is it?" Dillon said, making sure the irritation could be heard in her voice.

The door opened a crack, and Sylvia peeked her head in. "There's someone here that's demanding to talk to you immediately. Oh, and your sat phone keeps going off."

Dillon shook her head. Everyone needed to get in line. "Who wants to see me?"

"She says her name is Leslie," Sylvia said.

Leslie? What the hell would she want at a time like this?

"Says it's an emergency," Sylvia said.

Dillon's mind jumped to Skylar. No, that made no sense. Maybe she had insight into what happened to Cynthia.

Dillon stood. She put her hand on Alaina's shoulder. "I'll be back."

Alaina looked up at her with panic in her eyes.

Dillon wiped the hair away from Alaina's face that had stuck in the tears on her cheeks. "I promise."

Alaina nodded.

Dillon turned to Sylvia. "I'll talk to Leslie in the hallway. Please bring her and tell Jake to answer the sat phone." As Sylvia turned away, Dillon said, "And could you sit with Alaina? I'm worried about her."

"Sure."

Dillon smiled when Sylvia brought Leslie into the empty hallway. "What's wrong? You look like you've been hit by a truck." She hadn't looked that bad since she'd found Denise dead.

Leslie didn't speak until Sylvia slid into the office with Alaina. "Oh, Dillon, I've fucked everything up. I'm so sorry." Tears streamed down her face.

The last hour, Dillon had seen more tears than she'd seen in a month. Tensions were boiling over. Dillon took a step toward Leslie and touched her arm.

Leslie flinched and pulled back.

Whoa. That was an odd reaction. Dillon took two steps back to give Leslie space. "Talk to me, Leslie. I know you're aware that we have a situation here, and we're running out of time. I have to get back to my meeting." She wondered why Maria or Skylar couldn't have dealt with whatever was bothering Leslie. "Do the others know you're here?"

Leslie shook her head. "I came straight here as soon as I figured it out."

"Figured what out?" Dillon searched her mind but came up blank. Nothing was making any sense right now.

"I'm the traitor!" Leslie blurted out.

Dillon blinked. "What?"

"I'm the—" Leslie started.

Jake sprinted around the corner and stopped abruptly when he saw the two talking. "Um, Dillon is here talking with Leslie," he whispered into the phone, but it was still loud enough for her to hear.

The weirdness continued. "Could someone tell me what the hell is going on?" Dillon said.

Jake locked his gaze on Leslie as he came closer, and his hand slid toward his waistband.

"You know," Leslie said to him.

Jake nodded and held up the phone. "Katie figured it out."

Dillon's jaw dropped. "You're the traitor?" Dillon said to Leslie.

"That's what I was trying to tell you."

The air went out of Dillon as if she'd been punched in the gut. She'd said she'd pummel whoever the traitor was, but now she just wanted to vomit. "But why?"

Tears streamed down Leslie's cheeks. "I was so lost when Denise died. Everyone hid from me, not knowing how to manage their own grief, let alone mine." Leslie waved her hand. "Not that it's any excuse."

"But you betrayed us all," Dillon said, her voice full of hurt not anger.

"That's not what I meant to do." Leslie brushed the tears from her cheek. "One night, I couldn't sleep and was walking through the atrium when the voice called out over the computer. I answered. And we started talking about God and why he let so many people die. I was looking for answers. Denise was the best. Why her?"

Dillon's heart broke as she watched her friend struggle. "But you kept talking to them. Why?"

"They told me what I wanted to hear. Denise was watching me from heaven, and if I followed the right path, we would be reunited." Leslie met Dillon's gaze. "I'm so embarrassed now. I was so naive."

"You were in pain." Dillon took a step toward Leslie. Jake still stood with the phone, not saying anything. "When did you stop talking to them?"

"A couple months ago. I finally came to my senses and realized I was being played, and their version of religion was sick. I tried to back out, but they kept pushing me. Finally, one day, I said enough, and that was it."

"You haven't been in contact with them recently?"

"Oh, god, no. I prayed that nothing would

happen. I was so scared. I thought a million times that I should tell you, but then when each day passed, I started to get hopeful that they'd forgotten about me. About us. And then when we were attacked, I was sure it was Babcock, and I'd caused it."

"That was a lot to carry around. You could have told us."

"The time never felt right." Leslie averted her gaze. "Or I was just a coward. And then everyone was grieving, so the time wasn't right. That's why I wanted to come on this trip. I didn't trust that Babcock wouldn't do something. Stupid I know, but I thought if something came up, if they showed up, maybe I could talk to them since I knew at least one of them. God, I'm delusional! They're monsters. And now they've taken Cynthia, and it's all my fault."

Dillon shook her head. "No. Some things are your fault, but taking Cynthia isn't one of them. It had nothing to do with you. They're after Alaina."

"Alaina?" Leslie's eyes widened. "Why?"

"She ended up in Amarillo after she escaped the compound. They want her back. At least that's what the note said. I was in talking to her when you showed up." Dillon's eyes narrowed. "How did you know we were looking for the traitor?"

"Maria told me," Leslie said. "We were talking about Cynthia, and it slipped out. I knew I had to come tell you."

"Thank you for that." Dillon glanced at her watch. "We have until four p.m., and we're running out of time. I need to get back to Alaina. But this helps. We've wondered all along if she was playing us, but now I know she isn't."

"Can you ever forgive me?" Leslie said.

"I forgive you." Dillon closed the gap between them and wrapped Leslie in a hug. "While I'm not happy that it happened, I do understand. We're living through something none of us could ever have imagined. We've all done things we wish we wouldn't have."

"But this was big," Leslie said through her tears. "And I'm so sorry."

"It's okay. We'll sort it out, but I need to get back to Alaina."

Leslie squeezed Dillon tight and then stepped back. "Thank you. Go do what you need to do. Bring Cynthia back safely."

Dillon didn't have the heart to tell her what a long shot it was. She smiled and turned away.

She didn't have much time to think as she walked back to Alaina. How did it change things now that she knew Alaina wasn't the traitor? Everything Alaina had told them was true, although things still didn't add up. Why had they called off the strike? Surely, if they somehow discovered Alaina was here, they'd be happy to kill her with the rest of them. Why this elaborate stunt to get her back? Did they want her alive to punish her for leaving?

When Dillon opened the door, Sylvia was standing next to it. It didn't look as if there was any conversation happening between the two. Alaina's knees were pulled against her chest, and her head rested on them.

Sylvia smiled and slipped out the door.

Dillon filled Alaina in on her conversation with Leslie.

After she finished, Alaina said, "So now you believe I'm not scamming you."

"Yes," Dillon said, deciding not to lie and pretend that she'd never suspected her.

"Does that change anything?"

Perceptive. The calm cool version of Alaina had returned. "I'm not sure. Tell me why it should."

"Because you know I'm not playing you. That I don't have some ulterior motive for wanting to be exchanged."

"Cynthia would never forgive me if we gave you up." Dillon paused. "She's falling for you."

Pain flashed in Alaina's eyes. "I've already fallen for her, and I can't leave her there with those demons. You don't understand how evil they are."

"I've seen enough about them on TV and read enough to know their methods are unorthodox."

Alaina snorted. "Unorthodox. That's an interesting word to describe them. Unless you've been there, you will never understand. I can't be the reason Cynthia has to suffer at their hands."

Dillon fought against herself. She couldn't go along with Alaina's plans, even though she wanted to give in. They argued for several more minutes, but with every argument Alaina threw out, Dillon held her ground.

"You don't believe what monsters they are?" Alaina stood and started unbuttoning her shirt.

Dillon stared. "What are you doing?"

Alaina didn't speak but kept undoing her buttons. When she got to the bottom, she pulled off her shirt.

What the hell? Dillon's gaze darted around the room, looking for something to cover Alaina with. Had she lost her mind? Did she think throwing herself at Dillon sexually would help her get her way? Dillon stood frozen in horror.

Alaina turned her back to Dillon.

Dillon gasped. "Oh, my god. Did they do that to you?" Dillon took a step forward. Her stomach roiled, but she couldn't look away. Cords of raised scars crisscrossed Alaina's back. Despite herself, Dillon reached out and touched one of the angry red bumps. *Monsters.*

Alaina stood with her back to Dillon. Her shoulders shook, but she said nothing.

Dillon needed to say something but what? What would Cynthia want her to do? Dillon took another step forward and wrapped her arms around Alaina from behind. Although Alaina was shirtless, there was nothing sexual about the gesture.

Alaina must have known it, as well, because she melted against Dillon.

Still in that position, Alaina said, "Do you understand now why I can't leave Cynthia there?"

"Why did they do this to you?" Dillon choked down the bile that rose in her throat.

"Let's just say it's the next step when conversion therapy doesn't work."

"Oh, god." Dillon held Alaina tighter. "I can't send you back to this."

"They'll kill Cynthia," Alaina said, her voice full of pain. "But they'll make her suffer first. And they'll do it up big to make sure I know."

"But they'll do the same to you." Dillon's arms remained around Alaina.

"I've lived through it before." Alaina put her hands on Dillon's forearms and squeezed. "That's why I showed you. I learned how to go to a place in my mind that they can't find me. Cynthia doesn't have that skill.”

“Does Cynthia know about any of this?”

Alaina shook her head.

“But they’ll kill you.”

“No, they won’t,” Alaina said barely over a whisper.

“Of course they will.” Dillon released Alaina and backed up so she could see her eyes. Alaina pulled her shirt back on and began buttoning it. “They’ll use you as an example for anyone else that might think of escaping.”

“They won’t kill me,” Alaina said with conviction.

“Goddamn it, you know they will.”

“If I guarantee they won’t, will you let me go?”

“You’d say anything to get me to agree, but I can’t.”

Alaina took a step toward Dillon and stood toe to toe with her. “It’s my choice. And once and for all, they will *not* kill me.”

“You don’t know that.”

“I do.” Alaina looked to the floor. “The son of a bitch is my father.”

“Babcock?”

“Yes!”

Chapter Twenty-four

Skylar followed Sylvia down the hall, nearly jogging to keep up. She'd been sitting with the others when Sylvia burst in, demanding that Skylar come with her immediately. She still hadn't told her the reason, other than it was at Dillon's request.

This was strange. Skylar had not been allowed to be in any other meeting, so why now? As soon as she entered the room, her focus went to Dillon. She hoped the shock she felt didn't show on her face. Dillon's hair was disheveled, despite it being short. Her bloodshot eyes were vacant, and her normally confident posture held defeat.

What the hell was going on? Skylar wanted to rush to her, but she held back, instead taking in the rest of the room. Even stranger, Alaina sat next to Dillon holding her hand. She looked only slightly better than Dillon.

She met Jake's gaze, and he simply shook his head.

The two men she met earlier, Skeeter and Bobby, sat off in one corner talking quietly, and a couple of men from Washington rounded out the group.

Dillon finally noticed she'd entered and sprang to her feet. Skylar was thankful that a little life returned to Dillon's eyes.

"What's going on?" Skylar asked, no longer willing to wait for an explanation.

Dillon took her hand. "We've come up with a plan, and I needed for you to hear it."

An uneasy feeling washed over her. When she glanced around the table, no one would meet her gaze. She let Dillon lead her to a chair. When they sat, Dillon continued to hold her hand, but with her other took Alaina's again.

"General," Dillon said. "Could you run through it?"

Skylar's mouth fell open as she listened to him speak. Once he finished, she turned to Dillon and Alaina. "I don't get any say in this?"

Dillon rubbed her chest, her eyes full of sadness. "Not this time, babe. I'm sorry."

"How am I supposed to respond to that, Dillon?" Skylar let go of Dillon's hand and crossed her arms over her chest.

Dillon hung her head. "What else would you want me to do?"

General Morgan motioned to the others, and they quietly got up and left the room. Skylar was alone with Dillon and Alaina. "I don't know." Skylar let her head drop to her chest. "Is it the only way?"

Dillon nodded.

"But can't a soldier do it?"

Dillon shook her head. "They found another note. It has to be someone from our group."

"How would they know one of the soldiers wasn't ours?"

"It could be a bluff, but I'm not taking that chance with Cynthia's life."

Skylar turned to Alaina. "What will they do to you? It can't be safe."

Alaina met Skylar's gaze. "No. It won't be, but I'll survive."

As if her mind wasn't already blown, they told her that Braxton Babcock was Alaina's father. She simply stared, unable to come up with any words.

"Say something," Dillon said.

"You two might be the bravest or the stupidest people I've ever met. I'm not sure which." Tears rolled down Skylar's face. She wasn't dumb. The odds of Dillon returning safely weren't good. So many things could go wrong with someone as underhanded as Babcock.

She'd fallen hard for Dillon and wanted to spend a lifetime with her. The thought of not getting that chance immobilized her. What if she screamed or cried or refused to let Dillon do it? The thoughts overwhelmed her, and she put her head on the table and cried.

Dillon's strong arms wrapped around her while she sobbed. Arms that she'd come to feel so safe in. Her heart clenched. This could be the last time she felt them.

No! She wouldn't think this way. Dillon and Cynthia would both come home safely. Their plan would work. She'd not survived on the street all those years by being a downer. She'd always known something better would come out of her life, and it had. This time, it was no different. Dillon had the best chance of surviving if she were in a better head space, and worrying about Skylar wouldn't get her there.

Skylar lifted her head from the table and said, "I'm done now."

Dillon's mouth dropped open, and then her shoulders sagged. "With me?"

"No!" Skylar grabbed Dillon's hand. "Never with you. I'm done feeling sorry for myself and thinking the worst." She grabbed Dillon by the front of her shirt and pulled her closer. When they were only a couple inches apart, Skylar said, "You're going to do this and come back to me."

Dillon remained slack-jawed.

"Do you hear me?" Skylar said louder. "I will not lose you. I understand you have to do this, but failure is not an option. You're going to get that confidence back, and you're going to march out there and kick some bad guy ass." She shook Dillon by the collar. "Are you listening to me?"

Life slowly returned to Dillon's eyes, and a slight smile parted her lips. "I'm listening."

"Good." Skylar turned to Alaina. "You're all going to come through this. You will not let that psychopath defeat you! It's about time for good to triumph over evil."

Alaina nodded, then turned to Dillon. "We should have had her in here all along." Alaina put her hand over her heart. "This is the first time all day that I believe all's not lost."

"And I'm going with you," Skylar said.

Dillon sat up straighter. "You can't. It can only be the two of us."

"I know that. But the general will have a truck around the corner waiting to bring you back here. And I'm going, so I'll be there as soon as they pick you up."

"I'm sure he'll say no," Dillon said.

Skylar pointed at Dillon and then Alaina. "You two are the stars of the show, so stop letting him call the shots. Take charge."

A brief look passed between Dillon and Alaina. "You have to promise one thing," Dillon said.

"What is it?"

"Promise that you'll stay in the vehicle. I can't focus on what I need to do if I'm worried about you."

"I promise."

Dillon looked at her watch. "Ten minutes until show time."

"What about the others?" Skylar asked. "Are you going to tell them?"

"No, I can't handle any more emotional scenes." Dillon smiled. "Besides, you've already made it clear that nothing bad is going to happen."

"Exactly," Skylar said.

Chapter Twenty-five

The drive to the drop point was quiet. General Morgan had been furious at Dillon, but she didn't care. Having Skylar with gave her the confidence she needed to pull this off. It wasn't a long drive. It had taken them much longer to make their way back through the tunnels into the Mayan.

They couldn't risk being spotted coming out of Caesar's Palace when Babcock's people thought they were still sitting on tons of explosives at the Mayan.

As instructed, they parked in front of the MGM Grand. Alaina and Dillon would walk from there to the back of the Tropicana. Dillon was thankful that Skylar wouldn't be able to see anything from the truck.

Dillon gave Skylar a quick hug and kiss as she did every time she left. It wasn't lost on Dillon the symbolic nature of Skylar's reaction. It conveyed that this wasn't out of the ordinary, and Dillon wasn't walking into possible death.

Alaina took Dillon's hand as they walked. Another fuck you to her father, but Dillon didn't mind. She enjoyed the comfort of Alaina's touch. Her goal was to bring both Alaina and Cynthia home safely. No doubt a tall order, but Skylar had her believing it was possible.

Even though they wore hoodies, Dillon shivered. It was the coldest the desert ever felt, despite the seventy-degree temperature. She fought the urge to pull up her hood, knowing Babcock's people would take offense to it.

Dillon surveyed the area as they walked. Likely, eyes were on them already. She forced herself to stare straight ahead and not look up. It would do them no good to alert Babcock's people to her suspicions.

Dillon made eye contact with Alaina, and they picked up their pace. For their plan to work, they needed to get to the designated location before anyone stopped them. Babcock's people would expect them to stick close to the building, but that wasn't where they wanted to be.

They'd almost made it to their destination when Dillon heard the roar of an engine. "Keep moving," Dillon said to Alaina under her breath. "We just need to get another twenty yards or so."

They moved faster. Alaina squeezed Dillon's hand tighter. When they arrived at the spot next to the guardrail, Dillon breathed a sigh of relief. The roar of the engine became louder. "Are you sure he won't come himself?" Dillon asked.

"He's too much of a coward. It'll be his henchmen," Alaina said. "It'll be Brian. The leery son of a bitch."

"Are you ready to turn around?" Dillon asked. "They'll be upon us any second, and I'd like to see what we're dealing with."

"Let's do it."

Still holding hands, they turned. A van and a large pickup came their way. *Good.* It could have been worse. They could have had more manpower. Dillon assumed Cynthia was in the van.

The pickup continued driving toward them

without slowing. Were they simply going to run them over? Alaina tightened her grip. "Don't show fear. It's all for intimidation."

The truck skidded to a stop a few feet from them, kicking up rocks. A large stone shot up from the tires and hit Dillon in the shin. She flinched but hid any other signs of pain. The driver smirked as he threw the truck in reverse and backed up several yards. By the look on his face, he was debating whether to take another run at them. He killed the engine.

The large man jumped out of the truck. "Fucking queers. Let go of her hand." He pointed at Dillon.

"Hello, Brian," Alaina said in a calm voice. She continued to hold Dillon's hand.

He sneered. "Alaina. Why the fuck did you come all the way back here?"

Dillon needed to sell it. She put on her best puzzled look. "You guys said you'd kill everyone if we did anything stupid." She pointed to the building. "Figured you'd think we might have people hiding inside if we went too close, and we didn't want any trouble."

Brian grunted.

"I want to see Cynthia before we make the exchange," Alaina said.

"You do, do you?" Brian laughed. "Doesn't look like you're in any position to be making demands."

Alaina stared but didn't speak.

Brian turned to his passenger. "Stan, get the bitch."

Stan tumbled out of the truck. He was short but stocky. His crooked nose and prominent scars told her that he'd been in his share of fights. Neither he nor Brian would be someone she'd want to fight hand to hand; hopefully, they wouldn't have to. He trudged to the van, which gave Dillon the opportunity to examine it without causing suspicion.

The driver of the van stepped out. He didn't look much older than eighteen. His gaze flitted around the area, not focusing on any point, his fear evident.

The van driver met Stan at the back of the van. *Three men.* Unless there were others inside the van, which she doubted, the numbers were in their favor. Likely, there were more on the roof, but the distance should render them inconsequential. Hope rose in her. Brian's attempt at intimidation by driving the truck so close played into their hands. It gave them additional cover from the snipers, which increased their odds.

The van driver opened the back door, but she and Alaina were in no position to see inside. Without warning, Stan reached into the van and yanked something from inside. A figure draped in a hood stumbled and fell to the ground, landing hard on her side.

Dillon's jaw clenched, but she fought not to show any other reaction. Beside her, Alaina bit her lip. Dillon rubbed her thumb along the back of Alaina's hand, hoping to calm her.

Stan yanked off the hood, pulling Cynthia's hair as he did. She grimaced and let out a small squeak of pain. He tossed the hood at the driver before he bent and wrenched Cynthia to her feet. With her hands tied behind her back, she was helpless against his rough treatment. He goaded her to walk, and as she did, he shoved her from behind. She nearly lost her balance twice before he yanked her arms back to stop her.

Dillon's chest ached. She bit the inside of her

cheek. *Stay calm. Stay calm.*

Cynthia stared at the ground. Dillon suspected she'd been instructed how to conduct herself. Dillon wanted nothing more than to look into Cynthia's eyes. She pushed the thought out of her head. She needed to focus.

Stan slammed her against the front of the truck. "Want to say hi to your friends?" He sneered.

It must have been her cue. Cynthia looked up. Her face was bruised and one eye swollen shut.

Assholes. Alaina squeezed Dillon's hand. Dillon locked her gaze on Cynthia. Despite the bruises, she could still see the fire and fight in Cynthia's eyes. *Good.*

First, Cynthia made eye contact with Alaina. The look of love was undeniable. When she gazed at Dillon, the look wasn't so kind. She was angry. Of course she would be, she suspected that Dillon was turning Alaina over to Babcock. It gave Dillon even more incentive for their plan to work. She didn't want the last look they ever exchanged to be one full of such wrath.

"You've seen her. She's all yours." Brian snickered. "I guess she's not really yours because you'll be coming with us, Alaina."

Alaina let go of Dillon's hand and in one quick move reached into the back of her waistband and pulled out a small handgun.

What the hell? This wasn't part of their plan. Dillon looked into Alaina's eyes.

"Sorry, Dillon. It has to be this way."

Dillon's heart sank. She'd been a plant all along, but why was she doing this? It made no sense. Dillon shook her head. "I trusted you."

Then Alaina did something more unexpected. She put the gun to her own temple. "You still can. But don't you see? Look at her." She motioned toward Cynthia. "Do you really think they were going to let her live? My father wants me to see her die. My penance."

"Father. What the—" Cynthia said, but an elbow to the ribs stopped her cold. "Oof."

Alaina met Dillon's gaze one final time. There was softness and warmth in her ice blue eyes. "Thank you for everything. I will never forget your kindness. I love you both."

"Isn't that sweet?" Brian said in a mocking tone. He turned to Stan. "Looks like Alaina is going to need lots more conversion therapy."

Stan laughed and thrust his hips simulating sex. "Sign me up for that."

Suddenly, Dillon knew the truth. Alaina had no intention of being taken alive. Once Dillon and Cynthia were safe, she'd take her own life. She'd never allow herself to go back to a place that left the road map of scars on her back.

While the guys continued their crude jokes, Dillon said under her breath, "I love you, too. And I understand."

Alaina gave Dillon a quick smile. "Are you boys about done? Let's get on with this."

"We'll get on with this when I say we will." Brian puffed up his chest.

Alaina shrugged, the coolness back in her demeanor. Her earlier fear replaced by a calm acceptance. Dillon suspected that saving Cynthia was her only focus, so it would be up to Dillon to make the rest of their plan work.

"Untie Cynthia and send her over here," Alaina said.

"The bitch can still walk with her hands tied," Brian said. "Or maybe I should shoot her in the head to show you we mean business."

Alaina didn't flinch. "It's your funeral. I'm pretty sure if I blow my brains out, you wouldn't like what he'd do to you. Babcock wants his prized possession back."

A flash of fear danced in Brian's eyes, and the sneer was erased from his face. "Bitch," he said under his breath. He motioned to Stan. "Take her over there."

He walked Cynthia halfway there, her hands still tied.

"Stop," Alaina called out. "That's far enough. She can walk the rest of the way on her own."

Stan paused and glanced back at Brian.

Brian glared but said, "Let her go."

Cynthia walked the last few yards on her own, and Stan retreated.

"Dillon, untie her." Alaina squeezed Cynthia's arm but kept her gaze fixed on Brian.

"I said she can walk with her hands tied."

"But she can't run. I'm not stupid," Alaina said. "I know your orders are to either bring us both back alive or to kill her in front of me. But here's the deal, you can have Babcock pissed because you only accomplished one of your two objectives, bringing me in. Or you can fail at both. The choice is yours."

Brian's Adam's apple bobbed. "Untie her."

Dillon moved quickly and slid in behind Cynthia. Her hands white, the circulation cut off by the ropes. *Bastards.* They didn't need to make them this tight.

Dillon fought the urge to hug Cynthia. She had a job to do. She worked on the ropes for what seemed like an eternity before she pulled the rope off.

Once freed, Cynthia shook her hands, trying to get the circulation back. She turned to Alaina. "You can't do this."

With the gun still against her temple, Alaina briefly met Cynthia's gaze. Tears welled in Cynthia's eyes.

Pain radiated in Dillon's chest. The look had been so intimate that Dillon thought she should look away. So much had been conveyed in those few seconds.

With her gaze back on Brian, Alaina said, "Cynthia, I love you."

Brian yelled. "Enough of your queer bullshit. Let's get on with this."

Alaina pointed at Brian. "I will finish what I want to say."

He scowled.

"I love you with all my heart," Alaina said. "Don't be mad at Dillon, she's the best. You'll need each other."

Even though Alaina had turned the plan upside down, Dillon hoped they could still execute it. She brought her hand to her head and rubbed.

Brian yelled, "Hey, what the fuck are you doing? Stop it."

"Sheesh, I had a fucking itch. Chill out."

Dillon scratched her head a couple more times before bringing her hand back to her side. She wanted to look down over the railing but kept her gaze steady.

Cynthia reached out to Alaina, but Alaina backed up. "No, Cynthia. I can't let myself be distracted. They move quick." She pressed the gun harder against her temple.

"I love you, Alaina. Don't do this," Cynthia pleaded.

"Dillon," Alaina said. "Please, get Cynthia out of here."

"No," Cynthia said and made a move toward Alaina.

Although unscripted, this was perfect. All three men's focus was on the theatrics unfolding in front of them. Dillon decided to use the situation to her advantage. She grabbed Cynthia by the arm, spun her around, and shouted, "Damn it, Cynthia, would you stop it? Alaina said no."

Dillon didn't look at Cynthia but glanced past her at Alaina. Their gazes met, and Dillon saw recognition in her eyes. Dillon's heart raced.

"What the fuck, Dillon?" Alaina shouted. "You don't have to manhandle her. Those creeps did enough of that."

The men chuckled, and Brian called out, "Cat-fight."

Perfect.

"Make up your mind." Dillon glared, hoping it looked authentic. "How do you expect me to control someone six inches taller than me without using a little force?"

Cynthia struggled against Dillon's grasp. Although Dillon was much stronger, an upset Cynthia threatened to get the better of her.

Alaina must have recognized the problem and held up her hand toward Cynthia. "Stop. You need to get home to the gang. Starling and BJ miss you. And Tiffany said she'll make you your favorite pasta dish."

Dillon gaped. What the hell was Alaina talking about? Had the stress gotten to her? *Starling? BJ?* She remembered Tiffany was dead, didn't she?

Cynthia stopped straining against Dillon. "But Tiffany would want you there, too."

"I don't plan on seeing Tiffany any time soon, but you need to go with Dillon. Now." She made a slight motion with her head toward the guardrail. As soon as she did, she yelled and pointed at Brian. "And you will let her walk out of here, or I swear I'll shoot myself."

Cynthia glanced in the direction Alaina had nodded, and her eyes widened for a split second before they returned to normal.

Unbelievable. Good thing Cynthia was smart, she'd picked up what Dillon had missed. Alaina had communicated that things weren't what they seemed and that Alaina planned on living. By Cynthia's brief reaction when she glanced over the railing, the plan was in place. Dillon longed to check for herself, but it was too risky.

Cynthia's shoulders sagged. "Okay."

With that word, it was time to move. "Should we go now, Alaina?" Dillon said.

"Yes." Alaina answered but didn't turn to Dillon. On cue, Alaina broke into a rant at Babcock's goons.

Dillon took the opportunity to lean in toward Cynthia. "We have a plan," Dillon whispered. She wasn't lying; she just wasn't confessing that Alaina had thrown an unexpected kink into the plan. "I need you to do what I tell you."

Cynthia nodded.

Good. Cynthia was back on board, which was crucial for this to work. Dillon wasn't giving up her objective to get them all home safely, but it required a change of direction. It still could work. She just wished Alaina had let her in on her plans, but she understood why she hadn't. The window of time before Alaina pulled the trigger wasn't big. By the look in her eyes earlier, there was no way she would take the chance that the goons would take her alive.

"We're going over the guardrail. As soon as you slide down that embankment, I need for you to run as fast as you can toward the men. You saw them, didn't you?"

Cynthia nodded again.

"Do not stop or look back. It could get me or Alaina killed." Dillon hated to deliver the line, but she knew if Cynthia hesitated or tried to help, it would only lessen their chance of success. "Do you understand?"

Cynthia nodded.

The yelling between Alaina and Brian stopped. Alaina said, "Why are you still here? Go!"

With that, Dillon put her hand on Cynthia's back and helped her over the railing. She leapt it herself. Now was the tricky part. She surveyed the area. A steel post stuck out of the ground about two yards down. She had her target. "Get on your butt and slide down, then run," Dillon yelled. "Fast. We need to get out of here before they change their mind." Cynthia began her descent, sliding down the steep incline.

Dillon leapt in the air for show and began her slide. She had more momentum than she'd thought, so when she grabbed the steel post, she nearly wrenched her arm out of the socket but held on. She hoped she was far enough down that the goons couldn't see her. If not, her plan would fail.

She quickly glanced at Cynthia, who'd landed at the bottom and ran toward the storm drain. Out of the drain marched the battalion, the Washington military poured out side by side with the mole people.

No doubt the army would overtake Brian and his boys, but could she get Alaina to safety? Dillon clawed her way up the side of the incline. *Good.* Alaina was still only a foot from the guardrail. She and Brian were still exchanging heated words. Dillon hoped that her actions wouldn't cause Alaina to pull the trigger. Should she grab her or alert her with a sound first?

Dillon was still several feet from where Alaina stood. Her next step would make her visible to Brian. She clung to the incline, wishing she had better footing. It was now or never. She glanced to her side. An empty beer bottle shone in the sun. The Universe was smiling on her. She picked up the bottle. Her timing had to be impeccable.

Her softball days would hopefully come in handy. Blindly, she launched the bottle into the air as hard as she could. She threw it as if she were trying to gun down a runner at home plate from centerfield. As the bottle flew, she yelled Alaina's name and barreled up the side of the incline. She came up behind Alaina, who no longer held the pistol against her head. *Thank god.* Dillon grabbed her, pulled hard, and yanked her over the railing.

Alaina flew backward and landed on Dillon. The army that poured out of the storm drain had reached the incline, and Cynthia was no longer in sight. Dillon just needed to get Alaina to the bottom. Dillon rolled over and shielded Alaina's body from above and pushed off. They tumbled toward the bottom.

Everything was a blur. Yelling. The thundering

sound of boots running up the hill. Then a gunshot rang out. Two. Three. Dillon felt the pain in her back like a punch. She'd been hit. She tightened her grip on Alaina and kept moving. Only a little farther, she couldn't black out now.

Then gunshots filled the air.

Darkness. Silence.

Chapter Twenty-six

Dillon's eyes fluttered. Where was she? What happened? Everything came flooding back. She needed to get Alaina to safety. Something was holding her down; she thrashed at her restraints.

"Whoa, take it easy," a voice said.

Whose was it? She squeezed her eyes shut and then opened them. The room was bright. She was inside, not still out in the storm drain.

A hand gripped hers, then her other hand. Her vision was blurry. She blinked again, trying to clear it. She was lying on her back. Faces looked down at her. "Skylar," she croaked.

"Yeah, baby, I'm right here." Tears streamed down her face.

"Cynthia. Alaina. What happened?"

"I'm here." Cynthia's bruised face came into focus as she gazed down at Dillon.

Dillon winced at the sight of Cynthia's angry bruises. She reached up and lightly touched Cynthia's cheek. "Are you okay?"

"I am now," Cynthia said with a huge smile. "You scared the shit out of us."

Dillon frantically scanned the room. Nobody else was there. She struggled to sit up.

"Stop." Cynthia pushed her back down. "What are you doing?"

"Alaina?" Dillon searched the room, her eyes wild.

"What about Alaina?" a voice said from the door.

Dillon's gaze fell on Alaina. She wore a black button-down shirt, no longer dressed in her hoodie, and carried three bottles of water.

"Looks like I should have grabbed four," Alaina said with a twinkle in her eye.

"You're okay?" Dillon asked.

"Thanks to your dumb ass." Alaina walked to the bed and pointed down at Dillon. "If you ever do something like that again, I'm gonna kick your ass, and Cynthia's gonna help."

Dillon chuckled, but it caught in her throat when a blinding pain throbbed inside her skull. She grimaced and shut her eyes.

"Headache?" Cynthia asked.

Dillon nodded.

"You hit your head pretty hard on the way down."

The sharp pain passed. "Are you going to let her call me a dumbass?" Dillon said to Cynthia.

"If the shoe fits."

"Skylar?" Dillon said. "Make them stop."

Skylar squeezed her hand. "I'm afraid we have a consensus. We all think you're a dumbass."

Dillon groaned.

Skylar ran her hand over Dillon's forehead. "But we all love your dumb ass, anyway."

Dillon met Skylar's gaze. "Have I ever told you how beautiful you are?"

Skylar blushed.

"Jesus, Dillon," Cynthia said. "You're lying in

a hospital bed." Cynthia glanced around the room. "Well, a makeshift one, and you're putting the moves on Skylar? Who does that?"

Dillon glowered. "I'm not putting the moves on her. Get your mind out of the gutter. Just because you and Alaina are in the go-at-it-like-rabbits stage doesn't mean we are. I just wanted her to know how thankful I am to have her in my life."

"Sure, make me look like an idiot," Cynthia said with a grin.

"If the shoe fits," Dillon said, using the line Cynthia used on her a few minutes before.

They all laughed. The sound warmed Dillon's heart.

"What happened?"

"What do you remember?" Alaina asked.

"Grabbing you. Pulling you over the railing. I saw the soldiers pouring out of the drain, almost to us. My only thought was protecting you, so I wrapped myself around you, and we started tumbling down into the drain. Then I heard gunshots." Dillon's eyes widened. "Was I shot? I remember the horrible pain in my back." Dillon tried to twist and reach around to her backside, but pain stopped her.

"Yes," Cynthia said. "You were shot. Thank god for Skeeter and his storeroom of flak jackets."

Dillon gazed at Alaina. "I still can't believe Brian didn't think it was strange we were wearing hoodies in the middle of the desert."

"Or that I looked like I'd put on twenty pounds." Alaina laughed. "He's almost too stupid...was too stupid to dress himself."

"He's dead?"

"Yep!" Alaina said. "No tears from me." She

gestured toward her back. "He's responsible for a few of these."

Cynthia moved closer to Alaina and took her hand. Dillon made eye contact with her. Cynthia knew.

"Did we lose anyone?" Dillon said. Her heart raced.

Cynthia shook her head. "We have a couple with minor injuries, but everyone should be okay."

"Thank god." Dillon squirmed. "Can I sit up? It's weird having you three looking down at me."

"Always have to be in control," Cynthia teased.

Dillon felt heat rise in her cheeks. Cynthia knew her too well. She glared but didn't respond.

"Actually, you're fine to get up," Cynthia said. "You bumped your head pretty good. Likely a concussion. And you're going to be sore as hell for a few days. Should have a gigantic bruise where the bullet hit your flak jacket. Brian's gun packed some heat."

"Small penis," Alaina said.

They all turned to her in confusion.

"Big gun, small penis. Isn't that what they say?"

Skylar laughed. "I've never heard that, but I like it."

Dillon pushed back the covers. Her hoodie had been replaced by a soft cotton T-shirt. She still had on her blue jeans. "How long have I been out?"

"About an hour," Cynthia said.

Dillon sat up and dangled her feet off the side of the bed. Her head pounded, but she was glad to move. Skylar handed her a bottle of water. She gulped it, not realizing how thirsty she was.

"Whoa, slugger." Cynthia put her hand over

Dillon's that held the bottle. "Your system has had a shock. I don't recommend you guzzling anything."

Dillon wanted to chug the rest but decided to listen to Cynthia. Her back hurt bad enough without risking wrenching it if she vomited.

"The others are going to want to see you up and moving around," Skylar said.

"Can just the four of us sit here a little while longer?" Dillon asked.

"Of course." Skylar sat on the bed next to Dillon.

Dillon put her arm around Skylar's waist. She'd started to lift her arm over Skylar's shoulder, but the pain forced her to keep it lower.

"It's gonna hurt for a while," Cynthia said. "Your body will tell you what it can, or should I say can't, do."

"Yeah, it's speaking pretty loud and clear."

"Do you need something for the pain?" Cynthia asked.

Dillon shook her head. "Not yet. I want to be alert. I don't want to miss anything. And I want you guys to finish telling me what happened."

"That's right," Alaina said. "We got sidetracked talking about what a dumbass you were." She winked at Dillon. "Not a lot to tell, though. We landed at the bottom, and the army descended on the goons. A couple of them grabbed us and hauled us to safety." Alaina's eyes got misty, and she gazed up at Cynthia. "They pulled us into the storm drain tunnel out of the line of fire. That's where Cynthia was waiting for us."

Cynthia and Alaina had been standing shoulder to shoulder holding hands, but somehow, they managed to move in closer.

"Alaina told me everything. The plan. How she'd

adlibbed. And how you countered her adlib." Cynthia paused. "I'm sorry, Dillon."

Sorry? Dillon's eyes narrowed. "Why?"

"I was so angry at you." Cynthia shuffled her feet and stared down at them. "I thought you'd brought Alaina to the exchange. I should have known better."

"I'm sure you weren't exactly thinking clearly." Dillon motioned toward Cynthia's face. "It doesn't look like you'd been treated the best."

"We aren't talking about this." Cynthia touched her cheek. "Ever."

Dillon nodded. "Okay. For now."

"Do you know how much it took for me," Alaina said, "for us, to hold it together when we saw you looking like that?"

"I thought Alaina was going to squeeze my fingers off." Dillon chuckled. "And that jackass Brian hated that we were holding hands."

"Made it all the sweeter," Alaina said.

"No doubt."

"The battle, if you could call it that, only lasted a couple minutes. They took those three out quickly."

"What about the rooftops?" Dillon asked. "Were there snipers? Did the mole people get them?"

"Yep," Alaina said. "They were in position, and as soon as the first shot was fired, they had them immobilized in no time."

"By the way," Skylar said. "They have a new name."

"Who?" Dillon asked.

"The mole people. They're the Vegas people now. They've earned that respect."

"Oh, god, I'm sorry," Dillon said. "They've been the best. I never meant any disrespect."

Skylar patted her leg. "I know you didn't. Just

thought you'd want to know their new name."

"Thanks." Dillon smiled. "And the rest of Babcock's morons?"

"Their compound at Lake Las Vegas was invaded," Alaina said. "Heavy casualties on their side, none on ours."

"More good news," Dillon said.

"Braxton Babcock was taken alive," Cynthia added.

Dillon's gaze darted to Alaina. "Your father. How are you handling it?"

Alaina smiled up at Cynthia. "I can't believe that's the first thing she'd ask. You guys were right. She is the sweetest thing."

Cynthia put her finger to her lips. "Shh. Never tell her we said that. I'll deny it."

The words warmed Dillon. She struggled to do good by the others but always worried she'd not done enough. "I didn't hear a thing. But seriously, how are you doing?"

"Okay." Alaina smiled. "He can't hurt me anymore. Can't hurt anyone."

"He's been screaming that he wants to see her," Cynthia said.

"Are you going to?" Dillon asked.

"Not a snowball's chance in hell. My father's been dead to me for a long time. There's nothing he can say that would mean anything. Some things are unforgivable." Alaina shook her head. "Not that he'd sincerely ask for forgiveness, anyway. If he did, it would be part of a master game of manipulation."

"But don't you need closure? A way to let it go?" Dillon asked.

"Absolutely," Alaina said. "I just don't need

him to do it. It's the mistake so many people make. They think to heal they have to do it with the person or persons that caused them pain. It's backwards thinking to me."

Dillon studied Alaina, trying to understand her meaning. "Care to elaborate? I recently suffered a blow to the head, so I'm a bit slow on understanding."

Alaina smiled. She moved closer to where Skylar and Dillon sat on the bed and brought Cynthia with her. She looked directly at Skylar. "We've all suffered hurt, some worse than others. But in some cases, there is no redemption for those who hurt us. We must let go of the hurt and anger for our own sakes. I'm working on doing that. But I don't want to waste another minute revisiting the past."

Alaina took Dillon's hand and motioned with her eyes for Cynthia to take Skylar's. "This is where my healing begins, with people who love me. With people I trust. Who might make mistakes, but who will talk it out and make it better. You are my salvation, not some fucked-up father who claims to speak for God. I want to spend the rest of my life learning to accept my scars with you three. With the rest of the citizens of Whitaker Estate."

"Amen," Skylar said. "I couldn't have said it better.

"Group hug," Cynthia said. "Just watch out for gimpy's wounds."

Dillon smiled. "I love you, too, Cynthia."

Chapter Twenty-seven

Dillon drove slowly up the lane to Whitaker Estate. She remembered the first time she'd driven this path. CJ had been ecstatic that she'd finally agreed to come out of her self-induced isolation. Dillon had taken her wife's death hard and hadn't known if she'd ever be able to enjoy life again or find love. But the world, as they knew it, had changed so much. She'd changed so much. It seemed like a million years ago, but it had been less than nine months. Not even enough time to have a baby.

Babies. She and Skylar had talked more on their drive home about having a child. Nothing was decided, but she believed that soon they'd be parents. If CJ had told her during their drive to Whitaker Estate that she'd fall in love and be thinking about having a baby, she would have laughed and told CJ she'd lost her mind. Imagine if CJ told her the rest of what would happen, she'd have driven her straight to the nearest hospital for a psychiatric evaluation.

That was the thing with life, nobody ever knew what was going to happen next, even though experts claimed they could. All the prognosticators made a living, making up stories about what would be, and usually they were wildly inaccurate. Probably somewhere, there was an obscure journalist who predicted the world would come to an end in this way, but then again, someone had been forecasting the end of the world for centuries.

But still. They would have been wrong. The world hadn't ended, had it? They were still here, as were the many new friends they'd made.

After taking down Babcock, they'd stayed in Vegas for another week, working on their new Constitution. They'd decided to call it The Proclamation. It had taken fifteen ballots to finally settle on the name. It hadn't been Dillon's favorite, but that was how democracy worked, wasn't it?

They had considerable work to do to finish The Proclamation. Maria was in her glory, having been assigned to represent Whitaker Estate on the committee. Dillon smiled. She would serve the team well. Leslie had joined Maria on the committee, and the two chattered nonstop about it. So much so that Dillon had learned to tune them out.

They were slated to meet again in three months, in Vegas, to finish their work. In the meantime, they would continue sharing snippets of ideas. Dillon was happy not to be a part of the writing of The Proclamation; the tedious legalese would have driven her crazy.

Funny how she'd changed. Before they'd arrived in Vegas, no way would she have agreed to this. She would have insisted on being part of the group that formed the new government. She'd have pressed on, thinking that was what a leader should do. But she wouldn't have done near the job Maria and Leslie would. She'd discovered a true leader knew how to put the right people in the right job, and she wasn't the best choice, but Maria and Leslie were.

Eventually, their way of life would change once

more. Negotiations about who should live where would continue. Likely, they would take on members from the smaller communities. But that would be down the line. The first step was to scour the country, looking for other survivors. Surely, there were still more.

The urgency to bring everyone to one location lessened since they'd learned that the Washington group had access to airplanes and pilots. Now the distance between the groups didn't seem quite so bad. They'd agreed to position a small air force at the Nellis base in Las Vegas and another at Scott Air Force Base in Illinois. Of course, the biggest fleet would remain in Washington.

Should anyone run into trouble, they need only call, and backup would be on the way. The twenty-three original colonies had grown to twenty-four. In a unanimous vote, the mole people, no the Vegas group, were voted in as an original colony. Skeeter and Bobby had beamed as they took their place at the table.

During the week, each group began working on their flags. The Whitaker Estate flag had been turned over to the group that remained at the estate. Anne, Katie, and Karen were working on converting part of one of Tiffany's paintings into their flag. Dillon couldn't wait to see what they came up with.

She, Skylar, and Jake had volunteered to join the search team, assigned to travel the country looking for other survivors. It could be dangerous work but much less so with the equipment at their disposal, courtesy of the Washington group. Besides, they wouldn't be alone. Each team would consist of twenty-five well-trained and well-armed troops. She was happy to be in the same region as the Vegas clan, so Bobby and his soldiers would be part of their unit.

There was much to do, but Dillon felt hopeful for the future. More hope than she'd felt since the crisis happened. The phoenix would rise from the ashes. She just hoped that this time, they'd learn how to get along despite their differences.

She glanced over at the sleeping Skylar, and her chest filled. Out of tragedy, good had prevailed. She never realized she could love another person this much. She wiped a strand of hair from Skylar's face, so she could see her better. Skylar had taught her to love again, and she'd taught Skylar to trust for the first time. Pieces of Skylar's past had come out over the past several months, with more revealed in Vegas. Dillon had wanted to be the one who heard all of Skylar's stories first, but now she was okay if she wasn't. She'd learned that it didn't mean Skylar loved her any less.

Alaina and Skylar had formed a bond. They'd both lived through things that neither Dillon nor Cynthia would ever truly understand. They could talk freely to each other, without fear of seeing a look of horror cross their lovers' faces. Not that Cynthia or Dillon would judge, but over a drink one night, Alaina and Skylar had been able to explain it to them.

Dillon checked the rearview mirror as she neared the bend to take them to the mansion. The other vehicles followed close behind. Surely, they all couldn't wait to see their loved ones. Willa had almost stayed in Vegas but had decided to return, at least for now. She'd shot so much footage of the first summit that she needed CJ's help to put it all together. She'd turned out to be a shining star. Everyone loved her, or at least her camera. There were smiles and cheers whenever she trained her lens on someone.

Despite several conversations, Leslie still wasn't completely back to normal. Dillon hoped a little TLC from her best friend, Karen, would do the trick. She had to let go of her guilt of being the traitor, even though in the end it hadn't brought harm. Dillon reminded her that her spirituality was needed more than ever and how much she'd helped Anne as she grieved the loss of Tiffany. Dillon secretly hoped that the two might eventually make a love connection, but it might be a while.

Dillon's chest tightened. *Tiffany.* She wished she'd lived to see this moment, but she would live on in all of them. The three people she loved most in this world, Skylar, CJ, and Cynthia, were all alive because of her. Dillon and Anne would make sure she was written about kindly in the history books.

Dillon pulled around the corner. The sun shone off the mansion like a beacon welcoming them home. *Home.* Dillon smiled. The front yard was full of balloons, decorations, and a gigantic banner that said, *WELCOME HOME! WE MISSED YOU.*

Dillon shook Skylar. "Sky, wake up. We're home."

Skylar groaned. "Home?"

"Yep. And it looks like there's going to be a party."

Skylar brushed her hair back and sat up. "Holy shit! Now that's a greeting."

"I bet Renee and Katie have a feast planned."

"God, I've missed their food."

"Me too."

Dillon rolled down her window, so she could hear the cheers and music. The beginning refrain from Queen's *We Are the Champions* blared from the speakers. She laughed. No doubt the song was courtesy of CJ, who channeled her inner Freddie Mercury whenever it played.

Dillon pulled to a stop. The others pulled up alongside her.

"Ready?" Dillon said to Skylar.

"More than ready." Skylar grinned.

Jake was already out of his truck and ran toward Lily and his family. Dillon's eyes filled with tears. She swore that Tad and Kelly had grown over the past two weeks.

Cynthia and Alaina walked up beside Dillon and Skylar.

Dillon noticed that Alaina had folded in on herself and looked hesitant.

Before Dillon could ask, Cynthia said, "Would you tell her everyone is going to love her?"

Skylar moved into action and wrapped her arm over Alaina's waist and led her toward the chaos. "I was an outsider once, so was Cynthia. This is the best group of people you'll ever meet. I'm sure CJ and Karen have already spread your story."

The group surged forward and engulfed them. There were so many hugs and welcomes that Dillon lost track. Alaina was swallowed up by the crowd. Dillon smiled at the sound of her laughter.

CJ and Karen pushed through the crowd. In typical CJ fashion, she glanced at Dillon and in a robotic voice said, "Welcome home."

"Get your ass over here." Dillon launched herself at CJ and wrapped her in a bear hug. CJ laughed and picked her up off the ground.

Dillon protested, which made CJ laugh harder.

Karen and Skylar joined the mix.

When they parted, Dillon said to CJ, "I've missed you."

"I've missed your goofy face, too," CJ said. "Even if it isn't logical."

Dillon laughed.

A scream filled the air. Dillon flinched; after their experience, likely screams would have that effect for a while.

Katie ran across the lawn carrying a large cake. Renee followed, trying to keep up. "No fair. You weren't supposed to show up when we were bringing out the food." She stopped and looked down at the cake in her hand as if it were the first time she'd seen it. She shoved it into CJ's hands before she grabbed Dillon.

The laughter and hugs continued. There was even dancing. Dillon's cheeks hurt from smiling so much.

Eventually, the music was cut, and Renee announced that the feast would be served.

Skylar took Dillon's hand and said, "It's good to be home, isn't it?"

Dillon smiled. "The best."

About The Author

Rita Potter has spent most of her life trying to figure out what makes people tick. To that end, she holds a Bachelor's degree in Social Work and an MA in Sociology. Being an eternal optimist, she maintains that the human spirit is remarkably resilient. Her writing reflects this belief.

Rita's stories are electic but typically put her characters in challenging circumstances. She feels that when they reach their happily ever after, they will have earned it. Despite the heavier subject matter, Rita's humorous banter and authentic dialogue reflect her hopeful nature.

In her spare time, she enjoys the outdoors. She is especially drawn to the water, which is ironic since she lives in the middle of a cornfield. Her first love has always been reading. It is this passion that spurred her writing career. She rides a Harley Davidson and has an unnatural obsession with fantasy football. More than anything, she detests small talk but can ramble on for hours given a topic that interests her.

She lives in a small town in Illinois with her wife, Terra, and their cat, Chumley, who actually runs the household.

Rita is a member of American Mensa and the Golden

Crown Literary Society. She is currently a graduate of the GCLS Writing Academy 2021. Sign up for Rita's free newsletter at:

www.ritapotter.com

If you liked this book?

Reviews help an author get discovered and if you have enjoyed this book, please do the author the honor of posting a review on Goodreads, Amazon, Barnes & Noble or anywhere you purchased the book. Or perhaps share a posting on your social media sites and help us spread the word.

Check out Rita's other books

Broken not Shattered - ISBN - 978-1-952270-22-2

Even when it seems hopeless, there can always be a better tomorrow.

Jill Bishop has one goal in life – to survive. Jill is trapped in an abusive marriage, while raising two young girls. Her husband has isolated her from the world and filled her days with fear. The last thing on her mind is love, but she sure could use a friend.

Alex McCoy is enjoying a comfortable life, with great friends and a prosperous business. She has given up on love, after picking the wrong woman one too many times. Little does she know, a simple act of kindness might change her life forever.

When Alex lends a helping hand to Jill at the local grocery store, they are surprised by their immediate connection and an unlikely friendship develops. As their friendship deepens, so too do their fears.

In order to protect herself and the girls, Jill can't let her husband know about her friendship with Alex, and Alex can't discover what goes on behind closed doors. What would Alex do if she finds out the truth? At the same time, Alex must fight her attraction and be the friend she suspects Jill needs. Besides, Alex knows what every lesbian knows – don't fall for a straight woman, especially one that's married…but will her heart listen?

Upheaval: Book One - As We Know It - ISBN - 978-1-

952270-38-3

It is time for Dillon Mitchell to start living again.

Since the death of her wife three years ago, Dillon had buried herself in her work. When an invitation arrives for Tiffany Daniels' exclusive birthday party, her best friend persuades her to join them for the weekend.

It's not the celebration that draws her but the location. The party is being held at the Whitaker Estate, one of the hottest tickets on the West Coast. The Estate once belonged to an eccentric survivalist, whose family converted it into a trendy destination while preserving some of its original history.

Surrounded by a roomful of successful lesbians, Dillon finds herself drawn to Skylar Lange, the mysterious and elusive bartender. Before the two can finish their first dance, a scream shatters the evening. When the party goers emerge from the underground bunker, they discover something terrible has happened at the Estate.

The group races to try to discover the cause of this upheaval, and whether it's isolated to the Estate. Has the world, as we know it, changed forever?

Survival: Book Two - As We Know It - ISBN - 978-1-952270-47-5

Forty-eight hours after the Upheaval, reality is beginning to set in at the Whitaker Estate. The world, As We Know It, has ended.

Dillon Mitchell and her friends are left to survive, after discovering most of the population, at least in the United States, has mysteriously died.

While they struggle to come to terms with their devastating losses, they are faced with the challenge of creating a new society, which is threatened by the divergent factions that may tear the community apart from the inside.

Even if the group can unite, external forces are gathering that could destroy their fragile existence.

Meanwhile, Dillon's budding relationship with the elusive Skylar Lange faces obstacles, when Skylar's hidden past is revealed.

Thundering Pines – ISBN – 978-1-952270-58-1

Returning to her hometown was the last thing Brianna Goodwin wanted to do. She and her mom had left Flower Hills under a cloud of secrecy and shame when she was ten years old. Her life is different now. She has a high-powered career, a beautiful girlfriend, and a trendy life in Chicago.

Upon her estranged father's death, she reluctantly agrees to attend the reading of his will. It should be simple—settle his estate and return to her life in the city—but nothing has ever been simple when it comes to Donald Goodwin.

Dani Thorton, the down-to-earth manager of

Thundering Pines, is confused when she's asked to attend the reading of the will of her longtime employer. She fears that her simple, although secluded life will be interrupted by the stylish daughter who breezes into town.

When a bombshell is revealed at the meeting, two women seemingly so different are thrust together. Maybe they'll discover they have more in common than they think.

Other books by Sapphire Authors

Finding Faith - ISBN - 978-1-952270-16-1

Faith Fitzgerald thought that if she got an education and became a high-powered attorney in Manhattan, maybe—just maybe—she'd gain the attention and respect of her absentee father. Considering he was the only parent she had left after her mother's suicide when Faith was just a child, she thought that's what it would take.

She was wrong.

What she dreamed would be glamorous and satisfying turned out to be grueling and thankless. Since she wasn't willing to play the game between the sheets, she was forced to stay in the cubicle jungle doing all the heavy lifting while the men got the credit and the rewards.

Deciding she is done, Faith packs up and, with the flip of the bird to the rearview mirror, leaves New York and heads home to Colorado. She has nothing there: no job, nowhere to live, no relationship with her father. Truth is, she barely has a relationship with herself.

On the drive home, she finds herself in Wynter, a tiny mountain town at the foot of the Rockies. Looking more like it belongs in a made-for-TV Christmas movie than on the map, Faith is utterly enchanted. When she tries her luck and buys a raffle ticket at Pop's, Wynter's charming café, her prize is far more than meets the eye—or the heart.

Enter Wyatt, a feisty, sexy southerner and waitress at Pop's, who just happens to be married to a local sheriff's deputy. All is not as it appears with the All-American boy and his Georgia peach.

A colorful cast of unforgettable and charming characters will teach the jaded attorney that sometimes to find yourself all you have to do is go back to the basics…and have a little Faith.

Survival – ISBN – 978-1-952270-18-5

After surviving a school shooting, Mona Ouellet moves from Montreal to Peterborough, switches her PhD discipline from English Literature to Psychology, and tries to move on with her life. Unfortunately, her nightmares follow her—and so do a host of "bad men" who seem to appear around every corner to make her life difficult. Her only escape is to fall into her research completely, where she soon becomes obsessed with retelling true crime case studies and enamoured by a waitress at a local diner.

Kerri Reznik is a waitress by day and horror writer by night, where she turns elements of her two-month long captivity in the wilderness with her survivalist father into stories to scare others. Though over a decade has passed, Kerri is still haunted by her brother Lee's absence in her life and her inability to reconcile with it. She seeks camaraderie with Absalom Lincoln, a detective on Peterborough police's force, where the two bond over mysteries, both true and imagined.

As Kerri and Mona's connection becomes stronger, their past traumas begin to intertwine and both of their worst nightmares begin to evolve and intensify. Each character must struggle to negotiate how to live in a world where survival is never guaranteed, and even when it is possible, there is always a cost.

Keeping Secrets – ISBN – 978-1-952270-04-8

What would you do if, after finally finding the woman of your dreams, she suddenly leaves to fight in the Civil War?

It's 1863, and Elizabeth Hepscott has resigned herself to a life of monotonous boredom far from the battlefields as the wife of a Missouri rancher. Her fate changes when she travels with her brother to Kentucky to help him join the Union Army. On a whim, she poses as his little brother and is bullied into enlisting, as well. Reluctantly pulled into a new destiny, a lark decision quickly cascades into mortal danger.

While Elizabeth's life has made a drastic U-turn, Charlie Schweicher, heiress to a glass-making fortune, is still searching for the only thing money can't buy.

A chance encounter drastically changes everything for both of them. Will Charlie find the love she's longed for, or will the war take it all away?